# THE
# STOLEN
# HEIR

# BY HOLLY BLACK

## THE FOLK OF THE AIR

## OTHER

# THE STOLEN HEIR

## A NOVEL OF ELFHAME

## HOLLY BLACK

LITTLE, BROWN AND COMPANY

NEW YORK BOSTON

Copyright © 2023 by Holly Black
Map and illustrations by Kathleen Jennings

Cover art copyright © 2023 by Sean Freeman. Cover design by Karina Granda.
Cover copyright © 2023 by Hachette Book Group, Inc.
Interior design by Karina Granda.

Little, Brown and Company
Hachette Book Group
1290 Avenue of the Americas, New York, NY 10104
Visit us at LBYR.com

First Edition: January 2023

Little, Brown and Company is a division of Hachette Book Group, Inc.
The Little, Brown name and logo are trademarks of Hachette Book Group, Inc.

The publisher is not responsible for websites (or their content) that are not owned by the publisher.

Little, Brown and Company books may be purchased in bulk for business, educational, or promotional use. For information, please contact your local bookseller or the Hachette Book Group Special Markets Department at special.markets@hbgusa.com.

Library of Congress Cataloging-in-Publication Data
Names: Black, Holly, author.
Title: The stolen heir / Holly Black.
Description: First edition. | New York : Little, Brown and Company, 2023. |
Series: The stolen heir | Audience: Ages 14+. | Summary: "The changeling queen Suren must venture back into the Court of Teeth with the help of the Prince of Faerie, Oak."—Provided by publisher.
Identifiers: LCCN 2022037583 | ISBN 9780316592703 (hardcover) |
ISBN 9780316422260 (ebook)
Subjects: CYAC: Fantasy. | LCGFT: Fantasy fiction. | Novels.
Classification: LCC PZ7.B52878 St 2023 | DDC [Fic]—dc23
LC record available at https://lccn.loc.gov/2022037583

ISBNs: 978-0-316-59270-3 (hardcover), 978-0-316-42226-0 (ebook), 978-0-316-54330-9 (int'l),
978-0-316-54351-4 (Walmart exclusive edition), 978-0-316-51904-5 (B&N exclusive edition)

Printed in the United States of America

LSC-C

Printing 1, 2022

*For Robin Wasserman, who has the*
*curse (and blessing) of True Sight*

One evening, too, by the nursery fire,

We snuggled close and sat round so still,

When suddenly as the wind blew higher,

Something scratched on the window-sill,

A pinched brown face peered in—I shivered;

No one listened or seemed to see;

The arms of it waved and the wings of it quivered,

Whoo—I knew it had come for me!

Some are as bad as bad can be!

All night long they danced in the rain,

Round and round in a dripping chain,

Threw their caps at the window-pane,

Tried to make me scream and shout

And fling the bedclothes all about:

I meant to stay in bed that night,

And if only you had left a light

They would never have got me out!

—Charlotte Mew,
"The Changeling"

# PROLOGUE

A passerby discovered a toddler sitting on the chilly concrete of an alley, playing with the wrapper of a cat-food container. By the time she was brought to the hospital, her limbs were blue with cold. She was a wizened little thing, too thin, made of sticks.

She knew only one word, her name. Wren.

As she grew, her skin retained a slight bluish cast, resembling skimmed milk. Her foster parents bundled her up in jackets and coats and mittens and gloves, but unlike her sister, she was never cold. Her lip color changed like a mood ring, staying bluish and purple even in summer, turning pink only when close to a fire. And she could play in the snow for hours, constructing elaborate tunnels and mock-fighting with icicles, coming inside only when called.

Although she appeared bony and anemic, she was strong. By the time she was eight, she could lift bags of groceries that her adoptive mother struggled with.

By the time she was nine, she was gone.

As a child, Wren read lots of fairy tales. That's why, when the monsters came, she knew it was because she had been wicked.

They snuck in through her window, pushing up the jamb and slashing the screen so silently that she slept on, curled around her favorite stuffed fox. She woke only when she felt claws touch her ankle.

Before she could get out the first scream, fingers covered her mouth. Before she could get out the first kick, her legs were pinned.

"I am going to let you go," said a harsh voice with an unfamiliar accent. "But if you wake anyone in this house, you will most assuredly be sorry for it."

That was like a fairy tale, too, which made Wren wary of breaking the rules. She stayed utterly quiet and still, even when they released her, although her heart beat so hard and fast that it seemed possible it would be loud enough to summon her mother.

A selfish part of her wished it would, wished that her mother would come and turn on a light and banish the monsters. That wouldn't be breaking the rules, would it, if it was only the thundering of her heart that did the waking?

"Sit up," commanded one of the monsters.

Obediently, Wren did. But her trembling fingers buried her stuffed fox in the blankets.

Looking at the three creatures flanking her bed made her shiver uncontrollably. Two were tall, elegant beings with skin the gray of stone. The first, a woman with a fall of pale hair caught in a crown of jagged obsidian, wearing a gown of some silvery material that wafted around her. She was beautiful, but the cruel set of her mouth warned Wren not to trust her. The man was matched to the woman as though they were pieces on a chessboard, wearing a black crown and clothes of the same silvery material.

Beside them was a huge, looming creature, spindly, with mushroom-pale skin and a head full of wild black hair. But what was most notable were her long, clawlike fingers.

"You're our daughter," one of the gray-faced monsters said.

"You belong to us," rasped the other. "We made you."

She knew about *birth parents*, which her sister had, nice people who came to visit and looked like her, and who sometimes brought over grandparents or doughnuts or presents.

She had wished for birth parents of her own, but she had never thought that her wish could conjure a nightmare like this.

"Well," said the woman in the crown. "Have you nothing to say? Are you too in awe of our majesty?"

The claw-fingered creature gave an impolite little snort.

"That must be it," said the man. "How grateful you will be to be taken away from all of this, changeling child. Get up. Make haste."

"Where are we going?" Wren asked. Fear made her sink her fingers into her bedsheets, as though she could hang on to her life before this moment if she just gripped hard enough.

"To Faerie, where you will be a queen," the woman said, a snarl in her voice where there ought to have been cajoling. "Have you never dreamed of someone coming to you and telling you that you were no mortal child, but one made of magic? Have you never dreamed about being taken from your pathetic little life to one of vast greatness?"

Wren couldn't deny that she had. She nodded. Tears burned in the back of her throat. That's what she had done wrong. That was the wickedness in her heart that had been discovered. "I'll stop," she whispered.

"What?" asked the man.

"If I promise never to make wishes like that again, can I stay?" she asked, voice shaking. "Please?"

The woman's hand came against Wren's cheek in a slap so hard that it sounded like a crack of thunder. Her cheek hurt, and though tears pricked her eyes, she was too shocked and angry for them to fall. No one had ever hit her before.

"You are Suren," said the man. "And we are your makers. Your sire and dam. I am Lord Jarel and she, Lady Nore. This one accompanying us is Bogdana, the storm hag. Now that you know your true name, let me show you your true face."

Lord Jarel reached out to her, making a ripping motion. And there, underneath, was her monster self, reflected in the mirror over her dresser—her skimmed milk skin giving way to pale blue flesh, the same color as buried veins. When she parted her lips, she saw shark-sharp teeth. Only her eyes were the same mossy green, large and staring back at her in horror.

*My name isn't Suren*, she wanted to say. *And this is a trick. That's not me.* But even as she thought the words, she heard how similar Suren was to her own name. Su*ren*. Ren. Wren. A child's shortening.

*Changeling child.*

"Stand," said the huge, looming creature with nails as long as knives. *Bogdana.* "You do not belong in this place."

Wren listened to the noises of the house, the hum of the heater, the distant scrape of the nails of the family dog as it pawed at the floor restlessly in sleep, running through dreams. She tried to memorize every sound. Her gaze blurry with tears, she committed her room to memory, from the book titles on her shelves to the glassy eyes of her dolls.

She snuck one last pet of her fox's synthetic fur and pressed him down, deeper under the covers. If he stayed there, he'd be safe. Shuddering, she slid out of the bed.

"Please," she said again.

A cruel smile twisted up the corner of Lord Jarel's face. "The mortals no longer want you."

Wren shook her head, because that couldn't be true. Her mother and father *loved* her. Her mother cut the crusts off her sandwiches and kissed her on the tip of her nose to make her giggle. Her father cuddled up with her to watch movies and then carried her to bed when she fell asleep on the couch. She knew they loved her. And yet the certainty with which Lord Jarel spoke plucked at her terror.

"If they admit that they wish for you to remain with them," said Lady Nore, her voice soft for the first time, "then you may stay."

Wren padded into the hall, her heart frantic, rushing into her parents' room as if she'd had a nightmare. The noise of her shuffling feet and her ragged breaths woke them. Her father sat up and then startled, putting an arm up protectively over her mother, who looked at Wren and screamed.

"Don't be scared," she said, moving to the side of the bed and crushing the blankets in her small fists. "It's me, Wren. They did something to me."

"Get away, monster!" her father barked. He sounded frightening enough to send her scuttling back against the dresser. She'd never heard him shout like that, certainly never at her.

Tears tracked down her cheeks. "It's *me*," she said again, her voice breaking. "Your daughter. You love me."

The room looked exactly as it always had. Pale beige walls. Queen-size bed with brown dog fur dirtying their white duvet. A towel lying beside the hamper, as though someone had thrown and missed. The scent of the furnace, and the petroleum smell of some cream used to remove makeup. But it was the distorted-mirror nightmare version, in which all those things had become horrible.

Below them, the dog barked, sounding a desperate warning.

"What are you waiting for? Get that thing out of here," her father growled, looking toward Lady Nore and Lord Jarel as though he was seeing something other than them, some human authority.

Wren's sister came into the hall, rubbing her eyes, clearly awakened by the screaming. Surely Rebecca would help, Rebecca who made sure no one bullied her at school, who took her to the fair even though no one else's little sister was allowed. But at the sight of Wren, Rebecca jumped onto the bed with a horrified yelp and wrapped her arms around her mother.

"Rebecca," Wren whispered, but her sister only dug her face deeper into their mother's nightgown.

"Mom," Wren pleaded, tears choking her voice, but her mother wouldn't look at her. Wren's shoulders shook with sobs.

"*This* is our daughter," her father said, holding Rebecca close, as though Wren had been trying to trick him.

Rebecca, who'd been adopted, too. Who ought to have been exactly as much theirs as Wren.

Wren crawled to the bed, crying so hard that she could barely get any words out. *Please let me stay. I'll be good. I am sorry, sorry, sorry for whatever I did, but you can't let them take me. Mommy. Mommy. Mommy, I love you, please, Mommy.*

Her father tried to push her back with his foot, pressing it against her neck. But she reached for him anyway, her voice rising to a shriek.

When her little fingers touched his calf, he kicked her in the shoulder, sending her to the floor. But she only crawled back, weeping and pleading, keening with misery.

"Enough," rasped Bogdana. She yanked Wren against her, running one of her long nails over Wren's cheek with something like gentleness. "Come, child. I will carry you."

"No," Wren said, her fingers winding themselves in the sheets. "No. No. No."

"It is not meet for the humans to have touched you in violence, you who are ours," said Lord Jarel.

"Ours to hurt," Lady Nore agreed. "Ours to punish. Never theirs."

"Shall they die for the offense?" Lord Jarel asked, and the room went quiet, except for the sound of Wren sobbing.

"Should we kill them, Suren?" he asked again, louder. "Let their pet dog in and enchant it so that it turns on them and bites out their throats?"

At that, Wren's crying abated in astonishment and outrage. "No!" she shouted. She felt beyond the ability to control herself.

"Then hear this and cease weeping," Lord Jarel told her. "You will come with us willingly, or I will slay everyone on that bed. First the child, then the others."

Rebecca gave a little frightened sob. Wren's human parents watched her with fresh horror.

"I'll go," Wren said finally, a sob still in her voice, one she couldn't stop. "Since no one loves me, I'll go."

The storm hag lifted her up, and they were away.

Wren was discovered in the flashing lights of a patrol car two years later, walking along the side of the highway. The soles of her shoes were as worn as if she'd danced through them, her clothing was stiff with sea salt, and scars marred the skin of her wrists and cheeks.

When the officer tried to ask her what had happened, she either wouldn't or couldn't answer. She snarled at anyone who came too close, hid beneath the cot in the room they brought her into, and refused to give a name or an address as to where her home had been to the lady they brought with them.

Their smiles hurt. Everything hurt.

When they turned their backs, she was gone.

CHAPTER

1

The slant of the moon tells me that it's half past ten when my un-sister comes out the back door. She's in her second year of college and keeps odd hours. As I watch from the shadows, she sets down an empty cereal bowl on the top step of the splintery and sagging deck. Then she glugs milk into it from a carton. Spills a little. Squatting, she frowns out toward the tree line.

For an impossible moment, it's as though she's looking at me.

I draw deeper into the dark.

The scent of pine needles is heavy in the air, mingling with leaf mold and the moss I crush between my bare toes. The breeze carries the smell of the sticky, rotten, sugary dregs still clinging to bottles in the recycling bin; the putrid something at the bottom of the empty garbage can; the chemical sweetness of the perfume my unsister is wearing.

I watch her hungrily.

Bex leaves the milk for a neighborhood cat, but I like to pretend it's me she's leaving it for. Her forgotten sister.

She stands there for a few minutes while moths flit above her head and mosquitoes buzz. Only when she goes back inside do I slink closer to the house, peering through the window to watch my unmother knit in front of the television. Watching my unfather in the breakfast nook with his laptop, answering email. He puts a hand to his eyes, as though tired.

In the Court of Teeth, I was punished if I called the humans who raised me my mother and father. *Humans are animals*, Lord Jarel would say, the admonishment coming with a breathtakingly hard blow. *Filthy animals. You share no blood with them.*

I taught myself to call them unmother and unfather, hoping to avoid Lord Jarel's wrath. I keep the habit to remind myself of what they were to me, and what they will never be again. Remind myself that there is nowhere that I belong and no one to whom I belong.

The hair on the back of my neck prickles. When I look around, I note an owl on a high branch, observing me with a swivel of its head. No, not an owl.

I pick up a rock, hurling it at the creature.

It shifts into the shape of a hob and takes off into the sky with a screech, beating feathered wings. It circles twice and then glides off toward the moon.

The local Folk are no friends to me. I've seen to that.

Another reason I am no one, of nowhere.

Resisting the temptation to linger longer near the backyard where I once played, I head for the branches of a hawthorn at the edge of town. I stick to the dimness of shadowed woodland, my bare feet finding their way through the night. At the entrance to the graveyard, I stop.

Huge and covered in the white blooms of early spring, the hawthorn towers over headstones and other grave markers. Desperate locals, teenagers especially, come here and tie wishes to the branches.

I heard the stories as a kid. It's called the Devil's Tree. Come back three times, make three wishes, and the devil was supposed to appear. He'd give you what you asked for and take what he wanted in return.

It's not a devil, though. Now that I have lived among the Folk, I know the creature that fulfills those bargains is a glaistig, a faerie with goat feet and a taste for human blood.

I climb into a cradle of branches and wait, petals falling around me with the sway of the tree limbs. I lean my cheek against the rough bark, listening to the susurration of leaves. In the cemetery that surrounds the hawthorn, the nearby graves are more than a hundred years old. These stones have weathered thin and bone pale. No one visits them anymore, making this a perfect spot for desperate people to come and not be seen.

A few stars wink down at me through the canopy of flowers. In the Court of Teeth, there was a nisse who made charts of the sky, looking for the most propitious dates for torture and murder and betrayal.

I stare up, but whatever riddle is in the stars, I can't read it. My education in Faerie was poor, my human education, inconsistent.

The glaistig arrives a little after midnight, clopping along. She is dressed in a long burgundy coat that stops at the knees, designed to highlight her goat feet. Her bark-brown hair is pulled up and back into a tight braid.

Beside her flies a sprite with grasshopper-green skin and wings to match. It's only a bit larger than a hummingbird, buzzing through the air restlessly.

The glaistig turns to the winged faerie. "The Prince of Elfhame? How interesting to have royalty so close by..."

My heart thuds dully at *prince*.

"Spoiled, they say," the sprite chirps. "And wild. Far too irresponsible for a throne."

That doesn't sound like the boy I knew, but in the four years since I saw him last, he would have been inducted into all the pleasures of the High Court, would have been served up a surfeit of every imaginable debauched delight. Sycophants and toadies would be so busy vying for his attention that, these days, I wouldn't be allowed close enough to kiss the hem of his cloak.

The sprite departs, darting up and away, thankfully not weaving through the branches of the tree where I crouch. I settle in to observe.

Three people come that night to make wishes. One, a sandy-haired young man I went to fourth grade with, the year before I was taken. His fingers tremble as he ties his scrap of paper to the branch with a bit of twine. The second, an elderly woman with a stooped back. She keeps wiping at her wet eyes, and her note is tearstained by the time she affixes it with a twist tie. The third is a freckled man, broad-shouldered, a baseball cap pulled low enough to hide most of his face.

This is the freckled man's third trip, and at his arrival, the glaistig steps out of the shadows. The man gives a moan of fear. He didn't expect this to be real. They seldom do. They embarrass themselves with their reactions, their terror, the sounds they make.

The glaistig makes him tell her what he wants, even though he's written it three separate times on three separate notes. I don't think she ever bothers to read the wishes.

*I* do. This man needs money because of some bad business deal. If he doesn't get it, he will lose his house, and then his wife will leave him. He whispers this to the glaistig, fidgeting with his wedding ring as he does so. In return, she gives him her terms—every night for seven months and seven days, he must bring her a cube of fresh human flesh. He may cut it from himself, or from another, whichever he prefers.

He agrees eagerly, desperately, foolishly, and lets her tie an ensorcelled piece of leather around his wrist.

"This was crafted from my own skin," she tells him. "It will let me find you, no matter how you try to hide from me. No mortal-made knife can cut it, and should you fail to do as you have promised, it will tighten until it slices through the veins of your arm."

For the first time, I see panic on his face, the sort that he ought to have felt all along. Too late, and part of him knows it. But he denies it a moment later, the knowledge surfacing and being shoved back down.

Some things seem too terrible to seem possible. Soon he may learn that the worst thing he can imagine is only the beginning of what they are willing to do to him. I recall that realization and hope I can spare him it.

Then the glaistig tells the freckled man to gather leaves. For each one in his pile, he'll get a crisp twenty-dollar bill in its place. He'll have three days to spend the money before it disappears.

In the note he attached to the tree, he wrote that he needed $40,000. That's *two thousand* leaves. The man scrambles to get together a big enough pile, searching desperately through the well-manicured graveyard. He collects some from the stretch of woods along the border and rips handfuls from a few trees with low-hanging branches. Staring at what he assembles, I think of the game they have at fairs, where you guess the number of jelly beans in a jar.

I wasn't good at that game, and I worry he isn't, either.

The glaistig glamours the leaves into money with a bored wave of her hand. Then he's busy stuffing the bills into his pockets. He races after a few the wind takes and whips toward the road.

This seems to amuse the glaistig, but she's wise enough not to hang around to laugh. Better he not realize how thoroughly he's been had. She disappears into the night, drawing her magic to shroud her.

When the man has filled his pockets, he shoves more bills into his shirt, where they settle against his stomach, forming an artificial paunch. As he walks out of the graveyard, I let myself drop silently out of the tree.

I follow him for several blocks, until I see my chance to speed up and grab hold of his wrist. At the sight of me, he screams.

Screams, just like my unmother and unfather.

I flinch at the sound, but the reaction shouldn't surprise me. I know what I look like.

My skin, the pale blue of a corpse. My dress, streaked with moss and mud. My teeth, built for ease of ripping flesh from bone. My ears are pointed, too, hidden beneath matted, dirty blue hair, only slightly darker than my skin. I am no pixie with pretty moth wings. No member of the Gentry, whose beauty makes mortals foolish with desire. Not even a glaistig, who barely needed a glamour if her skirts were long enough.

He tries to pull away, but I am very strong. My sharp teeth make short work of the glaistig's string and her spell. I've never learned to glamour myself well, but in the Court of Teeth I grew skilled at breaking curses. I'd had enough put on me for it to be necessary.

I press a note into the freckled man's hands. The paper is his own, with his wish written on one side. *Take your family and run,* I wrote with one of Bex's Sharpies. *Before you hurt them. And you will.*

He stares after me as I race off, as though I am the monster.

I have seen this particular bargain play out before. Everyone starts out telling themselves that they will pay with their own skin. But seven months and seven days is a long time, and a cube of flesh is a lot to cut from your own body every night. The pain is intense, worse with each new injury. Soon it's easy to justify slicing a bit from those around you. After all, didn't you do this for their sake? From there, things go downhill fast.

I shudder, remembering my own unfamily looking at me in horror and disgust. People who I believed would always love me. It took me the better part of a year to discover that Lord Jarel had *enchanted* their love away, that his spells were the reason he was so certain they wouldn't want me.

Even now, I do not know if the enchantment is still on them.

Nor do I know whether Lord Jarel amplified and exploited their actual horror at the sight of me or created that feeling entirely out of magic.

It is my revenge on Faerie to unravel the glaistig's spells, to undo every curse I discover. Free anyone who is ensnared. It doesn't matter if the man appreciates what I've done. My satisfaction comes at the glaistig's frustration at another human slipping from her net.

I cannot help them all. I cannot prevent them from taking what she offers and paying her price. And the glaistig is hardly the only faerie offering bargains. But I try.

By the time I return to my childhood home, my unfamily has all gone to bed.

I lift the latch and creep through the house. My eyes see well enough in the dark for me to move through the unlit rooms. I go to the couch and press my unmother's half-finished sweater to my cheek, feeling the softness of the wool, breathing in the familiar scent of her. Think of her voice, singing to me as she sat at the end of my bed.

*Twinkle, twinkle, little star.*

I open the garbage and pick out the remains of their dinner. Bits of gristly steak and gobs of mashed potatoes clump together with scattered pieces of what must have been a salad. It's all mixed in with crumpled-up tissues, plastic wrap, and vegetable peels. I make a dessert of a plum that's mushy on one end and the little bit of jam at the bottom of a jar in the recycling bin.

I gobble the food, trying to imagine that I am sitting at the table with them. Trying to imagine myself as their daughter again, and not what's left of her.

A cuckoo trying to fit back into the egg.

Other humans sensed the wrongness in me as soon as I set foot in the mortal world. That was right after the Battle of the Serpent, when the Court of Teeth had been disbanded and Lady Nore fled. With nowhere else to go, I came here. That first night back, I was discovered by a handful of children in a park who picked up sticks to drive me off. When one of the bigger ones jabbed me, I ran at him, sinking my sharp teeth into the meat of his arm. I opened up his flesh as though he were a tin can.

I do not know what I would do to my unfamily if they pushed me away again. I am no safe thing now. A child no more, but a fully grown monster, like the ones that came for me.

Still, I am tempted to try to break the spell, to reveal myself to them. I am always tempted. But when I think of speaking with my unfamily, I think of the storm hag. Twice, she found me in the woods outside the human town, and twice she hung the strung-up and skinned body of a mortal over my camp. One who she claimed knew too much about the Folk. I don't want to give her a reason to choose one of my unfamily as her next victim.

Upstairs, a door opens and I freeze. I fold up my legs, circling my arms around my knees, trying to make myself as small as possible. A few minutes later, I hear a toilet flush and let myself breathe normally again.

I shouldn't come. I don't always—some nights, I manage to stay far away, eating moss and bugs and drinking from dirty streams. Going through the dumpsters behind restaurants. Breaking spells so that I can believe I'm not like the rest of them.

But I am lured back, again and again. Sometimes I wash the dishes in the sink or move wet clothes to the dryer, like a brownie. Sometimes I steal knives. When I am at my angriest, I rip a few of their things into tiny shreds. Sometimes I doze behind the couch until they all leave for work or school and I can crawl out again. Search through the rooms for scraps of myself, report cards and yarn crafts. Family photos that include a human version of me with my pale hair and pointy chin, my big, hungry eyes. Evidence that my memories are real. In one box marked *Rebecca*, I found my old stuffed fox and wonder how they explained away an entire room of my belongings.

Rebecca goes by Bex now, a new name for her fresh start in college. Despite her probably telling everyone who asks that she's an only child, she's in nearly every good memory I have of being a kid. Bex drinking cocoa in front of the television, squishing marshmallows until her fingers were sticky. Bex and I kicking each other's legs in the car until Mom yelled at us to stop. Bex sitting in her closet, playing action figures with me, holding up Batman to kiss Iron Man and saying: *Let's get them married, and then they can get some cats and live happily ever after.* Imagining myself scrubbed out of those memories makes me grind my teeth and feel even more like a ghost.

Had I grown up in the mortal world, I might be in school with Bex. Or traveling, taking odd jobs, discovering new things. That Wren would take her place in the world for granted, but I can no longer imagine my way into her skin.

Sometimes I sit up on the roof, watching the bats twirl in the moonlight. Or I watch my unfamily sleep, reaching my hand daringly close to my unmother's hair. But tonight, I only eat.

When I am done with the scavenged meal, I go to the sink and stick my head underneath the tap, guzzling the sweet, clear water. After I have my fill, I wipe my mouth with the back of my hand and slip out onto the deck. At the top step, I drink the milk my unsister put out. A bug has fallen in and spins on the surface. I drink that, too.

I am about to slink back into the woods when a long shadow comes from the side yard, its fingers like branches.

Heart racing, I pad down the steps and slide beneath the porch. I make it just moments before Bogdana lopes around the corner of the house. She is every bit as tall and terrifying as I remember her being that first night, and worse, because now I know of what she is capable.

My breath catches. I have to bite down hard on the inside of my cheek to keep quiet and still.

I watch Bogdana drag one of her nails across the sagging aluminum siding. Her fingers are as long as flower stalks, her limbs as spindly as sticks of birch. Weed-like strands of black straight hair hang over her mushroom-pale face, half-hiding tiny eyes that gleam with malice.

She peers in through the glass panes of a window. How easy to push up a sash, to creep in and slit the throats of my unfamily as they sleep, then flense the skins from their bodies.

My fault. If I had been able to stay away, she wouldn't have scented my spoor here. Wouldn't have come. *My fault.*

And now I have two choices. I can stay where I am and listen to them die. Or I can lead her from the house. It's no choice at all, except for the fear that has been my constant companion since I was stolen from the mortal world. Terror seared deep in my marrow.

Deeper than my desire to be safe, though, I want my unfamily to *live.* Even if I no longer belong with them, I need to save them. Were they gone, the last shred of what I was would be gone with them, and I would be set adrift.

Taking a deep, shuddery breath, I kick out from underneath the porch. I run for the road, away from the cover of woods, where she would easily gain on me. I am heedless in my steps across the lawn, ignoring the snapping of twigs beneath my bare feet. The crack of each one carries through the night air.

I do not look back, but I know that Bogdana must have heard me. She must have turned, nostrils flaring, scenting the breeze. Movement draws the eye of the predator. The instinct to chase.

I wince against the headlights of the cars as I hit the sidewalk.

Leaves are tangled into the muddy clots of my hair. My dress—once white—is now a dull and stained color, like the gown one would expect to adorn a ghost. I do not know if my eyes shine like an animal's. I suspect they might.

The storm hag sweeps after me, swift as a crow and certain as doom.

I pump my legs faster.

Sharp bits of gravel and glass dig into my feet. I wince and stumble a little, imagining I can feel the breath of the hag. Terror gives me the strength to shoot forward.

Now that I have drawn her off, I must lose her somehow. If she becomes distracted for even a moment, I can slip away and hide. I got very good at hiding, back at the Court of Teeth.

I turn into an alley. There's a gap in the chain-link fence at the end, small enough for me to wriggle through. I run for it, feet sliding in muck and trash. I hit the fence and press my body into the opening, metal scratching my skin, the stink of iron heavy in the air.

As I race on, I hear the shake of the fence as it's being climbed.

"Stop, you little fool!" the storm hag shouts after me.

Panic steals my thoughts. Bogdana is too fast, too sure. She's been killing mortals and faeries alike since long before I was born. If she summons lightning, I'm as good as dead.

Instinct makes me want to go to my part of the woods. To burrow in the cave-like dome I've woven from willow branches. Lie on my floor of smooth river stones, pressed down into the mud after a rainstorm until they made a surface flat enough to sleep on. Cocoon myself in my three blankets, despite them being moth-eaten, stained, and singed by fire along a corner.

There, I have a carving knife. It is only as long as one of her fingers, but sharp. Better than either of the other little blades I have on my person.

I dart sideways, toward an apartment complex, running through the pools of light. I cut across streets, through the playground, the creak of swing chains loud in my ears.

I have more skill at unraveling enchantments than making them, but since her last visit I warded around my lair so that a dread comes upon anyone who gets too close. Mortals stay away from the place, and even the Folk become uneasy when they come near.

I have little hope that will chase her off, but I have little hope at all.

Bogdana was the one person that Lord Jarel and Lady Nore feared. A hag who could bring on storms, who had lived for countless scores of years, who knew more of magic than most beings alive. I saw her slash open and devour humans in the Court of Teeth and gut a faerie with those long fingers over a perceived insult. I saw lightning flash at her annoyance. It was Bogdana who helped Lord Jarel and Lady Nore with their scheme to conceive a child and hide me away among mortals, and many times she had been witness to my torment in the Court of Teeth.

Lord Jarel and Lady Nore never let me forget that I belonged to them, despite my title as queen. Lord Jarel delighted in leashing me and dragging me around like an animal. Lady Nore punished me ferociously for any imagined slight, until I became a snarling beast, clawing and biting, barely aware of anything but pain.

Once, Lady Nore threw me out into the howling wasteland of snow and barred the castle doors against me.

*If being a queen doesn't suit you, worthless child, then find your own fortune,* she said.

I walked for days. There was nothing to eat but ice, and I could hear nothing but the cold wind blowing around me. When I wept, the tears froze on my cheeks. But I kept on going, hoping against hope that I might find someone to help me or some way to escape. On the seventh day, I discovered I had only gone in a great circle.

It was Bogdana who wrapped me in a cloak and carried me inside after I collapsed in the snow.

The hag carried me to my room, with its walls of ice, and set me down on the skins of my bed. She touched my brow with fingers twice as long as fingers ought to be. Looked down at me with her black eyes, shook her head of wild, storm-tossed hair. "You will not always be so small or so frightened," she told me. "You are a queen."

The way the hag said those words made me raise my head. She made the title sound as though it was something of which I ought to be proud.

When the Court of Teeth ventured south, to war with Elfhame, Bogdana did not come with us. I thought to never see her again and was sorry for it. If there was one of them who might have looked out for me, it was her.

Somehow that makes it worse that she's the one at my heels, the one hunting me through the streets.

When I hear the hag's footfalls draw close, I grit my teeth and try for a burst of speed. My lungs are already aching, my muscles sore.

Perhaps, I try to tell myself, perhaps I can reason with her. Perhaps she is chasing me only because I ran.

I make the mistake of glancing back and lose the rhythm of my stride. I falter as the hag reaches out a long hand toward me, her knife-sharp nails ready to slice.

No, I don't think I can reason with her.

There is only one thing left to do, and so I do it, whirling around. I snap my teeth in the air, recalling sinking them into flesh. Remembering how good it felt to hurt someone who scared me.

I am not stronger than Bogdana. I am neither faster nor more cunning. But it's possible I am more desperate. I want to live.

The hag draws up short. At my expression, she takes a step toward me, and I hiss. There is something in her face, glittering in her black eyes, that I do not understand. It looks triumphant. I reach for one of the little blades beneath my dress, wishing again for the carving knife.

The one I pull out is folded, and I fumble trying to open it.

I hear the clop of a pair of hooves, and I think that somehow it is the glaistig, come to watch me be taken. Come to gloat. She must have been the one to alert Bogdana to what I was doing; she must be the reason this is happening.

But it is not the glaistig who emerges from the darkness of the woods. A young man with goat feet and horns, wearing a shirt of golden scale mail and holding a thin-bladed rapier, steps into the pool of light near a building. His face is expressionless, like someone in a dream.

I note the curls of his tawny blond hair tucked behind his pointed ears, the garnet-colored cloak tossed over wide shoulders, the scar along one side of his throat, a circlet at his brow. He moves as though he expects the world to bend to his will.

Above us, clouds are gathering. He points his sword toward Bogdana.

Then his gaze flickers to me. "You've led us on a merry chase." His amber eyes are bright, like those of a fox, but there is nothing warm in them.

I could have told him not to look away from Bogdana. The hag sees the opening and goes for him, nails poised to rip open his chest.

Another sword stops her before he needs to parry. This one is held in the gloved hand of a knight. He wears armor of sculpted brown leather banded with wide strips of a silvery metal. His blackberry hair is cropped short, and his dark eyes are wary.

"Storm hag," he says.

"Out of my way, lapdog," she tells the knight. "Or I will call down lightning to strike you where you stand."

"You may command the sky," the horned man in the golden scale mail returns. "But, alas, we are here on the ground. Leave, or my friend will run you through before you summon so much as a drizzle."

Bogdana narrows her eyes and turns toward me. "I will come for you again, child," she says. "And when I do, you best not run."

Then she moves into the shadows. As soon as she does, I try to dash to one side of him, intent on escape.

The horned man seizes hold of my arm. He's stronger than I expect him to be.

"Lady Suren," he says.

I growl deep in my throat and catch him with my nails, raking them down his cheek. Mine are nowhere near as long or sharp as Bogdana's, but he still bleeds.

He makes a hiss of pain but doesn't let go. Instead, he wrenches my wrists behind my back and holds them tight, no matter how I snarl or kick. Worse, the light hits his face at a different angle and I finally recognize whose skin is under my fingernails.

Prince Oak, heir to Elfhame. Son of the traitorous Grand General and brother to the mortal High Queen. Oak, to whom I was once promised in marriage. Who had once been my friend, although he doesn't seem to remember it.

What was it the pixie had said about him? *Spoiled, irresponsible*, and *wild*. I believe it. Despite his gleaming armor, he is so poorly trained in swordplay that he didn't even attempt to block my blow.

But after that thought comes another one: I have *struck* the Prince of Elfhame.

Oh, I am in trouble now.

"Things will be much easier if you do exactly as we tell you from this moment forward, daughter of traitors," the dark-eyed knight in the leather armor informs me. He has a long nose and the look of someone more comfortable saluting than smiling.

I open my mouth to ask what they want with me, but my voice is rough with disuse. The words come out garbled, the sounds not the ones I intended.

"What's the matter with her?" he asks, frowning at me as though I am some sort of insect.

"Living wild, I suppose," says the prince. "Away from people."

"Didn't she at least talk to herself?" the knight asks, raising his eyebrows.

I growl again.

Oak brings his fingers to the side of his face and draws them back with a wince. He has three long slashes there, bleeding sluggishly.

When his gaze returns to me, there's something in his expression that reminds me of his father, Madoc, who was never so happy as when he went to war.

"I told you that nothing good ever came out of the Court of Teeth," says the knight, shaking his head. Then he takes a rope and ties it around my wrists, looping it through the middle to make it secure. He doesn't pierce my skin like Lord Jarel used to, leashing me by stabbing a needle threaded with a silver chain between the bones of my arms. I am not yet in pain.

But I do not doubt that I will be.

As I trudge through the woods, I think about how I will escape. I have no illusions that I won't be punished. I *struck the prince*. And if they knew about the curses I've been unraveling, they'd be even more furious.

"Next time you'll remember not to drop your guard," the knight says, observing the wounds on Oak's cheek.

"My vanity took the worst of the blow," he says.

"Worried about your pretty face?" the knight asks.

"There *is* too little beauty in the world," says the prince airily. "But that is not my area of greatest conceit."

It can't be coincidence that they turned up clad in armor and prepared to fight at nearly the same time Bogdana started poking around my unfamily's home. They were all looking for me, and whatever the reason, it cannot be one I will like.

I breathe in the familiar scent of wet bark and kicked-up leaf mold. The ferns are silvery in the moonlight, the woods full of shifting shadows.

I wriggle my wrists experimentally. Unfortunately, I am tied well. Flexing my fingers, I try to slip one underneath the binding, but the knots are even too tight for that.

The knight snorts. "Not sure this is the luckiest start to a quest. If the hob hadn't spotted your little queen here, that hag might be wearing her skin for a coat."

The owl-faced hob. I grimace, not certain whether I ought to be grateful. I have no idea what they mean to do to me.

"Isn't that the very definition of luck—to have arrived in time?" Oak throws a mischief-filled glance in my direction, as though at some feral animal he wonders if it would be fun to tame.

I think of him in the High Court, as I was about to be sentenced for my crimes as queen of the traitorous Court of Teeth. I was eleven, and he'd just turned nine. I was bound then, as now. I think of him at thirteen, when he met me in the woods and I sent him away.

At seventeen, he has grown tall, towering over me, lithe and finely muscled. His hair catches the moonlight, warm gold threaded with platinum, bangs parting around small goat horns, eyes of shocking amber, and a constellation of freckles across his nose. He has a trickster's mouth and the swagger of someone used to people doing what he wanted.

Faerie beauty is different from mortal beauty. It's elemental, extravagant. There are creatures in Faerie of such surpassing comeliness that they're painful to look at. Ones that possess a loveliness so great that mortals weep at the sight of them or become transfixed, haunted by the desire to see them even once more. Maybe even die on the spot.

Ugliness in Faerie can be equally extravagant. There are those among the Folk so hideous that all living things shrink back in horror. And yet others have a grotesquerie so exaggerated, so voluptuous, that it comes all the way around to beauty.

It isn't that mortals can't be pretty—many of them are—but their beauty doesn't make you feel pummeled by it. I feel a little pummeled by Oak's beauty.

If I look at him too long, I want to take a bite out of him.

I turn my gaze to my muddy feet, scratched and sore, then Oak's hooves. I recall from a stolen school science book that hooves are made from the same stuff that makes up fingernails. Keratin. Above them, a dusting of fur the same color as his hair disappears into a pant cuff hitting just below his knees, revealing the odd curve of his lower legs. Slim-fitting trousers cover his thighs.

I shiver with the force of keeping myself from thrashing against my bindings.

"Are you cold?" he asks, offering his cloak. It's embroidered velvet, with a pattern of acorns, leaves, and branches. It's beautifully stitched and looks wildly out of place this far from Elfhame.

This is a pantomime I am familiar with. The performance of gallantry while keeping me in restraints, as though the chill in the air is what I am most worried about. But I suppose this is how princes are expected to behave. Noblesse oblige and all that.

Since my hands are tied, I am not sure how he expects me to put it on. When I say nothing, he drapes it over my shoulders, then ties it at my throat. I let him, even though I am used to the cold. Better to have something than not, and it's soft.

Also, it hangs over my hands, shielding them from view. Which means that if I *do* manage to get my wrists loose from the knots, no one will know until it's too late.

That's twice he's been foolish.

I try to concentrate on escape and on not allowing hopelessness to sweep over me. Were my hands free, I would still need to get away. But if I did, I think I could prevent them from tracking me. The knight may have been taught how to follow a trail, but I have had years of experience obscuring mine.

Oak's skills—if he has any outside of being a lordling—are unknown to me. It's possible that despite all his big talk and his pedigree, the prince has brought the knight along to make sure he doesn't trip and impale himself on his own fancy sword.

If they leave me alone for a moment, I can bring my arms down and step backward through the circle of them, bringing my bound hands to the front of my body. Then I'd chew through the rope.

I cannot think of any reason they will give me that chance. Still, under cover of Oak's cloak, I fidget with my bindings, trying to stretch them as far as I am able.

When we depart the woods, we step onto an unfamiliar street. The houses are farther apart than in my unfamily's neighborhood and more run-down, their lawns overgrown. In the distance, a dog is barking.

Then I am guided onto a dirt road. At the very end is a deserted house with boarded-up windows and grass so tall a mower might choke on it. Outside stand two bone-white faerie steeds, the gentle curve of their necks longer than those of mortal horses.

"There?" I ask. The word comes out clearly enunciated, even if my voice still sounds rough.

"Too filthy for Your Highness?" the knight asks, raising his brows at me as though I am unaware of the dirt on my dress and mud on my feet. As though I don't know I am no longer a queen, that I do not remember Oak's sister disbanding my Court.

I hunch my shoulders. I'm used to word games like this one, where there is no right answer and every wrong answer leads to punishment. I keep my mouth shut, my gaze going to the scratches on the prince's cheek. I have made enough mistakes already.

"Ignore Tiernan. It's not so awful inside," Oak says, giving me a courtier's smile, the kind that's supposed to convince you it's okay to relax your guard. I tense up even further. I have learned to be afraid of smiles like that. He continues, with a wave of one hand. "And then we can explain the necessity for our being so wretchedly impolite."

*Impolite.* That was one way to refer to tying me up.

The knight—*Tiernan*—opens the door by leaning his shoulder against it. We go inside, Oak behind me so there's no hope of running. The warped wooden floorboards groan beneath the tread of his hooves.

The house has obviously been empty for a long time. Graffiti sprawls across floral wallpaper, and a cabinet under the sink has been ripped out, probably to get at any copper pipes. Tiernan guides me toward a cracked plastic table that's in a corner of the kitchen along with a few scuffed-looking chairs.

In one is a soldier with a wing where an arm ought to be, light brown skin, a long fall of mahogany hair, and eyes the startling purple of monkshood. I do not know him, but I think I know the curse. Oak's sister, the High Queen, had the unrepentant soldiers who followed Madoc turned into falcons after the Battle of the Serpent. They were cursed so that if they wanted to return to their true forms, they couldn't hunt for a year and a day, eating only what they were given. I do not know what it means that he seems *half*-cursed now. If I squint, I can see the trailing threads of magic around him, winding and coiling like roots trying to regrow.

No easy spell to unmake.

And against his mouth, I see the thin leather straps and golden fastenings of a bridle. A shudder of recognition goes through me. I know *that*, too.

Created by the great smith Grimsen, and given to my parents.

Lord Jarel placed that bridle on me long ago, when my will was an inconvenience to be cleared away like a cobweb. Seeing the bridle brings back all the panic and dread and helplessness I'd felt as the straps slowly sank into my skin.

Later, he'd tried to use it to trap the High King and Queen. He failed and it fell into their hands, but I am horrified that Oak would have made a prisoner wear it, casually, as though it were nothing.

"Tiernan *captured* him outside your mother's Citadel. We needed to know her plans, and he's been immensely helpful. Unfortunately, he's also immensely dangerous." Oak is speaking, but it's hard to see anything but the bridle. "She has a motley crew of vassals. And she has stolen something—"

"More than one something," says the bridled former falcon.

Tiernan kicks the leg of the falcon's chair, but the falcon only smiles up at him. They can make that bridled soldier do anything, say anything. He is trapped inside himself far more securely than he could be bound by any rope. I admire his defiance, however useless.

"Vassals?" I echo the prince's statement, my voice scratchy.

"She has reclaimed the Citadel of the Court of Teeth and, since that Court is no more, has made a new one," Oak says, raising his brows.

"And she has an old magic. She can *create* things. From what we understand, mostly creatures from twigs and wood, but also parts of the dead."

"How?" I ask, horrified.

"Does it matter?" Tiernan says. "*You* were supposed to keep her under control."

I hope he can see the hate in my eyes. Just because the High Queen forced Lady Nore to swear fealty to me after the battle, just because I *could* command her, didn't mean I'd had the first idea of what to actually do.

"She was a kid, Tiernan," Oak says, surprising me. "As was I."

A few embers glow in the fireplace. Tiernan huffs and moves to kneel beside it. He adds logs from a pile, along with balled-up pages he rips from an already-torn cookbook. The edge of a page catches, and flames blaze up. "You'd be a fool to trust the former queen of the Court of Teeth."

"Are you so sure you know our allies from our enemies?" Oak takes out a long stick from the pile of wood, thin enough to be kindling. He holds it in the fire until the end sparks. Then he uses it to light the wicks of candles set around the room. Soon warm pools of light flicker, making the shadows shift.

Tiernan's gaze strays to the bridled soldier. It rests there a long moment before he turns to me. "Hungry, little queen?"

"Don't call me that," I rasp.

"Grouchy, are we?" Tiernan asks. "How would you like this poor servant to address you?"

"Wren," I say, ignoring the taunt.

Oak watches the interaction with half-lidded eyes. I cannot guess at his thoughts. "And do you desire repast?"

I shake my head. The knight raises his eyebrows skeptically. After a moment, he turns away and takes out a kettle, already blackened by fire, and fills it from the tap in the bathroom sink. Then he hangs it on a prop stick they must have rigged up. No electricity, but the house still has running water.

For the first time in a very long while, I think about a shower. About how my hair felt when it was combed and detangled, my scalp spared from the itch of drying mud.

Oak walks to where I am sitting, my tied wrists forcing my shoulders back.

"Lady Wren," he says, amber eyes like those of a fox meeting mine directly. "If I undo your bindings, may I rely upon you to neither attempt escape nor attack one of us for the duration of our time in this house?"

I nod once.

The prince gives me a quick, conspiratorial grin. My mouth betrays me into returning the smile. It makes me recall how charming he was, even as a child.

I wonder if somehow I have misread this situation, if somehow we could be on the same side.

Oak takes a knife from a wrist guard hidden beneath his white linen shirt and applies it to the rope behind me.

"Don't cut it," the knight warns. "Or we'll have to get new rope, and we may have to restrain her again."

I tense, expecting Oak to be angry at being told what to do. As royalty, it is out of order for him to be directed by someone of lower status, but the prince only shakes his head. "Worry no more. I'm only using the point of my blade to help me pry apart your too-clever knots."

I study Tiernan in the half light of the fire. It is hard to gauge age among the Folk, but he looks to be only a little older than Oak. His blackberry hair is mussed; one of his pointed ears has a single piercing through it, a silver hoop.

I bring my hands to my lap, rubbing my fingers over the indentations the rope left in my skin. Had I not been straining so hard against the bindings, they wouldn't be half so deep.

Oak puts the knife away and then says with great formality, "My lady, Elfhame requires your assistance."

Tiernan looks up from the fire but does not speak.

I don't know how to reply. I am unused to attention and find myself flustered to be the focus of his. "I have already sworn fealty to your sister," I manage to croak out. I wouldn't be alive if I hadn't. "I am hers to command."

He frowns. "Let me try to explain. Months before the Battle of the Serpent, Lady Nore managed to cause an explosion underneath the castle."

I glance over at the former falcon, wondering if he was part of it. Wondering if I should remember him. Some of my memories of that time are terribly vivid, while others are blotted out like ink running over paper.

"At the time, it was thought to be an attack on Elfhame's spies and a coincidence that Queen Mab's resting place was disturbed." Oak pauses, watching me as though he's trying to determine if I am following along. "Most faerie bodies break down into roots and flowers, but Mab's did not. Her remains, from her ribs to her finger bones, were imbued with a power that kept them from crumbling—a power to bring things to life. That's what Lady Nore stole, and that's what she's drawing her new power from."

The prince gestures toward the bridled soldier. "Lady Nore has attempted to recruit more Folk to her cause. For those who were cursed to be falcons, if they come to her Citadel, she offers to feed them from her own hand for the year and a day during which they are forbidden from hunting. And when they return to their original form, she demands their loyalty. Between them, her own Folk who remained loyal to her, and the monsters she's making, her plans for revenge on Elfhame seem well under way."

I look at the prisoner. The High Queen granted clemency to any soldier who repudiated what they'd done and swore fealty to her. Anyone who repented. But he'd refused.

I recall standing before the High Queen myself the night Oak spoke on my behalf. *Remember when you said we couldn't help her. We can help her now.* Pity in his voice.

I'd bragged to the High Queen that I knew all Lady Nore and Lord Jarel's secrets, hoping to be useful, thinking that since they spoke in front of me heedlessly, treating me as a dumb animal instead of a little girl, they'd kept nothing back. Still, they'd never spoken of this. "I can't recall any mention of Mab's bones."

Oak gives me a long look. "You lived in the Ice Needle Citadel for more than a year, so you must know its layout, *and* you can command Lady Nore. You're her greatest vulnerability. No matter her other plans, she has good reason to want to eliminate you."

I shudder at that thought because it should have occurred to me before now. I remember Bogdana's long nails, the panic of her chasing me through the streets.

"We need you to stop her," Oak says. "And you need our help to fend off whomever she sends to kill you."

I hate that he's right.

"Did you make Lady Nore promise you anything before she left Elf-hame?" Tiernan asks hopefully.

I shake my head, looking away in shame. As soon as she was able, Lady Nore slipped off. I never had a chance to tell her anything. And when I realized she was gone, what I felt had been mostly relief.

I think of the words she swore before the High Queen, when Jude demanded she give me her vow: *I, Lady Nore, of the Court of Teeth, vow to follow Suren and obey her commands.* Nothing about not sticking a dagger in my back, unfortunately. Nothing about not sending a storm hag after me.

Tiernan frowns, as though my failing to give Lady Nore any orders has confirmed his suspicion that I am untrustworthy. He turns to Oak. "You know the grudge Lady Nore bears against Madoc, justified or not. Who knows what slights *this one* won't forget."

"Let's not discuss my father right at the moment," Oak returns.

Madoc, the traitor who marched on Elfhame with the Court of Teeth. Before that, the Grand General who was responsible for the slaughter of most of the royal family. And Oak's foster father.

Madoc had sought to put Oak on the throne, where he could rule through him. Though the crown would have rested on Oak's head, all the power would have belonged to the redcap. At least until Lord Jarel and Lady Nore tricked Madoc and took over.

I know how precarious it is to be a queen without power, controlled and thoroughly debased. That could have been Oak's fate. But if the prince bears his father any ill will, it doesn't show on his face.

Tiernan leans forward to take the metal kettle off the prop stick with a poker, setting it gingerly on a folded-up towel. It steams steadily.

Then he takes out several foam containers of instant ramen from a kitchen cabinet, along with an already-opened box of mint tea. Noticing me looking, he nods toward Oak. "The prince introduced me to this delicacy of the mortal world. Bollockses up your magic for a while—all that salt—but I can't deny it is addictive."

The smell makes me recall the satisfaction of something burn-your-mouth hot, something straight from an oven instead of congealed in a garbage bin.

I don't take one of the noodle cups, but when Oak hands me a mug of tea, I accept that. I stare into the depths and see silt at the bottom. *Sugar*, he would tell me if I asked, and at least some of it would be, but I can't be sure the rest isn't a drug of some kind, or a poison.

*They do not want me dead*, I try to tell myself. *They need me.*

And I need them, too, if I want to live. If Lady Nore is hunting me, if Bogdana is helping her, the prince and his companion are my only hope of staying out of reach.

"So, what would you have me to do?" I am proud to get the whole sentence out without my voice cracking.

"Go north with me," Oak says, sitting on the plastic chair beside mine. "Command Lady Nore to tie a big bow around herself and make a present to Elfhame. We'll steal back Mab's bones and end the threat to—"

"With *you*?" I stare at him, sure I have misunderstood. Princes stay in palaces, enjoying revels and debauchery and the like. Their necks are too valuable to risk.

"And my brave friend Tiernan." Oak inclines his head toward Tiernan, who rolls his eyes. "Together, the four of us—counting Hyacinthe—will take back the Citadel and end the threat to Elfhame."

Hyacinthe. So that's the cursed soldier's name.

"And when we complete our quest, you can ask a boon of me, and if it is within my power and not too terrible, I will grant it." I wonder at the prince's motive. Perhaps ambition. If he delivers Lady Nore, he could ask a boon of his own from the High King and cement his position as heir, effectively cutting any future children out of the line of succession.

I can imagine a prince might do a lot for an unwavering path to the throne. One that by some accounts should have been his in the first place.

And yet, I cannot help thinking of the sprite saying he would be unsuitable as a ruler. Too spoiled. Too wild.

Of course, since she's a companion of the glaistig and the glaistig is awful, perhaps what she thinks shouldn't matter.

Tiernan takes out a wooden scroll case carved with a pattern of vines. It contains a map, which he unfurls on the table. Oak weighs down the edges with teacups, spoons, and a brick that might have been thrown through one of the windows. "First we must go a ways south," the prince says. "To a hag who will give us a piece of information that I hope will help us trick Lady Nore. Then we head north and east, over water, into the Howling Pass, through the Forest of Stone, to her stronghold."

"A small group is nimble," Tiernan says. "Easier to hide. Even if I think crossing through the Stone Forest is a fool's notion."

Oak traces the route up the coast with a finger and gives us a roguish grin. "I am the fool with that notion."

Neither seems inclined to tell me more about the hag, or the trickery she is supposed to inspire.

I stare at the path, and at its destination. The Ice Needle Citadel. I suppose it is still there, gleaming in the sun as though made of spun sugar. Hot glass.

The Stone Forest *is* dangerous. The trolls living there belong to no Court, recognize no authority but their own, and the trees seem to move of their own accord. But everything is dangerous now.

My gaze goes to Hyacinthe, noting his bird wing and the bridle sinking into his cheeks. If Oak leaves it on him long enough, it will become part of him, invisible and unable to be removed. He will forever be in the prince's thrall.

The last time I wore it, Lady Nore and Lord Jarel's plan to move against the High Court was the only reason they cut the bridle's straps from my skin, leaving the scars that still run along my cheekbones. Leaving me with the knowledge of what they would do to me if I disobeyed them.

Then they marched me before the High Queen and suggested that I be united in marriage with her brother and heir, Prince Oak.

It is hard to explain the savagery of hope.

I thought she might agree. At least two of Oak's sisters were mortal, and while I knew it was foolish, I couldn't help thinking that being mortal meant they would be kind. Maybe an alliance would suit everyone, and then I would have escaped the Court of Teeth. I kept my face as blank as possible. If Lady Nore and Lord Jarel thought the idea pleased me, they would have found a way to turn it to torment.

Oak was lounging on a cushion beside his sister's feet. No one seemed to expect him to act with any kind of formal decorum. At the mention of marriage, he looked up at me and flinched.

His eldest sister's lip curled slightly, as though she found the thought of me even coming near him repulsive. *Oak shouldn't have anything to do with these people or their creepy daughter*, she said.

In that moment, I hated him for being so precious to them, for being cosseted and treated as though he was deserving of protection when I had none.

Maybe I still hate him a little. But he was kind when we were children. It's possible there's a part of him that's still kind.

Oak could always remove the bridle from Hyacinthe. As he might, if he decides he wants to put it on *me*. If I am Lady Nore's greatest vulnerability, then he might well consider me a weapon too valuable to chance letting slip away.

It is too great a risk to think of a prince as so kind that he wouldn't.

But even if he wouldn't use the bridle to control me, or invoke his sister's authority, I still have to go north and face Lady Nore. If I don't, she will send the storm hag again or some other monster, and they will end me. Oak and Tiernan are my best chance at surviving for long enough to stop her, and they are my only chance at getting close enough to command her.

"Yes," I say, as though there was ever a choice. My voice doesn't break this time. "I'll go with you."

After all, Lady Nore ripped away everything I cared about. It will give me no small pleasure to do the same to her.

But that doesn't mean that I don't know that, no matter how courteously they behave, I am as much a prisoner as the winged soldier. I can command Lady Nore, but the Prince of Elfhame has the authority to command me.

CHAPTER

3

The night after Madoc, Lady Nore, and Lord Jarel failed to arrange our marriage, Oak snuck to the edge of where Madoc's traitorous army and the Court of Teeth had made camp. There, he found me staked to a post like a goat.

He was perhaps nine, and I, ten. I snarled at him. I remember that.

I thought he was looking for his father and that he was a fool. Madoc seemed the sort to roast him over a fire, consume his flesh, and call it love. By then, I had become familiar with love of that kind.

He looked upset at the sight of me. He ought to have been taught better than to let his emotions show on his face. Instead, he assumed that others would *care* about his feelings, so he didn't bother to hide them.

I wondered what would happen if, when he got close enough, I pinned him to the ground. If I beat him to death with a rock, I might be rewarded by Lord Jarel and Lady Nore, but it seemed equally likely that I would be punished.

And I didn't want to hurt him. He was the first child I'd met since coming to Faerie. I was curious.

"I have food with me," he said, coming closer and taking a bundle out of a pack he wore over one shoulder. "In case you're hungry."

I was always hungry. Here in the camp, I mostly filled my belly by eating moss and sometimes dirt.

He unwrapped an embroidered napkin on the ground—one made of spider silk finer than anything I wore—to reveal roasted chicken and plums. Then he moved away. Allowing me space to feed, as though he were the frightening one.

I glanced at the nearby tents and the woods, at the banked fire a few feet away, embers still glowing. There were voices, but distant ones, and I knew from long experience that while Lord Jarel and Lady Nore were out, no one would check on me, even if I screamed.

My stomach growled. I wanted to snatch the food, though his kindness was jarring and made me wonder what he'd want in return for it. I was used to tricks, to games.

I stared at him, noting the sturdiness of his body, solid in a way that spoke of having enough to eat and running outside. At the alienness of the little goat horns cutting through his soft bronze-and-gold curls and the strange amber of his eyes. At the ease with which he sat, faun legs crossed, hooved feet tipped in covers of beaten gold.

A woolen cloak of deep green was clasped at his throat, long enough to sit on. Underneath, he wore a brown tunic with golden buttons and knee-length trousers, stopping just above where his goat legs curved. I could not think of a single thing I had that he could want.

"It's not poisoned," he said, as though that was my worry.

Temptation won out. I grabbed a wing, tearing at the flesh. I ate it down to the bone, which I cracked so I could get at the marrow. He watched in fascination.

"My sisters were telling fairy tales," Oak said. "They fell asleep, but I didn't."

That explained *nothing* about his reasons for coming here, but his words gave me a strange, sharp pain in my chest. After a moment, I recognized it as envy. For having sisters. For having stories.

"Do you talk?" he asked, and I realized how long I'd been silent. I had been a shy child in the mortal world, and in Faerie nothing good had ever come from my speaking.

"Not much," I admitted, and when he smiled, I smiled back.

"Do you want to play a game?" He shuffled closer, eyes bright. Reaching into his pocket, he produced some little metal figures. Three silver foxes resting in the middle of his callused palm. Inset chips of peridot sparkled in their eyes.

I stared at him in confusion. Had he really come all this way to sit in the dirt and show me his toys? Maybe he hadn't seen another kid in a while, either.

I picked up one of the foxes to examine it. The detail work was very fine. "How do we play?"

"You throw them." He formed a cage of his hands with the foxes inside, shook it up, and then tossed them into the grass. "If they land standing, you get ten points. If they land on their backs, you get five points. If they land on their side, no points."

His landed: two lying on their sides, and one on its back.

I reached out eagerly. I wanted to hold those foxes, feel them fall from my fingers.

When they did and two landed on their backs, I gasped in delight.

Over and over, we played the game. We made tally marks in the dirt.

For a while, there was only the joy of escaping from where I was and who I was. But then I remembered that as little as he might want from me, there was plenty I needed.

"Let's play for stakes," I proposed.

He looked intrigued. "What will you bet?"

I was not so foolish as to ask for anything much that first time. "If you lose, you tell me a secret. Any secret. And I will do the same for you."

We played, and I lost.

He leaned in, close enough for me to smell the sage and rosemary his clothes had been wrapped with before he wore them, close enough to bite out a chunk of flesh from his throat.

"I grew up in the mortal lands," I said.

"I've been there." He seemed amused to discover we had something in common. "And eaten pizza."

It was hard to imagine a prince of Faerie journeying to the human world for anything but a sinister reason, but eating pizza didn't seem that sinister.

We played again, and this time he lost. His smile dimmed, and he dropped his voice to a whisper. "This is a *real secret*. You can't tell any-one. When I was little, I glamoured my mortal sister. I made her hit herself, a lot of times, over and over, and I laughed while she did. It was awful of me, and I never told her that I regretted it. I am afraid of making her remember. She might get really mad."

I wondered which sister he'd glamoured. I hoped not the one who sat on a throne now, his life in her hands.

His words stood as a reminder, though, that no matter how soft he seemed or how young, he was as capable of cruelty as the rest. But cruel or not, his help could still be won. My gaze went to the stake to which I was bound. "This time, if my score is better, you cut the rope and free me. If *your* score is better, you can . . . ask me to do something, anything, and I will."

A desperate bargain for me, but hope had made me reckless.

He frowned. "If I free you," he said, "what happens then?"

He must have wondered if I had been tied here because I was *dangerous*. Maybe he wondered if, once free, I would run at him and hurt him. I supposed he was not so stupid after all. But if he wanted me to swear myself into his service, I could not.

All Courts pledge fealty to their ruler and that ruler pledges fealty to the High Court. When High King Cardan came to power, because I was hidden, and Queen of the Court of Teeth, my failure to give him an oath of loyalty was the reason Lady Nore and Lord Jarel were able to betray him. They would kill me on the spot if I pledged myself to anyone, because I would have become useless to them.

"We can go to the palace, and you can show me your other games," I told him. I would hide there for as long as I could, perhaps long enough to get away from Lady Nore and Lord Jarel.

He nodded. "You toss first."

I cupped the foxes in my hand and whispered to them softly. "Please."

They fell, one on its back, one standing, and one on its side. A total of fifteen points. Good, but not great.

Oak picked them up, shook, and tossed. They all fell on their feet. Thirty points.

He laughed and clapped his hands. "Now you have to do whatever I want!"

I thought of what he'd made his sister do for his amusement and shuddered. At that moment the secret he'd told me seemed less a confession and more a warning.

"Well?" I growled.

Oak frowned, clearly trying to think of something. Then his brow cleared, and I dreaded what was to come next.

"Sing a song," he said with a wicked smile.

I glanced over at the camp in panic. "They'll hear," I protested.

He shook his head, still grinning. "You can sing quietly. And we've been talking all this time. It doesn't have to be any louder than that."

My mind went blank. Only perhaps a year before, my unsister and I were dancing around the house to songs from movies with brave princesses, but at that moment I could think of none of their words. All I could recall were bloodthirsty ballads from the Court of Teeth. But when I opened my mouth, the tune was from a song my unmother had sung when she was putting me to bed. And the lyrics were a mishmash of the two.

"*Sing a song of sixpence,*" I sang as softly as I could. "*Pocket full of snakes. If they take my head off, that'll cure my aches.*"

Oak laughed as though my song was actually funny and not just some weird, grim doggerel. But however poorly done, my debt was paid, which meant I had another chance to win my freedom.

I grabbed up the foxes to play again before he could change the stakes.

Mine landed with one standing, two on their sides. Five measly, stupid, useless points. Nearly impossible to win with. I wanted to kick the figurines into the dirt, to throw them at Oak. I would owe him twice over and still have nothing. I could feel the old burn of tears behind my eyes, the taste of salt in my mouth. I was an unlucky child, ill-fated and—

On Oak's toss, the foxes all landed on their sides for zero points.

I caught my breath and stared at him. I won. *I won.*

He didn't seem disappointed to have to pay the forfeit. He got up with a grin and took out a knife from a sheath I hadn't noticed, hidden in the sleeve of his shirt. The blade was small and leaf-shaped, its handle chased in gold, its edge sharp.

It barely parted the strands of the heavy rope, though, each one taking minutes of sawing to slice through. I had tried my own teeth on them before, with little success, but I hadn't realized how tough they really were.

"There's some kind of enchantment on this," he said, frustrated.

"Cut faster," I said, and received an annoyed look.

My fingers vibrated with the tension of waiting. Before he was a quarter of the way through, the thunder of horses and the rattle of a carriage made me realize that my win had come too late. Lady Nore and Lord Jarel were returning to camp. And they would check to make certain I was where they'd left me. Oak began to hack at the rope frantically, but I knew escape was impossible.

"Go," I told him, disappointment bitter in my mouth.

He caught hold of my hand, pressing one of the silver foxes into my palm. "I'll come back tomorrow," he said. "I promise."

I sucked in my breath at that casually given vow. Faeries couldn't break their promises, so I had no choice but to believe him.

The next night the entire Court of Teeth was preparing for what Lord Jarel had announced with great smugness was to be a celebratory feast. The mortal High Queen had agreed to accept the bridle, along with their offer of a truce. I had been given a dress and told not to get it dirty, so I stood rather than sat on the ground.

I worried that Oak wouldn't get there in time to keep me from being carted off to the feast. I was dreaming up ways to beseech him at the castle when he emerged from the woods. He dragged a sword behind him, too long to wear at his side. It made me recall that he'd jumped in front of his mother when the serpent king darted toward her, a prince from a fairy tale facing down a dragon. He might have been soft and cherished, but he could be brave.

Oak winked at me, and I wondered if he was brave because he didn't understand the danger he was in.

I glanced at the camp, then at him, widening my eyes in warning. But he came to my side anyway, drew the sword, and started to saw away at my bindings.

"The sword's name is Nightfell," he whispered. "It belongs to Jude."

His sister. The High Queen. It was such a different way to be royal, to have a family that you would consider by their relationship to you before their title. Whose weapon you wouldn't be afraid to steal.

The blade was sharp and must have been well made, since it sliced through the enchanted rope much faster than the little knife.

"Her human father was a blacksmith," he went on. "He forged the sword before she was born."

"Where is he now?" I wondered if she had her own unfamily somewhere.

"Madoc killed him." Oak's tone made it sound as though he was aware that was *bad*, but not *so bad* that his sister would bear a grudge. I don't know what I ought to have expected; Oak might make an exception for his sisters, might have enjoyed the pizza, but that didn't mean he thought much of mortal lives.

My gaze went in the direction of the main camp, where Madoc's tent would be. Inside, he'd be preparing for the banquet. Preparing to trick Jude, his foster daughter, whose sword this was and whose father he'd slain. Oak seemed to be laboring under the illusion that Madoc cared about him enough that Oak would be safe if he got caught, but I doubted that was the case.

The last strand of rope parted, and I was free, although it still braceleted my leg.

"They'll be traveling to the banquet," I whispered. "They might spot us."

He took my hand and pulled me toward the woods. "Then we better go fast. Come on, we can hide in my room."

Together, we ran through the mossy forest, past white trees with red leaves and streams holding pale-eyed nixies that watched us as we went by.

This felt a little bit like one of Lady Nore and Lord Jarel's games. Sometimes they would act in a way that suggested affection, then behave as though they had never felt anything but disgust. Leave out something I desperately desired—food, a key to a room in the Citadel where I might hide, a storybook to hide with—and then punish me for taking it.

But I ran anyway. And clutched his fingers as though he could drag me into a world where other kinds of games were possible. Hope lit my heart.

We slowed at certain points when we spotted another one of the Folk. This far from the camp of the Court of Teeth, the soldiers we were avoiding belonged to Elfhame. That did little to reassure me, though. No harm would come to Oak at their hands, but they might well lock me up in their dungeons or take me to their Tower of Forgetting.

At the palace, we passed our first set of guards. They bowed to Oak, and if they were surprised to see him with another child trailing a piece of dirty rope, they kept it to themselves. The palace of Elfhame was a grassy hill, set with windows. Inside, there were stone walls, occasionally covered in plaster or packed earth. Nothing like the cold, carved ice chambers of the Citadel. We climbed one flight of stairs, and then another, when a knight stepped out in front of us.

She was dressed all in green, with armor cleverly shaped into leaves. Celery-colored hair was pulled back from an angular, insect-like face.

"Prince," said the knight. "Your lady mother seeks you. She wanted to be sure you were safe."

Oak nodded stiffly. "You may tell her I've returned."

"And where ought I say you were...?" The knight eyed me and then the stolen sword. I feared I saw a flash of recognition in her eyes.

"Tell her that I'm well," the prince said, seeming to deliberately misunderstand her.

"But by what name ought I call—" the knight began, attempting to interrogate him and be deferential to his position all at once.

Oak seemed to have come to the end of his patience.

"Call us whatever you like!" he interrupted her to say. Then he grabbed my hand again, and we hurried up the stairs and into his room, where we slammed the door. We collapsed against it.

He was grinning, and looking at him, I had the strangest urge to laugh.

The room was large and painted a bright white. A round window let in light from the lamps outside. I heard strains of music, probably from the banquet, which was sure to start soon. A bed sat along one wall, topped with a velvet coverlet. A painting hung above it, of deer eating apples in a forest.

"This is your room?" I asked. Nothing about it spoke of him, except for a few paperback books on a small table and playing cards scattered beside an armchair.

He nodded but seemed a bit cautious about it. "I've only just gotten back to the isles. I was staying in the mortal world with one of my sisters. Like I told you last night."

That wasn't exactly what he'd said. I had thought he'd *visited* the place, not that he'd lived there and definitely not so recently.

I looked out the window. He had a view over the woods and to the sea beyond, the dark water rippling in the moonlight. "Are you going back?" I asked.

"I guess." He knelt and opened a dresser drawer to reveal a few games and some toy bricks. "We couldn't bring much with us."

I supposed he wouldn't be sure of anything, what with the unlikelihood of his sister keeping her crown, with so many forces conspiring against her.

"You have Uno," I said, picking up the card game and staring at it as though it was the relic of some fallen city.

He grinned, delighted at my recognizing it. "And Nine Men's Morris, Sorry!, and Monopoly, but that takes *forever*."

"I've played some of those." I felt shy now that we were in the palace, his territory. I wondered how long he would let me stay.

"You pick one," he said. "I am going to see what I can swipe from the kitchens. The cooks ought to have plenty to spare, considering how much food they made for tonight."

After he left, I reverently took the Sorry! game out of its box, sliding my fingers over the plastic pieces. I thought about playing with my unfamily one night when Rebecca sent me to Start three times in a row and teased me about it, back before I learned how much there really was to lose. I'd cried, and my unfather had told Rebecca that it was as important to be a good winner as a good loser.

I wanted Oak to give me an opportunity to be a good winner.

When he returned, it was with a whole pie and a pitcher of cream. He'd forgotten spoons and plates and cups, so we had to scoop handfuls of blueberry filling and crust into our mouths and drink from the jug. We stained our fingers and then the edges of the game cards.

So lost in the joy of that moment, I didn't think of danger until the latch of the door turned. I was barely able to roll underneath Oak's bed, putting my sticky, stained fingers over my mouth, before Oriana came into the room.

I tried to remain as still as possible. Madoc's wife had camped with us when we were in the north and would know me instantly if she saw me.

For a moment, I even considered throwing myself on her mercy. I might have made a useful hostage. If Oriana turned me over to the High Queen, she might not be cruel. Certainly, I had heard no rumors of her being awful in that way.

But if there were to be a truce, then I would be handed back to Lord Jarel and Lady Nore. The High Queen would want to give them all the easy things they asked for so that she'd have half a chance at denying them the hard ones.

Moreover, I wasn't entirely sure whose side Oriana was on.

"Where were you?" she asked Oak, voice sharp. "Is this what Vivi and that Heather girl let you get up to in the mortal world? Running off without telling anyone?"

"Go away," Oak said.

"The guards said you had someone with you. And there's a rumor that monster child from the Court of Teeth is missing."

He gave her a bored look.

"You are not to go near her alone."

"I am the prince," he said. "I can do whatever I like."

Oriana looked momentarily surprised, then hurt. "I left Madoc's side for you."

"So what?" He didn't appear at all sorry. "I don't have to listen to you or do what you say. And I don't have to tell you anything."

I expected her to slap him or call the guards to do it for her, but then I realized the guards would follow the prince's commands over those of Lady Oriana. He was the one his sisters loved and they had all the power now.

But I could not have predicted how his mother went to him and touched his forehead, fingers pushing back his dark gold hair from his horns. "I know," she said. "I cannot hope for one side to win, either. I used to wish that Madoc never went looking for those girls, and now all I wish is that we could be together again as we once were."

Despite what he'd told her, Oak leaned his head against her hand and closed his eyes. In that moment, I understood how little I knew about any of them. But I recognized love, and I envied the brush of her hands through his hair.

She sighed. "Stay in your room tonight, if not because I ask you, then because the banquet will be dull and your sister cannot handle one more distraction."

With a kiss upon his brow, she left.

The closing of the door recalled me to the precariousness of my position. I needed to find a way to persuade Oak to keep me in the palace. A reason for him to stand up to his mother and sisters in my behalf. I was certain I knew the mortal games better than he did, even if he'd been in the mortal world more recently, and moreover, I knew how to cheat at them. I could count the number of blueberry stains, could shuffle so that the first few cards most benefited me. Rebecca used to do that all the time.

"Let's play Go Fish," I said.

He appeared relieved that I didn't ask him questions about his mother, like why he was upset with her or why she'd been kind despite it. I wondered again if he'd been looking for Madoc when he found me the night before.

I began to shuffle the cards and talked as I did so he wouldn't notice my hands. "What else was there in the kitchens?"

He frowned a little, and it made me nervous until I realized he was just concentrating. "Pheasant," he said. "Acorn cakes. Oh, and I think I have Ring Pops somewhere here, from trick-or-treating. I went as myself."

There was something horrifying about that, but some part of me wished I could have done it, too.

I dealt to him from the bottom of the deck and to myself from the top, where I'd been careful to put plenty of matches. He won once anyway. But I won twice.

He let me hide under his bed that day, and the next, after I learned that there hadn't ever been a chance at peace, that the Court of Teeth had lost the war, and that Lord Jarel, my father, was dead.

That was the first time in over a year that I slept through the night and deep into the afternoon without waking.

I will always be grateful for that, even after guards dragged me out of his room three days later in chains. Even after the High Queen sent me away from Elfhame, and Oak said not a single word to stop her.

# CHAPTER

# 4

Behind the abandoned house, two faerie horses chew on dandelions as they wait for their riders. Slight as deer, with a soft halo of light surrounding their bodies, they glide between the trees like ghosts.

Oak goes to the first. Her coat a soft gray, her mane braided into something that looks like netting, and which is hung with gold beads. Tooled leather saddlebags rest against her flanks. She nuzzles into his hand.

"Have you ridden before?" he asks me, and I return him the look he deserves.

In the Court of Teeth, I was instructed on almost none of the things that a child of royalty ought to know. I was barely taught to use my own magic, leaving me as I am, with weak spells, poor etiquette, and no familiarity with faerie horses.

"No? And yet you would look so well with your hair whipping behind you," Oak says. "Wild as the Folk of old."

I feel the tightening coils of embarrassment in my gut. Although he may intend it as mockery, I am pleased as much as shamed by his words.

Tiernan has his hand on Hyacinthe's back, guiding him across the grass. An odd way of touching a prisoner. "You can't help trying to charm every snake you come upon, no matter how cold-blooded or vicious. Let that one be."

I want to bare my teeth, but I feel it will only justify Tiernan's words.

"I think you're giving me the advice you ought to have given yourself years ago," Oak returns without real annoyance, and I can see from Tiernan's expression that arrow struck true. The knight's eyes narrow.

Oak rubs a hand over his face and, in that moment, looks exhausted. I blink, and his features shift to mildly amused. I am left to wonder if I imagined the whole thing. "Making pleasant conversation with one's traveling companions leads to less miserable travel, I find."

"Oh, do you?" says Tiernan in a parody of the prince's drawl. "Well, then, by all means—carry on."

"Oh, I *shall*," Oak returns. Now they're both obviously annoyed with each other, although I have no idea why.

"What's your horse's name?" I ask in the long silence that follows. My voice rasps only a little.

Oak strokes fingers over the velvet nap of her flank, visibly pushing off his mood. "My sister Taryn called her Damsel Fly when we were young, and it stuck. I'll hand you up."

"Isn't that sweet?" Hyacinthe says, the first words I've heard him speak. "Riding your sister's horse into battle. Have you anything of your own, prince? Or just girls' castoffs and scraps?"

"Get up," Tiernan tells Hyacinthe gruffly. "Mount."

"As you command," the cursed soldier says. "You do delight in giving orders, don't you?"

"To you, I do," Tiernan returns, heaving himself up behind the prisoner. A moment later he seems to realize what he's said, and his cheeks pink. I don't think Hyacinthe can see him, but I can.

"He calls his horse Rags," Oak goes on as though neither of the others spoke, although ignoring them must take some effort.

Tiernan sees me glance in his direction and gives me a look that reminds me that, were it up to him, he'd have me bound and gagged and dragged along behind them.

"I need to get my things," I tell them. "From my camp."

Oak and Tiernan share a look. "Of course," Oak says after whatever silent communication passed between them. "Lead the way, Lady Wren."

Then the prince clasps his fingers together to make a step so I can hop up onto the horse. I do, scrambling to throw my leg over. He swings up in front of me, and I do not know where to put my hands.

"Hold on," Oak urges, and I have no choice but to dig my nails into the flesh of his hip bones, just below the scale mail, and try not to fall off. The warmth of his skin is scalding through the thin cloth he's wearing beneath the gold plates, and embarrassment pulls that heat to my cheeks. The faerie horse is supernaturally fleet of foot, moving so fast that it feels a little like flying. I try to speak into Oak's ear, to give him directions, but I feel as though half the things I say are swept into the wind.

As we get close to my woven willow hut, the horse slows to a trot. A shiver goes through the prince as he hits the spell I wove to protect this place. He turns with a swift accusatory look and then reaches into the air and swipes it away as easily as if it were cobwebs.

Does he think I meant to use it to escape? To harm him? When he stops, I slide down with relief, my legs wobbly. Usually, this would be the hour when I slept, and I am more exhausted than usual as I stagger to my little home.

I feel Oak's gaze on me, evaluating. I cannot help but see this place through his eyes. The den of an animal.

I grit my teeth and crawl inside. There, I scrounge around for an old backpack scavenged from a dumpster. Into this, I shove items, without being sure what I might need. The least-stained of my three blankets. A spoon from my unparents' kitchen drawers. A plastic bag with seven licorice jelly beans in it. A bruised apple I was saving. A scarf, the ends unfinished, which my unmother was still knitting when I stole it.

Oak walks through a pattern of mushroom rings nearby, studying my packing from a distance.

"Have you been living here since last we spoke?" he asks, and I try not to read too much into the question. His expression isn't disgusted or anything like that, but it is too carefully neutral for me to believe he isn't hiding what he thinks.

Four years ago, it was easier to disguise how far I'd fallen. "More or less," I tell him.

"Alone?" he asks.

Not entirely. I'd made a human friend at twelve. I'd met her rooting through trash behind a bookstore, looking for paperbacks with their covers stripped off. She'd painted my toenails a bright glittering blue, but one day I saw her talking to my sister and hid from her.

And then Bogdana showed up a few months later, hanging a human pelt over my camp and warning me not to reveal any of our secrets. I stayed away from mortals for a year after that.

But there'd been a boy I saved from the glaistig when I was fourteen and he, seventeen. We'd sit together by a pond a few miles from here, and I would carefully avoid telling him anything I thought the storm hag wouldn't like. I think he was half-sure that he'd conjured me with his vape pen, an imaginary girlfriend. He liked to start fires, and I liked to watch. Eventually, he decided that since I wasn't real, it didn't matter what he did to me.

Then I demonstrated that I was very real, and so were my teeth.

The storm hag came again after that, with another pelt, and another warning about mortals, but by then I hardly needed it.

There was a silver-haired banshee I visited sometimes. As one of the sluagh, the other local faeries avoided her, but we would sit together for hours while she wept.

But when I thought of telling Oak any of that, I realized it would make my life sound worse, instead of better. "More or less," I say again.

I pick up things and then put them down, wishing to keep them with me but knowing they won't all fit. A chipped mug. A single earring hanging from a branch. A heavy textbook of poetry from seventh grade, with *REBECCA* written in thick Sharpie on the side. The butcher knife from the family kitchen, which Tiernan eyes skeptically.

I stick with the two little knives I have on my person.

There is one last thing I take, swiping it fast, so neither of them sees. A tiny silver fox with peridot eyes.

"The Court of Moths is a savage place, risky even for a prince of Elfhame," Tiernan informs Oak from where he sits on a log, cutting bark from a branch with a wicked little blade. I sense this is not the first time they've had this conversation. "Sure, they're your sister's vassals, but they're violent as vultures. Queen Annet eats her lovers when she tires of them."

Hyacinthe kneels at the trickle of a nearby stream to drink. With only one hand to support himself and not a second to make a cup with, he puts his mouth directly into the water and gulps what he can. At Tiernan's words, he lifts his face. Alert, perhaps, to an angle for escape.

"We only need to speak with the Thistlewitch," Oak reminds him. "Queen Annet can grant us a way to navigate her swamps and find the hag. The Court of Moths is only half a day's ride, down and east, toward the sea. We won't dally. We can't afford to."

"The Thistlewitch," Tiernan echoes. "She's seen two queens dead in the Court of Termites. Rumor is, she had a hand in engineering it. Who knows what her game is now."

"She was alive during Mab's reign," Oak says.

"She was *old* during Mab's reign," Tiernan supplies, as though that makes his point for him. "She's dangerous."

"The Thistlewitch's dowsing rod can find anything." There is a deep anxiety under the surface of this conversation. I am too well acquainted with the feeling not to recognize it. Is he more afraid than he's letting on, a prince on his first quest, riding his sister's pretty horse?

"And then what?" Tiernan says. "That's a tricky gambit you're considering."

Oak heaves a heavy sigh and does not answer, leaving me to wonder about his motives all over again. Leaving me to wonder what part of his plan he has elided, that he needs a hag to find something for him.

Tiernan returns to whittling and doesn't issue any further warnings.

I wonder how hard it is to keep Oak out of trouble, and if Tiernan does it out of friendship or loyalty to Elfhame. If Oak is the sunlight filtering through trees in the woods, all shifting gold and shadow, then Tiernan seems like those same woods in winter, the branches barren and cold.

As I move to rise, I notice something white is tucked into the edge of my hut, pushed into the weave of the woods. A wadded-up piece of paper, unmarked by dirt. As they speak, I manage to smooth it out beneath one of my filthy blankets so I can read what's written there.

*You cannot outrun fate.*

I recognize Bogdana's spidery handwriting. I hate the thought of her intruding on the place where I feel most safe, and the note itself makes me angry. A taunt, to make it clear that she hasn't given up hunting me. A taunt, like giving me a head start in a game she is sure to win.

I crumple the note and shove it into my backpack, settling it beside the little silver fox.

"Got everything?" Oak asks, and I straighten up guiltily, slinging my bag across one shoulder.

A gust of wind makes my threadbare dress blow around me, its hem dirtier than ever.

"If you thought we went fast before—" the prince begins to say, his smile full of mischief. Reluctantly, I walk to the horse and resign myself to getting on her back again.

That's when arrows fly out of the dark.

One hits the trunk of a nearby maple tree, just above my head. Another strikes the flank of the knight's horse, causing her to let out a horrible whinny. Through my panic, I note the rough, uneven wood of the shafts, the way they are fletched with crow feathers.

"Stick creatures!" the winged soldier shouts.

Tiernan gives him a look of banked fury, as though this is somehow his fault. "Ride!"

Oak reaches for my hand, pulling me up onto Damsel so that I am seated in front, my back against his metal-covered chest. I grab for the knots of the horse's mane, and then we're racing through the night, the horse thundering beneath us, arrows hissing through the air at our heels.

The stick creatures come into view, beasts of branches and twigs—some shaped like enormous wolves, others like spiders, and one with three snapping heads, like nothing I have seen before. A few in vaguely human shapes, armed with bows. All of them crawling with moss and vine, with stones tucked into packed earth at their centers. But the worst part is that among those pieces of wood and fen, I see what appear to be waxy mortal fingers, strips of skin, and empty mortal eyes.

Terror breaks over me like a wave.

I throw a panicked glance back at the wounded horse riding after us, carrying Tiernan and Hyacinthe. Blood stains her flank, and her steps are stumbling, uneven. Though she is moving fast, the wicker creatures are swifter.

Oak must know it, because he pulls on the reins and Damsel wheels around, back toward our attackers. "Can you get behind me?" he says.

"No!" I shout. I am having a hard enough time hanging on, pressing my thighs against the horse's flanks as firmly as I can and clinging to its neck, my fingers tangled in its mane.

His arm encircles my waist, pressing me to him. "Then crouch down as low as you're able," he warns. With his other hand, he pulls a small crossbow from a saddlebag and notches a bolt with his teeth.

He fires, missing spectacularly. The bolt strikes the dirt between

Tiernan and the wicker men's deer. There isn't time to reload, and the prince doesn't try, just takes a sharp, expectant breath.

My heart sinks, desperately wishing for some talent other than curse breaking. Had I the storm hag's power, I could call down lightning and singe them to cinders. Had I better control of my own magic, perhaps I could hide us behind an illusion.

Then the bolt Oak shot explodes into blue shimmering fire, and I realize he didn't miss after all. Burning stick men fall from the backs of their stick mounts, and one of the spidery creatures darts off, aflame, into the woods.

Tiernan's horse has nearly caught up to ours when we gallop away. I feel Oak tense behind me and I turn, but he shakes his head, so I concentrate on holding on.

It was one thing to have Lady Nore's power described, but seeing the stick creatures with their bits of flesh made me all too aware of how easy it would be to harvest human parts from cities like she might take rocks from quarries, and carve armies from forests. Elfhame should worry. The mortal world should fear. This is worse than I imagined.

The horses break free of the woods, and we find ourselves on suburban roads, then crossing a highway. It's late enough that there's little traffic. Tiernan's glamour settles over us, not quite a disguise but a piece of misdirection. The mortals still observe something out of the corner of their eyes, just not us. A white stag, perhaps. Or a large dog. Something they expect and that fits into the world they can explain. The magic makes my shoulders itch.

We ride on for what feels like hours.

"Oak?" the knight calls as we come to a crossroads. His gaze goes to me. "When was the prince hit?"

I realize that the weight on my back has grown heavier, as though Oak slumped forward. His hand is still around me, but his grip on the reins has loosened. When I shift in the saddle, I see that his eyes are shut, lashes dusting his cheeks, limbs gone slack.

"I didn't know—" I begin.

"You *fool*," mutters Tiernan.

I try to turn in the saddle and grab for the prince's body so it doesn't fall. He slumps against me, large and warm in my arms, his armor making him heavier than I am sure I can manage. I dig in my fingers and hope I can hold him, although it is all too easy to imagine the prince's body dropped in the dirt.

"Halt," Tiernan says, slowing his horse. Damsel slows, too, keeping pace with the knight's mount.

"Get down," he tells Hyacinthe, then pokes him in the back.

The winged soldier slides off the horse with the sort of ease that suggests he's ridden many times before.

"So this is who you follow?" he asks sullenly, with a glare in the prince's direction.

Tiernan dismounts. "So you're suggesting I throw in my lot with those *things*?"

Hyacinthe subsides, but he studies me as though he wonders if I might be on his side. I am not, and I hope my look tells him so.

Tiernan strides to Damsel. He reaches up, taking Oak's weight in his arms and easing the prince onto the leaf-covered earth.

I slip off the saddle gracelessly, hitting the ground hard and staggering to one knee.

A bit of blood shows that one of the arrows struck Oak just above the shoulder blade. It was stopped by the scales of his golden armor, though; only the very tip punctured his flesh.

It must have been poisoned.

"Is he...?" I can see the rise and fall of his chest. He's not dead, but the poison could still be working its way through his system. He might be dying.

I don't want to think of that. Don't want to think that were he not behind me, I would have been the one struck.

Tiernan checks Oak's pulse. Then he leans down and sniffs, as though trying to identify the scent. Takes a bit of blood on his finger and touches it to his tongue. "Deathsweet. That stuff can make you sleep for hundreds of years if you get enough in your system."

"There can't have been more than a little bit on the arrow," I say, wanting him to tell me that couldn't possibly have been enough.

Tiernan ignores me, though, and rummages in a bag at his belt. He takes out an herb, which he crushes under the prince's nose and then presses onto his tongue. Oak has enough consciousness to jerk his head away when the knight's fingers go into his mouth.

"Will that fix him?" I ask.

"We can hope," Tiernan says, wiping his hand on his trousers. "We ought to find a place to shelter for the night. Among mortals, where Lady Nore's stick things are unlikely to look."

I give a quick nod.

"It shouldn't be too long a walk." He lifts the prince, draping Oak back over his steed. Then we proceed, with Tiernan leading Damsel Fly. Hyacinthe walks behind him, and I am left to lead the knight's mount.

The bloodstain on her flank has grown, and her limp is noticeable. So, too, is the piece of an arrow still embedded in her side. "Was she poisoned, too?"

He gives a curt nod. "Not enough to bring this tough girl down yet, though."

I reach into my backpack and take out the bruised apple I brought. I bite pieces off for both horses, who snuffle gently into my hands.

I stroke the hair over Rags's nose. She doesn't seem to be in too much pain from the arrow, so I choose to believe she'll be okay.

"Maybe it would be better if he did sleep for a hundred years," Tiernan says, although he seems to be talking more to himself. "Lady Nore is going to be hunting us as surely as we're hunting her. Asleep is better than dead."

"Why *is* Oak really doing this?" I ask.

The knight gives me a hard look. "Doing what?"

"This task is *beneath* him." I don't know how else to say it. In the Court of Teeth, Lady Nore made me understand that *she* might pierce my skin to make a leash of silver mesh run through it, might cause me agony so great that my thoughts shrunk to those of an animal, but any disrespect of me by a *commoner* was punished by death. Being royal mattered.

Surely, even at her worst, the High Queen cannot value the prince less than Lady Nore valued me. Jude ought to have sent a dozen knights rather than her own brother, with only a single guard to protect him.

"Maybe there's a lady he wants to impress with his heroics," the knight says.

"His sister, I imagine," I say.

He laughs at that. "Or Lady Violet, with lips of carmine and a crown of living butterflies in her hair, according to a poem written about her. Oak spent three days in her bed before a jealous lover appeared, waving around a dagger and making an ugly scene. There was a Lady Sibi, too, who will declare dramatically to anyone likely to listen that Oak made her mad with passion and then, once he tired of her, splintered her heart into shards.

"Actually, now that I think on it, he'd be well served not to impress Sibi more than he already has. But there's any of the other two dozen beauties of Elfhame, all of whom are very willing to be awed by his heroics."

I bite the inside of my cheek. "That's a ridiculous reason."

"Some people are ridiculous," says Tiernan with a glance back at the sullen Hyacinthe in the bridle, trudging along. "Especially when it comes to love."

Not a flattering assessment of Oak, but he is currently slung over the back of a horse. He also, possibly, saved the knight's life. And mine.

"Is that what you truly believe?" I ask.

"What? That there's a girl? Of that, I'm certain. There always is. But I'm equally certain that bravery shouldn't be beneath a prince," Tiernan tells me.

There are rumors that Cardan never wanted the throne, that he will hand it over to Oak willingly at some vague future time. But when I think of High King Cardan with his black curls and cruel mouth, the way he behaves—silly and dangersome all at once—I don't believe he would relinquish power. He might, however, trick Oak into going on a quest he wouldn't return from. Build him up with stories of honor and valiant deeds. "If the High King and Queen let him go without no more protection than you, someone wants him dead."

Tiernan's eyebrows raise. "You've got a suspicious mind."

"Says the lover of a traitor." I hadn't been certain I was right, but then I saw Tiernan glance at Hyacinthe when he spoke of love, and recalled what Oak said to him before about trust.

It's satisfying when I see the blow land.

Tiernan gapes at me, stunned, as though it never occurred to him that just because my voice is scratchy with disuse, just because I seem more beast than girl, it doesn't mean I haven't been paying attention.

Hyacinthe gives a hollow laugh.

"You think the High King is making a move against Oak through me?" asks the knight.

I shrug. "I think that even if you want to take every risk for the prince, there's only one of you. And I think it's odd for the royal family to allow a prince to gamble on glory with his life."

The knight looks away and does not respond.

We walk on for the better part of a mile before Oak makes a low moan and tries to sit up. *"Jude,"* he mutters. *"Jude, we can't just let him die."*

"You're all right," Tiernan says, putting a hand on his shoulder. "We lost them."

The prince opens his tawny fox eyes and looks around. When he sees me, he slumps back down, as though relieved that I am still here.

Near dawn we come to a windswept beach.

"Wait here with the prince," Tiernan tells me as we close on a jetty of black stone. "Hyacinthe, your commands stand. My enemies are yours. Defend her if necessary."

The prisoner gives a thin-lipped smile. "It's not I who has forgotten all I vowed."

I cannot see Tiernan's face, so I cannot tell if Hyacinthe's bitterness bothers him.

The air is thick with salt. I lick it off my top lip and watch as Tiernan leads his wounded horse onto the sand. Rags's hoof touches the edge of a wave. At the brush of sea-foam, she tosses her mane and gives a whinnying sound that causes the hair to stand up along my arms.

Hyacinthe turns to me. The crash of the surf makes it impossible for him to be heard by Tiernan, but he lowers his voice anyway. "There are things I could tell you, were I not bridled. Free me, and I'll help you."

I say nothing. I pity him, bridled as he is, but that doesn't make him my ally.

"Please," he says. "I would not live like this. When I was caught, Oak removed the curse, but he didn't have the power to keep it from creeping back. First my arm, then I know not what. It is worse than being a falcon entire, to lose oneself again slowly."

"Let me be clear. I *hate* Lady Nore," I say, a snarl in my voice, because I don't want to listen to him. I don't want to sympathize with him more than I do already. "And if you're loyal to her, I hate you, too."

"I followed Madoc," Hyacinthe says. "And now I am his son's prisoner. Because I was more constant, not less. More loyal than my lover, who became twisted around the finger of another and forswore me. Lady Nore promised to remove the curse on any falcon who would join her, but I never gave her any oath. You can trust me, lady. Unlike the others, I will not play you false."

Across the beach, Tiernan's horse charges into the black water, heedless of the swells breaking over her.

*More loyal than my lover, who became twisted around the finger of another.*

"Is Rags *drowning*?" I ask.

Hyacinthe shakes his head. "The sea folk will take her back to Elfhame, and she will be made well there."

I let out my breath. My gaze goes to Oak, his cheek pillowed on Damsel's flank. His armor glinting in the moonlight. The flutter of his lashes. The calluses on his hands. "Removing the bridle will neither halt nor hasten your curse," I remind Hyacinthe.

"Do not fall under Prince Oak's spell," he warns as the knight climbs up the rocks to us. "He's not what he seems."

Several questions are on the tip of my tongue, but there is no time to ask them. As Tiernan draws close, I look out at the sea. Rags has disappeared. I can't see so much as her head above the waves.

"We're down to one steed," Tiernan informs us.

We don't have a place to rest, either. I study the shadowy space beneath the boardwalk. We could curl up there on the cool, soft sand without being bothered. Just the thought of it makes me freshly aware of how exhausted I am.

The knight points up toward the road. "There's a motel that way. I saw the sign from the shoreline."

He takes the reins of Oak's horse and leads her up the hill. I follow, ahead of the winged soldier. I note how stiff they are with each other, how carefully they keep separate, as magnets must keep a safe distance or be slammed together by their very nature.

We walk, fading stars overhead, brine in the air. I wonder if the hum of traffic or the smell of iron bothers them. I am used to it. So long as we remain here, I am on solid ground. Once we get to the Court of

Moths, we will be far enough into Faerie for things to grow slippery and uncertain.

At the thought, I kick a desiccated fast-food drink cup, sending it spinning along the gutter.

A few blocks and we come to a motel with scrubby weeds pushing through the cracks of the parking lot. A few run-down cars are parked near the one-level stucco building. A sign overhead promised vacancies, cable, and little else.

The prince attempts to sit up again.

"Just stay where you are," says Tiernan. "We'll be back with the keys."

"I'm fine," Oak says, sliding off the horse and immediately collapsing onto the asphalt.

"*Fine?*" the knight echoes, eyebrows raised.

"I couldn't say it if it wasn't true," says the prince, and manages to stagger to his feet. He leans heavily on a nearby car.

"Hyacinthe," Tiernan says, pointing. "Do not let him fall again. Wren, you're with me."

"I could only dream of letting so important a personage drop," Hyacinthe sneers. "Or I would never dream. Or something."

"Flying is what you ought to dream of, falcon," Oak says, with enough heat that I wonder if he overheard part of our conversation.

Hyacinthe flinches.

"Wren," Tiernan says again, beckoning toward the motel.

"I'm bad at glamours," I warn him.

"Then we won't bother with one."

The reception area stinks of stale cigarettes despite the NO SMOKING sign over the door. Behind the desk is an exhausted-looking woman playing a game on her phone.

She glances up at us, and her eyes go wide. Her mouth opens to scream.

"You see totally normal people here for totally normal reasons," Tiernan tells her, and as I watch, her features smooth out into a glassy-eyed calm. "We want two rooms, right next to each other."

I think of how my unparents were glamoured and hate this, even though he's not asking her to do anything awful. Yet.

"Sure," says the woman. "Not too many tourists this time of year; you'll have most places to yourselves."

The knight nods vaguely as the woman shoves a blank motel key into the machine.

She says something about how she still needs a card for incidentals, but a few words later, she's forgotten all about that. Tiernan pays with bills that don't have the suspiciously crisp look of glamoured leaves. I cut him a strange glance and pocket a matchbook.

Outside, our remaining horse stands on a patch of scrubby grass, glowing softly, eating a dandelion. No one seems inclined to tie Damsel up.

Oak sits on the bumper of a car, looking a bit better. Hyacinthe leans against a dirty stucco wall.

"That money," I ask. "Was it real?"

"Oh, yes," the prince confirms. "My sister would be wroth with us otherwise."

"Wroth." I echo the archaic word, although I know what it means. Pissed off.

"*Super* wroth," he says with a grin.

To faeries, mortals are usually either irrelevant or entertainment.

But I suppose his sister can be relegated to neither. Many of the Folk must hate her for that.

Tiernan leads us to our rooms—131 and 132. He opens the first and ushers us all inside. There are two twin beds, with scratchy-looking coverlets. A television sits on the wall over a saggy desk that's been bolted to the floor, causing the carpet to be stained with small circles of rust around the screws. The heater is on, and the air smells vaguely of burning dust.

Hyacinthe stands beside the door, wing closed tight to his back. His gaze follows me, possibly to avoid resting on the knight.

Oak crawls onto the nearest bed but doesn't shut his eyes. He smiles up at the ceiling instead. "We learned something of her capabilities."

"And you want me to tell you that was worth you being poisoned?" the knight demands.

"I'm always being poisoned. Alas, that it wasn't blusher mushroom," the prince says nonsensically.

Tiernan nods his chin at me. "That girl thinks you're a fool for even being here."

I scowl, because that's not what I meant.

"Ah, Lady Wren," Oak says, a lazy smile on his mouth. Marigold hair brushing his forehead, half-hiding his horns. "You wound me."

I doubt I hurt his feelings. His cheeks are still slashed from my nails, though. Three lines of dried blood, pink around the edges. Nothing he says is a lie, but all his words are riddles.

Tiernan kneels and starts to unbuckle the sides of Oak's armor. "Give me a hand, will you?"

I squat on the other side of the prince, worried I am going to do something wrong. Oak's gaze slants to me as, with fumbling fingers, I try to work off the scale mail where it has stuck to his wound. He makes a soft huff of pain, and I can see the way his lips are white at the edges, from being pressed together as he bites back whatever other sounds he wants to make.

Underneath, his stained linen shirt is pushed up over the flat plane of his stomach, the dip of his hip bones. His sweat carries the scent of crushed grass, but mostly he smells like blood. He watches me, lashes low over his eyes.

Without his golden armor, he almost looks like the boy I remember.

Tiernan gets up, gathering towels.

"How did Lady Nore know you were coming for me?" I ask, trying to distance myself from the strange intimacy of the moment, from the heat and nearness of his body.

If she'd sent both Bogdana and stick creatures, she must suddenly want me very much, after ignoring me for eight years.

Oak tries to sit up higher on the pillows and winces, a hectic flush on his cheeks. "She's likely to have realized that asking you to come with me would be the clever thing to do," he says. "Or she could have had spies that saw the direction in which we were headed when we left Elfhame."

Tiernan nods toward Hyacinthe from the bathroom, where he's soaking cloth under steaming water from the tap. "Spies like him, I imagine."

I frown at the bridled former falcon.

"There's not a lot of work for birds out there," Hyacinthe says, putting up his hand in defense. "And I didn't spy on *you*."

Tiernan brings over the towels, picking one up as though he intends to wash the prince's wound. Before he can, Oak takes and presses it to his own shoulder, closing his eyes against the pain. The water trickles down his back to stain the sheets pink.

"We're within a few days' ride of the Court of Moths, but we're down to one horse," Tiernan says.

"I'll bargain for another," Oak tells us distractedly. I am not sure he realizes that in the mortal world, horses are not something you can just pick up at a local farmers' market.

When the prince begins to bind up his wound, Tiernan nods in my direction. "Come," he says, ushering me out of the room. "Let's leave him to dream of all the things he will do tomorrow."

"Like issue a royal decree that you won't mock me when I've been poisoned," says Oak.

"Keep dreaming," Tiernan tells him.

I glance back at Hyacinthe, since it doesn't seem to me that the knight is wrapped around the prince's finger. If anything, they seem like friends who've known each other a long time. But the former falcon is picking his fingernails with a dagger and ignoring all of us.

Tiernan uses his second key to open the way to a nearly identical space. Two beds, one television. Rust stains where the bolts have sat in contact with the rug. A polyester coverlet that looks as though spilled water might bead up on top of it.

There, the knight loops rope around my ankle, tying me to the bed with enough slack that I can lie down, even roll over. I hiss at him as he does it, pulling against the bonds.

"He might trust you," says Tiernan. "But I trust no one from the Court of Teeth."

Then he speaks a few words over the knot, a bit of enchantment that

I am almost certain I can break, what with all the practice I've had at unraveling the glaistig's spells.

"Sleep tight," he tells me, and goes out, closing the door hard after him. He's left his pack behind, and I bet he's planning on returning and sleeping here, where he can keep an eye on me. And where he can avoid whatever he's feeling about Hyacinthe.

Spitefully, I get up and throw the bolt lock, letting the rope pull taut.

Dawn has lengthened into day, and all around the motel, the mortal world is coming awake. A car engine fires to life. Two people argue near a vending machine. A slammed door sounds from the room next to mine. I peer out the window, imagining slipping away into the morning and disappearing. Imagining the look on Tiernan's face when he returns to find me gone.

But I would be foolish to try to face the storm hag or Lady Nore on my own. I would have been felled by the same poison that struck the prince, except without armor, the bolt would have sunk deeper into my flesh. And no one would have been there to give me an antidote or carry me on a horse.

Still, I don't want to be dragged along like an animal, worrying about being put on a leash.

If I cannot have respect, if I cannot be treated as their equal, then at least I want Oak to see that I have as much right as he does to this quest, more reasons to hate Lady Nore, and the power to stop her.

But it's hard to think of how I will manage to convince them of that when my ankle is tied to the leg of the bed, and my thoughts are woolly with exhaustion. Taking one of the blankets from my bag, I scrabble into the dusty space between mattress and floor, curling up there. The awareness of the slats over me and the familiar, forest smell of my blanket is comforting.

Pillowing my head on my arms, I try to settle in. It ought to be hard to fall asleep in this unfamiliar place, filled with strange sounds. My thighs hurt from the ride, and my feet are sore from walking. But as warm, buttery sunlight flows into the room like yolk from a cracked egg, my eyes drift closed. I do not even dream.

When I wake, the sky is dark. I crawl out from underneath the bed, hunger gnawing my belly.

Tiernan must have been in and then gone without my noticing, because the bolt lock is undone, his pack missing. I make quick work of his stupid enchanted knot, then go into the bathroom and fill the plastic cup I find there with water. I guzzle it, refill it, and drink again.

As I look up, I catch sight of my own reflection and take an automatic step back. Unglamoured, my skin is the pale blue-gray of hydrangea blooms, smeared with dirt along one cheek and across my nose. My hair is so woven with leaves and twigs and mud that it would be almost impossible to know that underneath it is an even darker blue. I have the same pointy chin I had when I thought I was mortal. A thin face, with large eyes, and an expression of startlement, as though I expect someone else when I look in the mirror.

At least my eyes could pass for human. They're green, deep and dark.

I smile a little to see the awfulness of my sharp teeth. A mouth full of knives. They make even the Folk flinch.

My gaze goes to the tub, thinking about what I must seem like to Oak, now that we're both grown. Turn the faucet and let the hot water run over my hand. As dirt washes off, I see that the skin underneath is a warmer, lighter blue.

But I am no Court lady with lips of carmine and butterflies in my hair. I am scrawny, like a stick bug.

I put the stopper in the tub and let it fill. Then slowly I lower myself in. The heat is almost more than I can bear. Still, I scrub at my skin with my jagged nails. In minutes the water is so filthy that I have to let it drain out. Then I do it again. Sinking my fingers into my hair, I try to pick apart the tangles. It's painful, and slathering it with the contents of the tiny bottle of conditioner does little to help. I am still not totally clean when I get out of the water, despite the fine layer of grit remaining behind in the tub.

Now that I've washed, my dress looks dirtier than ever, worn as thin as tissue in places, and discolored by both sun and mud. There's nothing else, so I pick it up and run it under the tap of the sink, scrubbing at it gently with soap and hoping it doesn't tear. Then I drape it over the shower-curtain rod and aim the hair dryer onto it. It's still damp when I take it down.

I start stepping into it when I see a shadow move outside the window.

I drop to the floor, but not before I recognize the long fingers. As I crawl naked underneath the bed, I hear the sound of nails scratching against glass. I brace for Bogdana to shatter the window or kick in the door.

Nothing happens.

I draw in a breath. Then another.

Minutes later, there's a knock. I don't move.

Oak's insistent voice comes from the other side. "Wren, open up."

"No," I shout, crawling out from underneath the bed and scrambling into my clothes.

I hear shuffling and a thud, and then something metal slides down the gap between door and jamb. It opens.

"I thought you were…" I start to explain, but I am not sure he's paying attention. He's put away what he was using to jimmy the door and is gathering back up a cardboard drink holder of coffees and a large paper bag.

When he looks up, he freezes for a moment, an unreadable expression on his face. Then he averts his gaze, turning it toward something just over my shoulder.

I glance down, at the way the damp cloth of my dress has stuck to my body, and flinch. My breasts are visible, even my nipples. Could he think I did this for his attention? Shame heats my cheeks, crawls down my neck.

Walking past me, he sets down the sack on the bed. His golden curls are only slightly mussed, his fresh linen shirt white and unwrinkled, as though he'd never been poisoned, or shot, or fallen off a horse. He certainly hadn't cleaned his clothes in the sink. And his mouth is twisted in an expression of insufferable amusement.

I wrap myself in the coverlet from the bed.

"I wasn't sure what you liked." Oak proceeds to take out a mango, three green apples, a handful of dried figs, a bag of crackers in the shapes of goldfish, frozen pizza bites, and four foil-wrapped hot dogs. He does all this without looking at me. "They seem like meat, but they're not."

I am hungry enough to accept one of his weird vegan hot dogs. "You don't eat meat? Your father must hate that."

He shrugs, but there's something in his face that tells me it's been discussed before. "More for him."

Then I am distracted by eating. I gobble three out of the four hot dogs so quickly that when I stop, I see Oak has his hand curved protectively over the remaining one. I pick up a fig and try to take smaller bites.

Leaving the remainder of the food on the mattress, he goes to the door. "Tiernan told me I should be grateful for your unwillingness to drop me on my head, however tempted you were," he says. "They'll sing ballads to your restraint."

"And why would you think I was tempted?" There's a growl in my voice I can't seem to get out.

"Many are. It must be something about my face." He smiles, and I think of the jealous lover with the knife.

"Maybe you keep dragging them on quests," I say.

He laughs. "This isn't how I thought to see you again."

"I imagine you thought you'd *never* see me again," I say, to remind myself of the many, many differences between our positions in life.

His grin slides off his mouth. "That did seem to be what you wanted."

I wish it didn't bother me that he isn't smiling anymore, but it does.

The door opens. Tiernan is on the other side, glowering at us. "Let's get moving. We've got a lot of ground to cover."

Outside, I see that we have acquired a new horse, black as ink and smelling of seawater. Oak's faerie steed shies away from it, blowing panicked breaths from flared nostrils.

The new mount catches my eye hungrily, and I realize what I'm looking at. The creature is one of the solitary Folk, a devourer of flesh. A kelpie.

# CHAPTER
## 5

"G et on up," Tiernan says impatiently, nodding toward the kelpie. The thing doesn't even have a saddle, no less reins. I look longingly at Damsel and wonder if the knight is forcing me onto a carnivorous monster out of sheer dislike.

But Oak goes to it willingly enough, patting its flank absently. Then he swings onto the kelpie's back and reaches down a hand to me. He is wearing his golden armor again, the boy who'd been my friend disappearing into a man I don't know.

The knight heaves me up behind the prince. As my hands go to Oak's waist, I am aware of the warmth of his skin even through the scale armor, of his body pressed against my thighs, and while the cloak he loaned me covers the thinness of my gown, it cannot protect me from that.

"Hope you're feeling rested after all that deathsweet," Tiernan tells Oak. "Because you're mutilating our timetable."

Oak gives him a look that makes me suspect the prince will finally call him to account for his familiarity. But if so, this is not the moment.

I wonder how hard it is for the kelpie not to run directly into a pond and drown us both. But, as one of the solitary fey, he has very likely made vows of obedience to Elfhame, and I can only hope those hold. I barely have time to wrap my arms around the prince's waist and try not to fall. Then we're off, thundering through the late afternoon without cease.

Through the sap-smeared woods of the Pine Barrens, crossing highways filled with the bright headlights of cars, we ride. My hair whips behind me, and when Oak glances back, I have to look away. Circlet at his brow, sword at his belt, in his shining mail, he looks like a knight from a child's imaginings, out of a storybook.

Break of day comes in pinks and golds, and the sun is high above us when we come to a stop. My thighs are sorer than before from rubbing against the kelpie's flanks, and even my bones feel tired. My hair is knotted worse than ever.

We make camp in a forest, quiet and deep. The distant hiss of traffic tells me that mortal roads are near, but if I don't listen too closely, I could mistake that for the sounds of a stream. Oak unpacks and unrolls blankets while Tiernan starts a fire. Hyacinthe watches, as if daring to be asked to help.

I slip away and return with handfuls of persimmons, two dryad's saddle mushrooms as large as helmets, wild garlic, and spicebush twigs. Even Tiernan pronounces himself impressed by my finds, although I think he's annoyed that Oak allowed me to wander off.

The prince ignores him and rigs up a way to cook the mushrooms. They've brought cheese and good black bread, and while we eat, Oak tells us stories of the Court. Ridiculous parties held by the High King. Pranks Oak has personally played and been punished for. No mention of his lovers, but he recounts a tragicomic romance involving a phooka, a pixie, and one of the king's counselors that was still playing out when he left.

Even Tiernan seemed different in the firelight. When he poured tea for Hyacinthe, he added honey without being asked, as though he'd made it that way many times before. And when he handed it over and their fingers met, I recognized in his face the sharp pain of longing, the unwillingness to ask for what you knew you would be denied. He hid it quickly, but not quickly enough.

"Will you tell me what this hag in the Court of Moths is supposed to find for us?" I ask when the stories come to an end.

I want the answer, but more than that, I want to know if they trust me enough to give me one.

Tiernan looks in Oak's direction, but the prince is looking directly at me, clear-eyed. "The limits of Lady Nore's power, I hope. The This-tlewitch lived during the time of Mab, and there was a curse on Mab's bones, if I understand right."

"So not an object?" I ask, thinking of their conversation in the woods.

Oak shrugs. "That depends on what she tells us."

I mull over his answer as I bed down in some of the prince's blankets. They are perfumed with the scents of Elfhame, and I pull my own muddy covering close to my nose to blot out the smell.

That afternoon there is another long, exhausting ride, with only a brief break for food. By the time we stop, I feel ready to fall off the kelpie's back and not care if it starts nibbling on me.

Nearby a wide, brackish river froths, bubbling around rock. Tall, slender saw palmettos make lonely islands of rubble and root. On a steep slope, a single wall of a five-story concrete building stands. It looks like a castle cut out of construction paper, flat instead of three-dimensional.

"The entrance to the Court of Moths is supposed to be here somewhere," Tiernan says.

I slide off the kelpie and lie down in the weeds while Oak and Tiernan debate where to find the entrance to the brugh. I breathe in the fine mist from the water, the scents of loam and clotted river grass.

When I open my eyes, a young man is standing where the kelpie was. Brown hair the color of mud in a riverbed and eyes the murky green of stagnant water. I startle, scuttling away, and reach into my pack for a knife.

"Greetings," he says expansively, bowing. "You must wish to know the name of the one who carried you on his back, who so stalwartly aided a young prince in his time of need, before the beginning of his true reign—"

"Sure," I say, interrupting him.

"Jack of the Lakes," he says with a menacing grin. "A merry wight. And whom do I have the honor of addressing?" He looks at me.

"Wren," I say, and immediately wish I hadn't. It's not my true name, but all names have some power.

"You have an unusual voice," he says. "Raspy. Quite fetching, really."

"I damaged my vocal cords a long time ago," I inform him. "Screaming."

Oak steps between us, and I am grateful for the reprieve. "What a fine gentleman you make, Jack."

Jack turns to the prince, his sinister smile dropping back into place. "Oak and Wren. Wren and Oak. Delightful! Named for woodland creatures, but neither of you so simple." He glances at Tiernan and Hyacinthe. "Not nearly as simple as these two."

"That's enough," Tiernan says.

Jack's gaze stays on Oak. "Will you caper for the pleasure of the Queen of Moths? For she is a grim ruler, and her favor hard to win. Not that you need to concern yourself with impressing anyone, Your Highness."

I get a cold feeling at his words.

"I don't mind a caper," Oak says.

"That's enough impertinence," says Tiernan, inserting himself into the conversation. He stands with his shoulders back and his arms folded, the picture of the officer in Madoc's army that he must have once been. "You had the privilege of carrying the prince a ways, and that's that. Whatever we see fit to give you in recompense, be it a coin or a kick in the teeth, you'll take it and be grateful."

Jack of the Lakes sniffs, offended.

Hyacinthe's eyes glitter with anger, as though he feels the knight spoke directly to him.

"Nonsense," Oak tells Jack. "Your hooves were swift and sure. Come with us to the Court, rest your feet, and take some refreshment." He claps his hand on Tiernan's shoulder. "We're the ones with reason to be grateful, isn't that so?"

The knight pointedly ignores him, clearly not experiencing the awe of Prince Oak that he expects of Jack of the Lakes.

"This way," the prince says, and ushers us along the bank. I follow, trying not to slide on the wet mud.

"Decide for yourself how well they repay gratitude," says Hyacinthe to the kelpie, touching the leather strap of the bridle he wears. "And do not give them cause for too much of it."

Tiernan rolls his eyes.

There's solid concrete blocking our path, with the river on one side and a hill covered in poisonous manchineel trees on the other. The remains of the old building have no door, only large windows that show an even more forbidding and swampy landscape beyond. And yet I can feel the stillness in the air, the crackling presence of magic. Oak stops, frowning. I am sure he can feel it, too.

The prince presses his hand against the concrete, like he's trying to find the source.

Jack of the Lakes is wading in the water, looking eager to drag someone down into its depths.

Hyacinthe moves to stand nearby, his free hand clenching as though missing something. I wonder what weapon he used when he was a soldier. "I bet you think you're all great friends now."

I lower my voice to a rasp, remembering our conversation by the sea. "I am not under anyone's spell."

His gaze goes to the prince, standing on a windowsill, and then back to me. "He seems like an open book, but that's the game he plays. He keeps plenty of secrets. For instance, did you know he received a message from Lady Nore?"

"A message?" I echo.

He smiles, satisfied he has rattled me.

Before I can press him for details, Oak turns to us with a grin that calls for an answer. "Come look."

A meadow of flowers flows impossibly from the other side of the window. There is no river there, no scrub grass or mud. Just endless blooms, and among them scattered bones, as white as petals.

He hops into the meadow, hooves sinking beneath the flowers, and then reaches up for me.

*Do not fall under his spell.*

I remind myself that I knew Oak when we were children, that we have the same enemies. That he has no reason to play me false. Still, thinking of Hyacinthe's words, I shake my head at Oak's offer of help and climb down myself.

"It's beautiful, no?" he asks, a little smile on his face. A light in his fox eyes.

It is, of course. All of Faerie is beautiful like this, with carnage hidden just beneath. "I am sure the Queen of Moths will be delighted that the Crown Prince thinks so."

"You're in a prickly mood," he tells me.

As though I am not all-over briars at all times.

We walk through a landscape with no sun or moon above us until we come to a patch of earth with a deep pit half-hidden by swirling fog. There cut into the dirt are steps spiraling down into darkness.

"The Court of Moths," says Jack of the Lakes softly.

As I glance back at the field, the bones bother me: signs of death strewn among a carpet of flowers. I wish we had not come here. I have a dread that feels like premonition.

I notice that Oak has his hand on his sword as he begins his descent.

We follow, Tiernan behind the prince, then me and Jack, with Hyacinthe bringing up the rear, bridle tight against his cheeks. I hold my knife against my belly, inhale the rich scent of earth, and remember all the times I broke curses, all the tricks I played on the Folk.

We step into a long hall of packed dirt, with pale roots forming a latticework along the ceiling. Occasional glowing crystals light our way. I find myself growing more uncomfortable the deeper we go into the hill. I feel the weight of the earth above me, as though the passageway could collapse, burying us all. I bite my lip and keep going.

Finally, we step into a high-ceilinged cavern, its walls shining with mica.

There stands a green-skinned troll woman, with piercings through her cheeks and two sets of black horns protruding from her head. Sabers hang on either side of her hips. She wears armor of leather, carefully worked so that it seems as though there are a dozen screaming mouths on her chest plate.

At the sight of us, she scowls. "I guard the passage to the Court of Moths. Declare your name and your purpose in coming here. Then I will very likely kill you."

The expression on Tiernan's face hardens. "Do you not know your own sovereign? This is Prince Oak, heir to Elfhame."

The troll's gaze goes to Oak, looking as though she could eat him in three bites. Finally, she makes a reluctant, shallow bow. "You do us honor."

The prince, for his part, appears genuinely pleased to meet her and not the least bit afraid, bespeaking either great arrogance or foolishness, or both. "The honor is ours," he says, looking ready to kiss her hand if she offered it to him. I cannot imagine being so certain of one's welcome.

Just imagining it makes my stomach hurt.

"We seek the Thistlewitch, who dwells in Queen Annet's lands. We understand that without permission to see her, supplicants become lost in her swamp for a hundred years," Oak says.

The troll tilts her head, as if still evaluating his deliciousness. "Some don't make it back at all."

The prince nods, as though she's confirming his suspicions. "Alas, we don't have time for either of those options."

The troll smiles a little despite herself, at the silliness of his words. "And your companions?"

"Sir Tiernan," says the knight, pointing to himself. "Jack of the Lakes. Lady Wren. Our prisoner, Hyacinthe."

The troll's gaze glides over Hyacinthe and Jack to rest on me for an uncomfortably long moment. My lip curls in automatic response, to reveal the points of my teeth.

Far from looking discomfited, the troll woman gives me a nod, as though appreciative of their sharpness and my mistrust.

"Queen Annet will wish to greet you personally," the troll says, kicking the wall behind her three times. "She is fain to fete you in her hall and all that sort of thing. I've summoned a servant to bring you to some rooms. There, you may refresh yourselves and dress for the evening's revel. We will even lock up your prisoner for the night."

"There's no need for that," Oak says.

The troll grins. "And yet we will do it."

Hyacinthe glances in Tiernan's direction, perhaps looking to his former lover to speak in his behalf. I feel all around me the closing of a trap, and yet I do not think I am the one who is meant to be caught.

"We would be delighted to enjoy the hospitality of the Court of Moths," Oak says. If he hopes to get what he came for, it would be impossible for him to say anything else.

The troll guard's smile grows impossibly wide. "Good. You may follow Dvort."

I note her gaze and turn, startled to see that one of the Folk has crept in behind us. His skin and beard are the same color as the roots winding down from the ceiling, his eyes a bloodshot pink. His ears are long, like those of a rabbit, and his clothes appear to be covered in a layer of moss, heavier on his shoulders. He does not speak, only bows, then turns and shuffles down the passageway.

Hyacinthe bumps my shoulder with his. "Before they take me, let me prove what I've said and give you at least this much information. The prince's mother was a gancanagh. A *love-talker*. Honey-mouths, we used to call them back at Court."

I give a quick shake of my head, dreading what he will say next.

"You've not heard of them? A love-talker is able to quicken such desire in mortals that they die of it. The Folk might not find the passion lethal, but we still feel it. Oak's first mother charmed the High King Eldred *and* his son Dain into her bed. Oak's half brother is said to have made both Jude and her twin, Taryn, his lovers and stolen Cardan's former betrothed from his side. What do you suppose the prince is able—"

Hyacinthe bites off his last words because we have stopped in front of four doors, all of them of stone with spiraling metal hinges.

But I can't help finishing the sentence for him, the way I fear it would have gone. *What do you suppose the prince is able to do to someone like you?* A shudder goes through me, a recognition of a desire that I would have preferred to deny.

Was that how he made everyone feel? No wonder there was always a girl. No wonder Hyacinthe believes Tiernan is wrapped around his finger.

Dvort bows again, gesturing toward the rooms, then gives Hyacinthe a shove to keep moving into one of three branching passageways.

"He stays with us," Oak says.

"You heard *His Majesty.*" Despite the sneer in his voice when he speaks of Oak, Hyacinthe obviously doesn't want to be taken. He attempts to move around the page, toward the prince. But the silent page blocks his way.

Oak's hand goes to the hilt of a blade.

"Enough," Tiernan says, grabbing the prince's arm. "They want you to break hospitality. Stop it. It shouldn't hurt Hyacinthe to cool his heels in the queen's prison for one night. I'll accompany him and make sure he's comfortable enough."

"Unseelie is as Unseelie does," says Jack of the Lakes with some relish.

I watch them go, panic rising as our party is cleft in two. When I am ushered into my room, I only feel worse.

It is a grim chamber, its walls carved of stone and earth. There is a rough bed in one corner, heaped with blankets and opulent cushions, and hung with tapestries. Each curtain depicts hunted creatures bleeding out in forests of colorful foliage, their bodies full of arrows.

There's a jug of water and a washbasin on a stand, and a few hooks on the wall. I take a turn about the room, looking for spy holes, secret passageways, and hidden dangers.

The place makes my skin itch. Though it is warm here, and nothing is ice, it reminds me entirely too much of the Court of Teeth. I want to be away.

I sit on the bed, counting to one hundred, hoping that the panicky feeling will pass.

Just as I get to number eighty-eight, Oak opens the door. "I've arranged for you to see the royal seamstress."

My gaze alights on the hollow of his throat just above his collar. I try to avoid his eyes.

*Love-talker.*

"I don't want to go." All I want is to curl up in a corner until we can leave.

He looks incredulous. "You can hardly attend the revel like that."

Shame heats my cheeks, looking at him in all his finery.

It's not fair. I am cleaner than I've been in weeks. It's true that there are holes in my dress, the hem is ragged, and there are places where the fabric has worn thin enough to tear. Still, it's *mine.*

"If you think I will embarrass you, leave me to this room," I growl, hoping he agrees.

"If you go as you are, it will appear as though Elfhame does not value you, and that's perilous in the Court of Moths," he says.

I scowl, unwilling to be reasonable.

The prince sighs, pushing hair out of his fox eyes. "If you remain in this room, Tiernan must stay to watch over you, and he has a hankering to drink the sweet wines and hear the songs of the Court of Moths. Now, up. You can put your old dress back on tomorrow."

Humiliated, I rise and follow him.

Someone sings an eerie little song on the other side of the seamstress's door, and I feel the pull of magic, thick clots of it. Whatever is inside has power.

I shoot Oak a look of warning, but he knocks anyway.

The song stops.

"Who calls at Habetrot's chamber?" comes a whispery voice.

Oak raises his eyebrows at me, as though he intends me to answer.

Fine, if that's what he wants. "Suren, whose garb has been deemed inadequate by an obnoxious prince, despite the fact I've seen people go *naked* to revels."

Rather than be insulted, Oak laughs delightedly.

The door opens to reveal a woman with frog-green skin, a wide lower lip, and wild eyebrows. Dressed in a black garment large enough to swallow up her body, she's bent so far over that her fingers nearly touch the ground.

She looks at me and blinks wet black eyes. "Come, come," she calls.

"I'll leave you to it," says Oak with a departing bow.

I bite my lip against snarling and follow the faerie into a tunnel that's so low-ceilinged that I have to stoop.

When we emerge, it is into a chamber filled with bolts of cloth resting on shelves that go up high enough to be shrouded in darkness. What light there is comes from candles set in sconces around the room, covered in globes of cloudy glass.

"You know what they say about me?" Habetrot whispers. "That instead of sewing garments, I pluck them out of dreams. Raiments such as I create have never been seen before, or since. So, what do you dream of?"

I frown down at my tattered dress in confusion.

"Forest girl, is that what you were? One of the solitary fey brought to Court?"

I nod, because that's true enough, in a way.

"Perhaps you want something of bark and furs?" she asks, walking around me, squinting a little as though seeing some vision of what she will put me in.

"If that's appropriate," I say, unsure.

She grabs hold of my arm, encircling it with her fingers to measure. "Surely you would not insult me with such a lack of extravagance?"

I am at a loss. Even if she could see into my dreams, she would find no garment of the sort she would have me imagine. "I don't know what I want." The words come out a whisper, too true by half.

"Destruction and ruin," she says with a clack of her tongue. "I can practically smell it on you."

I shake my head, but I can't help thinking of the satisfaction I felt wrecking the glaistig's spells. Sometimes it feels as though there's a knot inside me, and were it to come apart, whatever emerged would be all teeth.

Habetrot regards me with her bead-black eyes, unsmiling. Then starts searching among her bolts of cloth.

Once, the thing I am wearing was a sundress, with fluttery sleeves. A diaphanous white gown that flowed around me when I spun. I found it in a shop late one night. I'd stripped off the clothes given to me in the Court of Teeth, left them behind, and put that on instead.

I liked the dress so much that I wove myself a crown of hellebores and danced through the night streets. I stared at myself in puddles, convinced that so long as I didn't smile, I might even be pretty. I know it doesn't look like that anymore, but I can no longer picture myself in anything else.

I wish Oak could have seen the dress as it was, even though it hasn't looked that way in a long time.

A few minutes later, Habetrot comes over with a fabric in a soft, deep gray that seems to shift in her hands between brown and blue when she turns it in the light. My fingers stray to the cloth, petting the nap of the velvet. It is as soft as the cloak that the prince draped over my shoulders.

"Yes, yes," she says. "This will do. Arms out like a bird. There."

As I stand there, letting her drape me in fabric, my gaze goes to her collections of buttons and fiber and cloth. To the spindle resting in one corner and the shimmer of the thread in it, bright as starlight.

"You," Habetrot says, poking me in the side. "Shoulders back. Don't crouch like an animal."

I do what she tells me but bare my teeth at her. She bares her teeth in return. They are blunt, blackened along the gums.

"I have dressed queens and knights, giants and hags. I will dress you, too, and give that for which you were too afraid to ask."

I don't see how that is possible, but I do not argue. I think instead of the way we came. I counted the passages, and I am almost certain I know the way back to the fog-shrouded hole in the ground. I go over them again and again to fix them in my memory in case I have to run. In case we all have to run.

When she has my measurements and perhaps my measure, she goes to her table and begins to rip and stitch, leaving me to awkwardly wander the room, peering at ribbons, some of which seem to be made of woven hair, others of toad skin. I pocket a pair of sharp-looking scissors with a handle in the shape of a swan. They are lighter than my knives and much easier to conceal.

I cannot deny that though I have avoided the Folk, I am fascinated by them. Despite them being deceivers, and dangerous.

My gaze alights on a button the exact shining golden bronze of Oak's hair. Then another the purple of Hyacinthe's eyes.

I think of him in the dungeons. Hyacinthe, half-cursed, wearing that awful bridle, so desperate that he would seek help even from me.

"Come and try this on," says Habetrot, surprising me out of my thoughts.

"But it's only been a few moments," I say, puzzled.

"Magic," she reminds me with a flourish, then ushers me behind a screen. "And give me that dress you're wearing. I want to burn it."

I pull the worn fabric over my head, letting it fall to the floor between us and fixing her with a look that dares her to wrest it from me. I feel as vulnerable as a selkie taking off her skin.

Habetrot pushes the soft blue-purple-gray garment into my hands. I put it on carefully, feeling the slide of the lining smooth against my skin, feeling the comforting weight of fabric.

It is a gown, but one such as I have never seen before. It is composed mostly of the cloth she showed me, but there are strips of other material running through it, some diaphanous and others satiny, some patterned in butterfly wings, some felted wool. Dangling threads hang from torn edges, and a few pieces of thin fabric have been wadded up to give them a new texture. The swirling patchwork she has created is at once tattered and beautiful.

As I look at it, I am not sure what to think. It is mockery that makes her dress me thus, in rags and scraps, no matter how deftly put together?

But perhaps that's what she thought would best suit me. Perhaps it is Oak who is the fool, who caught a wolf and thought that by putting it in a gown and speaking to it as though it were a girl, it would become one.

At least the hem of the skirt doesn't drag impractically on the floor. I can still run in it as I howl at the moon.

"Come out, come out," she says.

I step from behind the screen, taking a sharp breath as I do so, dreading seeing myself in the mirror and feeling the burn of further humiliation.

The little seamstress pushes me toward a polished bronze thing that looks like a shield. My reflection stares back at me.

I am taller than I remembered. My hair is a wild tangle despite my attempts at finger-combing and washing it back at the motel. I never got out all the knots. My clavicle shows at the top of the collar, and I know I am too thin. But the dress clings to my chest and waist, skirt flaring over my hips. The tattered edges give it a haunting elegance, as though I am wrapped in the shadows of dusk. I look the picture of a mysterious courtier, rather than someone who sleeps in dirt.

Habetrot drops boots beside me, and I realize how long I've been standing there, staring at myself. A different kind of shame heats my cheeks.

I twist my hands in the skirt. The dress even has pockets.

"I knew I kept these," she says, indicating the footwear. "If he's half as taken with you as you are with yourself, I imagine he'll be well pleased."

"Who?" I demand sharply, but she only shrugs and presses a bone comb into my hand.

"Fix your hair," she says, then shrugs again. "Or make it wilder. You look lovely either way."

"What will you want for all this?" I ask, thinking of all the faerie bargains I've overheard, and of how much I like the dress I am wearing, how I could use the boots. I understand the temptation felt by every fool in a forest.

Her bead-black eyes study me, then she shakes her head. "I serve Queen Annet, and she bade me gift whatever the prince of the High Court asked, were it within the scope of my talents."

Of course someone must have told Oak where Habetrot's chambers were and assured him that she could do what he asked. So it is not Habetrot I owe, but Oak. And he owes Queen Annet in turn. My heart sinks. Debt is not easily dismissed in Faerie.

And the Court of Moths are showing off what good hosts they are.

"The gown is the most gorgeous thing I've ever seen," I say to her, as I can pay her no other way without insult. It has been a long time since I have been given a gift, barbed though it may be. "It does feel as though it might come from a dream."

That makes Habetrot's cheeks pink. "Good. Maybe you will come back and tell me how the Prince of Sunlight liked the Queen of Night."

Embarrassed, I step out into the hall, wondering how she could believe that a dress—no matter how beautiful—could make me into an object of desire. Wondering if everyone at the revel would think that I was dangling after Oak and laugh behind their hands.

I stomp back through the hall to my room and swing open the door, only to find Oak lounging in one of the chairs, his long limbs spread out in shameless comfort. A flower crown of myrtle rests just above his horns. With it, he wears a new shirt of white linen and scarlet trousers embroidered with vines. Even his hooves appear polished.

He looks every bit the handsome faerie prince, beloved by everyone and everything. Rabbits probably eat from his hands. Blue jays try to feed him worms meant for their own children.

He smiles, as though not surprised to see me in a beautiful gown. In fact, his gaze passes over it quickly, to rest with an odd intensity on my face. "Striking," he says, although I do not see how he could have possibly given it enough attention to know.

I feel both shy and resentful.

*The Prince of Sunlight.*

I do not bother telling him what he looks like. I am sure he already knows.

He brushes one hand through his golden curls. "We have an audience with Annet. Hopefully we can persuade her to send us to the Thistlewitch swiftly. Until then, we have been invited to roam her halls and eat from her banquet tables."

I sit on a stool, pull on my new boots, and then tie up the laces. "Why do you think she took Hyacinthe?"

Oak rubs a hand over his face. "I believe she wanted to show she could. I hope there's no more to it than that."

I take the comb from a pocket of my new dress and then hesitate. If I begin to untangle my nimbus of snarls, he will see how badly my hair is matted and be reminded of where he found me.

He stands.

Good. He will leave, and then I will be able to wrangle my hair alone.

But instead he steps behind me and takes the comb from my hands. "Let me do that," he says, taking strands of my hair in his fingers. "It's the color of primroses."

My shoulders tense. I am unused to people touching me. "You don't need to—" I start.

"It's no trouble," he says. "I had three older sisters brushing and braiding mine, no matter how I howled. I had to learn to do theirs, in self-defense. And my mother..."

His fingers are clever. He holds each lock at the base, slowly teasing out the knots at the very ends and then working backward to the scalp. Under his hands, it becomes smooth ribbons. If I had done this, I would have yanked half of it out in frustration.

"Your mother…," I echo, prompting him to continue in a voice that shakes only a little.

He begins to braid, sweeping my hair up so that thick plaits become something like his circlet, wrapping around my head.

"When we were in the mortal world, away from her servants, she needed help arranging it." His voice is soft.

This, along with the slightly painful pull against my scalp, the brush of his fingertips against my neck as he separates a section, the slight frown of concentration on his face, is overwhelming. I am not accustomed to someone being this close.

When I look up, his smile is all invitation.

We are no longer children, playing games and hiding beneath his bed, but I feel as though this is a different kind of game, one where I do not understand the rules.

With a shiver, I take up the mirror from the dresser. In this hair and with this dress, I look pretty. The kind of pretty that allows monsters to deceive people into forests, into dances where they will find their doom.

CHAPTER

6

A knock on the door announces a knight with hair the color of rotten vegetation and eyes like onyx, who introduces herself as Lupine. She tells us that she is to lead us to the revel happening in the great hall of the palace. When she speaks, I see that the inside of her mouth is as black as her eyes. "The Queen of Moths awaits you."

She appears to be one of the sluagh, the half-dead Folk. Banshees, who are said to be the souls of those who died in grief. Fetches, which mirror the faces of the dying and announce their doom. If the Gentry are proof that faeries can live forever, and be forever young, then the sluagh are proof they might even live on after that. I find them both disconcerting and fascinating in equal measure.

Tiernan and Jack have made themselves presentable. The kelpie slicked back his dark hair and affixed a flower just below the collar of his shirt. Tiernan wears a doublet he must have hunted up from one of his bags, brown velvet and slightly wrinkled, more that of a soldier than a courtier. He frowned when he saw Oak emerge from my room with me.

"Lead on," Oak tells Lupine, and with a shallow bow, she sets off, leaving us to trail behind.

The tunnels of the Court of Moths carry the scents of fresh-turned earth and seawater. As the southernmost Court on the coast, it is perhaps not surprising that we pass through sea caves, their walls studded with the sharp remains of barnacles. There is a wet, crashing sound, and for a moment I imagine the ocean rushing in and drowning us all. But it recedes, and I realize the waves must be far enough off not to be a danger.

A little farther and we come to an underground grove. The air is suffocatingly humid. We pass floss-silk trees, their thick gray trunks covered in thorns bigger than two of my fingers together. From them hang what appear to be woolen nests of white seedpods. A few wriggle as I study them, as though something more than seeds is trapped inside, trying to be born.

The next room has a still pool dipping down into unknown depths, with night-dark water. Jack of the Lakes goes toward it, dabbling his hand. Tiernan tugs sharply on the back of his doublet. "You don't want to go swimming in there, kelpie."

"Do you think there's an enchantment on it?" Jack asks, fascinated, squatting to look at his reflection.

"I think it's where the sea folk come in," says the knight grimly. "Swim too far, and you will find yourself in the Undersea, where they have little love for lake dwellers."

I kick my skirt ahead of me. My fingers dig deep into my pockets, running over what I stuffed into them. The sharp scissors I stole from

Habetrot, the matchbook, the fox figurine, a single licorice jelly bean. I hate the idea of my things remaining in the room and being pawed over by inquisitive servants, inventoried for the queen.

Three more turns, and then I hear strains of music. We pass a smattering of guards, one that smacks their lips at me.

"Did they let you see Hyacinthe?" I ask Tiernan, matching my step to his. I do not like the thought of the former falcon being confined when he was already desperate to be free. And I am worried over Queen Annet's plans, no less her whims.

Tiernan seems surprised I have spoken to him voluntarily. "He's well enough."

I study the knight. His expression is stiff, his broad shoulders set. A thin dusting of stubble darkens his jaw. His short black hair appears unbrushed. I wonder how long he remained in the prisons and how quickly he had to dress because of it.

"What do you think Queen Annet will do with him?" I ask.

Tiernan frowns. "Nothing much. The prince has promised—" He bites off the end of the sentence.

I give him a swift, sideways look. "Did you really trick Hyacinthe into being captured?"

He turns toward me sharply. "He told you that?"

"Why shouldn't he? Would you have used the bridle to keep him from speaking had you known what he would say?" I keep my voice low, but something in my tone makes Jack of the Lakes glance my way, a small smile at the edge of his mouth.

"Of course I wouldn't!" Tiernan snaps. "And I am not the one with command of him anyway."

That seems like splitting hairs, since Oak must have told Hyacinthe to obey the knight. He's issued plenty of orders in my hearing. Still, I hate the reminder that the prince is the one who owns the bridle. I want to like him. I want to believe that he's nothing like Madoc.

Up ahead, Lupine is telling Oak something about the crystalline structures, how there are rooms of ruby and sapphire near the prisons. She points toward an arched doorway, beyond which I can see steps down. The prince bends to say something in return, and her face changes, her eyes going a little glassy.

Love-talker.

"Is that where he's being held?" I ask, angling my head in the direction that Lupine indicated.

Tiernan nods. "You think I am terrible, is that it? Hyacinthe's father was a sworn knight of Lady Liriope—Oak's birth mother. When she was poisoned, he killed himself out of shame at having failed her.

"Hyacinthe swore to avenge his father. When Madoc proved to him that Prince Dain was responsible, he declared that he would be loyal thereafter to the general who caused his death. And Hyacinthe was fantastically loyal."

"That's why he chose to be punished rather than repent?" I ask.

Tiernan made a motion of uncertainty. "Hyacinthe had heard awful things of the new High King—that he pulled the wings off of Folk who wouldn't bow to him, that sort of stuff. And Cardan was the brother of Prince Dain. So yes, his loyalty to Madoc was some of it, but not all. He can't let go of his desire for revenge, even if he's no longer sure whom he blames."

"Is that why he's wearing the bridle?" I ask.

He frowns. "There was an incident. This punishment was better than the others."

This is the most Tiernan has ever spoken to me, and even now, I suspect he is mostly talking to himself.

Still, if he expects me to believe he bridled Hyacinthe for Hyacinthe's own sake, I will find that hard to do. In the Court of Teeth, everything terrible that happened to me was supposed to be for my benefit. They probably could have found a way to slit my throat and call it a gift.

We pause at the edge of the great hall.

"Allow me to escort you in?" Oak asks me, offering his arm.

Lupine sighs.

Awkwardly, I place my hand over his, as I see others doing. The pressure of his skin against my palm feels shockingly intimate. I note the three gold rings on his fingers. I note that his nails are clean. Mine are jagged in places or bitten.

I am unfamiliar with Faerie Courts in times of peace, and yet I do not think it is just that which makes me sense the pull toward violence that is in the air. Faeries spin in intersecting circle dances. Some are in garments of silk and velvet, leaping along with those in gowns of stitched leaves or bark, others in bare skin. Among the petals, grasses, silks, and embroidered fabrics are human clothes—t-shirts, leather jackets, tulle skirts. One of the ogres wears a silver-sequined gown over their leather trousers.

Giants move slowly enough for the crowd to part around them, a few goblins dance, a troll sinks her teeth into what appears to be a stag's liver, a redcap adjusts his gore-soaked hat, pixies flit up into the tangled roots of the domed ceiling, and nixies toss their still-wet hair as they cavort. I note a trio of hobs playing a game of chestnuts in a corner, perhaps to decide what will happen to a sprite that one of them is holding in a birdcage, her feet stuck in honey.

As we enter, Folk turn toward us. They do not look at me in horror, as they did in the Court of Teeth, where I was often paraded before them while I tried to bite my captors and pulled at my chains. I see curiosity in the gazes that follow me, not entirely unmixed with admiration—though that part is doubtless either for the gown or the prince on my arm.

The air is thick with the sweetness of flowers and overripe fruit, making me feel dizzy when it fills my lungs. Small faeries buzz through it like living dust motes.

Long, low tables are heaped with food—grapes as black as ink rest beside golden apples, cakes dusted with sugar and rose petals rise in towers, and pomegranates spill their red seeds onto the tablecloth—pale silk that trails its fringe onto the packed dirt of the floor. Silver goblets stand near carafes of wines—one as green as grass, another the purple of violets, and a third the pale yellow of buttercups.

Fiddlers and pipers spread out across the brugh play songs that ought to have been discordant, but instead the notes come together in a wild and delirious noise. It makes my blood sing.

There are performers nearby, jugglers who toss golden balls into the air that turn silver before being caught. A horned acrobat steps into a flower-covered hoop and arches her back while twisting her body, making it spin. A few Folk gasp in delight. The Gentry flash their haughty, superior smiles.

For me, who has been so much alone, it feels like drowning in a deluge of sights and sounds and smells.

I make a fist of the hand that is not touching Oak, sinking my ragged nails into the pad of my thumb to keep my expression neutral. The pain works, clearing my head.

*Do not scream*, I tell myself. *Do not bite anyone. Do not cry.*

The guide indicates a slightly raised dais, where the Unseelie queen sits on a throne of mangrove, roots of it spread out so that they seem like the tentacles of some enormous octopus. Queen Annet wears a gown that is half leather armor and half dramatic extravagance, making her look ready to rise and fight upon a stage. Her hair falls loose in a cascade of black curls, caught in a crown of magenta bougainvillea. Her stomach is round and heavy with child. One of her clawed hands spreads across her belly protectively.

I have learned many things in the woods. I could tell you the flight patterns of crows, how to collect water droplets off leaves after a storm. I could tell you how to unravel the spells of the half dozen Folk who seek to bind mortals into unfair bargains. But I have learned nothing of politics. And yet, I have an awful feeling that every move Queen Annet has made since we arrived was pure calculation.

At Oak's approach, Queen Annet rises and sinks into a curtsy.

"Please do not trouble yourself," he says too late. He makes a bow of his own, clearly much surprised to find her pregnant. Faeries do not reproduce easily or often, and rumor was that Queen Annet had spent decades longing in vain for a child.

I make a curtsy, too, lowering my head. I am not sure the exact etiquette relative to our stations, but I hope that if I go low enough and stay there long enough, it will serve.

"Your kindness in giving us rest and refreshment is more than we would have asked," Oak says, a phrase that could have come only from someone who has been tutored in courtesy, since he sounds polite, but underneath that, a lot is left unsaid.

"And how may we accommodate you further?" asks Queen Annet

while settling herself back in her throne with the help of a goblin attendant.

"I have heard that the Thistlewitch makes her home deep in a cypress swamp in your lands. We know that those who seek her there do so at their peril. We ask for a clear path to her, if you can grant us one."

"And for what purpose do you seek her?" The queen's gaze brooks little in the way of evasion.

"It is said she can find all lost things," says Oak. "Maybe even see into the future. But we wish to know about the past."

Queen Annet smiles in a way that makes me worried. "I do not seek to anger the High Court by misplacing their prince. I could give you a marking to write on your shoes that would lead you straight through the swamp."

Oak opens his mouth, looking ready to thank her and be off on our way.

"And yet," Queen Annet says. "Let us consider your traveling companions. A kelpie, your bodyguard, and a fallen queen." Her gaze goes to me. "Do not think I do not know you, Suren, daughter of ice."

My gaze meets hers, quick and hostile, before I can make myself otherwise.

"And Hyacinthe," Oak says. "Whose return I would appreciate."

"Your prisoner?" Queen Annet raises her eyebrows. "We will secure him for the time being so that you need not play jailer in my house."

"It is no hardship," Oak says. "Whatever else you think of me, I know my duty to a captured foe, especially considering that my father is more than a little responsible for his being cursed. I ought to be the one to look after him."

Queen Annet smiles. "Sometimes duty can be a hardship. As long as everyone is well behaved, I will return him anon. Headed north, then, are you?"

"I am." The prince looks wary.

"The High Court won't help your father, will they?" the queen goes on, studying Oak.

He doesn't answer, and she nods as though his silence is answer enough.

"So you're left to save Madoc yourself." The queen draws forward on her throne. "Does that sister of yours even know you've embarked on this quest?"

*Jude, we can't just let him die.* That was what Oak said when he was delirious and half-unconscious.

That's why he seems tired and anxious, why he's the one putting himself in danger with only a single knight at his side. Why he and Tiernan evaded so many of my questions. Because Lady Nore took his foster father prisoner. And since Madoc was a traitor, banished from Elfhame, no one else is willing to lift a finger to get him back.

"What a dutiful boy you are," says Queen Annet when he doesn't answer.

The tilt of his mouth goes sharp-edged.

My heart beats double time. If he hid this from me, he did it for a reason. Maybe it was only that he thought I had cause not to like Madoc, since he was allied with the Court of Teeth. Or maybe he knew that we would be at cross purposes when we arrived at the Citadel, me wishing to bring Lady Nore down, and him looking to negotiate.

"The High Court might not thank me for aiding you," Queen Annet says. "Might even punish me for my part in your plan. It seems you've brought trouble to my household, Oak of Elfhame. This is poor repayment for our generosity."

And now, after realizing the game Oak has been playing with me, I understand the game Queen Annet has been playing with him.

Faerie rules around hospitality are extremely specific. For example, invoking parlay is how Madoc got the High Court to allow him, Lord Jarel, and Lady Nore to walk right into Elfhame without anyone touching a hair on his head, even though he had an enemy army camped right at the edge of one of the islands.

But once he lifted a sword and broke the rules of hospitality, well, all bets were off.

The Court of Moths declared themselves to be our hosts, so they were obligated to take care of us. Unless we were bad guests. Then they'd be free to do whatever they liked.

But what could Annet want from him? A boon for her unborn child? The bridle? The head of the heir to Elfhame?

"If my sister bears anyone a grudge for this," Oak says, "it will be me and me alone."

Queen Annet considers this. "Give me your hand," she says finally.

He does, turning it palm up. She cuts the tip of her finger with a knife taken from a strap at her wrist, then writes a symbol on his skin. "Trace that onto your shoes, and you will find your way through the swamp."

The ease with which she has given us what we want makes it clear to me she anticipates getting something from us later. Something we would not give her now, if she asked for it.

"We are all gratitude." Oak inclines his head toward her. This seems like a cue to curtsy again.

"I take very seriously my obligations as a host," Queen Annet warns, then gives Oak a small, strange smile. "You may depart in the morning. For tonight, make merry in my halls. You will need a little warmth where you are going."

Somewhere nearby, a new group of musicians starts up, playing an eerie tune.

As we make our way from the dais, Tiernan puts his hand on Oak's arm. "I don't like this."

I push my way into the crowd. My thoughts are a tangle. I recall Hyacinthe referring to Lady Nore communicating with Oak. She would have had to if she wanted him to know she had his father. And whatever else he intended, whatever he told me, Oak wants to secure his father's freedom far more than he wants to stop Lady Nore. Were I his sister, I wouldn't send him north, not when his goals might not match her own.

His goals almost certainly don't match mine.

*"Elfhame requires your assistance."* I repeat his words back to him with a sneer.

He doesn't look half as guilty as he ought. "I should have explained, about Madoc."

"I wonder why you decided against it," I say in a tone that indicates just the opposite.

He meets my gaze with all the arrogance of royalty. "Everything I *did* tell you was true."

"Yes, you deceive the way all the Gentry do. With your tricks and omissions. It's not as though you have the option of lying."

Out of the corner of my eye, I note that Tiernan has backed away from our argument. He is moving in the direction of the banquet table and the wine.

Oak sighs, and finally I hear something like chagrin creep into his voice. "Wren, you have plenty of reasons not to trust me right now, but I do intend to stop Lady Nore. And I believe we can. Though I plan on bringing back Madoc, we will still have done a deed no one can deny was of service to Elfhame. Whatever trouble I will be in, you'll be a hero."

I am not sure anyone has considered me that, not even the people I've saved. "And if I decide to part ways? Are you going to tie my hands and drag me along with you?"

He looks at me with trickster eyes beneath arched golden brows. "Not unless you scratch me again."

"Why do you *want* to help him?" I ask. Madoc had been willing to use Oak as a path to power, at the least.

"He's my father," he says, as though that should be enough.

"I am going north for the sole purpose of destroying my parent, and you've never seemed to think I would so much as hesitate," I remind him.

"Madoc is not the father of my blood," he says. "He's the person who raised me. He's my *dad*. And yes, fine, he's complicated. He always craved conquest. Not even power, really, but the fight itself. Maybe because he was a redcap, or maybe it's just how he was, but it's like a compulsion."

I am not sure it makes it better, to think of it as a compulsion.

"Strategy was dinner-table conversation. It was game play. It was everything. From the minute he met my mother and learned who sired me, learned that I could be the heir to Elfhame, he couldn't help scheming.

"After he got exiled to the mortal world, stuck with that geas that kept him from picking up a weapon, he was completely at a loss. Started working shifts at a slaughterhouse just for the smell of blood. Trained me in the combat he was barred from. Got involved in playing politics with the neighbors in his apartment building. Had them all at each other's throats inside of a month. Last I heard, one of the old ladies stabbed a young guy in the neck with a pen."

Oak shakes his head, but it's clear he loves Madoc, even knowing he's a monster. "It's his nature. I can't deny that he brought an army to Elfhame's shores. He's the reason Folk were killed. He made himself an enemy of the High Court. He would have *murdered* Cardan if he'd had a chance. And so, no matter how much my sister loves our dad, she can't ask her sworn subjects to help him. It would look terrible, to ask Folk to risk their lives for his when he put them in danger. But someone has to do it or he's going to die."

Now I am paying attention to what he doesn't say. "Did she *tell* you she wanted to help him?"

"No," he admits slowly.

"And does she want *you* to help him?"

He's caught and knows it. "Jude didn't know what I was planning, but if I were to guess how she's feeling right now—I'd go with enraged. But Madoc would have come for us if we were the ones that were trapped."

I've seen the High Queen angry, and no matter how she loves him, I am not sure she will forgive choosing their father over her. When she punishes the prince, though Oak believes otherwise, she will very probably punish those who helped him, too.

But when he reaches for my hand, I take it and feel the nervous, awful pleasure of his fingers threading through mine. "Trust me, Wren," he says. "Help me."

Love-talker.

Schemer.

My gaze goes to the scratches on his cheek, still raw-looking. My doing, for which he has not rebuked me. However secretive his nature, however foolish his reasons for loving his father, I like that he does. "I'll come with you," I say. "For now."

"I'm glad." The prince looks out at the hall, at the Gentry of the Court of Moths, at the dances and the revelry. Then he gives me his quicksilver smile, the kind that makes me feel as though we are friends conspiring together. "Since you're in a benevolent mood, perhaps you'll also dance with me."

My surprise must be evident. *"Why?"*

He grins. "To celebrate you continuing with this quest. Because we're at a party. So that Queen Annet believes we've got nothing to hide."

"Do we have something to hide?" I ask.

He smiles wider, giving me a tug toward the revelers. "Always."

I hesitate, but there is a part of me that wants to be convinced. "I don't know how."

"I have been trained in all the arts of the courtier," he says. "Let me show you."

I allow him to lead me into the crowd. Instead of going into one of the circle dances, though, he steers me to one side of them, so that we have room to practice. Turns me in his arms and shows me a movement, waiting for me to mirror it.

"Do you ever think about what it would be like to be a queen again?" he whispers against my cheek as we practice the steps.

I pull away to glare at him.

He holds up his hands in surrender. "It wasn't meant to be a trick question."

"You're the one that's going to rule," I remind him.

"No," he says, watching the other dancers. "I don't think I will."

I suppose he's been avoiding the throne for most of his life. I think of cowering beneath the bed in his room during the Battle of the Serpent and shove the memory from my mind. I don't want to think about *back then*. Just as I do not want to think about how, despite Hyacinthe's warnings, I am ready to eat out of the prince's hand as tamely as a dove.

It's too easy. I'm hungry for kindness. Hungry for attention. I want and want and want.

"We ought to eat something," I say. "We have a long journey ahead of us."

Although he must know it is an excuse, he releases me from his arms.

We wend through the crowd to a banquet table laden with delicacies. Oak takes a tart filled with golden faerie fruit and cuts it in half, giving a portion to me. Though I was the one who suggested food, I realize how hungry I am only after taking the first bite. Self-consciously, I pour a glass of water from the pitcher set out to mix with the wine and gulp that down.

Oak pours himself wine, undiluted.

"Will you tell me how you came to be living…" He stops, as if trying to find the words. "As you were."

I remember the care I'd given that he not know. How could I explain the way time seemed to slip from my fingers, the way I became incrementally more detached, more unable to reach out a hand to take anything I wanted? I will not allow him to pity me any more than he does.

"You could have come to see me," he says. "If you needed something."

I laugh at that. *"You?"*

He frowns down at me with his amber eyes. "Why not?"

The enormity of the reasons catches in my mouth. He's a prince of Elfhame, and I am the disgraced child of traitors. He befriends everyone, from the troll guard at the entrance to all those Tiernan mentioned back in the High Court, while I have spent years alone in the woods. But most of all, because he could have asked his sister to allow me to stay on the Shifting Isles and didn't.

"Perhaps I wanted to save that favor you still owe me," I say.

He laughs at that. Oak liking me is as silly as the sun liking a storm, but that doesn't stop my desire for it.

Me, with my sharp teeth and chilly skin. It's absurd. It's grotesque.

And yet, the way he looks at me, it almost seems possible. I imagine that's his plan. He wants me to be charmed by him so that I will stay by his side and do what he asks of me. No doubt he believes that a little attention and a few smiles will be all it requires of him. He expects me to be as malleable as one of the ladies of the Court.

So much of me wants to give in and pretend with him that it makes me hot with rage.

If he wants to charm me, the least I can do is make it cost him. I won't settle for smiles and a dance. I am going to call his bluff. I am going to prove to myself—prove to us both—that his flirtation isn't sincere. I lean toward him, expecting him to unconsciously move away. To be repulsed. But he only watches me curiously.

As I draw closer, his eyes widen a little.

"Wren," he whispers. I am not sure if it's a warning or not. I hate that I don't know.

At every moment, I expect him to flinch or pull back as I put one hand on his shoulder, then go up on my toes, and kiss him.

This is ridiculous. Kissing him is profane. It gives me all the horrible satisfaction of smashing a crystal goblet.

It's quick. Just the press of my dry mouth against his lips. A brief sense of softness, the warmth of breath, and then I pull away, my heart thrumming with fear, with the expectation that he will be disgusted.

With the certainty that I have well and truly punished him for trying to flirt with me.

The angry, feral part of me feels so close to the surface that I can almost scent its blood-clotted fur. I want to lick the scratches I made.

He doesn't look alarmed, though. He's studying my face, as though he's trying to work something out.

After a moment, his eyes close, pale lashes against his cheek, and he dips forward to press his mouth to mine again. He goes slower, one of his hands cupping my head. A shivery feeling courses down my spine, a flush coming up on my skin.

When he draws back, he is not wearing his usual complicated smile. Instead, he looks as though someone just slapped him. I wonder if a kiss from me is like being clawed on the cheek.

Did he force himself to go through with it? For the sake of keeping me on this quest? For the sake of his father and his plans?

I thought to punish him, but all I have succeeded in doing is punishing myself.

I take a breath and let it out slowly. My gaze slides from his, and I spot Tiernan, coming toward us. I am not certain how much he saw, but I do not want to hear anything he might have to say just now. "Your pardon," I tell Oak. "But I've had enough dancing. I think I will take my leave."

The corner of his mouth quirks. "You know where to find me if you change your mind."

I hate the way those words make my skin flush.

I head into the crowd, hoping he will lose sight of me. Cursing myself for being foolish. Cursing him for addling my thoughts.

As my eyes slide across the dancers, I know I must talk to Hyacinthe.

*As long as everyone is well behaved, I will return him anon.* That was what Queen Annet said, but it was possible we had already failed at being well behaved. That coming here against the wishes of the High Queen might be excuse enough to keep him locked away.

Imprisoned as he is, though, I can go and speak with him *right now* with no one the wiser. He can give me his warning in full, can tell me everything he knows.

I scoop up a handful of roasted chestnuts and eat them slowly, dropping peels onto the floor as I move toward an exit. A cat-faced faerie tears at a piece of raw meat on a silver platter. A two-headed ogre drinks from a goblet that looks, pinched between his fingers, small enough to belong to a doll.

I aim a look in Oak's direction. He's being pulled into one of the dances by a laughing girl with golden hair and deer antlers. I imagine he will swiftly forget our kiss in her arms. And if the thought makes my stomach hurt, that only makes me think of getting to Hyacinthe again.

A mortal man leaps up onto a table near me, hair in thin locs. He has an expressive face and a rangy vulnerability that draws the eye. Pushing his glasses up higher onto his nose, he begins to play a fiddle.

The song he sings is of lost places and homes so far away that they are no longer home. He sings of love so intense it is indistinguishable from hate, and chains that are like riddles of old, no longer holding him, and yet unbroken.

Automatically, I look for ensorcellment, but there is none. He seems here of his own volition, although I dread to think how mistaken he may be in his audience. Still, Queen Annet says she is a fair host. So long as he keeps to the baroque rules of Faerie, he might find himself back in his bed in the morning, his pockets full of gold.

Of course, no one will tell him the rules, so he won't know if he breaks one.

Turning away at that thought, I move the rest of the way through the crowd as fast as I can.

CHAPTER

7

I pass bored guards, who throw hungry looks in my direction. They do not follow me, though, either because they are forbidden from leaving their post or because I look too stringy to make much of a meal.

Once they are out of sight, I begin to run. I veer through the three turns to where Lupine spoke of the gem-encrusted rooms near the prisons so fast that I nearly trip.

My thoughts are racing as fast as my feet. I kissed two people before Oak. There was the boy who liked fires and, later, one of the treefolk. Neither of those kisses felt quite as doomed as the one I shared with the prince, and they had been doomed enough.

This is the problem with living by instinct. I don't *think*.

The lower level has a damp, mineral smell. I hear guards ahead, so I creep carefully to the bend in the corridor and peer around it. The enormous, copper-banded door they guard is almost certainly to the prisons, as it is carved with the words *Let Suffering Ennoble*. One is a knight with hair the color of red roses. She seems to be losing a game of dice to a snickering, large-eared bauchan. Both wear armor. She has a long sword at her hip, while his is curved and strapped to his back.

I am used to sliding into and out of a forest without being observed, but I have little experience in the sort of fast-talking trickery that might get me past guards. I draw myself up, though, and hope that my tongue does not betray me.

Then I feel a tap on the shoulder. Spinning, swallowing a scream, I come face-to-face with Jack of the Lakes.

"I can guess what you're about," he says, looking maliciously pleased, like someone who has ferreted out a delicious bit of gossip. "You intend to free Hyacinthe."

"I just want to ask him some questions," I say.

"So you don't want to break him out of the prisons?" His green eyes are sly.

I'd like to deny that, but I cannot. Like all the Folk, my tongue seizes up when I start to lie, and unlike Oak, no clever deception comes easily to my lips. Just because I want to, though, it doesn't mean I will.

"Oooooooh," says Jack, correctly interpreting my silence for a confession. "Is he your lover? Is this a *ballad* we're in?"

"A murder ballad maybe," I growl.

"No doubt, by the end," he says. "I wonder who will survive to compose it."

"Have you come to gloat?" I ask, frustrated. "To stop me?" I am not sure how powerful a kelpie is out of the water and in the shape of a man.

"To surprise you," he says. "Aren't surprises wonderful?"

I grind my teeth but say nothing for a long moment. I may not be able to charm him with honey-mouthed words, but I understand resentment. "It must gall you, the way Tiernan talked to you."

Jack might be a merry wight, but I bet he's also a petty one.

"Maybe it wouldn't bother you so much to see him looking foolish in front of the prince? And if their prisoner was gone, the one noble knight who checked on him last would look very foolish indeed."

I don't plan on freeing Hyacinthe. I don't even think I can. Still, Jack doesn't need to know that. I am only playing into what he thinks about me.

He considers my words, a smile growing on his mouth. "What if I were to make a loud noise? Perhaps the guards would abandon their posts to follow. What would you give me to make the attempt?"

"What do you want?" I ask, digging in my pockets. I take out the swan-shaped scissors I stole from Habetrot. "These are pretty."

"Put them away," he scoffs. "It would be an insult to be stabbed by them."

"Then do not court that fate," I growl softly, rummaging a bit more, past Bogdana's note and the motel matchbook. I couldn't fit much in the pockets of my dress, and it is not as though I had much in the first place. But then my fingers close on the silver fox with the peridot eyes.

I take it out and hold it on my palm, reluctant to show it to him.

"What's this?" he asks.

I open my hand. "One of only three. A game piece of the Gentry." I am proud of my answer, which is both true and yet missing the most important detail. I am learning how to speak like them.

"You didn't steal it?" he asks, perhaps thinking of how disheveled I was when he first met me.

"It's mine," I tell him. "No one would dispute that."

He plucks it up between two fingers. "Very well. Now it shall be mine, I suppose, since you have nothing finer. And in return I will lead the guards on a merry chase."

I clench my hand to force myself not to snatch the little fox back. He sees the gesture and smiles. I can tell he likes the trinket better now that he knows I didn't want to give it to him.

"On my signal," he says. "Hide!"

"Wait," I caution, but he is already moving.

The hall is lit with orbs that glow a sickly green, giving the stone walls a mossy cast. The orbs are spaced far enough apart that it is possible for me to push myself into a bend of the corridor and be concealed by darkness, so long as no one looks too closely.

I hold my breath. I hear the pelting of hoofbeats, then a great and foolish whooping accompanied by shouts.

"That's my sword!" the rose-haired knight yells, and then I see Jack of the Lakes streak by, running hell-for-leather in his horse form, laughing and gripping a bright silver sword in his teeth.

The knight comes into view. "When I catch you, I am going to turn you inside out, like a toad!" she shouts as she gives chase. The bauchan follows at her heels, his blade drawn.

When they are far enough, I slip out of the dark.

I head swiftly to the copper-banded door to the prisons. The rocks around the door are studded with crystals that gleam bright against the dull gray stone.

I turn the latch and walk inside. All the rooms are like chambers of a cave, with massive stalagmites and stalactites functioning as bars. It appears not unlike looking at rows and rows of mouths with rows and rows of awful teeth.

Figures move in some of the cells, shifting to blink at me from the gloom within.

A clawed hand darts out, grabbing for my arm. I jump out of its reach, jerking the cloth of my dress from its grip. I step on, shuddering.

Most of the chambers are empty, but in one I see a merrow. The floor of his cell is wet, but not enough for him to be comfortable. His scales have grown dull and dry. He watches me with eyes that are pale all the way through, the pupils barely discernible from the irises or scleras.

There is a scuffing sound from the other side, and I see a girl tossing a piece of rock into the air and catching it. For a moment, I think I am looking at a glamour, but a moment later I realize that she's actually human.

She looks as though she might be around my age, with hair the color of straw. There's a bruise on her cheek. "Can I have some water? Will you tell me how much longer I have to be here?" Her voice trembles.

I follow her gaze to the wooden tub in the corner of the room, a copper ladle hanging off one side, its body streaked with verdigris. She pushes a ceramic bowl toward the bars and looks up at me plaintively.

"Is a man with a single wing for an arm here?" I ask.

The human comes eagerly to her feet. "You're not one of the guards."

I dip the ladle into the tub and haul up some water, then pour it into her bowl. Across the way, the merrow makes a low moan. I dip the ladle again and splash him.

"The winged guy?" the human whispers. "He's down there." She points toward the end of the corridor. "See? I can be helpful. Let me out, and I could be of service to you."

It is tragic that she has only me to beseech. Does she not see my predator's teeth? How afraid must she already be for me to seem like a possible ally?

I splash the merrow again. With a sigh, he sinks down to the floor, gills flexing.

I need to see Hyacinthe, but looking at the girl, I cannot stop myself from thinking of Bex, my unsister. Imagining her in a place like this, with no one to help her and no way out.

"How did you come to be here?" I ask, knowing that more information is only going to make it harder to walk away.

"My boyfriend," she says. "He was *taken*. I met a creature, and he told me I could win Dario back if I threatened to dig down into their—" She stops, possibly at the remembrance that I *am* one of them.

I nod, though, and that seems enough to get her speaking again. "I got a shovel and came out to the haunted hill, where everyone says weird things happen."

While she talks, I evaluate the stalagmites and stalactites of her prison. Perhaps one could be cracked if someone very strong swung something very heavy at it, but since these prisons must have been constructed to hold even ogres, there's no way I would be able to do it.

"Then I was grabbed. And these *things* said they were going to bring me before their queen, and she would punish me. They started naming what they thought she might order done. All their suggestions were like something out of the *Saw* movies." She gives a weird giggle, one that tells me she's fighting off hysteria. "You've got no idea what I'm talking about, right?"

Living in the mortal world as I did, I have some idea, but there's no point in telling her that. Better get her mind away from what could happen. "Wait here."

She scrubs a hand over her face. "You have to help me."

I find Hyacinthe's cell at the end of the corridor. He's sitting on the floor, on a carpet of hay. Beside him is a tray of oranges and sweetmeats, along with a bowl of wine set down so that he might lap from it like a dog. He looks up at me in surprise, his amethyst eyes wide. I am surprised, too, because he is no longer bridled.

"Where is it?" I blurt out, terrified that it is in the possession of Queen Annet.

"The bridle?" He rubs his cheek against his wing. I see a few fresh feathers at his throat. The curse is spreading slowly, but it is spreading. "The prince was afraid of it falling into the hands of the Court of Moths, so he had Tiernan remove it."

"Oak has it?" I ask, wondering if that was the real reason he ordered it taken off. Wondering what he was planning on doing with it.

Hyacinthe nods. "I suppose." Then he sighs. "All I know is that I don't have to wear it, at least until we depart the Court of Moths. Are we leaving? Is that why you're here?"

I shake my head. "Has Queen Annet asked anything of you?"

He takes two steps closer to the bars. "I think she wishes to delay Oak long enough to determine if there's a profit in returning him to the High Court, but that's only from what I overheard the guards saying."

"You think his sister wants him back?"

Hyacinthe shrugs. "Trussing him up and handing him over could bring Queen Annet some reward if Jude does, but it would not do to *cross* her if she and the High King turn out to support his mission. Discovering what they want takes time, hence the delay."

I nod, calculating. "If Elfhame wants to stop us..."

*If the High Court makes a captive out of the prince, from love or anger, then who will stop Lady Nore? Will I be held as well? And if not, then how long before Bogdana finds me?*

"I don't know," he says in answer to one or all the questions I do not ask.

I lower my voice even further. "Tell me about the prince's powers as a gancanagh? And what Lady Nore sent in her message? You're not constrained by the bridle."

"Free me," he says, eyes intent. "Free me, and I will tell you all I know."

Of course. Why else try to interest me in the information he had? Not for my benefit. He wanted to escape.

I ought to focus on my own survival. This isn't what I came to the prisons for. Helping Hyacinthe will only make it certain that I wear the bridle myself.

And yet, I do not know how I can turn and walk away from him, leaving him in a cage. Neither Oak nor Tiernan were cruel to him when he was their prisoner, and still I was horrified. The Court of Moths could be so much worse.

Oak would never forgive me, though.

Unless...he never found out that I was the one who helped Hyacinthe escape. No one saw me come in here, save for Jack of the Lakes. And Jack can hardly tell anyone, since he had a part in it.

Perhaps I could keep this secret, as Oak kept secrets from me.

"Promise you will tell no one—especially not Lady Nore—anything of Oak, or me, or Tiernan that would put us in danger or expose our plans." I try to convince myself that this plan might be to the prince's advantage and that he would benefit if Queen Annet's schemes were at least partially thwarted. After all, if Hyacinthe goes missing from her prisons after she insisted on keeping him, she can hardly call herself a good host.

If Oak finds out, he will not see my actions in that light. He'll believe that I kissed him to divert his attention from the way I was stabbing him in the back. He'll believe that everything Tiernan ever said about me was true.

But if I do nothing, then Queen Annet is likely to keep Hyacinthe, in the hopes she can detain Oak or lure him to return to her Court. I cannot stand the idea of anyone being kept as I was, locked away and helpless.

"Help me escape and I will tell no one—especially not Lady Nore— anything of you, or Oak, or Tiernan that would put you in any danger or expose your plans," Hyacinthe vows prettily and in full.

The gravity of this moment settles heavily on my shoulders.

"So how do I get you out?" I ask, trying to focus on that and not the dread I suddenly feel at taking fate in my own hand, mine and Hyacinthe's. I study the stalagmites instead, looking for a seam. "These jaws must *open* somehow, but I can't see the way."

Hyacinthe puts his fingers through the gap in the teethlike bars and gestures toward the ceiling. "There's something up there, written in the stone. One of the guards looked up when he spoke, like he was reading. He shuffled his feet, too, as though there's a particular place to stand."

"You didn't *hear* what he said?" I ask, incredulous.

He shakes his head. "That must be part of the enchantment. I saw his mouth move, but there was no sound."

I squint up and spot a few scratchy, thin lines of writing. I take two steps back, and am able to make it out. It is no password to open the teethlike bars, however. It's a riddle. And as I look, I note a different one above each of the cells.

I suppose that if each chamber requires a different word or phrase to open or close, it'd be useful to have a reminder, especially with new guards coming in all the time. Not everyone's memory is keen, and there's a risk that should a word be forgotten, the cell would cease to work forevermore.

"*Daughter of the sun,*" I read. "*Yet made for night, fire causes her to weep, and if she dies before her time, cut off her head and she may be reborn.*"

"A riddle," Hyacinthe groans.

I nod, thinking of the Folk's love of games. Of how Habetrot had called Oak the *Prince of Sunlight*. Of the word puzzles my unfamily would play—Scrabble, Bananagrams. Of the poems I memorized from Bex's schoolbooks and recited to squirrels.

I try to clear my head. "The moon?" Nothing happens. As I look down, I notice there's a circle etched into the floor, just a little beyond where I stand. I step into it and speak again. "Moon."

This time, the jaws creak, but instead of opening, the cell shrinks, as though biting down on its prisoner.

Hyacinthe bangs on the toothlike stone bars, panicked. "How is the moon *beheaded*?"

"It thins to a sliver," I say, horrified at what I'd nearly done. "But it comes back. And it could be seen as the daughter of the sun—I mean, reflected light and all that."

No number of explanations for why I thought my answer was right can change that it almost got him crushed. Even now that the movement ceased, I am still left afraid that it will snap closed, grinding him to pieces.

"Be careful!" he hisses.

"Give me your answer, then," I growl.

He is silent at that.

I think more. Perhaps a *rose*? I have a vague recollection of being with my unmother at one of her friends' houses, playing in the backyard while the friend trimmed her rosebushes. There had been something about cutting off the flower heads so there would be more blooms the following year. And daughter of the sun—well, plants liked sun, right? And they didn't like fire. And, well, people thought of roses as romantic, so maybe they were made for night because people romance one another mostly at night?

That last seems like a stretch, but I can think of nothing better.

"I have something," I say, my lack of confidence clear in my voice.

He gives me a wary look, then heaves a sigh. "Go ahead," he tells me.

I move to the spot and take a deep breath. "A rose."

The teeth grind lower, the ceiling dropping so fast that Hyacinthe sprawls on the floor to avoid getting hit. I hear a sound that might be laughter from the merrow's cell, but the winged soldier is deathly silent.

"Are you hurt?" I ask.

"Not yet," he says carefully. "But I don't think there's room for the cell to close farther without cracking me like a nut."

It was different to lie in wait for the glaistig and rip apart her spells, knowing I was the one in danger. To sneak through mortal houses or even run from hags. But to think that because of a mistake of mine, a life could be snuffed out like a—

*Daughter of the sun. Made for night. Cut off her head and she's reborn.*

"Candle," I blurt out.

The stone cavern shifts with a groaning sound, and the bars spring apart like a mouth, like some enormous carnivorous flower. We stare at each other, Hyacinthe moving from terror to laughter. He springs to his feet and spins me around in one arm, then presses a kiss to the top of my head. "You delightful, amazing girl! You did it."

"We still have to get past the guards," I remind him, uncomfortable with the praise.

"*You* freed me from the prison. *I* will free us from the hill," he says with an intensity that I think might be pride.

"But first," I say, "tell what you know about Oak. All of it, this time."

He makes a face. "On the way."

I shake my head. "Now."

"What is it he's supposed to tell you?" the human girl asks from her cell, and Hyacinthe gives me an exasperated look.

"Not here," he says, widening his eyes to suggest the reason should be obvious: *The girl can hear us. So can the merrow.*

"We're going to get them out, too, so it doesn't matter," I say. After all, it wasn't as though I could be in *more* trouble if I were discovered.

He stares at me, wide-eyed. "That would be unwise."

"My name is Gwen," the girl calls. "Please. I promise I won't tell anyone what I overheard. I'll do whatever you want if you take me with you."

I look up at the writing over the door to her cell. Another riddle. *It gorges, yet lacks a maw. Well-fed, it grows swift and strong. Give it a draught, though, and you give it death.*

No mouth, but eats...

"Wren, did you hear me?" Hyacinthe demands.

"They're witnesses," I tell him. "Leaving witnesses behind would also be *unwise.*"

"Then give me your knife," he says, frowning. "I'll take care of them."

Gwen has come to the edge of the stalagmites. "Wait," she says, her voice edged with desperation. "I can help you. There's lots of stuff I can do."

*Like navigate the human world.* I don't want to hurt his pride to say it, but she might be able to hide him in places the Folk are unlikely to look. Together, they can escape more easily than either of them could alone.

"The knife," Hyacinthe says, putting out his hand as though he really expects me to give him one and let him do it.

I turn, frowning. "You still haven't told me anything useful about the prince."

"Very well," he says. "When Lady Nore took Madoc, she sent a message to the High Court, asking for something in return for the old general's freedom. I don't know what she wanted, only that the king and queen refused her."

I nod. Oak spoke to me of desiring Lady Nore's defeat, though an exchange of messages suggests he might be willing to appease her instead. For a moment, I wonder if it is *me* that she wants. But if so, he hardly needs to go to the Thistlewitch. He knows exactly where I am. And the High Court would give me up immediately.

"What about being a gancanagh?" I ask.

Hyacinthe huffs out a frustrated sigh, clearly wishing to be away from here. "I will tell you what I know as quickly as I am able. He inherited some of Liriope's power, and she was able to kindle strong emotions in the people who got close to her, feelings of loyalty and desire and adoration. I am not certain how much of it was conscious and how much of it was just a tide all around her, sweeping people who got too close onto the shoals. Oak will use you until you're all used up. He will manipulate you until you don't know what's real and what isn't."

I remember what Tiernan said about Hyacinthe's father.

"Forget this quest. You will never know what the prince is thinking behind his smiles," Hyacinthe says. "You are a coin to be spent, and he is a royal, used to throwing around gold."

My gaze goes to the riddle above Gwen's door again, which suddenly seems easier to solve than any of my other problems.

What eats but doesn't drink? My gaze drifts to the water, to the verdigris. Then to gorging. To hungry mouths.

Mouths like the one that the bars represent, ready to devour Gwen if I get the answer wrong. The cell that Hyacinthe was in gave me three tries, but I note that the ceiling of Gwen's is lower. I might have only two guesses before she's crushed.

And since the guards may come in at any moment, it's possible I have less time than that.

I am terrified of coming up with the wrong answer and yet equally worried we will be caught. Both thoughts are distracting, creating a loop of nerves.

*Give it a draught and you give it death.*

I think of splashing the merrow with water. I think of the sea.

I think of the answer to the other door, a candle. It gorges, and giving it a drink would put out its flame. Could both riddles have the same answer? Could all the cells be opened the same way?

I open my mouth to speak, but caution stops me. *Well-fed, it grows swift and strong.* Candles do not grow. I almost spoke the wrong word again.

No, not a candle, but something like one. A candle might not grow, but its flame could.

"Fire," I whisper, and Gwen's cell opens, disgorging her.

She stumbles out, looking around the room as though this might be a trick. She studies Hyacinthe warily, perhaps worried he might use a knife on her after all.

"You're going to take her with you," I inform him. "Instead of me."

He looks at me as if I have lost my mind. "And why would I do that?"

"Because I am asking you to, and I got you out of prison," I say, fixing him with what I hope is a firm look.

He is not intimidated by me, however. "Nowhere in your price was helping a foolish mortal."

Panic churns in my gut. "What if I take the curse off you?"

"Impossible," he says. "Even Oak couldn't permanently remove it, and he is from the High Court."

The prince hasn't had the practice I have in removing curses, though. And perhaps he hadn't *wanted* it completely gone.

"But if I could...," I ask in my rough voice.

Grudgingly he nods.

I turn to Gwen and show her my teeth, pleased when she flinches. "You solve the riddle to release the merrow. Do not get it wrong."

Then I reach for Hyacinthe's wing.

I feel the feathers in my hands, the softness and lightness of the bones underneath. And I sense the curse reknitting itself inside Hyacinthe, as though it were a living thing.

I reach into the magic and am surprised by the stickiness of the threads. It's like tugging at a spiderweb. The harder I pull, the more the curse seems to attach itself to me, trying to transform me, too. I feel the draw of the enchantment, the shimmer and burn of it, tugging at something inside me.

"What are you doing?" Hyacinthe asks. His wing pulls free of my fingers.

I open my eyes, only then realizing I'd closed them. "Did it hurt?"

"No—I don't know," he says. "It felt like you were touching—under my skin."

I take a breath and return to the work of pulling apart the curse. But each time I attempt to break it, the strands of the spell slip through my fingers. And each time I am drawn further in, until I feel as though I am choking on feathers. Until I am drowning. The knot inside me, at the center of my magic, is coming undone.

"Stop," Hyacinthe says, shaking my shoulder. "Enough."

I find myself on the ground with him kneeling beside me. I can't seem to get my breath back.

The glaistig's spells were simple compared with this webbing of enchantment. I grit my teeth. I might be good enough among the solitary fey of the mortal world, but it was sheer arrogance to think that meant I could unstitch the magic of the High Court.

A few feet away, I see Gwen and the merrow looking over at me. He blinks, his nictating membrane following a moment later.

"We puzzled out the riddle together," Hyacinthe says with a frown at Gwen. "Now let's go."

"But—" I start.

"I'll take her," he says. "The mortal girl. I will get her out of here, and that creature, too. Just get up."

I ought to do that. But his words seem to come from far away as I reach for the magic again, and this time when it tries to draw me into it, I pull it into me instead. I let it drag me under. I take the whole curse in a rush.

Everything stops. No air is in my lungs. There is a pain in my chest, as though my heart cannot beat. As though something inside me is cracking. As though I am going to come apart.

I concentrate on the curse. On wrestling that sticky, grasping enchantment and quashing it down until it is a solid thing, heavy and cold. And then I press it further, into nothing.

When I open my eyes, my ragged nails are digging into the skin of Hyacinthe's arm. His *arm*, which is no longer feathered, no longer a wing. He is on his knees, still. I am trembling all over, so light-headed that I can barely remember where I am.

"You did it. You broke the curse. My lady, I swear fealty to you." His words take a moment to sink in, and when they do, horror sweeps over me. "To you and you alone. I was wrong to doubt."

"No," I manage to choke out.

I do not want that responsibility. I have seen what power does to people. And I have seen how those who pledge loyalty come to resent those oaths and wish for the destruction of the one who holds them. I was never less free than when I ruled.

"I am your servant forevermore," he says, heedless, pressing his dry lips to the back of my hand. His dark brown hair falls forward in a curtain, brushing my arm like silk. "Obedient to your command."

I shake my head, but the vow is made. And I'm too tired to even be able to explain why that worries me. My mind feels too adrift.

I look up at the three prisoners I freed and am suddenly, acutely aware of how much trouble I made. I didn't realize how much I have changed from that terrified girl, forever looking for a place to hide in the Court of Teeth. Breaking spells on mortals has made me rebellious.

And for a moment, I am viciously glad. It doesn't feel good exactly, to be in danger, but it does feel good to be the cause of events rather than being swept along into them.

"Take off your shoes," I tell the girl, my voice rasping worse than ever.

She looks down at her sneakers. "What for?"

I give her a commanding look, and she toes them off.

I push myself up, trying to remember my half a plan. Hyacinthe grabs my arm as I sway, and my pride urges me to snap at him, but I am too grateful.

"So that your steps will be quiet," I explain. "You three can fit behind the water trough. It's dark, and if you crouch down, you won't be seen."

Hyacinthe pauses. "And you?"

I shake my head. "I said I wasn't coming. I'll keep the guards busy. Can you find your way out from here?"

He nods, briefly. He's a soldier, hopefully trained for situations not totally unlike this. Then he frowns. "If you stay behind, you will be in great danger," he tells me.

"I'm not going," I say.

"He won't forgive you for this."

If Oak discovers what I've done, Hyacinthe is probably right. But I still have to face Lady Nore or she will hunt me down. Nothing about this changes that.

"You swore to me," I remind him, although his words echo my fears. "Moments ago. What I ask is for you to get yourself and Gwen out of the Court of Moths alive. And get the merrow to the sea cave. It's on the way."

"Send me north, to Lady Nore, then," Hyacinthe tells me, almost whispering. "Should you make it there, at least you'll have an ally."

"And that is why you ought not dramatically vow to obey someone," I say, a growl in my voice. "They seldom ask for what you hope they will."

"I know about faeries and bargains," Gwen says to me, foolishly. "You're going to ask something from me, too, right?"

I look her over. I hadn't planned on asking for anything, but that was unwise. She probably has little on her, but her clothes and sneakers would allow me to pass into the mortal world more easily, if I had to do so. And there are other things. "Do you have a phone?"

Gwen appears surprised. "I thought you would ask for a year of my life, or a cherished memory, or my voice."

What would I do with any of that? "Would you prefer to give me a year of your life?"

"I guess not." Gwen reaches into her pocket and pulls out her phone, along with a plug-in charger she detaches from a key chain. "There's no reception here."

"When you and Hyacinthe get to safety, let me know," I say, taking it. The metal-and-glass object is light in my hand. I haven't held one in a long time.

"I was going to call my boyfriend," she tells me. "Once, he picked up, and I could hear their music in the background. If he calls—"

"I'll tell him to get out," I say. "Now hide, and when they come in, you leave."

Hyacinthe gives me a speaking look as he guides the mortal toward the darkness.

It is the merrow that takes my hand. "Lady of the land," he says, voice even raspier than mine, skin chilly. "The only gift I have to give you is knowledge. There is a war coming in the waves. The Queen of the Undersea has grown weak, and her child is weaker. When there comes blood in the water, the land would be well served to stay away. Cirien-Cròin is coming."

Then he lurches toward the water barrel.

And at his warning, I walk to the copper-banded door and turn the knob. I still feel wobbly and breathless, as though I have cast off a long fever. No breaking of a curse ever felt like this before, and it frightens me.

But the bauchan and the rose-haired knight on the other side scare me even more. At the sight of me, she reaches for her sword, which I note she retrieved. I hope that means that Jack of the Lakes dropped it and not that he was caught.

"How did you—" the bauchan begins.

I cut them off with the firmest voice I can summon. "The cursed soldier—the prince's prisoner—he's not in his cell!" Which is true enough, since I let him out.

"That doesn't explain what *you're* doing where you're not supposed to be," the rose-haired knight says.

"When I came, there was no one guarding the entrance," I say, letting that accusation hang in the air.

The rose-haired knight strides past me impatiently, a blush coloring her cheeks. She stalks to the end of the prison where Hyacinthe ought to be. I follow, carefully keeping my gaze from the shadows.

"Well?" I say, hand on my hip.

The panic in their eyes tells me that Queen Annet has earned her reputation for brutality honestly.

"*The girl*," the rose-haired knight says, realizing the human is gone, too.

"And the *spy* from the Undersea." The bauchan speaks a word to open the merrow's cell, then walks around it. Letting all the prisoners out has confused their suppositions about what happened, at least.

"You saw nothing?" the rose-haired knight asks.

"What was there to see?" I return. "What did *you* see, to leave your post?"

The bauchan gives the knight a look, seeming to will her to silence. Neither of them speaks for a long moment. Finally, the knight says, "Tell no one of this. We will catch the prisoners. They must never make it out of the Court of Moths."

I nod slowly, as though I am considering her words. I lift my chin as I have seen the Gentry do, as Lady Nore did. No one would have believed the part I am playing were I in my rags, with my wild hair, but I see the guards believe me now. Perhaps I could come to like this dress for more than its beauty.

"I must rejoin the prince," I say. "I will keep this from him as long as I can, but if you don't find Hyacinthe before we depart for the Thistle-witch at dawn, there will be no hiding that he's gone."

Heart thundering, I walk out into the hall. Then I retrace my steps to the revel, pressing my hands to my chest to still their trembling.

I head to a table and pour myself a long draught of green wine. It smells like crushed grass and goes straight to my head, drowning out the sour taste of adrenaline.

I spot Oak, a wine bottle in one hand and the cat-headed lady I saw before in his arms. She reaches up to pet his golden curls with her claws as they dance. Then there is a change of partners, and a crone moves into the cat lady's place.

The prince takes her withered hand and kisses it. When she leans in to kiss his throat, he only laughs. Then sweeps her away into the steps of the gavotte, his inebriated smile never dipping or faltering.

Until the ogre dancing with the cat-headed lady abruptly pulls her out of the spinning circle. He pushes her roughly through the throng toward a second ogre.

Oak stops dancing, leaving his partner as he strides across the floor to them.

I follow more slowly, unable to make the crowd part for me as he did.

By the time I get anywhere close, the cat-headed lady is standing behind Oak, hissing like a snake.

"Give her over," says one of the ogres. "She's a little thief, and I'll have it out of her hide."

"A thief? Purloining hearts, perhaps," says Oak, making the cat lady smile. She wears a gown of the palest pink silk with panniers on either side and earrings of crystals hanging from her furred ears. She looks too wealthy to need to steal anything.

"You think because you've got that good royal blood in you, you're better than us," says the ogre, pressing one long fingernail against the prince's shoulder. "Maybe you are. Only way to be sure is to have a taste."

There's a drunken wobble to Oak's movements as he pushes off the ogre's hand and obvious contempt in his voice. "The difference in flavor would be too subtle for your palate."

The cat-headed lady presses a handkerchief to her mouth and steps delicately away, not sticking around to witness the consequences of Oak's gallant defense of her.

"I doubt it will be much trouble to bleed you and find out," one ogre says, causing the other to laugh and close in. "Shall we put it to a test?"

At that, the prince edges back a little, but the second ogre is directly behind him. "That would be a mistake."

The last thing Oak ought to do is show them he's afraid. The scent of weakness is headier than blood.

Unless he *wants* to be hit.

Should he be drawn into a fight, he would violate guest etiquette. But if one of the ogres struck first—then it would be the host who had made the misstep. Judging by the size of the ogres, though, a single blow might knock the prince's head off his shoulders.

Not only are they large, but they look trained for violence. Oak wasn't even able to block my hand when I scratched his face.

I must have made some impulsive, jerky movement, because the prince's gaze goes to me. One of the ogres turns in my direction and chuckles.

"Well, well," he says. "She looks delicious. Is she yours? Since you defended a thief, perhaps we ought to show you what it feels like to be stolen from."

Oak's voice hardens. "You're witless enough not to know the difference between eating a rock and a sweetmeat until your teeth crack, but know this—she is not to be touched."

"What did you say?" asks his companion with a grunt.

Oak's eyebrows go up. "Banter isn't your strong suit, is it? I was attempting to indicate that your friend here was a fool, a muttonhead, a clodpate, an asshat, an oaf—"

The ogre punches him, massive fist connecting with Oak's cheek-bone hard enough to make him stagger. The ogre hits him again, blood spattering from his mouth.

An odd gleam comes into the prince's eye.

Another blow lands.

Why doesn't he hit back? Even if Oak wanted them to strike first, they've done it. He would be well within his rights to fight. "Queen Annet will punish you for attacking the Crown Prince!" I shout, hoping the ogre will come to his senses before Oak gets hurt worse.

At my words, the other ogre clamps down on his friend's shoulder, restraining him from a third blow. "The boy's had enough."

"Have I?" Oak asks, wiping his mouth with the back of his hand. His smile grows, showing red teeth.

I turn to him in utter disbelief.

Oak stands up straighter, ignoring the bruise blooming beneath one eye, pushing away the hair hanging in his face. He looks a little dazed.

"Hit me again," the prince says, daring them.

The two ogres share a look. The companion seems nervous. The other makes a fist.

"Come on." Oak's smile does not seem to belong to him. It's not the one he turned on the dancers. Not the one he turned on me. It's full of menace, his eyes shining like a blade. *"Hit me."*

"Stop it!" I scream, so loud that several more people turn toward me. "Stop!"

Oak appears chagrined, as though he were the only one I was yelling at. "Your pardon," he says.

They allow him to stumble over to me. Whether he's punch-drunk or just plain drunk, I cannot tell.

"You're hurt," I say, foolishly.

"I lost you in the crowd," Oak says. There's a bruise purpling at the corner of his mouth, and a few specks of blood mixed with his freckles.

The same mouth that I kissed.

I nod, too stunned to do more. My heart is still racing.

"Shall we put our dance practice to some purpose?" he asks.

"Dance?" I ask, my voice coming out a little high.

His gaze goes to the circles of leaping and cavorting Folk. I wonder if he is in shock.

I have just come from betraying him. I feel rather shocked myself.

I put my hand in his as if mesmerized. There is only the warmth of his fingers against my chilly skin. His amber fox eyes, pupils wide and dark. His teeth catch his lip, as though he's nervous. I reach up and touch his cheek. Blood and freckles.

He's shaking a little. I guess if I'd done what he did, I'd still be shaking, too.

"Your Highness," comes a voice.

I drop his hand. The rose-haired knight has pushed her way through the crowd, three more heavily armored soldiers behind her. Their expressions are grim.

My stomach drops.

The knight bows. "Your Highness, I am Revindra, part of Queen Annet's guard. And I bring news that your—that one of your companions broke into our prison and released Lady Nore's spy as well as one of Queen Annet's mortals and a merrow from the Undersea."

I say nothing. There's nothing for me to say.

"What evidence do you have?" Oak asks with a quick glance in my direction.

"A confession from a kelpie that he gave her aid. She paid him with this." Revindra opens her palm to show the silver fox with the peridot eyes.

His jaw tightens. "Wren?"

I don't know how to answer for what I did.

Oak takes the playing piece, an abstracted expression coming over his face. "I thought never to see this again."

"We're here to take Suren," Revindra goes on. "And we will take it ill if you attempt to prevent us."

The gaze that Oak slants toward me is as cold as the one he bestowed on the ogres.

"Oh," he says. "I wouldn't dream of stopping you."

# CHAPTER

# 8

At fourteen, I learned to make tea out of crushed spruce needles along with bee balm flowers, boiled over a fire.

"Would you like a cup, Mr. Fox?" I asked my stuffed animal solicitously, as though we were very fancy.

He didn't want any. Since stealing Mr. Fox back from my unparents' boxes, I'd cuddled up with him every night, and his fur had become dingy from sleeping on moss and dirt.

Worse, there were a few times I'd left him behind when I went to sit underneath windows at Bex's school or the local community college, repeating probably useless poems and snatches of history to myself, or doing sums by tracing the numbers in the earth. One night when I returned, I found he'd been attacked by a squirrel looking for material to nest in and most of his insides had been pulled out.

Since then, I'd stayed at my camp, reading him a novel about an impoverished governess I'd taken from the library when I'd picked up

*Foraging in the American Southeast.* There was a lot about convalescing and chilblains, so I figured it might make him feel better.

Mr. Fox looked uncomfortably like the skins Bogdana hung up to dry after her kills.

"We'll get you some new guts, Mr. Fox," I promised him. "Feathers, maybe."

As I flopped down, my gaze tracked a bird in the tree above us. I'd gotten fast and vicious in the wild. I could catch it easily enough, but it would be hard to be sure the feathers were clean and parasite-free. Maybe I should consider ripping apart one of my unfamily's pillows instead.

Out in the woods, I'd often think of the games Rebecca and I used to play. Like once, when we were pretending to be fairy-tale princesses. We carted out props—a rusty axe that had probably never been taken from the garage before, two paper crowns I'd made from glitter and cut-up newspaper, and an apple, only slightly bruised, but shiny with wax.

"First, I am going to be a woodsman and you are going to plead for your life," Rebecca told me. "I'll be sympathetic, because you're so pretty and sad, so I'll kill a deer instead."

So we played that out, and Rebecca hacked at weeds with the axe.

"Now I'll be the evil queen," I'd volunteered. "And you can pretend to give me—"

"*I'm* the evil queen," Rebecca insisted. "And the prince. And the woodsman."

"That's not fair," I whined. Rebecca could be so bossy sometimes. "You get to do everything, and all I get to do is cry and sleep."

"You get to eat the apple," Rebecca pointed out. "And wear a crown.

Besides, you *said* that you wanted to be the princess. That's what princesses do."

Bite the bad apple. Sleep.

Cry.

A rustling sound made my head come up.

"Suren?" a shout came through the woods. No one should have been calling me. No one should have even known my name.

"Stay here, Mr. Fox," I said, tucking him into my dwelling. Then I crept toward the voice.

Only to see Oak, the heir to Elfhame, standing in a clearing. All my memories of him were of a merry young boy. But he'd become tall and rawboned, in the manner of children who have grown suddenly, and too fast. When he moved, it was with coltish uncertainty, as though not used to his body. He would be thirteen. And he had no reason to be in my woods.

I crouched in a patch of ferns. "What do you want?"

He turned toward my voice. "Suren?" he called again. "Is that you?"

Oak wore a blue vest with silver frogging in place of buttons. Beneath was a fine linen shirt. His hooves had silver caps that matched two silver hoops at the very top of one pointed ear. Butter-blond hair threaded with dark gold blew around his face.

I glanced down at myself. My feet were bare and dark with filth. I couldn't remember how long it had been since I washed my dress. A bloodstain marred the cloth near my waist, from where I'd snagged my arm on a thorn. Grass stains on the skirt, near my knees. I recalled him finding me staked to a post, tied like an animal outside the camp of the Court of Teeth. I could not bear more of his pity.

"It's me," I called. "Now go away."

"But I've only just found you. And I want to talk." He sounded as though he meant it. As though he considered us friends, even after all this time.

"What will you give me if I do, Prince of Elfhame?"

He flinched at the title. "The pleasure of my company?"

"Why?" Though it was not a friendly question, I was honestly puzzled.

He was a long time in answering. "Because you're the only person I know who was ever a royal, like me."

"Not like you," I called.

"You ran away," he said. "I want to run away."

I shifted into a more comfortable position. It wasn't that I'd run. I hadn't had anywhere else but here to go. My fingers plucked at a piece of grass. He had everything, didn't he? "Why?" I asked again.

"Because I am tired of people trying to assassinate me."

"I would have thought they'd prefer you on the throne to your sister." Killing him didn't seem as though it would accomplish anything useful to anyone. He was replaceable. If Jude wanted another heir, she could have a baby. She was human; she could probably have a lot of babies.

He pressed the toe of his hoof into the dirt, digging restlessly at the edge of a root. "Well, some people want to protect Cardan because they believe that Jude means to murder him and think my not being around would discourage it. Others believe that eliminating me is a good first step to eliminating her."

"That doesn't make any sense," I said.

"Can't you just come out so we can talk?" The prince turned, frowning, looking for me in the trees and shrubs.

"You don't need to see me for that," I told him.

*"Fine."* He sat among the leaves and moss, balancing his cheek on a bent knee. "Someone tried to kill me. Again. Poison. Again. Someone else tried to recruit me into a scheme where we would kill my sister and Cardan, so I could rule in their place. When I told them no, *they* tried to kill me. With a knife, that time."

"A poisoned knife?"

He laughed. "No, just a regular one. But it hurt."

I sucked in a breath. When he said there had been attempts, I assumed that meant they'd been prevented in some way, not that he merely *hadn't died.*

He went on. "So I am going to run away from Faerie. Like you."

That's not how I'd thought of myself, as a runaway. I was someone with nowhere to go. Waiting until I was older. Or less afraid. Or more powerful. "The Prince of Elfhame can't up and *disappear.*"

"They'd probably be happier if he did," he told me. "I'm the reason my father is in exile. The reason my mother married him in the first place. My one sister and her girlfriend had to take care of me when I was little, even though they were barely more than kids themselves. My other sister almost got killed lots of times to keep me safe. Things will be easier without me around. They'll see that."

"They *won't,*" I told him, trying to ignore the intense surge of envy that came with knowing he would be missed.

"Let me stay in your woods with you," he said with a huff of breath.

I imagined it. Having him share tea with me and Mr. Fox. I could show him the places to pick the sweetest blackberries. We would eat burdock and red clover and parasol mushrooms. At night we would lie on our backs and whisper together. He would tell me about the constellations, about theories of magic, and the plots of television shows he'd seen while in the mortal world. I would tell him all the secret thoughts of my heart.

For a moment, it seemed possible.

But eventually they would come for him, the way that Lady Nore and Lord Jarel came for me. If he was lucky, it would be his sister's guards dragging him back to Elfhame. If he wasn't, it would be a knife in the dark from one of his enemies.

He did not belong here, sleeping in dirt. Scrabbling out an existence at the very edges of things.

"No," I made myself tell him. "Go home."

I could see the hurt in his face. The honest confusion that came with unexpected pain.

"Why?" he asked, sounding so lost that I wanted to snatch back my words.

"When you found me tied to that stake, I thought about hurting you," I told him, hating myself. "You are not my friend."

*I do not want you here.* Those are the words I ought to have said, but couldn't, because they would be a lie.

"Ah," he said. "Well."

I let out a breath. "You can stay the night," I blurted out, unable to resist that temptation. "Tomorrow, you go home. If you don't, I'll use the last favor you owe me from our game to force you."

"What if I go and come back again?" he asked, trying to mask his hurt.

"You won't." When he got home, his sisters and his mother would be waiting. They would have worried when they couldn't find him. They'd make him promise never to do anything like that again. "You have too much honor."

He didn't answer.

"Stay where you are a moment," I told him, and crept off through the grass.

I had him there with me for one night, after all. And while I didn't think he was *my* friend, it didn't mean I couldn't be his. I brought him a cup of tea, hot and fresh. Set it down on a nearby rock, with leaves beside it for a plate, piled with blackberries.

"Would you like a cup of tea, prince?" I asked him. "It's over here."

"Sure," he said, walking toward my voice.

When he found it, he sat down on the stone, settling the tea on his leg and holding the blackberries in the palm of one hand. "Are you drinking with me?"

"I am," I said.

He nodded, and this time he didn't ask me to come out.

"Will you tell me about the constellations?" I asked him.

"I thought you didn't like me," he said.

"I can pretend," I told him. "For one night."

And so he described the constellations overhead, telling me a story about a child of the Gentry who believed he'd stumbled onto a prophecy that promised him great success, only to find that his star chart was upside down.

I told him the plot of a mortal movie I'd watched years ago, and he laughed at the funny parts. When he lay down in a pile of rushes and closed his eyes, I crept up to him and carefully covered him in dry leaves so that he would be warm.

When I woke up in the afternoon, he was already gone.

# CHAPTER

# 9

I am dragged through the halls and brought not to the prisons, as I supposed I would be, but to the bedroom where I readied myself for the revel. My bag is still on the hook where I left it, the comb Oak used still on the dresser. Revindra, the rose-haired knight, pushes me inside hard enough that I hit the floor with my shoulder. Then she kicks me in the stomach, twice.

I curl around the pain, gasping. I reach into the folds of my dress, hand closing over the scissors I stole from Habetrot's rooms.

Here is what I learned in the Court of Teeth. It seemed, in the beginning, that fighting back would only bring me further pain. That's the lesson they wanted me taught, but soon I realized I would be hurt anyway. Better to hurt someone else when I had a chance. Better to make them hesitate, to know it would cost them something.

Revindra is wearing armor, so when I go for her, I slash where she is most unprotected—her face.

The sharp edge slices her cheek, down over the corner of her lips. Her eyes go wide, and she pulls away from me with a wild shout. Her hand goes to her mouth, wiping and staring at her fingers as though it were impossible for the wetness she's feeling to be her own blood. Another knight grabs my throat, holding me in place while a third slams my wrist on the ground until I let go of the scissors with a cry of pain.

*It would be an insult to be stabbed by them*, I recall Jack of the Lakes saying. I hope he's right.

When Revindra kicks me in the back of the head, I don't bother trying to muffle my anguished moan. In the Court of Teeth, they liked to hear me scream, cry out, and howl. Enjoyed seeing bruises, blood, bone. I've embarrassed Revindra, twice over. Of course she's angry. There is no profit in giving her anything but what she wants.

At least until she gives me another opening.

"Whatever your punishment is, I will ask to be the one to administer it, little worm," she tells me. "And I will do so with lingering thoroughness."

I hiss from the floor, scuttling back when she comes toward me again.

"See you very soon." Then she goes out, the other knights with her.

I crawl to the bed and curl up on it miserably.

I should have kept my temper, and I know it. If it gives me satisfaction to cause pain, that means only that I am more akin to Lady Nore and Lord Jarel than I like to suppose.

Seeking distraction from the agony in my wrist and my side, seeking a reason not to think about Oak's expression when he took his old gaming piece or to gauge the likelihood I will be executed in one of the ways that so horrified Gwen, I reach into my pocket for her phone. The glass isn't cracked. It lights up as my fingers travel over it, but there is no message from Hyacinthe. As I stare at the glowing screen, I think of my home number, the one my unparents made me repeat over and over back when Bex was Rebecca and I was their child.

We are far enough underground that the signal is very faint. A single little bar, occasionally two when I tilt it at an uncertain angle. I punch in the number. I do not expect it to ring.

"Hello." My unmother's voice is staticky, as though farther away than ever. I shouldn't have done this. I have to try to be emotionless when they come to hurt me again, and my unmother's voice makes me feel too much. It would be better to disconnect from everything, to float free from my body, to be nothing in an endless night of nothing.

But I want to hear her in case I never have a chance again.

"Mom?" I say so softly that I imagine she doesn't hear me, the connection being as bad as it is.

"Who's this?" she asks, voice sharp, as though she suspects me of playing a joke on her.

I don't speak, feeling sick. Of course this must seem like a wrong number or a prank. In her mind, she has no other daughter. I stay on the line another moment, though, tears burning the back of my eyes, the taste of them in my throat. I count her breaths.

When she doesn't hang up, I put the phone on the bed, speaker on. Lie down beside it.

Her voice quavers a little. "Are you still there?"

"Yes," I whisper.

"Wren?" she asks.

I hang up, too afraid to know what she might say next. I would rather hold her saying my name to my heart.

I press the palm of my hand to the cold stone of the wall to ground myself, to try to remember how not to feel again.

I don't know how long I lie there, but long enough to doze off and wake, disoriented. Fear crawls into my belly, clawed and terrible. My thoughts have to push through a fog of it.

And yet they come. I am afflicted with the memory of kissing Oak. Whenever I recall what I did, I wince with embarrassment. What must he think of me, to have thrown myself at him? And why kiss me in return, except to keep me docile?

Then comes the memory of Hyacinthe urging me to come with him, warning me I wouldn't be safe.

And again and again, I hear my unmother saying my name.

When the grind of the stone and the creaking of the hinges comes, I feel like a cornered animal, eager to strike. I shove the phone back into my pocket and stand, brushing myself off.

It's the rose-haired knight, Revindra. "You're to come and be questioned."

I say nothing, but when she reaches out to grab my arm, I hiss in warning.

"Move," she tells me, shoving my shoulder. "And remember how much pleasure it will give me if you disobey."

I walk into the hall, where two more knights are waiting. They march me to an audience chamber where Queen Annet sits on a throne covered in powdery white moths, each one fluttering its wings a little, giving the whole thing the effect of a moving carpet. She is dressed in simpler black than she was when I saw her last, but Oak is in the same clothes, as though he hasn't slept. His hands are clasped behind him. Tiernan stands at his side, his face like stone.

I realize how used to seeing Oak's easy smile I am, now that he no longer wears it. A bruise rests beneath one of his eyes.

I think of him staggering back from the ogre's blow, blood on his teeth, looking as though he was waiting for another hit.

"You stole from me." Annet's eyes seem to glint with barely concealed rage. I imagine that losing a mortal and a merrow was embarrassing enough, not to mention losing Hyacinthe, whom she had practically bullied Oak into letting her keep. She must especially mislike being humiliated in front of the heir to the High Court, even if I have given her an excuse to delay him a little longer. Still, she cannot make any legitimate claim that *he* was a party to what I did.

At least I don't think she can.

If Revindra is angry with me, Annet's rage will be far greater and much more deadly.

"Do you deny it?" the queen continues, looking at me with the expression of a hunting hawk ready to plunge toward a rat.

I glance at Oak, who is watching me with a feverish intensity. "I can't," I manage. I am trembling. I bite the inside of my cheek to ground myself in pain that I cause. This feels entirely too familiar, to wait for punishment from a capricious ruler.

"So," the Unseelie queen says. "It seems you conspire with the enemies of Elfhame."

I will not let her put that on me. "No."

"Then tell me this: Can you swear to being loyal to the prince in all ways?"

I open my mouth to speak, but no words come out. My gaze goes to Oak again. I feel a trap closing in. "No one could swear to that."

"Ahhh," says Annet. "Interesting."

There has to be an answer that won't implicate me further. "The prince doesn't need Hyacinthe, when he has me."

"It seems *I* have you," Queen Annet says, making Oak look at her sideways.

"Won't he go immediately to Lady Nore and tell her everything we plan?" asks Oak, speaking for the first time. I startle at the sound of his voice.

I shake my head. "He swore an oath to me."

Queen Annet looks at the prince. "Right under your nose, not only does your lady love take him from you, but uses him to build her own little army."

My cheeks heat. Everything I say just makes what I've done sound worse. Much, much worse. "It was wrong to lock Hyacinthe up like that."

"Who are you to tell your betters what is right or wrong?" demands Queen Annet. "You, traitorous child, daughter of a traitorous mother, ought to be grateful you were not turned into a fish and eaten after your betrayal of the High Court."

I bite my lip, my sharp teeth worrying the skin. I taste my own blood.

"Is that really why you did it?" Oak asks, looking at me with a strange ferocity.

I nod once, and his expression grows remote. I wonder how much he hates that I was called his lady love.

"Jack of the Lakes says that you were to escape with Hyacinthe," the queen goes on. "He was very eager to tell us all about it. Yet you're still here. Did something go wrong with your plan, or have you remained to commit further betrayal?"

I hope Jack of the Lakes' pond dries up.

"That's not true," I say.

"Oh?" says Annet. "*Didn't* you mean to escape, too?"

"No," I say. "Never."

She leans forward on her throne of moths. "And why is that?"

I look at Oak. "Because I have my own reasons to go on this quest."

Queen Annet snorts. "Brave little traitor."

"How did you persuade Jack to help you?" Oak asks, voice soft. "Did he truly do it for the game piece? I would have paid him more silver than that to tell me what you intended."

"For his pride," I say.

Oak nods. "All my mistakes are coming home to me."

"And the mortal girl?" asks Queen Annet. "Why interfere with her fate? Why the merrow?"

"He was dying without water. And Gwen was only trying to save her lover." I may be in the wrong by the rules of Faerie, but when it comes to Gwen, at least, I am right by any other measure.

"Mortals are liars," the Unseelie queen says with a snort.

"That doesn't mean everything they say is a lie," I return. My voice shakes, but I force myself to keep speaking. "Do you have a boy here, a musician, who has not returned to the mortal world in days, and yet through enchantment believes far less time has passed?"

"And if I have?" Queen Annet says, as close to an admission as I am likely to get. "Liar or no, you will take her place. You have wronged the Court of Moths, and we will have it out of your skin."

I shiver all over, unable to stop myself.

Oak's gaze goes to the Unseelie queen, his jaw set. Still, when he speaks, his voice is light. "I'm afraid you can't have her."

"Oh, can't I?" asks Queen Annet in the tone of someone who has murdered most of her past lovers and is prepared to murder again if provoked.

His grin broadens, that charming smile, with which he could coax ducks to bring their own eggs to him for his breakfast. With which he could make delicate negotiations over a prisoner seem like nothing more than a game. "As annoyed as you may be over the loss of Hyacinthe, it is I who will be inconvenienced by it. Wren may have stolen him from your prisons, but he was still *my* prisoner. Not to say that you weren't a wronged party." He shrugs apologetically. "But surely we could get you another mortal or merrow, if not something better."

Honey-mouthed. I think of how he'd spoken to that ogre in the brugh, how he could have used this tone on him but didn't. It appears to work on the Unseelie queen. She looks mollified, her mouth losing some of its angry stiffness.

It's a frightening power to have a voice like that.

She smiles. "Let us have a contest. If you win, I return her *and* the kelpie. If you fail, I keep them both, and *you* as well, until such time as Elfhame ransoms you."

"What sort of contest?" he asks, intrigued.

"I present you with a choice," she tells him. "We can play a game of chance in which we have equal odds. Or you can duel my chosen champion and bet on your own skill."

A strange gleam comes into his fox eyes. "I choose the duel."

"And I shall fight in your stead," Tiernan says.

Queen Annet opens her mouth to object, but Oak speaks first. "No. I'll do it. That's what she wants."

I take a half step toward him. She must have heard of his poor performance the night before. He's still got the bruise as evidence. "A duel isn't a contest," I say, cautioning. "It's not a game."

"Of course it is," Oak replies, and I am reminded once again that he is used to being the beloved prince, for whom everything is easy. I don't think he realizes this won't be the polite sort of duel they fought in Elfhame, with plenty of time for crying off and lots of deference given. No one here will feign being overcome. "To first blood?"

"Hardly." Queen Annet laughs, proving all I feared. "We are Unseelie. We want a bit more fun than that."

"To the *death*, then?" he asks, sounding as though the idea is ridiculous.

"Your sister would have my head if you lost yours," says Queen Annet. "But I think we can agree that you shall duel until one of you cries off. What weapon will you have?"

The prince's hand goes to his side, where his needle of a sword rests. He puts his hand on the ornate hilt. "Rapier."

"A pretty little thing," she says, as though he proposed dueling with a hairpin.

"Are you certain it's a fight you want?" Oak asks, giving Queen Annet a searching look. "We could play a different sort of game of skill—a riddle contest, a kissing contest? My father used to tell me that once begun, a battle was a living thing and no one could control it."

Tiernan presses his mouth into a thin line.

"Shall we set this duel for tomorrow at dusk?" Queen Annet inquires. "That gives us both time to reconsider."

He shakes his head, quelling her attempt at a delay. "Your pardon, but we are in a hurry to see the Thistlewitch, now more than ever. I'd like to have this fight and be on my way."

At that, some of Queen Annet's courtiers smile behind their hands, although she does not.

"So sure of winning?" she asks.

He grins, as though in on the joke despite it being at his expense. "Whatever the outcome, I would hasten it."

She regards him as one would a fool. "You will not even take the time to don your armor?"

"Tiernan will bring it here," he says, nodding toward the knight. "Putting it on won't take long."

Queen Annet stands and motions to her knight. "Then let us not detain you longer—Revindra, fetch Noglan and tell him to bring the slenderest and smallest sword he owns. Since the prince is in haste, we must make do with what he can find."

Tiernan bends toward me. He lowers his voice so that only I can hear. "You should have left with Hyacinthe."

I look down at my feet, at the boots that the Court of Moths gave me for the prince's sake. If I were to reach up to my head, I know I would be able to feel the braid he wove into my hair. If he dies, it will be my fault.

It is not long before the hall is filled with spectators. Watching the heir to Elfhame bleed will be a rare treat.

As Tiernan helps Oak into his scale-mail shirt, the crowd parts for an ogre I instantly recognize. The one that punched Oak twice the night before. He's grinning, walking into the room with insufferable swagger. He looms over the spectators in his leather-and-steel chest plate, his heavy pants tucked into boots. His arms are bare. His lower canines press into his top lip. *This* must be Noglan.

He bows to his queen. Then he sees me.

"Hello, morsel," he says.

I dig my fingers into my palm.

His gaze goes to the prince. "I guess I didn't hit you hard enough last time. I can remedy that."

Queen Annet claps her hands. "Clear some space for our duel."

Her courtiers arrange themselves in a wide circle around an empty patch of packed earth.

"You don't have to do this," I whisper to Oak. "Leave me. Leave Jack."

He gives me a sidelong look. His face is grave. "I can't."

Right. He needs me for his quest to save his father. Enough to make himself kiss me. Enough to bleed to keep me.

Oak strides to a place opposite where the ogre has chosen to stand. The ogre jests with a few folks in the eager, bloodthirsty crowd—I can tell because they laugh, but I am too far to hear what he says.

I think of Oak's father, who I saw in war councils. Mostly, his eyes went past me, as though I were like one of the hunting hounds that might lounge under a table, hoping to have bones tossed to them. But there was a night when he saw me sitting in a cold corner, worrying at my restraints. He knelt down and gave me the cup of hot spiced wine he had been drinking, and when he rose, he touched the back of my head with his large, warm hand.

I'd like to tell Oak that Madoc isn't worth his love, but I don't know if I can.

The cat-headed lady pushes herself to the front and offers Oak her favor, a gauzy handkerchief. He accepts it with a bow, letting her tie it around his arm.

Queen Annet holds a white moth on her open palm.

"If he's hurt...," Tiernan tells me, not bothering to finish the threat.

"When the moth takes flight, the duel shall begin," the queen says.

Oak nods and draws his blade.

I am struck by the contrast of his gleaming golden mail, the sharpness of his rapier, the hard planes of his body with the softness of his mouth and amber eyes. He scrapes one hoofed foot on the packed earth of the floor, moving into a fighting stance, turning to show his side to his opponent.

"I borrowed a toothpick," Noglan the ogre calls, holding up a sword that looks small in his hand but is far larger than what the prince wields. Despite Oak's height, the ogre is at least a foot taller and three times as wide. Muscles cord his bare arms as though rocks are packed beneath his skin.

At that moment, I see something waver in the prince's eyes. Perhaps he finally realizes the danger he's in.

The moth flutters upward.

Oak's expression changes, neither smiling nor grim. He looks blank, empty of emotion. I wonder if that's how he appears when he's scared.

The ogre strides across the circle, holding his thin sword like a bat. "Don't be shy, boy," he says. "Let's see what you've got." Then he swings his blade toward Oak's head.

The prince is fast, ducking to the side and thrusting the point of his rapier into the ogre's shoulder. When Oak pulls it free, Noglan roars. A dribble of blood trickles over the ogre's bicep.

The crowd sucks in a collective breath. I am stunned. Was that a lucky shot?

But I cannot continue to believe that when Oak spins to slash across the ogre's belly, just below his chest plate. The prince's movements are precise, controlled. He's faster than anyone I've seen fight.

There's a gleam of wet pink flesh. Then Noglan crashes to the floor, knocking other faeries out of his way. There are screams from the spectators, along with astonished gasps.

The prince steps to the other side of the circle. "Don't get up," he warns, a tremor in his voice. "We can be done with this. Cry off."

But Noglan pushes himself to his feet, snorting in pain. There is a bloodstain growing on his pants, but he ignores it. "I am going to eviscerate—"

"Don't," the prince says.

The ogre runs at Oak, slashing with his sword. The prince turns the slim rapier so that it slides straight up the blade, the sharp point sinking into the ogre's neck.

Noglan's hand goes to his throat, blood pooling between his fingers. I can see when the light goes out of his eyes, like a torch thrown into the sea. He slumps to the floor. The crowd roars, disbelief on their faces. The scent of death hangs heavily in the air.

Oak wipes his bloody blade against his glove and sheaths it again.

Queen Annet would have heard the story of Oak not defending himself against Noglan. She'd come to the same conclusion that I had, that there was no fight in him. That there was nothing sinister hidden behind Oak's easy smile. That he was the coddled prince of Faerie he seemed, spoiled by his sisters, doted on by his mother, kept in the dark regarding his father's schemes.

I had supposed he might not even know *how* to use his sword. He'd acted the fool, that his enemies might believe he was one.

How could I have forgotten that he'd been weaned on strategy and deception? He was a child when murders over the throne began, and yet not so young that he didn't remember. How had I not considered that his father and sister would have been his tutors in the blade? Or that if he was a favorite target of assassins, he might have had reason to learn to defend himself?

Queen Annet's expression is grim. She expected this match to go her way, with Noglan knocking around the prince, her honor restored, and us imprisoned long enough for her to get a message from her contacts at the High Court.

Tiernan turns a fierce look on me and shakes his head. "I hope you're pleased with what you wrought."

I am not sure what he means. Oak is clearly unharmed.

Seeing my expression, his only grows angrier. "Oak was never taught to fight any way but to kill. He doesn't know any elegant parries. He cannot show off. All he can do is deal death. And once he starts, he doesn't stop. I'm not sure he can."

A shiver goes through me. I remember the way his face went blank and the awfulness of his expression when he saw Noglan spread out on the ground, as though surprised by what he had done.

"Long, I wished for a child." Queen Annet's gaze goes to me again, then back to Oak. The shock seems to be wearing off, leaving her seeing that she must speak. "Now that one comes, I hope mine will do as much for me as you do for your sire. It pleases me to see a Greenbriar with some teeth."

I assume that last is a dig at the High King, well known for leaving the fighting to his wife.

"Now, Lady Suren, I promised to return you to the prince, but I don't recall promising you'd be alive when I handed you over." Then the Unseelie queen smiles without amusement. "I understand you like riddles, having solved so many in my prisons. So let us have one more contest of skill. Answer, or suffer the riddle's fate and leave Prince Oak with only your corpse: *Tell a lie and I will behead you. Tell me the truth and I will drown you. What is the answer that will save you?*"

"Queen Annet, I caution you. She is no longer yours to toy with," Oak says.

But her smile does not dim. She waits, and I am without any choice but to play her cruel little game.

Despite my mind having gone blank.

I take a shuddery breath. Queen Annet posited that there was a solution to the riddle, but it's an either-or situation. Either drowning or beheading. Either lying or truth. Two very bad outcomes.

But if the truth results in drowning and a lie results in beheading, then I have to find a way to use one of those against her.

I am tired and hurting. My thoughts are in knots. Is this one of those chicken-or-egg questions, a trap to seal my doom? If I were to choose drowning and it's the *truth*, then she'd have to do it. Which means beheading is the fate of a liar. So...

"I must say, 'You will behead me,'" I tell her. Because if she does it, then I am a truth-teller and she ought to have drowned me. There's no way to execute me properly.

I let out a sigh of relief—since there *is* an answer, whatever she might have wanted to do, she must now let me go.

Queen Annet gives a tight smile. "Oak, take your traitor with the blessings of the Court of Moths." As he takes a step toward me, she continues. "You may think that Elfhame will look ill on my attempts to keep you here, but I promise you that your sister would like it far less well to find I'd let you leave with Lady Suren, only to discover she sliced open your throat."

Oak winces.

Annet notes his reaction. "Exactly." Then she turns away with a swirl of her long black skirts, one hand on her gravid belly.

"Come," the prince commands me. A muscle in his jaw twitches, as though he's clenching his teeth too hard.

It would be safer if I hated him. Since I cannot, perhaps it is good that he now hates me.

They release Jack of the Lakes outside of the hill. His face is bruised. He slinks toward us, swallowing any witty comments. He goes to his knees before Oak, reminding me uncomfortably of Hyacinthe when he swore to me.

Jack says nothing, only bowing so low that his forehead touches Oak's hoof. The prince is still clad in his armor. The golden mail glitters, making him seem both royal and remote.

"I am yours to punish," says the kelpie.

Oak reaches out a hand and cups it lightly over Jack's head, as though offering a benediction.

"My debt to you is paid, and yours to me," Oak says. "We will owe each other nothing going forward, save friendship."

I wonder at his kindness. How can he mean it when he is so angry with me?

Jack of the Lakes rises. "For the sake of your friendship, prince, I would carry you to the ends of the earth."

Tiernan snorts. "Since Hyacinthe spirited off Damsel Fly, maybe you should take him up on his offer."

"It is tempting," Oak says, a half smile on his face. "And yet, I think we will make our own way from here."

I study the tops of my boots, avoiding eye contact with absolutely everyone.

"If you change your mind, you have only to call on me," says the kelpie. "Wheresoever you are, I will come."

Then Jack transforms into a horse, all mossy black and sharp-toothed. As he rides off into the waning afternoon, despite everything, I am sorry to see him go.

# CHAPTER
## 10

Clouds of mosquitoes and gnats blow through the hot, wet air of the marsh where the Thistlewitch lives. My boots sink into the gluey mud. The trees are draped heavily in creeper and poisonous trumpet vine, swaths of it blocking the path. In the brown water, things move.

"Sit," Oak says when we come to a stump. This is the first time he's spoken to me since we left Queen Annet's Court. From his pack, he takes out a brush and a pot of shimmering gold paint. "Stick out a foot."

Tiernan walks ahead, scoping the area.

The prince marks the bottom of my one boot, then the other, with the symbol we were given. His fingers hold my calves firmly in place. A treacherous heat creeps into my cheeks.

"I know you're angry with me...," I begin.

"Am I?" he asks, looking up at me as though there is a bitter taste in his mouth. "Maybe I'm glad that you gave me an opportunity to be my worst self."

I am still sitting on the stump, pondering that, when Tiernan returns and yanks a twist of hair from my head.

I hiss, coming to my feet, teeth bared, hand going for a knife that I no longer have.

"You know how the bridle works as well as anyone," Tiernan says, low, so that Oak, busy drawing symbols on the bottoms of his hooves, does not seem to hear. He holds three pale blue strands of my hair in his hand. "Do not betray us again."

A chill goes through me at those words. The great smith Grimsen forged that bridle, and like all his creations, it has a corrupt secret. There is another way than wearing it to be controlled—wrapped hair, and a few words—that was how Lady Nore and Lord Jarel had hoped to trick the High Queen into binding herself along with the serpent king.

The strands of my hair between Tiernan's fingers are a reminder that even if they don't put it on me, I am not safe from it. I should be grateful that I am not wearing it already.

"Were it up to me," he says, "I'd have left you behind and taken my chances against Lady Nore."

"It's not too late," I say.

"Don't tempt me," the knight growls back. "If not for you, Hyacinthe would still be with us."

Even though I know he has reason to be cross with me, I am suddenly angry, too. Hyacinthe, with his half-broken curse, reminded me too much of myself, of my desire to have someone free me, whether I was deserving of it or not. "No one in chains could ever truly love you."

He glares. "Do you expect me to believe you know *anything* about love?"

The truth of that hits like a blow.

I turn away and tromp along through the muck and rotted vegetation, the song of frogs loud in my ears, reminding me that the sharpness of the knight's tongue already cost Oak the loyalty of Jack of the Lakes. He throws his words around like knives. Recklessly. Heedlessly.

Whatever the opposite of being honey-tongued might be.

A slithering snake catches my eye, its body as black as the serpent the High King became. Out in the water, something that is perhaps the head of a crocodile, if not more monstrous, breaks the surface. The creature's skin has become green with vegetation.

I trust that the others see it, too, although they do not slow their step.

The air is overwarm and close, and I am exhausted from the events of the night before. My ribs hurt where they met Revindra's boot. But I bite the inside of my cheek and keep going.

We walk for a long time before we come to a clearing where a few mismatched and rusty human chairs sit. A few steps farther and we see a shriveled and ancient faerie squatting beside a fire. Over it is a spit, and threaded on the metal rod is a skinned rat. The Thistlewitch turns it slowly, making the meager fat sizzle.

The braided weeds and briars of her hair fall around her, serving as a cape. Large black eyes peer out from the tangle. She wears a gown of drab cloth and bark. When she moves, I see her feet are bare. Rings shine on several of her toes.

"Travelers," she rasps. "I see you have made your way through my swamp. What is it that you seek?"

Oak steps forward and bows. "Honored lady, finder of lost things, we have come to ask you to use your power in our behalf." From his pack, he pulls a bottle of honey wine, along with a bag of powdery white doughnuts and a jar of chili oil, and sets them down on the earth in front of her. "We've brought gifts."

The Thistlewitch looks us over. I do not think she is particularly impressed. When her gaze falls on me, her expression changes to one of outright suspicion.

Oak's glance goes to me, frowning in puzzlement. "This is Wren."

She spits into the fire. "Nix. Naught. Nothing. That's what you are. *Nix Naught Nothing.*" Then she indicates the gifts with a wave of her hand. "What will you have of me that you think to buy my favor so cheaply?"

Oak clears his throat, no doubt not liking how this is going so far. "We want to know about Mab's bones and Mellith's heart. And we want to find something."

*Mellith's heart?* I think of Hyacinthe's warnings and the unseen message from Lady Nore. Is this the ransom she asked for in exchange for Madoc? I have heard nothing of it before.

As I look at the prince's face, soft mouth and hard eyes, I wonder how important playing the part of the feckless courtier might be, if to show competence would be to endanger his sister?

Wonder how many people he's killed.

"Ahhhhh," says the Thistlewitch. "Now, there's a story."

"Mab's bones were stolen from the catacombs under the palace of Elfhame," the prince says. "Along with the reliquary containing them."

The Thistlewitch's ink-drop eyes watch him. "And you want them back? That's what you mean to ask me to find for you?"

"I know where the bones are." Beneath Oak's calm is a grim resignation, writ in the furrow of his brow, the slant of his mouth. He means to get his father back, whatever the cost. "But not how Lady Nore can use them for what she has. And not why Mellith's heart matters. Baphen, the Court Astrologer, told me some of the story. When I asked Mother Marrow for more, she sent me to you."

The Thistlewitch shuffles to one of the chairs, her body hidden by the cape of her hair and all the briars and vines in it. I wonder, had I stayed in the woods long enough, if I might have found my hair turned into such a garment. "Come sit by my fire, and I will tell you a tale."

We drag over a few more chairs and seat ourselves. In the light of the flames, the Thistlewitch looks more ancient than ever, and far less human.

"Mab was born when the world was young," she says. "In those days, we Folk were not so diminished as we are now, when there is so much iron. Our giants were as tall as mountains, our trolls like trees. And hags like myself held the power to bring all manner of things into being.

"Once a century, there is a convocation of hags, where we, the witches and enchanters, the smiths and makers, come together to hone our craft. It is not for outsiders, but Mab dared enter. She besought us all for what she wanted, the power to *create*. Not a mere glamour or little workings, but the great magic that we alone possessed. Most turned her away, but there was one who did not.

"That hag gave unto her the power to create from nothing. And in return, she was to take the hag's daughter and raise the witch child as her heir.

"At first, Mab did as she was bid. She took for herself the title of the Oak Queen, united the smaller Seelie Courts under her banner, and began bestowing sentience on living things. Trees would lift their roots at her beckoning. Grass would scurry around, confusing her enemies.

Faeries that had never existed before grew from her hands. And she raised three of the Shifting Isles of Elfhame from the sea."

Oak frowns at the dirt. "Has the High King inherited some of her power? Is that why he can—"

"Patience, boy," says the Thistlewitch. "Prince or not, I will tell you in full or not at all."

The prince puts on an imp's grin of apology. "If I seem eager, it is only because the tale is so compelling and the teller so skilled."

At this, she smiles, showing a cracked tooth. "Flatterer."

Tiernan looks amused. He has his elbow propped on the arm of his chair and rests his head on his hand. When he isn't concentrating on keeping his guard up, he looks like another person entirely. Someone who isn't as old as he wants the people around him to believe, someone vulnerable. Someone who might have feelings that are deeper and more desperate than he lets on.

The Thistlewitch clears her throat and begins to speak again. "Mab called the child Mellith, which means 'mother's curse.' Not an auspicious beginning. And yet, it was only when her own daughter was born that she began to think of ways to weasel out of the bargain."

"Clovis," Oak says. "Who ruled before my grandfather, Eldred."

The Thistlewitch inclines her head. "Indeed. In the end, it was a simple trick. Mab boasted again and again that she had discovered a means for Clovis to rule until the rumors finally found their way to the hag. Enraged, she swore to kill Clovis. And so, the hag crept up on where the child slept in the night and fell upon the girl she found there, only to discover that she had murdered her own daughter. Mab had bested her."

I shudder. The poor kid. Both kids, really. After all, if the hag had been a bit more clever, the other girl could have just as easily died. Just because a pawn is better treated doesn't make it safer on the board.

The Thistlewitch goes on. "But the hag was able to put a final enchantment on her daughter's heart as it beat its last, for her daughter was a hag, too, and magic sang through her blood. The hag imbued the heart with the power of annihilation, of destruction, of unmaking. And she cursed Mab, so that piece of her child would be forever tied to the queen's power. She would have to keep the heart by her side for her magic to work. And should she not, its power would unmake all that Mab created.

"It is said that Mab put a curse on the hag, too, although that part of the story is vague. Perhaps she did; perhaps she didn't. We are not easy to curse."

The Thistlewitch shrugs and pokes the rat with a stick. "As for Mab, you know the rest. She made an alliance with one of the solitary fey and founded the Greenbriar line. A trickle of her power passed down to her grandson, Eldred, granting him fecundity when so much of Faerie is barren, and to the current High King, Cardan, who pulled a fourth isle from the deep. But a large amount of Mab's power stayed trapped with her remains, confined to that reliquary."

Oak frowns. "So Lady Nore needs this thing. The heart."

The Thistlewitch picks off a piece of rat and puts it into her mouth, chews. "I suppose."

"What can she do *without* it?" Tiernan says.

"Mab's bones can be ground to powder, and that powder used to do great and mighty spells," says the Thistlewitch. "But when the bones are used up, that will be the end of their power, and without Mellith's heart, all that's done will eventually unravel...."

She lets the moment dramatically linger, but Oak, rebuked once, does not hurry her on.

"Of course," the Thistlewitch intones, "that unraveling could take a long time."

"So Lady Nore doesn't need Mellith's heart?" I ask.

The witch fixes me with a look. "The power of those bones is great. Elfhame shouldn't have been so careless with them. But they would be far more useful accompanied by the heart. And no one is quite sure what the heart can do alone. It has great power, too, power that is the opposite of Mab's—and if it could be extracted, then your Lady Nore could style herself as both Oak Queen and Yew Queen."

A horrifying thought. Lady Nore would desire power of annihilation above all else. And if she could have *both*, she'd be more dangerous than Mab herself. Lady Nore would unmake everyone who had ever wronged her, including the High Court. Including me. "Is that really possible?"

"How should I know?" asks the Thistlewitch. "Open the wine."

Oak takes out a knife, using it to pry off the foil, then sticks the point of the blade into the cork and turns. "Have you a glass?"

I half-expect her to swig from the neck of the bottle, but instead, she gets to her feet and trundles off. When she returns, she's carrying four dirty jars, a chipped platter, and a basket with two melons in it, one green and the other brown.

Oak pours while the Thistlewitch removes the rat from the spit and sets it out on the platter. She begins cutting up the melon.

"Mellith's heart was supposed to be buried with Mab's bones beneath the castle of Elfhame," the prince says. "But it isn't there. Can you tell me where it is?"

When the hag is done arranging things to her liking, she pushes the platter toward us and picks up her jar of wine. She takes a long slug, then smacks her lips together. "You want me to discover its location with my dowsing rod? You want me to send eggshells spinning down the river and tell you your fate? But what then?"

Tiernan pulls a leg off the rat and chews on it delicately, while Oak helps himself to a slice of melon. I eat one of the doughnuts.

"I see you there, unnatural creature," the Thistlewitch informs me.

I narrow my eyes at her. She's probably angry I took a doughnut.

"Then I will use Lady Nore's desire for it to get my father back. What else?" Oak asks.

The Thistlewitch grins her wicked grin. She eats the tail of the rat, crunching on the bones. "Surely you know the answer, Prince of Elf-hame. You seize the power. You have some of Mab's blood in you. Steal her remains and find Mellith's heart, and perhaps you can be Oak King and Yew King as well."

His sister would forgive him then, certainly. He wouldn't just return a hero. He would return a god.

After we eat, the Thistlewitch rises and dusts the bits of burned fur and powdered sugar off her skirts. "Come," she says to the prince. "And I will give you the answer you came here for."

Tiernan begins to rise as well, but she motions for him to sit.

"Prince Oak is the seeker," she says. "He will receive the knowledge, but he must also pay my price."

"I will pay it in his stead," Tiernan declares. "Whatever it is."

Oak shakes his head. "You will not. You've done enough."

"What is the point of bringing me along to protect you if you won't let me risk myself in your place?" Tiernan asks, some of his frustration over the fight in the Court of Moths obviously bleeding into his feelings now. "And do not give me some silly answer about companionship."

"If I get lost in the swamp and never return, I give you leave to be very cross with me," Oak says.

Tiernan's jaw twitches with the force of holding back a response.

"So, what will you have?" Oak asks the Thistlewitch.

She grins, her black eyes shining. "Ahhhhh, so many things I could ask for. A bit of your luck, perhaps? Or the dream you hold most dear? But I have read your future in the eggshells, and what I will have is this—your agreement that when you become king, you will give me the very first thing I request."

I think of the story the Thistlewitch told and the perils of bargaining with hags.

"Done," Oak says. "It hardly matters, since I will never be king."

The Thistlewitch smiles her private smile, and the hair stands up all along my arms. Then she beckons to Oak.

I watch them go, his hooves sinking into the mud, his hand out to support her, should she need it. She does not, scampering over the terrain with great spryness.

I take another doughnut and do not look in Tiernan's direction. I know he's still furious over Hyacinthe, and as mad as probably he is with Oak right now, I don't want to tempt him to snarl at me.

We sit in silence. I watch the crocodile creature rise in the water again and realize it must have followed us. It is larger than I supposed earlier and watches me with a single algae-green eye. I wonder if it was waiting for us to get turned around in the swamp and what might have happened if we had.

After long minutes, they return. The Thistlewitch carries a gnarled

dowsing rod in her hand, swinging at her side. Oak's expression is haunted.

"Mellith's heart is not in a place Lady Nore is likely to find it," Oak says when he draws close enough for us to hear him. "Nor should we waste our time looking for something we can't get. Let's depart."

"You weren't really going to give it to her, were you?" I ask.

He does not meet my eyes. "My plans require keeping it out of her reach. Nothing more."

"But—" Tiernan begins.

Oak cuts off whatever he was about to say with a look.

Mellith's heart must have been what Lady Nore demanded in exchange for Madoc in the correspondence Hyacinthe was talking about. And if Oak was even considering turning it over, then I have every reason to be glad it's impossible to get. But I also have to remember that, as much as he wants to take Lady Nore down, she has something over him. In a moment of crisis, he might choose her side over mine.

At the edge of the swamp, the hob-faced owl is waiting for us, perched on the stringy roots of a mangrove tree. Nearby is a patch of ragwort, its flowers blooming caution-tape yellow.

Oak turns toward me, a grim set to his mouth. "You're not going to continue on with us, Wren."

He can't mean it. The prince fought and killed an ogre to keep me with them.

Tiernan turns to him, evidently surprised as well.

"But you need me," I say, ashamed of how plaintive I sound.

The prince shakes his head. "Not enough for the risk of bringing you. I don't plan on dueling my way up the coast."

"She's the only one who can control Lady Nore," says Tiernan grudgingly. "Without her, this is a fool's errand."

"*We don't need her!*" Oak shouts, the first time I have really seen his emotions out of his control. "And I don't want her."

The words hurt, the more because he cannot lie.

"Please." My arms wrap around myself. "I didn't try to run away with Hyacinthe. This is my quest, too."

Oak lets out a long breath, and I realize he looks even more exhausted than I am. The bruise under his eye from the punches he took has darkened, the purple yellowing at the edges, spreading over the lid. He pushes a stray lock of hair back from his face. "I hope you don't intend to continue to help us the way you did in the Court of Moths."

"I helped the *prisoners*," I tell him. "Even if it inconvenienced you."

For a long moment, we just stare at each other. I feel as though I've been running, my heart is beating so hard.

"We head straight north from here," he says, turning away. "There's a faerie market near the human city of Portland, in Maine. I've visited it before; it's not far from the Shifting Isles. Tiernan will buy a boat, and we'll gather other supplies to make the crossing into Lady Nore's lands."

Tiernan nods. "A good place to set off from. Especially if we need to lose anyone following us in the crowds."

"Good," says the prince. "At Undry Market, we can decide Wren's fate."

"But—" I start.

"It's four days of travel up the coast to get there," he says. "We pass through the territory of the Court of Termites, the Court of Cicadas, and half a dozen other Courts. Plenty of time for you to convince me of the mistake I am making."

He strides off to the patch of ragwort, taking a stalk of the plant and enchanting it into a fringed skeletal beast. When he has two, he gestures for us to mount. "We can cover a lot more distance in the sky."

"I hate these things," Tiernan complains, throwing a leg over the back of one.

The owl-faced hob alights on the prince's arm, and he whispers to it for a moment before it takes to wing again. Off on some secret mission.

I climb onto the ragwort steed behind Oak, putting my hands around his waist, feeling shame at being dismissed, along with anger. No matter how fast Oak's swordplay or how loyal Tiernan or how clever they might be, there are still only two of them. The prince will realize it makes more sense to bring me along.

As we rise into the air, I find myself as unnerved by ragwort horses as Tiernan is. They seem alive now, and though they are not an illusion, they are not quite what they seem, either. They will become ragwort stalks again and fall to earth, with no more awareness of what they were than any other plucked weed. Half-living things, like the creatures Lady Nore enchanted.

I try not to grip Oak too tightly as we fly. Despite the strangeness of the creature whose back I am on, my heart thrills in the air. The dark sky, dotted with stars, mirrors the lights of the human world below.

We glide through the night, a few of my braids coming loose and undone. Tiernan may distrust the ragwort steeds, but he and Oak sit astride them with immense ease. In the moonlight the prince's features are more fey, his cheekbones sharper, his ears more pointed.

We make camp beside a stream in a wood redolent of pine resin, on a carpet of needles. Oak coaxes the taciturn Tiernan into telling stories of jousts. I am surprised to find that some of them are funny and that Tiernan himself, when all attention is on him, seems almost shy.

Parts of the water are deep enough to bathe in, and Oak does, stripping off his armor and scrubbing himself with the sand of the bank while Tiernan boils up some of the pine needles for tea.

I try not to look, but out of the corner of my eye, I see pale skin, wet hair, and a scarred chest.

When it is my turn, I wash my hot face primly and decline to remove my dress.

We fly through another day and night. At the next camp, we eat more cheese and bread and sleep under the stars of a meadow. I find duck eggs, and Tiernan fries them with wild onions. Oak talks some about the mortal world and his first year there, when he used magic in foolish ways and nearly got himself and his sister into a lot of trouble.

The third night, we camp in an abandoned building. The air has grown chill, and we make a fire of cardboard and a few planks of wood.

Oak stretches out beside it, arching his back like a preening cat. "Wren, tell us something about your life, if you will."

Tiernan shakes his head, as though he thinks I won't do it.

His expression decides me. I stumble over the words in the beginning, but I give them the tale of the glaistig and her victims. In part, I suppose, to be contrary. To see if they will fault me for helping mortals and cheating one of the Folk out of her due. But they listen and even laugh at the times I get the better of her. When I am done talking, I feel strangely lighter.

Across the fire, the prince watches me, reflected flames flickering in his unreadable eyes.

*Forgive me*, I think. *Let me come with you.*

The following afternoon, Tiernan dons Oak's golden scale mail and sets off on his own, to set a false trail. We have a meeting place not far from the Undry Market, and I realize that I will have only one more night to persuade them to allow me to stay.

As we fly, I try to put together my arguments. I consider speaking them into Oak's ear as he can hardly escape me, but the wind would snatch my words. A faint drizzle dampens our clothes and chills our skin.

As the sun begins to set, I see a darkness that is not night coming on. Clouds form in the distance, billowing upward and barreling outward, turning the sky a sickly greenish gray. Inside, I can see the flicker of lightning. They seem to reach into the stratosphere, the top of the clouds in a shape like an anvil.

And beneath it, wind whirls, tornadoes forming.

I give a cry, which is whipped away. Oak wheels the ragwort horse downward as the air around us becomes thick. We plunge into the fog of clouds, their wet, heavy mist sinking into my lungs. The steed shivers beneath us. And then, without warning, the ragwort horse dips sharply, then drops.

We plummet through the sky, the speed of our descent shoving the scream back into my mouth. All I can do is hang on to the solid mass of Oak's body and wrap my arms around him as tightly as they will go. Thunder booms in my ears.

We plunge into a sheet of rain. It knocks us around, slicking our fingers and hair, making holding on difficult with everything so slippery. Coward that I am, I close my eyes and press my face into the prince's back.

"Wren," he shouts, a warning. I look up just before we hit the ground.

I am thrown off into mud, my breath knocked out of me. The ragwort steed crumbles away to the dried stalk of a plant under my bruised palms.

Everything hurts, but with a dull sort of pain that doesn't get worse when I move. Nothing seems broken.

Standing shakily, I reach out a hand to help Oak up. He takes it, levering himself to his feet. His golden hair is dark with rain, his lashes spiky with it. His clothes are soaked through. His scraped knee is bleeding sluggishly.

He touches my cheek lightly with his fingers. "You—I thought—"

I stare up into his eyes, puzzled by his expression.

"Are you hurt?" he asks.

I shake my head.

The prince turns away from me abruptly. "We need to get to the meeting spot," he says. "It can't be far."

"We need to find shelter." I have to shout to be heard. Above us, lightning cuts through the sky, striking into the woods just beyond us. Thunder cracks, and I see a dim thread of smoke curl upward from the site of the hit before the rain douses the fire. "We can find Tiernan when the storm lets up."

"At least let's walk in that direction," Oak says, lifting his pack and throwing it over one shoulder. Ducking his head against the storm, he walks deeper into the woods, using the trees for cover. He doesn't look back to see if I follow.

We go on like that for a while before I see a promising area to stop.

"There." I point at an area with several large rocks, not far from where the soil dips down into a ravine. There are two trees, less than six feet apart, with branches reaching toward one another. "We can make a lean-to."

He gives an exhausted sigh. "I suppose you are the expert. Tell me what I need to do."

"We find two huge sticks," I say, measuring with my hands. "Basically, as long as you are tall. They have to extend past the branches."

I discover one a few yards away that seems as though it could be partially rotted, but I drag it back anyway. Oak has caused another to bend helpfully, through some magic. I begin to tear the skirt of my dress into strips, trying not to think of how much I liked it. "Tie with this," I say, going to work on the other end.

Once they're in place, I use smaller sticks as ribs, stacking them to make a roof and then piling that with moss and leaves.

It is far from waterproof, but it's something. He's shivering by the time we crawl inside. Outside, the wind howls and thunder booms. I drag in a large log and start stripping away the bark to get at the drier wood within.

Seeing the slowness of my progress, he reaches into his boot and takes out a knife, then hands it over. "Don't make me regret giving you this."

"She wanted to delay you," I say softly, aware that he probably doesn't want to hear my justification.

"Queen Annet?" he asks. "I know."

"And you think she almost managed it because of me?" I ask. The insides of the log are drier, and I arrange the pieces I chip off on the stones in a pyramid shape, trying to keep the worst of the water off them.

He pushes wet hair out of his eyes, which are that strange fox color. Like gold that has been cut with copper. "I think you could have told me what you intended to do."

I give him a look of utter disbelief.

"Hyacinthe told you something about me, didn't he?" Oak asks.

I shiver, despite not being affected by the cold. "He said that you had a kind of magic where you could *make* people like you."

Oak makes an exasperated sound. "Is that what you believe?"

"That you inherited an uncanny ability to put people at ease, to convince them to go along with your desires? Should I not?"

His eyebrows go up. For a moment, he's quiet. All around us the rain falls. The thunder seems to have moved off. "My first mother, Liriope, died before I was born. After she was poisoned—at Prince Dain's orders—Oriana cut open her belly to save me. People do say that Liriope was a gancanagh, and her love-talking was how she caught the eye of the High King and his son, but it's not as though that power was much use to her. She paid for that charm with her life."

At my silence, he answers the question I did not ask. "Blusher mushroom. You remain conscious the whole time as your body slows and then stops. I was born with it in my veins, if you can call being torn out of your dead mother a birth."

"And Liriope and Prince Dain—"

"Were my dam and sire," he agrees. I knew that he was some part of the Greenbriar line, but I hadn't known the details. With that horrifying legacy, I suppose I can understand how Madoc would seem an admirable father, how he would adore the mother who rescued and raised him. "Whatever power I have of Liriope's, I don't use it."

"Are you sure?" I ask. "Maybe you can't help it. Maybe you do it without knowing."

He gives me a slow smile, as though I've just confessed to something. "I suppose you want to believe I charmed you into kissing me?"

I turn away, shame heating my face. "I could have done it to distract you."

"So long as you know that *you* did it," he says.

I frown at the mud, wondering how far he would have gone had I not pulled away. Would he have taken me to bed, loathing in his heart? Could I even tell? "You also—"

The sound of footsteps stops me. Tiernan stands in front of our lean-to, blinking at us in the downpour. "You're alive."

The knight staggers into the shelter, collapsing onto the ground. His cloak is singed.

"What happened?" Oak asks, checking his arm. I can see where the skin is red, but no worse.

"Lightning, very close to where I was waiting." Tiernan shivers. "That storm isn't natural."

"No," agrees Oak.

I think on Bogdana's final words. *I will come for you again. And when I do, you best not run.*

"If we make it to the market tomorrow and get our ship," Tiernan tells Oak, "we can seek the Undersea's aid to take us through the Labrador Sea swiftly and without incident."

"The merrow told me—" I begin, and then stop, because both of them are staring at me.

"Go on," Oak says.

I try to recall his exact words, but I cannot. "That there's trouble in the sea, with the queen and her daughter. And warned me about someone, a name I didn't know."

Oak frowns, glancing at Tiernan. "So perhaps we take our chances and do not seek the Undersea's aid."

"I am not sure I trust Wren's informant," Tiernan says. "Either way, once we land, we ought to be able to travel from there on foot. The Citadel is perhaps thirty miles inland."

"Lady Nore will have those stick creatures patrolling everywhere but the Stone Forest," Oak says.

The knight shakes his head. "Going through those woods is a *bad plan*. It's cursed, and the troll king is mad."

"That's why no one will look for us there," says Oak, as though this was part of an ongoing game in which he'd made an excellent move.

The knight makes a gesture of exasperation. "Fine. We go through the Stone Forest. And when we're all about to die, I look forward to your apology."

Oak stands. "As I have not yet sealed our doom, I am going for supplies. It's hard to imagine I could feel any colder or wetter, and I saw the outskirts of a mortal town while we were in the air."

"Maybe the gale-force winds will clear your head," says the knight, wrapping his wet cloak more tightly around himself and appearing not even to consider volunteering to go along.

Oak makes an elaborate bow, then turns to me. "He's unlikely to make you any promises like Hyacinthe did, but if you get that fire going, he just might."

"Unfair," Tiernan growls.

Oak laughs as he tromps off through the wet forest.

I clear off some space on the ground to make a fire, piling up the dry bits of wood I stripped out of the center of the log. I fish in my pockets until I find the matchbook I took from the motel. I strike one against the strip of phosphorus, hoping it isn't too wet to work. When it flares to life, I cup my hand over it and try to set the small, dry pieces aflame.

Tiernan observes all this with a small frown.

"You're friends," I say, looking in the direction the prince went. "You and him."

He watches as the fire catches, smoke curling. "I suppose we are."

"But you're his guard, too, aren't you?" I am not sure if he's going to be offended by the question, or by my talking to him in general, but I am curious and tired of not knowing things.

Tiernan reaches out a hand to test the heat of the flames. "There were three before me. Two got killed protecting him. The third turned on him for a bribe. That's how Oak got the scar on his throat. At fourteen, he decided he didn't want any more guards. But his sister sent me anyway.

"First, he dragged me along to absurd parties, like he was going to embarrass me out of the job. Then I think he tried to bore me out of it by not going anywhere at all for weeks at a time. But I stayed. I was proud of being chosen for the position. And I thought he was nothing more than spoiled."

"That's what he wanted you to think," I say, having recently fallen for the same trick.

He nods to me in acknowledgment. "I didn't know that then, though. I just turned twenty myself and was more foolish than I like to remember. But it hardly matters, because a year later things went sideways. A mortal tried to stab Oak. I grabbed the guy, but he was meant to be a distraction. To my shame, it worked. A half dozen redcaps and goblins flooded the alley from the other direction, all well-armed. I told the prince to run.

"He stayed and fought like nothing I've ever seen before. Swift. Efficient. Brutal. He still wound up stabbed twice in the stomach and once in the thigh before the battle was over. I had failed him, and I knew it.

"He could have gotten rid of me after that, easily. All he would have had to do was tell anyone the truth of what happened that night. But he didn't. Got healing ointment in Mandrake Market so they wouldn't guess. I don't know when he would say I was his friend, but he was mine after that."

I look into the fire, thinking of Oak coming to see me in the woods, a year before he met Tiernan. I wonder if that was after his own guard turned on him and tried to cut his throat. Had I come out of hiding I might have noticed the newness of the scar.

Tiernan shakes his head. "Of course, that was before I realized *why* he hadn't wanted a guard. He'd taken up a new hobby. Decided to become a lure for the ambitious, anyone who might want to take a shot at the royal family. Did everything he could to make sure those shots were aimed at him."

I remember Oak coming to my woods. *Someone tried to kill me. Again. Poison. Again.* He'd been upset about the assassination attempts. Why would he court more of them? "Do they know?"

Tiernan doesn't bother asking whom I mean. "Certainly not. I wish the royal family would figure it out, though. It's exhausting to watch someone try to be a ship that rocks will break against."

I recall Oak's refusal to let Tiernan champion him in the Court of Moths, Oak's insistence that he be the one to take on the debt with the Thistlewitch. When I first met them, I thought Tiernan might grow tired of protecting Oak; now I see how hard he has to fight for an opportunity.

"Hyacinthe camped with the Court of Teeth during the war," Tiernan says, and I glance at him through my lashes, evaluating the meaning of his subject change. "He told me a little about it. Not a nice place to be a child."

I frown at my hands, but I can't just ignore his words. "Not a nice place to be anything."

"What do you suppose they were planning for you?"

I draw my legs up and shrug.

"Marry the prince and then kill him, is that right?" He doesn't sound accusatory, only interested.

"I don't think they meant either of us to live long."

To that, he doesn't reply.

I stare into the fire, watch the flames crackle.

I sit there for a while, feeding bits of the log to the blaze, watching them catch, embers blowing up into the sky like lightning bugs.

Then I get up, feeling restless. Living in the woods as long as I have, I ought to be gathering things. Perhaps there isn't much I can do to make up for freeing the prisoners, but I can build up our shelter at least.

"I'll gather some more wood," I say. "And see if I can find anything worth foraging."

"Remember that I have three strands of your hair," the knight says, but there's no real threat in his voice.

I roll my eyes.

Tiernan gives me a strange look as I walk off, gathering his wet cloak around himself.

As the night envelops me, I scent the air, drinking in the unfamiliar forest. I don't go far before I stumble on a patch of lemony wood sorrel and bullbrier. I gather some, tucking it into the pockets of my new dress. Pockets! Having them now, I cannot believe I went so long without them.

Idly, I pull the human's phone out. The screen is entirely black and will not wake. The battery has run down, and there's no way for me to charge it unless we stay in another mortal dwelling.

I tuck the phone away. Perhaps this is better, not having it work. It allows me to imagine that Hyacinthe and Gwen are safe, that my unmother was happy to hear from me. That perhaps she even called the number back.

Wandering farther into the woods, I discover a tree of loquats and pick them by the handful, eating as I go and filling my bag. I walk on, hoping to find chanterelles.

There's a rustling. I look up, expecting to see Tiernan.

But it is Bogdana who stands between the trees, her long fingers wrapped in the nearby branches. The storm hag looks down on me with her shining black eyes and smiles with her sharp, cracked teeth.

There is a rushing in my ears, and for a moment, I can hear only the thundering of my blood.

I take a branch from the floor of the woods and heft it like a bat.

Into that moment, she speaks. "Enough foolishness, child. I've come to talk."

I wonder how she found me. Was there a spy in Queen Annet's Court? Was it the Thistlewitch herself, out of courtesy toward another ancient power?

"What do you want?" I growl, feeling like a beast again despite the finery I've been dressed in. "Have you come to kill me for my lady mother? Tell me, then, how am I to die?"

The hag raises her eyebrows. "Well, well, look who's all grown up and throwing accusations around."

I make myself breathe. The branch is heavy and wet in my hand.

"I have come to fetch you," Bogdana says. "There is little profit in fighting me, child. It is time to separate your allies from your enemies."

I take a step back, thinking to put some distance between us. "And *you* are my ally?"

"I could be," the storm hag says. "Surely you'd prefer that to making me your opponent."

I take another step, and she grabs for me, nails slashing through the air.

I slam the branch against her shoulder as hard as I am able. Then I run. Through the night, between the trees, my boots sliding in the mud, thorned bushes tearing at my skin and branches catching on my clothes.

I slip, putting my foot wrong in a puddle. I crash down onto my hands and knees. Then I am up and running.

The solid weight of her comes down on my back.

We crash together, rolling on the carpet of wet leaves and pine needles, rocks digging into my bruises. Her nails digging into my skin.

The storm hag grabs my chin in her long fingers, pressing the back of my head against the forest floor. "It ought to sicken you to travel with the Prince of Elfhame." Her face is very close to mine, her breath hot. "Oak, whom you might have forced to cower at your side. To have to take orders from him is an affront. And yet, if he does disgust you, you have done well hiding it."

I struggle, kicking. Trying to pull away. Her nails scratch my throat, leaving a trail of burning lines on my flesh.

"But maybe he doesn't disgust you," Bogdana says, peering into my eyes like she sees something more there than her reflection. "They say that he can talk flowers into opening their petals at night, as though his face were that of the sun. He'll steal your heart."

"I doubt he would have the least interest in anything like that," I tell her, flinching away from her fingers.

This time she lets me go, grabbing one of my braids instead. She hauls me to my feet, using it like a leash.

I reach into my pockets and find the knife that Oak lent me to strip the log and pull it from its sheath.

The hag's eyes flare with anger at the sight of me with a weapon pointed at her. "The prince is your *enemy*."

"I don't believe you," I shout, slashing through the braid she's holding me by. Then I take off through the woods again.

And again, she gives chase.

"Halt," she calls to me, but I don't even slow. We crash through the brush. I have lost track, but I think I am headed in the direction of the lean-to. I hope I am headed toward the mortal town.

"Halt," she calls. "Hear me out, and when I am done, you may choose to stay or go."

Twice before she has nearly had me. I slow my step and turn, knife still gripped in my palm. "And no harm will come to me or my companions by your hand?"

She gives a wicked smile. "Not this day."

I nod but still make sure to leave plenty of space between us.

"You'd be well served to listen, child," she says. "Before it's too late."

"I'm listening," I say.

The hag's smile grows. "I'll wager your prince never told you the bargain Lady Nore offered. That she would trade Madoc to the prince in exchange for the very thing he is bringing north. A foolish girl. *You.*"

I shake my head. That can't be true.

No, Lady Nore must have asked for Mellith's heart. That was why he went to the Thistlewitch to find it. What use would Lady Nore have for me, who could command her? But then I recall Oak's words in the abandoned human house: *You're her greatest vulnerability. No matter her other plans, she has good reason to want to eliminate you.*

If Lady Nore wants me, she wants me dead.

And hadn't I wondered if it was me she asked for, when I was in the prisons with Hyacinthe? Suspected and then dismissed the idea. I hadn't wanted to believe it.

But the more I think on it, the more that I realize Oak never *said* that Lady Nore had asked for Mellith's heart. Only that he hoped to use her need for it against her. That he planned to trick her.

If it were *me* that Lady Nore wanted, I can see why he would have hidden so much of his plan. Why he was willing to risk his own neck to keep me out of Queen Annet's hands. Maybe even why he'd gone looking for Mellith's heart, if he thought that was something he could give to Lady Nore instead.

He must have wavered between wanting to save his father and knowing that turning me over to Lady Nore was monstrous.

*At Undry Market, we can decide Wren's fate.* That was what he said. And now I know what decision he will come to.

"Do not forget your place." She pokes me in the side. "You're not his servant. You're a queen."

"No longer," I remind her.

"Always," she says.

But my thoughts are on Oak, on the power I have over Lady Nore, and on how my death might be worth Madoc's life.

"I don't understand—why did she send those creatures against us if Oak was doing as she asked?"

Bogdana grins. "The message was sent to the High Queen, not to Oak. By the time the prince began his quest, Lady Nore had become frustrated, waiting. You need to wake up to the danger you're in."

"You mean from someone other than you?" I ask.

"I am going to tell you a story," Bogdana says, ignoring my words. "Would that I could say more, but certain constraints on me prevent it."

I blink at her, but I find it hard to concentrate on what she's saying, when her accusations toward Oak hang heavily in the air.

"It's a fairy tale of sorts," the storm hag begins. "Once upon a time, there was a queen who desperately wanted a child. She was the third bride of a king who'd murdered the two before her when they failed to conceive, so she knew her fate if she could not give him an heir. His need for a child was different than that of most monarchs in fairy tales—he planned for his issue to be his means of betraying the High Court—but his desire was as acute as any stemming from family feeling. And so the queen consulted alchemists, diviners, and witches. Being magical herself, she wove spells and brought she and her husband together on propitious nights, on a bed spread with herbs. And yet no child quickened in the queen's womb."

No one had ever spoken to me of my birth before, nor of the danger Lady Nore had been in from Lord Jarel. I had heard none of this, and my skin prickles all over with the premonition that whatever comes next, I won't like it.

Bogdana points a clawed finger at me. Behind her in the sky, I see a strike of lightning. "In time, they sought out a wise old hag. And she told them that she could give them the child that they'd wanted, but that they would have to do exactly what she said. They promised her any reward, and she only smiled, for her memory was long."

"What did you—" I start, but she holds up her finger in warning, and I close my mouth on the question.

"The wise old hag told them to gather up snow and form it into the shape of a daughter.

"They did this. The girl they made was delicate in form, with eyes of stone, and lips of frozen rose petals, and the sharply pointed ears of their people. When they finished sculpting her, they smiled at each other, captivated by her beauty.

"The hag smiled, too, for other reasons."

This seems like a bad jest. I am not made of snow. I am not some being who was sculpted just as Lord Jarel and Lady Nore wished. I never captivated them with my beauty.

And yet, Bogdana is telling me this story for a reason. *Sluagh.* Is that what I am? A soul given a body, one of the half-dead Folk that wail outside houses or promise doom in mirrors.

"*Now we must give her life,* the hag told them. *For this, she needs a drop of blood, for she is to be your child. Second, she needs my magic.*

"The first was easy to supply. The king and queen pricked their fingers and let their blood stain the snow.

"The second was easy for them as well because I gave it willingly.

When my breath blew across the girl, the spark of life lit within her, and they could see her eyelashes twitch, her tresses shiver. The child began to move. Her little limbs were slender and nearly as pale a blue as the reflection of the sky on the snow she'd been made from. Her hair, a deeper blue, like the flowers that grew nearby. Her eyes, that of the lichen that clung to rocks. Her lips, the red of that fresh-spilled blood.

"*You will be our daughter*, the king and queen told her. *And you will give us Elfhame.*

"But when the girl opened her mouth and spoke for the first time, they were afraid of the thing that they had made."

I shake my head. "That can't be true. That can't be how I was born."

I don't want to be a *creature*, shaped by their hands and quickened with their blood. Something made like a doll, from snow and sticks. An assemblage of parts, stranger even than the sluagh.

"Why tell me this now?" I ask her, trying to keep my voice even. "Why tell me this at all?"

"Because I need you," says Bogdana. "Lady Nore is not the only one who can seize power. There is myself as well. Myself, to whom you owe your life far more than you owe it to her. Forsake the others. Come with me, and we can take everything for ourselves."

I think of the Thistlewitch and the tale she told of Mab and Mellith's heart. Could *Bogdana* have been the hag who slaughtered her own daughter? Perhaps it is only that I heard the story days before, but Lady Nore must have been told about the bones from *someone* who remembered what had happened, who knew their true value.

And if Bogdana was that hag, then her belief that I owe her my life puts me in greater danger than ever. She murdered her own child, and even though it was by accident, I can only imagine what she'd be willing to do to something like me.

My ability to command Lady Nore is more curse than blessing. Anyone who wants Mab's bones will find me the easiest means to get them.

"You spoke of constraints," I say. "What are they?"

The storm hag gives me a fierce look. "For one, I may not harm that Greenbriar boy, nor any of the line."

I shiver. That would explain why she fled at the sight of him. Why she sent lightning only at Tiernan. And it would be the sort of curse that Mab might have put on the hag who'd intended the murder of her daughter.

I must keep my wild thoughts in check. "Is this story of my origins what you came to tell me that night on my unfamily's lawn?"

She gives me a crooked, frightening smile. "I came to warn you that Prince Oak was coming so that you could avoid him."

"Not about Lady Nore's stick creatures?" I demand.

Bogdana snorts. "Those, I thought you could handle on your own. Perhaps they'd wake you up to what you could be."

More likely, they would have shot me through with arrows, or the stick spiders would have ripped me apart. "You've told me your story. I listened. Now I am going to go. That was our agreement."

"Are you certain?" Her eyes are hard, and she asks the question with such weight in her voice that I am certain there will be consequences for my answer.

I nod, feeling as though that is safer than speaking. Then I begin to turn away.

"You know, the girl saw me."

I freeze. "What girl?"

Her smile is sly. "The mortal one whose house you creep around."

"Bex?" I was so sure she was asleep in bed. She must have been terrified to see a monster on her lawn.

"When the prince started waving his little toothpick sword, I doubled back. I thought I'd seen her face in the window. But she was outside."

I can barely breathe.

"She didn't scream. She's a brave girl." The storm hag seems to enjoy drawing out this moment. "Said she was looking for you."

"For me?"

"I told her that last I saw, you were in the company of a prince, and that he had taken you prisoner. She wanted to help, of course. But mortals will make a muddle of most anything, don't you find?"

"What did you do?" My voice is almost all breath.

"Gave her some advice, is all," says Bogdana, stepping into the shadows of the trees. "And now I am giving you some. Get away from that Greenbriar boy before it's too late. And when I see you again, you'd best do what I ask. Or I can snuff out that spark I put inside you. And snuff out your little unfamily, too, while you watch."

I am shaking all over. "Don't you dare touch—"

At that moment, Tiernan steps through the branches. "Traitor!" he shouts at me. "I caught you."

# CHAPTER

# 11

Tiernan looks across the clearing at me, his sword drawn. I take a step back, unsure if I ought to race off into the night.

Bogdana has disappeared into the woods, leaving behind only the distant hiss of rain.

I shake my head vehemently, holding up my hands in warding. "You're wrong. Bogdana surprised me. I ran from her again, but she said she wanted to talk...."

He peers into the forest, as if expecting to find the storm hag still lurking there. "It seems obvious you were conspiring with her."

My mind is reeling, thinking of how puzzled Tiernan was when Oak suggested we part ways. Thinking of how clever it was to let me believe I was on this quest of my own free will.

I recall Tiernan tethering me in the motel. Barely speaking with me. Now I can guess the reason. He'd always considered me a sacrifice, something to look away from, something to which one ought not become attached. I shake my head. What defense can I give, when telling the truth would expose their deception?

"She warned me about continuing north," I say. "And she thought I should help her instead of Oak. But I never agreed to it."

He frowns, perhaps realizing all the things he would be unable to deny. Together we walk back to the camp. I pick up new wood as I go.

And as awful as it is to think about Oak handing me over, everything in me shies away from the story of my making. Am I no more than the sticks I carry and a little magic? Am I like a ragwort steed, something with only the appearance of life?

I feel sick and scared.

When we arrive back at the camp, Tiernan sets about moving the fire out from beneath the lean-to so it doesn't set the whole thing ablaze once the sticks dry out. To keep my hands busy, I weave branches together and knot them with more pieces of my dress to create a mat for our dwelling. Everything is still wet, droplets falling from trees with every gust of wind, causing the fire to smoke and sputter. I try not to think about anything but what I am doing.

Eventually, the heat dries things out enough for Tiernan to stretch out on my dampish mat, kick off his soaked and muddy boots, and warm his wet feet by the fire. "What did she offer you for your help?"

I reach out my hand to the fire. Since I was formed of snow, I wonder if I will melt. I hold my fingers close enough to burn, but all that happens when I snatch them back is that the tips are reddened and they sting.

"Stop that," Tiernan says.

I look over at him. "Bogdana's offer was to not murder me and my family."

"That had to be tempting," he says.

"I'd prefer greater politeness than I've gotten from anyone who wants to use me for my power," I tell him, knowing that what he wants to use me for is very different.

I think Tiernan hears a secret in my voice. But he cannot possibly guess what I have to hide. He cannot know what I am, nor why the storm hag believes I owe her. And if he wonders whether she told me that I am meant to be Madoc's ransom, he will try to convince himself otherwise. If he didn't like looking into my face knowing I was a sacrifice, how much worse would it be to look at me if I knew as well?

I am under no illusions that Bogdana would make for an easy ally, either. Too easily I can picture Bex confronting the storm hag, standing on her lawn in the moonlight. She must have felt dizzy with terror, the way I did when I first saw one of the Folk.

And yet Bex would not have been nearly afraid enough. I think about the phone in my pocket, now wishing that I could steal away and charge it, call her, warn her.

I stand and reach for Tiernan's cloak. He gives me a sharp look.

"You should hang it to dry," I say.

He undoes the clasp and lets me take it. I walk a short way to drape it over a branch, my fingers skirting over the cloth, looking for the strands of my hair he took. Such fine things, so easy to hide. Easy to lose, too, I hope, but I do not find them.

Oak's whistling alerts us to his return. His hair is dry, and he's wearing fresh clothes—jeans that are a little too short in the ankle, along with a cable-knit sweater the color of clotted cream. Over one shoulder he has the straps of a hiker's backpack. Perching on the other is the owl-faced hob.

The creature eyes me with evident dislike and makes a low, whistling animal noise, then flies off to a high branch.

Oak dumps the pack beside the fire. "The town would be lovely during the day, I think, although it lacked something by night. There was a vegetarian place called the Church of Seitan and a farm stand that sold peaches by the bushel. Both closed. A nearby bus station, where various entertainments could be gotten in trade. Sadly, nothing I was in the market for."

I glance up at the moon, visible since the storm cleared off. We began flying on the ragwort horses at dusk, so it must be well past midnight now.

Oak unpacks, taking out and unfolding two tarps. On them, he places an assortment of groceries and a pile of mortal clothes. Nothing has tags, and one of the tarps has a small tear in it. He's brought back a half-eaten rotisserie chicken in a plastic container. Peaches, despite his saying the stand was closed. Bread, nuts, and figs packed in a crumpled plastic bag from a hardware store. A gallon of fresh water, too, which he offers first to Tiernan. The knight takes a grateful swig from what ought to have been a milk jug, according to the sticker on the side.

"Where did you get all this?" I ask, because it obviously wasn't from the shelves of any store. My voice comes out with more edge than I intended.

Oak gives me a mischievous smile. "I met the family at the farm stand, and they were enormously generous to a stranger caught in a storm on a windy night. Let me take a shower. Even blow-dry my hair."

"You vain devil," Tiernan says with a snort.

"That's me," Oak affirmed. He slides the strap of his own bag over his head and sets it down not too far from the fire. But not with the communal offerings from the backpack, either. That bag is where he must keep the bridle. "I persuaded the family to let me have a few things from their garage and refrigerator. Nothing they'll miss."

A shiver goes through me at the thought of him glamouring that family, or making them love him. I imagine a mother and father and child in the kitchen of their home, caught in a dream. A chubby toddler crying in a high chair while they brought the prince food and clothes, the baby's cries seeming to come from farther and farther away.

"Did you hurt them?" I ask.

He looks at me, surprised. "Of course not."

But then, he might have a very limited idea of what *hurting them* meant. I shake my head to clear it of my own imaginings. I have no reason to think he did anything to them, just because he is planning to do something to me.

Oak reaches into the pile and pushes a black sweater, leggings, and new socks toward me. "Hopefully they'll fit well enough for travel."

Oak must see the suspicion I feel writ in my features.

"When we return from the north," he promises, hand to his heart in an exaggerated way that lets me know he considers this a silly vow rather than a solemn one, "they will wake to find their shoes filled with fine, fat rubies. They can use them to buy new leggings and another roast chicken."

"How will they sell *rubies*?" I ask him. "Why not leave them something more practical?"

He rolls his eyes. "As a prince of Faerie, I flatly refuse to leave cash. It's inelegant."

Tiernan shakes his head at both of us, then pokes at the foodstuffs, selecting a handful of nuts.

"Gift cards are worse," Oak says when I do not respond. "I would bring shame on the entire Greenbriar line if I left a gift card."

At that, I can't help smiling a little, despite my heavy heart. "You're ridiculous."

Hours ago, I would have thought he was generous, to joke with me after what happened at the Court of Moths. But that was before I knew he was going to trade me for his father, as though I were one of those gift cards.

I pick at a wing of the chicken, pulling off the skin, then meat, then crunching the bird's bones. A jagged bit cuts the inside of my mouth, but I keep eating. If my mouth is full, I will not speak.

When I am done, I take the clothes that Oak brought back for me and duck behind a tree to change. My beautiful new dress is coated in mud, not to mention ripped up all along the hem. Already well on its way to being worse than my last one. My skin feels clammy as I pull it off.

It has been many years since I wore mortal clothes like these. As a child, I was often in leggings and shirts, with sparkly sneakers and rainbow laces. My younger self would have delighted in having naturally colorful hair.

As I pull the sweater over my head, I hear Tiernan speaking quickly under his breath to Oak. He must be telling him about spotting Bogdana with me.

As I return to our lean-to with the weight of suspicion on my shoulders, with the schemes of Lady Nore and Bogdana and Oak winding around me, I realize that I cannot wait for fate to come to me.

I must leave them now, before they discover what I know. Before the moment when Oak admits to himself that he plans to give me to Lady Nore. Before he realizes that everything will be easier if I am bridled. Before I go mad, waiting for the inevitable blow to fall and hoping that I find a way to avoid it when it does.

Better to go north on my own from here and kill my mother, the one who shaped me from snow and filled my heart with hate. Only then will I be safe from her and all those who would use my power over her, no matter their reasons. I am a solitary creature, fated to be one and better as one. Forgetting that is what got me into trouble.

Once I realize the path I must take, I feel lighter than I have since Bogdana caught me in the woods. I can enjoy the sweet stickiness of the peach nectar, the slight plastic flavor of the water.

Tiernan gives a sigh. "Suppose we *do* go through the Stone Forest," he says. "Despite the deep pits that lead to oubliettes, the trees that move to make you lose your way, the ice spiders that wrap their prey in frozen gossamer, the mad king, and the curse. Then what? We don't have Hyacinthe to get us inside the Ice Needle Citadel."

"It's supposed to be very beautiful, the Citadel," Oak says. "Is it beautiful, Wren?"

When the light went through the ice of the castle, it made rainbows that danced along its cold halls. You could almost see through the walls, as though the whole place was one large, cloudy window. When I was brought to it for the first time, I thought it was like living inside a sparkling diamond.

"It's not," I say. "It's an ugly place."

Tiernan looks surprised. I am sure he is, since, if he stole Hyacinthe from Lady Nore, he knows exactly what the Citadel looks like.

But when I think of it, what I recall is grotesque. Making people betray themselves was Lady Nore's favorite sport, and one in which she was very skilled. Tricking her supplicants and prisoners into sacrificing that which they cared most about. Breaking their own instruments. Their own fingers. The necks of those they loved best.

Everything died in the Ice Citadel, but hope died first.

*Laugh, child,* Lady Nore commanded, not long before our trip to Elfhame. I do not remember what she wanted me to laugh at, although I am sure it was something awful.

But by then I had retreated so far inside myself that I don't think she was certain I'd even heard her. She slapped me and I bit her, ripping open the skin of her hand. That was the first moment I thought I saw a flicker of fear in her face.

That is the place I need to return to, that cold place where nothing can reach me. Where I can do anything.

"For now," Oak says, "let's concern ourselves with getting to Undry Market. I don't think we can risk ragwort again, even if we could find another patch. We're going to have to go on foot."

"I'll leave first," the knight says. "And start arranging for the boat. You take a different route to confuse our trail."

Somewhere on Tiernan's person—or in his pack—are strands of my hair. But even if I found them, can I be sure they don't have more? Can I be certain there isn't one stuck on the cloak Oak draped over my shoulders? Can I be sure Oak didn't pilfer another when he was brushing my hair?

My gaze goes to the prince's bag. I wouldn't need to care about the strands of hair if there was nothing that could be done with them.

If I snatched the bridle and ran, when I got to Lady Nore, I could be the one to make her wear it.

Oak sits by the fire, singing a song to himself that I catch only snatches of. Something about a pendulum and fabric that's starting to fray. The firelight limns his hair, turning the gold dark, the shadows making his features sharp and harsh.

He's the kind of beautiful that makes people want to smash things.

Tonight, while they sleep, I will steal the bridle. Hadn't Oak talked about a bus station, one that appeared to be open, no matter the hour? I will go there and begin my journey as a mortal might. I have Gwen's phone. I can use it to warn my unfamily of what's coming.

While I am thinking through this plan, Oak is telling Tiernan about a mermaid he knows, with hair the silver of the shine on waves. He thinks that if he could speak to her, she might be able to tell him more about what's going on in the Undersea.

Eventually, I curl up in my blanket, watching Tiernan cover the lean-to with Oak's burgled tarps. Then he climbs a tree, settling himself in its branches like a cradle.

"I'll take first watch," he volunteers gruffly.

"Titch can guard us for a few hours," says Oak, nodding to the owl-faced hob in the tree. It nods, its head rotating uncannily. "We could all use the rest."

I try to tamp down my rising panic. Surely Titch will be easier to get past than Tiernan would have been. But I had not counted on *any-one* standing watch. An oversight that makes me wonder what other obvious thing I have overlooked. What other foolish mistake is there to make?

Oak rolls himself up in his damp cloak. He looks at me as though he wants to say something, but when I refuse to meet his gaze, he settles down to sleep. I am glad. I am not as skilled at hiding my feelings as I would like.

At first, I count the stars, starting in the east and then moving west. It isn't easy, because I can't tell if I've counted some already and keep going back and starting again. But it does while away time.

At last, I close my eyes, counting again, this time to a thousand.

When I get to 999, I sit up. The others appear asleep, the gentle susurrations of their breaths even and deep. Above me, Titch's golden eyes blink, staring into the dark.

I creep over to Oak's bag, lying beside his sword. The fire has burned down to embers. Starlight shines on his features, smoothed out in slumber.

Kneeling, I slide my finger into the sack, past a paperback book, granola bars, candles, a scroll, and several more knives, until I feel the smooth strap. My fingers tremble at the touch of the leather. The enchantment on it seems to spark.

I tug the bridle out as gently and slowly as I am able.

Nearby, a fox calls. Frogs bellow at one another from the ferns.

I risk a look at the owl-faced hob, but it is still watching for danger outside the camp. There is no reason, I tell myself, for it to believe that I am doing anything more than rooting for a snack. I am no threat.

I don't have a bag like Oak's to hide the bridle in, but I do have a scarf, and I wind it up in that and then tie it around my waist like a belt. My heart is beating so fast that it seems as though it's skipping, like stones across a pond.

I stand and take a step, so certain I am about to be caught that the anticipation makes me dizzy.

Two more steps, and the tree line is in sight.

That's when I hear Oak's voice behind me, thick with sleep. "Wren?"

I turn back, attempting not to panic, not to snarl and run. I can't let him see how afraid I am that he's caught me.

"You're awake," he says, sitting up.

"My mind keeps going around in loops," I say, keeping my voice low. That much is certainly true.

He beckons to me. Reluctantly, I come over and sit beside him. Leaning forward, he pokes the fire with a stick.

I can't help but see his face, soft from slumber, and remember what it was like to kiss him. When I recall the curve of Oak's mouth, I must force myself to think of the way it looks pulled into a sneer.

*I don't want her.* I remind myself of his words. And if there's any part of him that does, it's because I am, as Hyacinthe said, *a coin to be spent.*

I take a deep breath. "You're not really going to send me away, are you?"

"I should," he says. "This is a grievously foolhardy scheme."

I wonder if he believes the thought of being parted from him is what kept me awake. "I knew that from the first."

"I should never have gotten you into this," he says, self-loathing in his voice. Perhaps he is slipping a little, tired as he is. He cannot like what he plans to do. He is not that much of a monster.

"I can stop Lady Nore," I remind him.

He gives me a smile, a strange light in his eyes. "If we were capable of putting mistrust aside, we might be a formidable pair."

"We might," I say. "Were we sure of each other."

His hand touches my back lightly, making me shiver. "Do you know what I admire about you?"

Truly, I cannot imagine what he will say next.

"That you never stopped being angry," he tells me. "It can be brave to hate. Sometimes it's like hope."

I hadn't felt brave in the Court of Teeth. Or hopeful. I had felt only a clawing desperation, as though I was forever drowning in some vast sea, gulping seawater as I sank, and then just when I felt I was going to let myself drop beneath the waves, something would make me kick one more time. Maybe that thing was hate. Hating requires going on, even when you can no longer believe in any better future. But I am shocked that Oak, of all people, would know that.

"You will make an interesting High King," I tell him.

He looks alarmed. "I most definitely will *not*. The Folk adore Cardan, and they're terrified of my sister, two excellent things. I hope they rule Elfhame for a thousand years and then pass it down to one of a dozen offspring. No need for me to be involved."

"Honestly, you *don't* want to be the High King?" I ask, puzzled. It was all Lord Jarel and Lady Nore wanted, the entire focus of their ambition, the reason for my creation. It seemed almost an insult for him to shrink from it as though it was equivalent to eating an apple with a worm inside.

Even if I happened to agree with him.

"Cardan was smart not to want it before I slammed that crown on his head," Oak says, his mouth quirking at the memory, then flattening out again. "The desire to rule Elfhame ruined so many lives. Just being the heir is bad enough."

"What do you mean?" Watching him in the firelight, the sleep-mussed fall of gold curls against his cheeks and the curious intensity of his expression, I could almost believe he's telling me this because he wishes to be my friend, rather than knowing that the appearance of vulnerability is likely to make me drop my guard.

He stretches a little, like a cat. "Some people would prefer to see me on the throne, either because they think I'd be easier to manipulate or because they'd do anything not to be ruled by a mortal. They make no secret that were I to say the right word, they would pour poison in my ear and down my family's throats. Meanwhile, my sister Jude—I suspect she isn't having children to make it clear I will be next in line. She says not, but she's too good of a liar for me to know."

I picture the High Queen as she was in that final battle, blood flecked across her face. Chopping off the head of the serpent who'd once been her beloved, even if it doomed her side to failure, all to save a land that despised her.

Now, that was hate that was somehow also hope.

He laughs, surprising me. "I am grim tonight, am I not? Let me show you a trick."

I eye him suspiciously. But he only takes a quarter out of his pocket, then spins it on the edge of his finger.

I snort despite myself.

He tosses the coin up and catches it in the other hand, then opens both his palms. The coin is gone.

"Do you know where it is?" he asks.

"Magicked away into Faerieland?" I guess, but I am smiling.

With a grin, Oak reaches behind my ear, and I can feel the metal, warmed by his skin, against the side of my neck.

I am foolish for my delight, but I am delighted all the same.

"The Roach taught me that," he says, tucking the coin away. "I'm still practicing."

"I remember him," I say. "From your Court of Shadows."

Oak nods. "And before that, from the Court of Teeth. He wasn't just held there by himself, either."

The Bomb. I remember her, too. Lady Nore had called her Liliver. Considering how much the Court of Teeth corrupted, I can only admire their loyalty to each other. "They must have truly suffered."

Oak gives me an odd look. "As you did."

"We should try to sleep," I force myself to say. If I remain in his company any longer, I will *ask* if he intends to give me to Lady Nore. And then my plans will be discovered, and I, very likely, bridled.

He shakes his head, possibly at himself. "Of course. You're right."

I nod. *Yes. Go back to sleep, Oak. Please. Go to sleep before I change my mind about leaving.*

Though he means me harm, I will miss him. I will miss the way he moves through the world, as though nothing could be so terrible that he might not laugh at it.

I might even miss Tiernan's grumpiness.

I go back on my blankets and wait, counting to a thousand again. When I am certain the prince is asleep, I push myself up and walk steadily into the tree line. I do not look back to see if the owl eyes of the hob are on me. I must behave as though I am doing nothing of note, nothing wrong.

Once I am away from the camp and the hob gives no cry of alarm, I leave off caution and rush through the woods, then through the town, until I come to the bus station.

It takes me a full three minutes before my glamour is nearly good enough to allow me to pass for human. I touch my face and my teeth to be sure.

Then, taking a deep breath, I walk into the brightly lit station. It smells like gasoline and disinfectant. A few humans are sitting on metal benches, one with a garbage bag that seems to be stuffed full of clothes. A young couple with a single suitcase between them, whispering together. An elderly gentleman with a cane who has fallen asleep and may have already missed his bus.

According to the schedule, the next one is passing north and west, up toward Michigan. It's tricky to buy a ticket with glamoured money, because machines aren't unaware that you're feeding leaves into them, even if people are. Instead, I grab a receipt out of the trash and enchant it. It's only a rough approximation of a ticket, and I will have to glamour the driver to let me pass, but the role will be more convincing with something in my hand. My magic is wobbly enough to need all the help it can get.

When I look up, I see a man with dirty pants and an unkempt beard watching me. My heart speeds. Was he only noting that I'd been rooting around in the trash, or am I so unlucky as to run into one of the humans with True Sight? Or is he something else, something more?

I smile at him, and he flinches as though he can see the sharpness of my teeth. After that, he stops looking at me.

I plug Gwen's phone into the wall and wait.

I watch a girl kick a vending machine. A boy smokes a cigarette, pacing outside and talking to himself. An elderly man picks a penny off the floor.

Beside me, there is a sudden buzz. I look down and realize the screen of the phone has come back to life. I've missed ten calls while it was dead, none of them from numbers I know.

There are three texts from Gwen. The first reads: It's fucked to text my own phone, and even more because everything that happened seems like it can't be real, but I made it to my parents' house. That hot elf guy was kind of a dick bt he told me about his ex & the prince, and it sounds like your in trouble. Let me know your OK.

Below that there's a photo of her with the fiddler from the Court of Moths. They are draped over each other and smiling in the front seat of a car. The next message reads: MY BAE IS HERE. He says he woke up on the side of a hill. The last thing he remembers is someone who looked like a devil putting salt on his tongue. I don't know what you did, but THANK YOU THANK YOU THANK YOU.

And then: Are you OK? Please write to me so (a) I know you're good and (b) I didn't dream you.

I grin at the phone. Most of the people I broke curses for were as afraid of me as they were of the glaistig. It was strange to think that Gwen *liked* me. Fine, I had done something nice for her, but she still texted me as though we could be friends.

I text back: Hard to charge a phone in Faerieland. I made it to a bus station & am on my own. No princes. No knights. Glad you're okay and your boyfriend, too.

Then the smile fades off my face. Because I have to call home. I have to warn Bex.

I punch in the sequence of numbers from memory.

A man's voice picks up. My unfather. "Who is this?"

I watch the clock and the door, half-expecting Oak to come striding through and drag me back to the camp at sword's point. I remind myself that I have the bridle, and that even if he was looking for me, he'd have no reason to look here.

"Can I speak with Bex, please?" I ask, keeping my voice steady.

For a long moment, my unfather is quiet, and I think he's going to hang up. Then I hear him call for my unsister.

I bite my nails and watch the seconds tick by on the clock, watch the other people shuffle around the station.

She comes to the phone. "Yeah?"

"You have to listen to me," I tell her, keeping my voice low so that the whole bus station doesn't listen in. "You're in trouble."

She takes a sharp breath. *"Mom!"* she yells, then she sounds muffled, like she has her hand over the speaker. "She called back. No, it's *her.*"

I panic, worried that she's going to hang up. "Just hear me out. Before that monster comes for you."

Listen to *this* monster, not *that* one.

"Mom wants to talk."

I feel a little sick at the thought. "You. Just you. For now, at least. Please."

Her voice goes distant, as though she's speaking to someone other than me. "Wait. Yes, I'll tell her."

"Why did you go outside that night?" I ask.

There's a pause, footsteps, then I hear a door close. "Okay, I'm away from them."

I repeat my question, anxiety narrowing my focus to the gum on the floor, the smell of exhaust, the pinesap on my fingers, the sound of her sighs.

"I wanted to make sure you were okay," Bex says finally.

"You remember me?" I choke out.

"You lived with us for *seven years*," she says, accusation creeping into her voice. "After you went back to your birth family, we hoped we'd hear *something*. Mom used to cry on that made-up birthday she invented for you."

*"She told me to leave."* I growl out the words. I know it wasn't her fault, that she and Dad and Bex were glamoured. But how could I go back to them, make them face my monstrousness, allow them to reject me again? *"Dad kicked me."*

I look at the clock. It's nearly time for the bus to pull in.

Bex sounds angry. "That's not true."

I need to end this call. I pull the charging cord out of the wall and out of the base of the phone, then start to wind it up. Soon I will be on my way north. Soon I will be cold inside and out.

"You met the storm hag," I say. "You know that whatever story you heard can't be the whole of it. And you know that I was adopted, not a foster child any longer. I couldn't just up and return to my birth parents, nor could they come and take me away. Think about it, and the story falls apart. Because it's one that you were enchanted with to explain something unexplainable."

There's a silence from the other end, but I hear people in the background. I don't think the door is closed anymore.

"I thought you were a ghost the first time I spotted you," she says softly.

I feel foolish, thinking that no one saw me slipping in and out of the house. If you do anything for long enough, you're bound to be caught. "When?"

"About six months ago. I was up late reading, and I saw something moving outside. When I looked, it was like seeing your spirit, back from the dead. But then I thought you were in some kind of trouble. And I started to wait for you."

"And the milk," I say. "You left out milk."

"You aren't human, are you?" She whispers the words, as though she's embarrassed to say them aloud.

I think of my unmother's surprise at hearing my voice. "Did you tell—"

"No!" she interrupts me. "How was I supposed to? I wasn't even sure *what* I saw. And they're not happy with me right now."

I look at the clock. The bus should be here. For a heart-stopping moment, I think that I've missed it, that time has jumped while I've been speaking with Bex. But a quick glance around shows me that none of the people waiting have moved from their seats.

*The bus is late*, I tell myself. *It's coming. Just late.* But my heart keeps beating harder, and I shrink into myself, as though if I am still enough, anxiety will stop gnawing on my insides.

And if the bus is not the whole reason I feel the way that I do, it's enough of it.

"Listen," I say, my gaze going to the road, watching for headlights. "I don't know how long I have, but if Bogdana knows where you are, it's not safe. Fill your pockets with salt. Rowan berries will keep you from being glamoured by their magic. They hate cold-wrought iron. And they can't lie." I correct myself. "*We.* We can't lie."

"What are—"

I hear cloth rustling and my unmother's voice cutting off Bex. "Wren, I know you want to talk to your *sister*." She emphasizes the word as though I am about to deny it. "But I have something quick to say. If you're in some kind of trouble, we can help you. You just tell us what's going on. Bex made it sound like you were living on the streets."

I almost laugh at that. "I'm surviving."

"That's not enough." She gives an enormous shaky sigh. "But even if it were, I'd like to see you. I've wondered how you were doing. What you were doing. If you had enough to eat. If you were warm."

My eyes burn, but I can't imagine being there, in their living room, wearing my true face. I would horrify them. Maybe they wouldn't scream and shove me away at first, the way they did when they were enchanted, but it would quickly turn awful. I couldn't be the child that they had loved.

Not after everything that happened to me. Not after learning that I am made of sticks and snow.

Headlights swing into view. I am already moving by the time I hear the squeal of brakes.

"I never needed to be warm," I tell my unmother, my voice hard, full of the anger that has been gnawing at my insides for years.

"Wren," she says, stung.

I feel as though I am about to weep, and I am not even sure why.

"Tell Bex to remember the salt, the rowan, and the iron," I say, and hang up the phone, racing for the bus.

Only one person gets off, and then I get on, holding out my fake ticket to the driver and concentrating my magic on him. *Believe me*, I plead with all the force I possess. *Believe I have a ticket.*

He nods in a distracted fashion, and I flee to the back of the bus, still holding the phone. A few more people board, including the man who was watching me so strangely. My feelings are too tangled up for me to pay any of them much attention.

Once Lady Nore is dead, or perhaps wearing the bridle, maybe I will speak with Bex and my unmother and unfather again. Maybe, if I knew I could keep them safe from Bogdana. If I knew I could keep them safe from me.

Leaning my cheek against the glass, I slip my hand into the folds of the scarf, just to have the reassuring feel of the bridle's leather strap, to know I have a plan. I dig my fingers through the cloth, then reach around my body, scratching at my stomach, fresh panic flooding my chest.

The bridle isn't there.

Outside the window, Titch sits on the gutter of the bus station, blinking at me with golden eyes.

The bus begins to roll forward. I try to tell myself that I can still get away. That perhaps the bus will drive faster than the creature can fly. That Oak and Tiernan will not be able to follow.

That's when I hear a tire pop. The bus lurches to a stop, and I realize there is nowhere for me to go.

# CHAPTER

## 12

As I walk back through the woods, I am furious with all the world, but especially myself.

Even though I knew Oak had played the entire Court of Moths false and gotten himself punched in the face twice to convince them he was a vain, useless courtier, had preened and drank a trough of wine to hide his swordsmanship. Even though Oak told me the Roach had taught him the trick with the coin, still I didn't consider that the goblin might also have taught Oak the far more practical skill of *stealing*.

The prince was careful to speak to me as if nothing at all was the matter, even as he lifted the bridle from around my waist. Worked it off with such deftness that I hadn't felt more than a single touch. Lulled by his conversation, I let myself believe I had fooled him at the very moment he was fooling me.

He was as deceptive as the rest of his family. More, maybe.

He never let down his guard with me, not once.

Too late, I understand what's terrifying about his charm. He seems entirely open when he is unknowable. Every smile is painted on, a mask.

*Maybe I'm glad that you gave me an opportunity to be my worst self.*

The campsite is as quiet as when I left it. Tiernan remains draped in the tree, making soft snoring sounds. Titch shadows me with shining eyes. I stare at Oak, half-hoping he will turn over and confront me, and half-dreading it.

As I pass him, I note that his breaths are even, though I bet he sleeps the way cats do, lightly. If I got too close, I bet he would spring up, ready to fight.

That is, if he's sleeping at all.

I creep over to my own blankets and flop onto them. Despair drags me down into dreams, where I am back in the snow, walking in circles.

When I wake, it is to the smell of buttered rolls and coffee from town. Oak and Tiernan are eating and talking quietly. I hear Tiernan laugh, and I wonder how much of what they are saying is about my escape attempt, if they find my failure hilarious.

Oak wears mortal clothes over his shining golden mail. It peeks out at his collar and cuffs. Tiernan wears his armor without any cover.

When the prince glances over at me, nothing changes in his expression. Maybe that's because, to him, nothing *has* changed. He'd never believed I was anything but a potential adversary or a potential sacrifice.

I bite my tongue until it bleeds.

He smiles, and finally I see the flicker of anger in his eyes. It's satisfying that he, who hides so much, can't hide that. He walks over and sits beside me. "You knew I was a trickster."

Then, before I can react, he presses a finger to his lips, glancing sideways at Tiernan. It takes me a moment to understand that he *hasn't* told the knight that I attempted to steal the bridle. What I don't understand is why.

Tiernan rises and throws water onto the fire, causing a cloud of steam to rise. The late afternoon is bright, the sky almost aggressively blue after the storm.

I stick a roll in my mouth and pack up the remains of my gown, transferring the knife Oak lent me to my boot.

Tiernan mutters something and then heads off into the woods.

"Where is he going?" I ask.

"To Undry Market, ahead of us, to negotiate for the boat. Tiernan believes if the goblins know who I am, they will ask for outlandish things. We will take another path and see if anything follows." He pauses. "You don't mind, do you?"

I get up and brush off my legs. When someone thwarted your attempt to rob them, made it clear you were *their* prisoner, and then asks you a question like that, it's not really a question.

We walk for a while in silence.

"Do you remember what I said about us being formidable, were we able to put mistrust aside?" he asks.

I nod reluctantly.

"I see we were not able," he reminds me. "Now what, Wren?"

I feel helpless, as though he's herding me around a chessboard to checkmate. "Why are you asking me this?"

He lets out a frustrated huff. "Fine, I will be plain. If you wanted to leave, why not go any other night?"

Another trap. "Why should I tell you anything, when you're the one with so many secrets?"

"Everyone has secrets," he says, although there is something like despair in his voice.

"Secrets about me," I clarify.

"You've betrayed me. You've stolen from me. You met with the storm hag, and then hours later you snatch a powerful magical object and run. Do I deserve no answers?"

"I wanted the bridle," I say. "So that you could never make me wear it."

He kicks up a tornado of leaves. "What cause have I ever given you to accuse me of that?"

I look sullenly away.

He says nothing, merely waiting for my reply. The silence stretches on, and I am surprised that I am the one who breaks first and fills it.

"Tiernan told me he'd use the bridle on me if I betrayed you again." I fix him with a glare.

Oak blinks in surprise and is quiet for a long moment. "He doesn't understand why you freed Hyacinthe and the others," he says finally. "He can't believe you did it because you wanted to help them. Folk do not do such things where we come from."

I kick a rock, hard.

"If you want to go, go," the prince tells me with an elaborate swish of his hand toward the trees around us.

I look into the woods but am not so foolish as to take his offer at face value. "Then why not just let me leave last night?"

Oak gives me a slightly guilty look. "Because I don't like being the fool who'd been tricked. I like games, but I hate to lose."

I blink at him in surprise. "What?"

He shrugs impatiently. "It's not my best quality," he says. "And besides, it seemed worthwhile to *ask* you if you were working with Bogdana."

"I'm not," I say, and when he gives me a long look, I say it in full. "I am neither working for nor with Lady Nore. I am not allied with Bogdana. I want to go north and keep Lady Nore from making more monsters. I even want to see your father freed."

"Then why leave?" This is the difficulty with Oak. He invites you to trust him, makes you feel silly for doubting, and then you find yourself in a bus station, discovering how thoroughly you've been played.

"Rather than be sent to Elfhame, I decided I would go north without you and face my mother alone." I wonder if I can get away with saying only that.

When he glances in my direction, his fox eyes are bright. "That's even more foolish than our current plan."

My stomach twists.

"I don't understand it," he says, scrubbing his hand over his face. "I feel as though I ought to be angry with you, but I admired what you did back at the Court of Moths. Even when it did, as you say, *inconvenience* me."

I grimace a little at my own words, but then the import of what he's saying sinks in. "*You* ... admired *that*?"

"More than I'd like to admit." When he looks at me, I see that same intensity in his face that I remember from when he stood beside Queen Annet. "You cared about the mortal and the merrow and even Hyacinthe. You defied all of us and, as far as I can tell, got nothing in return."

I am not sure how to answer. "Did it weigh on you, keeping Hyacinthe prisoner?"

"He tried to kill the High King."

"What?" I recall Tiernan saying there'd been an incident.

Oak appears amused by the shock of my voice. "Once, my father said that conflicts seem as though they are between beliefs or desires. But more often conflicts are between rulers. Those that follow rulers can be perfectly nice, which is how you wind up with two perfectly nice people with daggers to each other's throats. Hyacinthe and I might have been friends, but for the part where we were set on opposite sides of a battlefield."

I think on that for a long moment, wondering if that's how he sees me as well. How it would be for him to discover that I am stitched together with magic, a manikin animated by a hag? Perhaps he would feel less guilty then.

I could take him at his word and attempt to leave. But he made no promises not to chase after me. Nor did he say he wouldn't make me wear the bridle.

I could slip away in Undry Market and find a place to hide. But I have no reason to believe that the Folk there would help me over their prince. Most likely they would give me up for a few coins.

Or I could try to get the truth out of him. "You like games," I tell him. "How about we play one?"

"What's the wager?"

"If I win," I say. "You answer my question. Without evasion."

Nothing about the way he looks at me suggests that he does not consider these to be large stakes. Still, he nods. "And what is the game?"

"You have the piece. Just as when we were children, let's see which of us throws better."

He nods again, taking it from his pocket. The peridot eyes glimmer. "And if I win?"

"What do you want?" I ask.

He studies me and I study him in return. No smile now can disguise the steel underneath. "You promise to dance with me so that our practice back in the Court of Moths won't be for nothing."

"Those are absurd stakes," I tell him, my cheeks hot.

"And yet they are mine," he says.

I nod quickly, unsettled. "Very well. You throw first."

We stop walking. He squats down and clears off the twigs and fallen leaves from a patch of grass. It feels like being children, like playing. It occurs to me that so many awful things in my life happened before that moment, and so many awful things in his life happened after.

The fox tumbles onto the ground, falling on its side. No points.

He looks over at me and raises his eyebrows.

I pick it up and throw, holding my breath. It falls on its side, too.

He reaches for it and I think he's going to throw again, but he sets the fox on its back, with its legs pointing up. "You win."

I shake my head, incredulous.

"You win," he says again, more firmly. "Ask."

Very well. If he is going to give me the game, I would be a fool not to take it. "Lady Nore asked for me in trade for Madoc, didn't she?" I brace myself for his answer, or for whatever he does in place of giving me one. "That's why you're really bringing me north."

His surprise is evident. "Is that what Bogdana told you?"

I nod.

He sighs. "No wonder you ran."

"Is it *true*?" I ask.

He frowns. "What did she say, exactly? So that I may answer without evasion."

"That Lady Nore offered to trade Madoc to the prince in exchange for *the very thing he is bringing north. A foolish girl.*"

"Well, it's accurate that Lady Nore offered to trade for what the storm hag *thinks* I am bringing north," Oak says. "Mellith's heart. That's what she asked for, and if I've managed to convince Bogdana that I have it, so much the better. Maybe Lady Nore will believe it as well. But what the storm hag told you—she meant to trick you with the way she put together those words."

I think over the tangle of what Bogdana said and what she didn't. Not simply *Lady Nore offered to trade Madoc for you.* If she'd been able to say that, she would have.

"So you *don't* have Mellith's heart and you're *not* going to give me— or it—to Lady Nore?" I need him to say the words.

He grins. "I am not planning on handing you over to anyone. Lady Nore did not ask for you in trade. As for Mellith's heart, I will show you what I intend when we reach the market. It's a nice bit of trickery, I think."

I stare into his fox eyes and feel relief so acute that I am dizzy with it.

I look up at the sky overhead, the intense blue that follows a storm, and let myself believe I am not in danger. Not right then. Not from him.

I pick up the gaming piece, and when he doesn't seem to notice or demand it back, I slip it into my pocket. Then we resume walking.

It's not far before a riot of colors shows through the trees. That must be Undry Market. In the wind, I hear the scrap of a song.

"What if," he says, mischief in his eyes, "in the interest of saving time, we pretend that we've played twice more and I won once, so you owe me a dance. But you won the second time, so if you have anything else to ask me, you may."

Those are teasing words, and I am suddenly in a teasing mood. "All right. Tell me about your girls, then."

He raises his eyebrows. *"Girls?"*

"Tiernan says there were two ladies in particular that you wanted to impress. Violet, I think. And Sibi. But he also says you fall in love a lot."

That surprises a laugh out of him, although he doesn't deny any of it. "There are certain expectations of a prince in Court."

"You cannot be serious," I say. "You feel *obliged* to be in love?"

"I told you—I am a courtier, versed in all the courtly arts." He's grinning as he says it, though, acknowledging the absurdity of the statement.

I find myself shaking my head and grinning, too. He's being ridiculous, but I am not sure *how* ridiculous.

"I do have a bad habit," he says. "Of falling in love. With great regularity and to spectacular effect. You see, it never goes well."

I wonder if this conversation makes him think of our kiss, but then, I was the one who kissed him. He'd only kissed back.

"As charming as you are, how can that be?" I say.

He laughs again. "That's what my sister Taryn always says. She tells me that I remind her of her late husband. Which makes some sense, since I would have been his half brother. But it's also alarming, because she's the one who murdered him."

Much as when he spoke about Madoc, it's strange how fond Oak can sound when he tells me a horrifying thing a member of his family has done. "Whom have you fallen in love with?" I ask.

"Well, there was you," the prince says. "When we were children."

"Me?" I ask incredulously.

"You didn't know?" He appears to be merry in the face of my astonishment. "Oh yes. Though you were a year my senior, and it was hopeless, I absolutely mooned over you. When you were gone from Court, I refused any food but tea and toast for a month."

I cannot help snorting over the sheer absurdity of his statement.

He puts a hand to my heart. "Ah, and now you laugh. It is my curse to adore cruel women."

He cannot expect me to believe he had real feelings. "Stop with your games."

"Very well," he says. "Shall we go to the next? Her name was Lara, a mortal at the school I attended when I lived with my eldest sister and her girlfriend. Sometimes Lara and I would climb up into the crook of one of the maple trees and share sandwiches. But she had a villainous friend, who implicated me in a piece of gossip—which resulted in Lara stabbing me with a lead pencil and breaking off our relationship."

"You *do* like cruel women," I say.

"Then there was Violet, a pixie. I wrote her terrible poetry about how I adored her. Unfortunately, *she* adored duels and would get into trouble so that I would have to fight for her honor. And even more unfortunately, neither my sister nor my father bothered to teach me how to sword fight for show."

I thought of the dead-eyed expression on his face before his bout with the ogre and Tiernan's angry words.

"That resulted in my accidentally killing a person she liked better than me."

"Oh," I say. "That is *three levels* of unfortunate."

"Then there was Sibi, who wanted to run away from Court with me, but as soon as we went, hated it and wept until I took her home. And Loana, a mermaid, who found my lack of a tail unbearable but tried to drown me anyway, because she found it equally unbearable that I would ever love another."

The way he tells these stories makes me recall how he's told me many painful things before. Some people laugh in the face of death. He laughs in the face of despair. "How old were you?"

"Fifteen, with the mermaid," he said. "And nearly three years later, I must surely be wiser."

"Surely," I say, wondering if he was. Wondering if I wanted him to be.

The threshold of Undry Market is announced by two trees leaning toward each other, their branches entangled. As we duck beneath, what had previously been scraps of song and spots of color lose their disguise and the entire panoply comes into view. Shops and stalls fill the clearing. The air is rich with perfumes, honey wines, and grilled fruits. We pass a tented area with lutes and harps, the vendor trying to call to us over the sound of one of his instruments recounting a terrible tale of how it was made.

As we walk, I see that the market stretches down to a rocky area near the shoreline, where a pier has been built out into the waves. A single ship bobs at the end of it. I wonder if that is what Tiernan is trying to buy from the goblins.

Then I am distracted by the hammering of smiths and a smattering of song. There is a forge not far from where we are standing, one with a display of swords in the front. And beside that, a maypole and a few dancers going around it, winding the ribbons. A stall selling cloaks in all the colors of the sky, from the first blush of dawn to deep as midnight and spangled with stars. A bakeshop hawking braided breads, their shining crusts decorated with herbs and flowers.

"Don't have gold?" calls an antlered shopkeeper. "Pay with a lock of hair, a year of your life, a dream you wish to never have again."

"Come!" calls another. "We have the finest jackets in a hundred leagues. Green as poison. Red as blood. Black as the heart of the King of Elfhame."

Oak stops to purchase cheese wrapped in wax paper, a half dozen apples, and two loaves of bread. He also gets us warmer clothes, along with hats and gloves. Rope, new packs, and a grappling hook, the tines of which fold down like the tentacles of a squid skimming through water.

We pass a fletcher, selling barrels of arrows with different feathers affixed to the ends. Crows and sparrows, even those from a wren. Pass a display of gowns in beetle-bright green, saffron, and pomegranate red. A stall with bouquets of drying herbs hanging upside down, beside seedpods. Then a bookseller, shelves of old tomes and empty, freshly bound books open to creamy pages waiting to be written in. One stall over, an alchemist displays a shelf of poisons, including poisoned ink. A row of oddly shaped skulls sits alongside them.

Oak pauses to purchase some explosives. "Just in case," he reassures me.

"Dear lady," says a faerie, coming toward us from a shop that sells jewels. He has the eyes of a snake and a forked tongue that darts out when he speaks. "This hairpin looks as though it were made for you."

It's beautiful, woven gold and silver in the shape of a bird, a single green bead in its mouth. Had it been in a display, my eyes would have passed over it as one of a dozen unobtainable things. But as he holds it out, I can't help imagining it as mine.

"I have no money and little to trade," I tell him regretfully, shaking my head.

The shopkeeper's gaze goes to Oak. I think he believes the prince is my lover.

Oak plays the part, reaching out his hand for the pin. "How much is it? And will you take silver, or must it be the last wish of my heart?"

"Silver is excellent." The shopkeeper smiles as Oak fishes through his bag for some coins.

Part of me wants to demur, but I let him buy it, and then I let him use it to pin back my hair. His fingers on my neck are warm. It's only when he lets go that I shiver.

He gives me a steady look. "I hope you're not about to tell me that you hate it and you were just being polite."

"I don't hate it," I say softly. "And I am not polite."

He laughs at that. "A delightful quality."

I admire the hairpin in every reflective surface we pass.

We cross a wide lawn where a puppet show is under way. Folk are gathered around a curtained box, watching an intricate paper cutout of a crow seem to fly above a mill. I spot a few human children and pause to wonder if they are changelings.

The crow puppet sweeps down to a painted papier-mâché tree. The hidden operator moves a pole, and the crow's beak opens and closes.

The bird sings:

> *Ca-caw, ca-caw,*
> *My mother she killed me,*

*My father he ate me,*
*My sister gathered my bones,*
*And buried them beneath the apple tree.*
*Behold! I hatched as a young crow.*
*Ca-caw, ca-caw, how beautiful a bird am I.*

I stop to watch. It turns out that the miller loves the song so much that he gives the crow a millstone in order to hear it again. And when the bird flies home, he drops the stone onto his stepmother's head and kills her.

The crowd is still clapping when I realize that Oak has gone on to the blacksmith shop. I arrive in time to see the bushy-eyebrowed smith returning from the back with what appears to be a metal-and-glass box, designed to display its contents. It is golden-footed and empty.

"What is that?" I ask as he carefully places it into his bag.

"A reliquary," he says. "Enchanted to keep whatever is inside forever preserved. It's much like the one that contained Mab's bones. I sent ahead Titch to commission it."

"And that's for—"

He signals me away from the shop. Together we walk toward the pier. "A deer heart," he says. "Because that's what I am going to bring Lady Nore. In a fancy reliquary, she won't know the difference for some amount of time, hopefully enough for us to be able to accomplish our goal and get you close to her."

"A deer heart?" I echo.

"That's what I am bringing north. A trick. Sleight of hand, like the coin."

I smile up at him, believing, for once, that we are on the same side.

When we come to the edge of the water, we find Tiernan still haggling with three goblins. One has golden hair and a pointy chin, the second has black hair and bushy eyebrows, and the third has very large ears and no hair on his head at all. The hairless one has a skin of wine and stares at me with the seriousness of the very drunk. He is passing his booze back and forth with a redheaded giant, who sits on the pier, dangling enormous feet in the sea.

The black-haired goblin holds up a silver-handled knife and tests its weight. "What else have you got?"

There is a small pile of treasure on a nearby boulder—a fat pearl, at least sixteen pieces of gold, and a stone that might be an emerald.

"You overestimate the value of what you're selling," says Tiernan.

The drunk goblin laughs uproariously.

In the water is a boat carved in the shape of a cormorant. At the front, the long curve of its neck makes it appear rampant, and the wings rise on either side, protecting those resting in the hull. It's beautifully made, and if I squint, I can see that it's also magical.

"Ahhhh," says the golden-haired goblin to Oak as we approach. "You must explain to your friend here that he cannot purchase one of our finest crafts with a few trinkets."

Tiernan is obviously frustrated. "We've come to a price, but I'm a little short of it, that's all. Now that you're here, we can make up the difference and go."

Whatever his reason for believing he would be better at negotiation than Oak, he's mistaken. It's not in his nature to dress up the truth, or slither around it.

The golden-haired goblin looks at us expectantly. "We would like the remainder of our payment now, please."

Oak reaches into his bag and pulls out several more gold coins, as well as a handful of silver ones. "Is this enough?"

"We'll have your rings," says the golden-haired goblin, pointing at the three encircling Oak's fingers.

I am not sure if they have any significance, but I suppose they mustn't since Oak heaves a sigh and starts to twist them off. Not only that, but he places his circlet beside them. Surely a crown is enough payment.

The golden-haired goblin shakes his head.

I see the shift of the prince's smile. Honey-tongued. "Mayhap your boat is too beautiful for our needs. We need seaworthy and little more."

Two of the goblins exchange glances. "Our craft is as seaworthy as they come," says the black-haired one.

"And yet, one might weep to see such a beautiful vessel as this battling the elements." Oak's expression turns thoughtful. "Perhaps you have something less fine you could sell us."

At this the black-haired goblin sniffs, offended. "We do not make ugly things."

"No, no," Oak says, acting as if he's disappointed. "Of course not."

I twig his game. "Maybe we should seek a boat elsewhere," I suggest.

Tiernan looks like he wants to strangle us. I can't decide if he's not sure what Oak is about or only skeptical that it will work.

The golden-haired goblin watches Oak. "You truly have nothing more to trade? I can hardly believe it, handsome travelers like yourselves. What's that in her hair?"

Oak frowns as I remove it from my braids. Regretfully, I set it down on the pile with the rest of our treasures. I tell myself that it doesn't matter. It would have been useless anyway, where we're going.

The bushy-browed goblin snorts, picking up the hairpin and turning it over. "Very well. If this assortment of baubles is all you can give us, I suppose we will take pity on you and make the trade. Your rings, the knife, the pearl, the coins, the emerald that's in no way the size of a duck egg, the circlet, and the hairpin. For these, we'll sell you the boat."

Smiling, Oak walks forward to shake the goblin's hand and seal the bargain.

Tiernan hops down into the sea craft, motioning for me to throw him down my bag. He looks relieved that the negotiations are finally over and we can get moving.

The drunk giant lumbers to his feet, fixing the prince with an accusatory stare. "Look at what he's wearing beneath his clothes. Armor of gold," he grunts. "We'll have that, too. Tell him!"

"We've agreed to a price," Tiernan warns.

Oak's hand goes to his sword hilt, and I see something wild in his eyes. "I don't want to fight," he says, and I am sure part of him means that.

"You meant to cheat us," the giant shouts.

Frantically, I kneel and begin to unknot the rope binding the boat to the dock. It is wet and pulled tight, with some magic on it besides.

"Rangi," one of the goblins says to the giant. "We've made a deal."

The giant is very drunk, though, too drunk to bother with further negotiations. He grabs for the prince, who jumps back, out of reach. Tiernan shouts a warning, although I am not sure to which of them. The prince's expression has turned cold and blank.

Finally, I get the knot loose and the boat begins to drift free of the moorings.

I grab for Oak's shoulder, and he looks at me with empty eyes. For a moment, I don't think he knows me at all.

"Can you swim?" I ask.

He nods once, as though coming out of a dream. A moment later, he lunges.

Not to stab the giant, as I expect. Or me. He grabs my hairpin. Then, turning, he races for the water.

"Thieves!" yells a goblin as we jump off the side of the pier together.

I land with a splash and a yelp about two feet from the boat. I go under, sinking until my feet hit the mud, then kick off toward the surface.

When I bob up through the waves, I see the prince holding on to the wing of the carved cormorant. He reaches out his hand.

I paddle toward him, spitting out muddy water.

Behind us, the goblins are shouting. Tiernan ignores them as he hauls me up onto the deck. Then he reaches for Oak.

Enraged, the giant jumps down and begins to wade through the waves.

The prince stumbles to the mast and unfurls a cloth sail. As soon as it goes up—despite the afternoon not being all that windy—it billows and then fills. Whatever magic speeds us out to sea cannot seem to be called back by the goblins. In moments, we are well out of the giant's reach.

I lick salt off my top lip. Tiernan takes the tiller, steering us away from the shoreline. With a whistling noise, Titch comes flying out of the market, circling once before settling on the mast.

It is not long before we are out of sight of the pier.

Oak walks to the prow, wrapping himself in a cloak. Staring into the sea.

I remember the voyage to the isles of Elfhame on a much larger boat. I was kept below for most of the trip but brought up once or twice to breathe the salty sea air and listen to the calls of gulls.

*If you marry the boy,* Lady Nore told me, *you can't carve out his heart right away. I know how bloodthirsty you are, but you'll have to be patient.* And she laughed a little.

I nodded, trying to look as though I was bloodthirsty, and that I could be patient. Wanting anything that would let me sit a little longer in the sun.

I wasn't looking forward to murdering a boy I had never met, but by then I hadn't thought much of it, either. If that was what she wanted me to do and it would spare me pain, I'd do it.

It's hard to believe how swiftly I became unrecognizable to myself.

I wonder how Oak sees himself when he's about to fight. And then I wonder how he sees himself after.

"Wren," Tiernan says, pulling me out of those thoughts. "What can you tell me about where we're going?"

I cast my mind further through that painful blur of time. "The Citadel has three towers and three entrances, if you count the aerial one." I sketch them with a wet finger on the wood of the hull.

Tiernan frowns.

"What?" I ask. "I know the place as well as Hyacinthe."

"I was only wondering over the aerial entrance," Tiernan says carefully. "I don't think I've heard that before."

I nod. "I mean, it's not a proper *door.* There's an arched opening in one of the towers, and flying things come in through it."

"Like birds," he says. "Hyacinthe might have mentioned that was what he used."

"There were guards at all the gates but that one," I say. "Mostly huldufólk then. Maybe stick creatures now."

Tiernan nods encouragingly, and I go on. "The foundation and the first level of the Citadel are all black rock. The walls beyond that are ice, translucent in some places—often closer to transparent—and opaque in others. It's hard to be certain there will be anywhere to hide where your shadow won't give you away," I say, knowing this fact all too well. "The prisons are in the black rock part."

Tiernan fishes a piece of lead from his pocket. "Here, see what you can draw with this."

I sketch out the garrison gate and the courtyard in the center of the Citadel in dull marks on the wood deck.

I know the Citadel, know where Lady Nore sleeps, know her throne room and banquet hall. Hyacinthe might have been better suited to explain its current defenses, but I know the number of steps to the top of every spire. I know every corner that a child could hide in, every place she could be dragged out from.

"If I could get into her chambers, I could command her," I say. "Lady Nore won't have many guards with her there."

What Lady Nore will have, though, is ferocity, ambition, and no hesitation about spilling an abundance of blood. She and Lord Jarel hated weakness as if it were a disease that could be caught.

I imagine the bridle sinking into Lady Nore's skin. My satisfaction at her horror. The moment before she realizes the trap is sprung, when she still wears her arrogance like armor, and the way her face will change as panic sets in.

Perhaps I am more like them than I would care to believe, to find the image pleasing.

At that upsetting thought, I rise and go to the prow of the boat, where Oak sits, wrapped in a sodden cloak.

Wet locks of hair kiss Oak's cheeks and are plastered to his throat and the small spikes of his horns. His lips look as blue as mine. "You should put on dry clothes," he tells me.

"Take your own advice, prince."

He looks down at himself, as though surprised to find himself half-frozen. Then he looks over at me. "I have something for you."

I put out my hand, expecting him to return my hairpin, but it's the bridle that he places in my palm.

"Why?" I ask, staring.

"One of us has to hold on to it. Let it be you," he says. "Just come to the Citadel by our side, and try to believe, whatever happens, whatever I say or do or have done, that my intention is for us to all survive this. For us to win."

I want to trust him. I want to trust him so much.

My hand closes over the leather straps. "Of course I'm coming to the Citadel."

His eyes meet mine. "Good."

I let myself relax into the moment, into friendship. "Now what about my hairpin?"

He grins and hands it over. I smooth my thumb over the silver bird, then use it to pull back *his* hair, instead of mine. As my fingers skim over his neck, threading through the silk of his locks, he shudders from something I do not think is cold. I am suddenly too aware of the physicality of him, his long legs and the curve of his mouth, the hollow of his throat and the sharp point of his ears, where earrings once hung. Of the hairs hanging loose from my pin, falling across one light brown horn to rest on his cheekbone.

When his eyes meet mine, desire, as keen as any blade, bends the air between us. The moment slows. I want to bite his lip. To feel the heat of his skin. To slide my hands beneath his armor and trace the map of his scars.

The owl-faced hob takes off from the mast, startling us. I stand up too quickly, jolted into awareness of where I am. I have to grab the wooden wings of the cormorant to keep from pitching into the sea.

Tiernan is perhaps twenty feet away, his gaze on the horizon, but my cheeks heat as though he can read my thoughts.

"Wren?" Oak is looking at me strangely.

I head to the cockpit, ducking under the boom as I go. But even with distance between us, the longing to touch him persists.

I can only be glad Oak does not follow me but heads below to put on dry clothes. Later, when he makes his way to the stern, he wordlessly takes the tiller from Tiernan.

The faerie boat, blown by unseen winds, flies across the sea. We catch sight of mortal schooners and tankers, pleasure barges, and fishing skiffs. Heading north, we skim the edge of the Eastern Seaboard, passing Maine on one side and the isles of Elfhame on the other. Then we sail farther north, through the Gulf of St. Lawrence to the Labrador Sea.

Everything ought to be as it was before, except it isn't. Whenever my hand brushes Oak's as he passes me a piece of bread or a skin of water, I can't help but notice. When we sleep in shifts, one of us left to navigate by the stars, I am drawn to watching his face, as though through his dreams, I will learn his secrets.

Something is very wrong with me.

On the third day, as we eat, I turn to throw an apple core into the sea and notice sharks circling the boat. Their fins cut smoothly through the swells. This close to the surface of the water, even their long, pale bodies are visible.

I suck in a breath.

Oak puts a hand up to shade his eyes from the sun just as a mermaid surfaces. Her hair is as silvery as the shine on the waves.

"Loana," he says with a smile that looks only slightly forced. I remember her name. She is one of the girls he fell in love with, the one who wanted to drown him.

I glance at Tiernan, who is gripping the hilt of his sword, though it is still sheathed. I do not think a blade is going to be particularly useful here.

"You sent for me and I came, Prince Oak. And lucky that I did, for the Undersea has challengers on all sides as Queen Orlagh weakens, each of them looking for an edge. Soon I may be your only friend beneath the waves."

"The treaty with the land still stands," Oak reminds her.

"For now, beautiful one." Her hair floats around her in a silver halo. Her eyes are the bright blue of chipped beach glass. Her tail surfaces lazily behind her, slapping the water before slipping beneath it again. "It is said that Nicasia intends to have a contest and marry the winning challenger."

"Ah," says Oak carefully. "Fun?"

"Or perhaps she will call on the treaty." A shark swims to the mermaid, and she strokes its side. I stare in fascination. The jaws of the beast look as though they could bite the boat in half. "And once she has all the contestants in one place, let the land destroy them."

"Alas," says Oak. "The land is trying to remedy its own problems. Which is why I sought your help. We would like to be concealed as we travel over the seas so that we may arrive onshore undetected."

"You could travel more swiftly beneath them." Her tone is all temptation.

"Nonetheless," he says.

Her expression turns into a pout. "Very well, if that's all you will have of me. I shall do as you ask for the price of a kiss."

"Oak—" Tiernan begins, a warning in his voice.

I take a step closer to the prince, who is going down on his knees on the hull.

"Easy enough," Oak says, but there is something in his face that cuts against those words. "And no hardship."

I spot a rope attached to the mast. As the prince speaks, I push the end in Oak's direction with my foot.

He does not look down when it hits his thigh. He loops it around one arm stealthily as he bends toward Loana.

She reached up with her webbed fingers, cupping the back of his head. Pressing her lips to his. They must be colder than the sea, colder than mine. His eyes almost close, lashes dipping low. Her tongue is in his mouth. Her grip on him tightens.

I hate watching, but I cannot look away.

Then she yanks him toward her sharply, thrashing with her tail. The rope goes taut, the only thing keeping him from being pulled into the sea.

He scrambles backward onto the boat, breathing hard. His shirt is wet with sea spray. His lips are flushed from her kiss.

"Come with me beneath the waves," she calls to him. "Drown with me in delight."

He laughs a little shakily. "A compelling offer, but I must see my quest to its conclusion."

"Then I will hasten to help you get it done," she says, diving down and away. The sharks follow, disappearing into the depths. I can see the shimmer of a mist just at the edges of my vision.

"I hope it was worth nearly being dragged down to the bottom of the sea," Tiernan says, shaking his head.

"We're concealed from Bogdana and Lady Nore," Oak says, but does not look either of us in the eye.

At nightfall we sail past floating chunks of ice, landing on a wind-swept beach just short of the Hudson Strait. Oak pulls the sea craft high onto the black rocks. Tiernan secures a rope to keep it there when the tide comes in. They do not ask me to help, and I do not volunteer.

Above us, a waning moon shines down on my homecoming.

I recall the words from the puppet show, when the crow sang for his millstone. *Ca-caw, ca-caw. How beautiful a bird am I.*

# CHAPTER
## 13

Winds rake over the mountains, sinking into the valley with an eerie whistling sound. The late-afternoon sun shines off Oak's golden hair, almost as bright as the snow.

Thick cloaks hang heavily over our backs. Titch huddles in the cowl at the prince's neck, occasionally peering out to scowl at me.

Snow is seldom still. It swirls and blinds. It clings to everything, glimmering and glittering, and when a gust comes, it turns into a white fog.

And it stings. First like needles, then like razors. Tiny particles of ice chafe the cheeks, and even when they settle, they hide pitfalls. I take too heavy a step and plunge down, one of my legs sinking deep and the other thigh bending painfully on the ice shelf.

Oak leans down to give me his hand, then hauls me up. "My lady," he says, as though handing me into a carriage. I feel the pressure of his fingers through both our gloves.

"I'm fine," I tell him.

"Of course you are," he agrees.

I resume walking, ignoring a slight limp.

The Stone Forest looms in front of us, perhaps twenty miles off and stretching far enough in both directions that it is hard to see how we could get around it. Tall pine trees, their bark all of silvery gray. They grow out of the snow-covered plain, rising up like a vast wall.

As we move along, we come to a stake in the ground, on which a troll's head has been mounted. The wooden shaft lists to one side, as though from the force of the wind, and the entire top is black with dried fluid. The troll's eyes are open, staring into nothing with cloudy, fogged-over irises. Its lashes are white with frost.

Written on the stake are the words: *My blood was spilled for the glory of the Kings of Stone who rule from beneath the world, but my body belongs to the Queen of Snow.*

I stare at the head, the rough-cut flesh at the neck and the splinter of bone visible just beneath. Then I look ahead into the snow-covered expanse, dotted with curiously similar shapes. Now that I know they are not fallen branches or slender trees, I see there are a half dozen at least, with a grouping of three in one spot and the others spread out.

As I am wondering what they mean, the thing opens its mouth and speaks.

"In the name of our queen," it creaks out in a whispery, horrible voice, "welcome."

I step back in surprise, slip, and land on my ass. As I scramble to get up, Tiernan draws his sword and slices the head in two. Half the skull falls into the snow, scattering frozen clumps of blood large enough to look like rubies.

The thing's lips still move, though, bidding us welcome again and again.

Oak raises his eyebrows. "I think we ought to assume that our presence is no longer secret."

Tiernan looks out at the half dozen similar shapes. He nods once, wipes his sword against his pants, and sheathes it again. "It's not far to the cave. There will be furs waiting for us and wood for a fire. We can plan from there."

"When did you provision all of that?" I ask.

"When I came here for Hyacinthe," Tiernan says. "Although we weren't the first to use it. There were already some old supplies, from the time when the Court of Teeth and Madoc's falcons made camp nearby."

As we trudge on, I consider Tiernan's answer.

I hadn't really thought about the *timing* of Hyacinthe's abduction before. I'd known that he was in Elfhame for long enough to try to murder Cardan and get put in the bridle. That had to have predated Madoc being kidnapped.

But Hyacinthe being in Elfhame when the general was taken seems odd, coincidental. Had he helped Lady Nore? Had he known it would happen and said nothing? Has Tiernan more reason to feel betrayed than I knew?

The third head we pass is one of the Gentry. His eyes are black drops, his skin bleached by blood loss. The same message about the Kings of Stone that was on the troll's stake is written on this one.

Oak reaches out to touch the frozen cheek of the faerie. He closes the eyes.

"Did you know him?" I ask.

He hesitates. "He was a general. Lihorn. One of the cursed falcons.

He used to come to my father's house when I was young, to drink and talk strategy."

Mercifully, this head does not speak.

Oak shivers beneath his cloak. Tiernan is doing little better. The heavy wool of their wrappings offers them some protection from the freezing temperatures, but not enough.

The sun turns the ice scarlet and gold as we begin making our way up the side of a mountain. It's a craggy climb. We heave ourselves over rocks, trying not to slip. I find it hard going, difficult enough that I am silent with concentration. Oak clambers behind me, his hooves slippery on the ice. Tiernan's training keeps his steps light, but his labored breathing gives away the effort of it. The air grows colder the darker the sky becomes. Oak's breath steams as Tiernan shivers. The cold burns through the fabric of their gloves to stiffen their fingers, making them clumsy. I am unaffected, except perhaps a bit more alive, a bit more awake.

Gusts of wind whip sharp needles of ice against our cheeks. We edge along, barely able to see the path forward among the scrubby trees, rocky outcrops, and icicles.

The thought comes to me, unbidden, that I am looking at what I was made from. Snow and sticks. Sticks and snow. Not a real girl. A paper doll of a child, to play with, then rip up and throw away.

I was meant for the purpose of betraying the High Court. Never to survive past that. If I am the cause of Lady Nore's fall, it will give me all the more pleasure for her never having anticipated it.

The cave entrance is wide and low, its ceiling a pocked sheet of ice. I duck my head as I enter. The owl-faced hob darts from the prince's cowl, flying into the darkness.

Oak digs out a stub of candle from his bag. He places four around the room and lights them. Their leaping flames send shadows in every direction.

A confusion of supplies is piled in the back: shaggy bear pelts, boxes, a small chest, and stacks of wood that have been here long enough to be covered in a thin layer of frost.

"Interesting stuff," Oak says, walking over to the chest and knocking the side lightly with his hoof. "Did you open any of it when last you were here?"

Tiernan shakes his head. "I was in a bit of a rush."

He would have been with Hyacinthe—still a bird, before Oak removed the curse. Had he been caught then, caged? Had he ridden on Tiernan's shoulder, sure he was being saved? Or had he gone, knowing he would help Lady Nore abduct Madoc? I frown over that, since I recall him telling me how loyal he'd been.

Oak is peering at the lock on the chest. "Once, the Bomb told me a story about poisonous spiders kept inside a trunk. When the thief opened it, he was bitten all over. Died badly. I believe she was trying to dissuade me from stealing sweets."

Tiernan kicks the stack of wood with one snow-covered boot. The logs tumble out of formation. "I am going to make a fire."

I lift a fur and turn it inside out, brushing my hand over the lining to check for rot or bugs. There's nothing. No discoloration, either, as there might be from poison. The only odor it contains is the faint smell of the smoke used to tan the hide.

A few uniforms from the long-disbanded army are in a gray woolen heap. I shake them out and assess them while Oak tries to pry apart the rusty chest. "There *probably* aren't any spiders," he says when I look in his direction.

Inside is a waxed wheel of cheese and ancient rolls, along with a skin of slushy wine. He appears disappointed.

Again, I find myself studying his face. The curve of his smiling mouth and the hard line of his jaw. What he wants me to see and what he wants to hide. After a moment, I turn away, heading to the front of the cave, where Tiernan is striking an ancient flint against the side of his sword, hoping to get a spark.

I wonder how much it bothers him to be back here, alone.

"How long were you with Hyacinthe?" I ask, pulling out my twice-soaked matchbook and handing it over, though it might be useless.

Tiernan sighs. "We met the summer before King Eldred abdicated, at a late-night revel—not a Court one, the informal kind. I was still hoping to be chosen for a knight."

I frown, not sure what he means. "Aren't you a knight?"

Tiernan grins, as amused as I've ever seen him. "Me? No. I was trained for it but never got the chance."

I glance at Oak, more confused than ever. I don't know a lot about the process, but I was fairly sure it involved some member of a royal family tapping you on the shoulder with a sword. Surely, this mission alone was cause for that.

"I joined the Court of Shadows," he says, answering the question I don't ask.

"You're a spy?" I think my mouth might be hanging open.

"Who else would my sister choose for a guard?" Oak interjects from the back. "She has a great fondness for spies who wanted to be knights, since she was one herself."

"I wasn't then, though. I was young and hopeful and a little drunk." He smiles at the memory. "Hyacinthe was standing half in shadow, and he asked me if I knew anything about prophecies. I think he was *very* drunk.

"We got lost together in a hedge maze and spoke of the great deeds we planned on doing, like the knights of old. I thought his quest for revenge was impossibly romantic." His mouth twists, as though it hurts for him to remember that version of himself, or a Hyacinthe who hadn't yet chosen vengeance over him.

The fire catches.

"And here you are, doing great deeds," I say.

He half smiles. "Sometimes life gives us the terrible gift of our own wishes come true."

Oak has peeled the wax from the cheese in the chest. He sits beside us, chewing a piece of it and grimacing.

"It's *aged*," the prince says, as though that might be cause to recommend it despite the taste.

I rifle through his bag for a granola bar and eat that instead.

"Tell her the rest," Oak says.

At Tiernan's frown, the prince grins. "Yes, I've heard the tale before. *Many times*. But Wren has not."

"What Oak wants me to tell you, I suppose, is that Hyacinthe and I spent the better part of two years together, before he left with Madoc's army. We made the sorts of promises lovers make." There's a stiffness to his speech. Tiernan seems to be the sort of person who, the more deeply he feels a thing, the harder it is for him to talk about—although apparently he's told plenty to Oak. "But when Hyacinthe wanted me to commit treason with him, I couldn't.

"His revenge ought to be done, I thought. Prince Dain was dead. The High King did seem a bit of a fop, but no worse than Eldred. He disagreed. We had a big row, Sin declared me a coward, and I didn't see him for another year."

*Sin*? I force myself not to grin at the nickname he'd managed to keep quiet until now.

"Yeah, when he came back to kill you," Oak says, then turns to me. "Hyacinthe would have been traveling with the Court of Teeth, like the rest of Madoc's army. And would have fought in the Battle of the Serpent. *Against* Tiernan."

"We didn't see each other," Tiernan clarifies. "No less fight. Not until after."

I think about myself, under Oak's bed. I wonder if that's what he's thinking about, too.

Tiernan goes on. "In the prisons. I was part of the Court of Shadows by then, and they let me visit him. We talked, and I thought—well, I didn't know what would happen, or whether there would be any mercy, but I promised that if he was going to be put to death, I would save him. Even if it meant betraying Elfhame after all.

"In the end, though, all he had to do was repent. And he wouldn't so much as do that." Tiernan puts his head in his hands.

"He was proud," Oak says. "And angry."

"Was I supposed to be less proud?" Tiernan demands.

Oak turns to me. "So here's where falcon Hyacinthe goes to Tiernan, who could have fed him and in a year had him back, but..."

He refused him.

"I regretted it," Tiernan said. "So, when I heard he'd gone to the Citadel, I came here and retrieved Hyacinthe. Brought him to Elfhame. Persuaded Oak to break his curse. Whereupon I got my thanks when he tried to kill the High King."

"No good deed goes unpunished, isn't that what they say?" Oak breaks off another piece of the horrible cheese and attempts to spear it onto something to melt over the fire.

"He worried about you," I tell Tiernan. "Hyacinthe, I mean."

He looks over warily. "In what way?"

"He believes you've been ensorcelled by Oak."

Tiernan sniffs, annoyed.

Oak laughs, but it sounds more forced than delighted. After a moment, he speaks again. "You know, until this trip, I thought I liked the cold. One can dress extravagantly when there's no risk of sweating— brocades, gold trims, hats. But I am reevaluating."

I can tell that Tiernan is grateful to have the attention off him. Oak's silly words, his smile, all dare me to play along.

I roll my eyes.

He grins. "*You* have an understated elegance, so no need to worry about weather."

When it is time to sleep, Tiernan and Oak wrap themselves in bearskins. Oak drapes one over my shoulders. I say nothing to indicate that I don't need it, that I am never too cold. When we lie down by the fire, he watches me. The light dances in his eyes.

"Come here," he says, beckoning with a hand.

I am not sure I know the me who moves, who shifts so that I am resting my head against his shoulder. The me who feels his breath against my hair and the pressure of his splayed fingers at the small of my back. His feet tangle with mine, my toes brushing against the fur just above his hooves. My fingers are resting against his stomach, and I cannot help feeling the hard planes of him, the muscles and the scars. When I move my hand, his breath catches.

We both go still. Tiernan, close to the fire, turns in his sleep.

In the firelight, the prince's amber eyes are molten gold.

I am aware of my skin in a way I have never been before, of the slight movements of my limbs, of the rise and fall of my chest. I can hear the beat of his heart against my cheek. I feel as though I am shouting *kiss me* with every restless shift of my body. But his does not, and I am too much of a coward to do more than lie there and yearn until my eyes drift closed at last.

When I wake in the afternoon, it is to Tiernan dragging in the body of a deer. He butchers it quickly, and he and I eat charred venison for breakfast.

Oak washes the heart clean of blood and puts it into the reliquary while still warm. Once it's secured, the prince fiddles with the lock, setting it carefully shut and adjusting something inside to keep it that way.

Then we set off again, the prince and Tiernan wrapping bear fur over their cloaks for greater warmth. The Stone Forest is ahead of us, light shining off the trees where ice encases their branches.

"We can't go in there," I say. "The trolls must be working with Lady Nore."

"Given what we saw yesterday, I must admit you were right to suggest we circle around this stretch of woods," Oak says, staring into the trees and frowning.

Tiernan gives a half smile. "I congratulate you on this wise decision."

We veer off to the east, skirting the edge of the forest. Even from this distance, it appears remarkable. Trees of ice grow blue fruits the size of peaches, encased in a frozen crust. Some have fallen and split open like candy apples. Their scent is that of honey and spice and sap. The leaves of the trees give off a haunting sound not unlike wind chimes when the air blows through the branches.

The longer we walk, the more we realize we cannot get away from the Stone Forest. Sometimes it seems as though the woods itself moves. Twice, I looked up and found myself surrounded by trees. The drag of the magic reminds me of the undertow on a beach: a strip of calm, dark water that seems innocuous but, once it has you, pulls you far from land.

We walk throughout the day, fighting to stay beyond the edges of the forest. We do not stop to eat but, fearing to be caught by the woods, walk while chewing supplies from our packs. At nightfall, our march is interrupted by something moving toward us through the snow.

Stick creatures, enormous and terrible, huge spiders made of brambles and branches. Monstrous things with gaping mouths, their bodies of burned and blackened bark, their teeth of stone and ice. Mortal body parts visibly part of them, as though someone took apart people like they were dolls and glued them back together in awful shapes.

"Make for the forest," Tiernan says, resignation in his voice. His gaze goes to me and then to Oak. "Now."

"But—" the prince begins.

"We're not mounted," Tiernan reminds him. "We have no chance on foot, unless we can get to someplace with cover. Let's hope your mad plan was the right one after all."

And then we stop fighting the forest and plunge into it.

We race past an enormous black boulder, then beneath a tree that makes a tinkling sound as the icicles threaten to fall. When I look over my shoulder, I am horrified to see the stick creatures lumbering toward us, faster than I expected.

"Here," Oak says, beside a fallen tree half-covered in snow. "We hide. Wren, get as far underneath as you can. If they don't see us, perhaps we can trick them into passing us by."

Tiernan kneels, putting his sword in the snow beside him and motions for me to come. I crouch in the hollow beneath the tree, looking up at the spangled sky and the bright scythe of a moon.

And the falcon, soaring across it.

"They have eyes in the air," I say.

Puzzled, Oak follows my gaze, then he understands. "*Tiernan*," he whispers, voice harsh.

Tiernan rolls to his feet and takes off running in the direction of the creatures, just as the bird screeches. "Get her away from here," he calls back to the prince.

A moment later, a rain of ice arrows flies from the trees.

The shaft of one slams into the earth beside my feet, tripping me. I stop so short that I fall in the snow.

Oak hauls me up. He's swearing, a streak of filthy words and phrases running into one another, some in mortal languages and some not.

The monstrous creatures are closing in. The nearer they get, the more clearly I can see the roots writhing through their bodies, the bits of skin and unblinking eyes, the great fang-like stone teeth.

"Keep going," he tells me, and whirls around, drawing his blade. "We're almost to the Citadel. If anyone can stop her, it's you."

"I can't—" I start.

His eyes meet mine. "Go!"

I run, but not far before I draw my borrowed knife and duck behind a tree. If I do not have Oak's skill, at least I have ferocity on my side. I will stab anything I can, and if something gets close enough, I will bite out whatever seems most like a throat.

My plan is immediately cut short. When I step out, an arrow skims over my leg, taking skin with it. A twisted creature with a bow lumbers toward me, notching another arrow. Aiming for my head.

Only to have its weapon cut in half as Oak strikes from the side, slashing through the bow and into the stick thing's stomach. Its mouth opens once, but no sound comes out as Oak pivots and beheads it. The creature goes down in a shower of dirt, berries, and blood that scatter across the snow.

Oak's face is still, but the frenzy of battle is back in his eyes. I think of his father, the redcap, whom he plans to rescue, and of how the prince must have been trained. I wonder if he has ever dipped a cap in someone's blood.

More of the stick creatures come at him, with their claws and fangs and stolen flesh, their shining ice arrows and black-stained blades.

Oak might be a great swordsman, but it seems impossible that any one person could hold them all off. Nonetheless, he looks prepared to try.

His gaze darts to me. "Hide," he mouths.

I scramble behind the black boulder and suck in a breath. The Stone Forest is so full of magic that even that is dizzying. A pulse of enchantment echoes off the trees and branches, ferns and rocks. I had heard the stories, but it was another thing to be inside it, to feel it surround me. *The whole forest is cursed.*

Before I can stop it, I am drawn into the spell. I can feel stone all around, and pressure, and thoughts that flow like honey.

*Let me be flesh again. Me. Me.* Two voices boom, loud enough to cause me to cover my ears, even though I hear the words only in my mind. Their raw power feels like touching a live wire. This boulder was once a troll king, turned to rock by the sun, and its twin is somewhere deeper in the forest. Their curse has grown, expanding to encompass the entire Stone Forest. I can smell it in the pine and the split blue fruit, so potent that I cannot understand how I could have not known before.

Anticipation whispers through the trees, like an indrawn breath. Urging me on.

I reach into the root of the enchantment, knotted tightly through everything around me. It started with the original curse of all trolls, to be turned to stone in the sunlight. As the magic has weakened, the trolls in Elfhame turn back to flesh at nightfall, but this curse is from a time when the magic was stronger, when stone was forever.

That curse grew outward, feeding on the magic of the troll kings. Nourished by their anger at being trapped, now their curse imprisoned their people and their people's descendants.

I can feel the magic trying to bind me into it, to pull me into its heart the way the woods tried to envelop us. I feel as though I am being buried alive. Digging through dirt, ripping apart the hairy roots that attempt to encircle my limbs like snakes. But even as I pull myself free, the curse on the Stone Forest itself remains as sure as iron.

But now that I have its attention, perhaps I can give the magic another target.

*There are invaders,* I whisper in my mind, imagining the stick creatures as clearly as I am able. *They will take your people from you.*

I feel the strands of magic curl away from me with a sigh. And then the earth itself cracks, the force of it enough to throw me back. I open my eyes to see a fissure splitting along the ground, wider than a giant's mouth.

A few minutes later, Oak stumbles out from between two trees, frost-covered ferns crackling beneath his steps. A wind blows through the branches to his left, sending a scattering of bladelike pieces of ice plummeting into the snow. The prince is bleeding from a cut on his shoulder, and both the bear fur and his cloak are gone.

I push myself to my feet. My hands are scratched raw, and my knee is bruised. The wound where the arrow grazed my leg is throbbing.

"What happened?" I ask.

A bellow comes from the forest.

"This place," he says, giving the crack in the ground a wide berth. "Some of them fell into the earth as it opened. I cut a few apart. But there are still more. We have to keep moving."

He reaches for my hand.

I take his, and together, we dart between trees. "Have you seen Tiernan?"

"Not yet." I admire how thoroughly he is not letting himself think of any other possibility.

The prince stops suddenly. In the clearing ahead, an enormous spider creature of sticks and earth is shambling toward us.

"Come on," I say, but he lets go of my hand. "What are you doing?"

"There's only the one," he tells me, holding his needle-thin blade aloft.

The spider is enormous, half as tall as one of the trees. It looms over us. One is more than enough. "Oak!"

As he rushes at it, I cannot help thinking of what Tiernan said, about how Oak wanted to be a ship that rocks broke against.

The spider lunges, with snapping fangs that appear to be made from broken femurs. It comes down on the prince, who rolls beneath it, slicing upward with his sword. Dirt rains down on him. It swipes with a thorn-tipped leg.

My heart is beating so hard that it hurts.

Oak climbs up, *into* the creature. Into the weaving of branch and bone, as though it were a piece of playground equipment.

The spider flips onto its back, the thorns on its legs tearing at its own chest. It's ripping out its own insides to get to him. Oak strikes out with his sword, hacking at it. Pieces shred off. It thrashes and bites at the air as it pulls itself apart. Finally, what remains of it goes still.

Oak climbs out of the husk, scratches all down his arms. He grins, but before I can say anything, there is a sound behind me. I whirl as three tall trolls step out from between the trees.

They have light green skin, golden eyes, and arrows tipped in bronze pointing directly at my chest. "You brought those monsters from the Citadel here," one says.

"They followed us," I sputter.

They wear armor of heavy cloth, stitched with a pattern of sworls like the map to a hedge maze or a fingerprint. "Come with us and meet our speaker," says the tallest of them. "She will decide what to do with you."

"It's kind to invite a pair of strangers back to your village," says Oak, walking to us, somehow misrepresenting their intention without actually lying. "But we've lost a friend in your woods and wouldn't want to go anywhere without him."

The tallest troll looks as though he is on the verge of turning his request into an order. Then, from the darkness, a knife catches the moonlight as it is placed to the base of the shortest troll's neck.

"Let's point those weapons elsewhere," Tiernan says.

The tallest troll's eyes narrow, and he lowers his bow. So does the other. The third, knife to his throat, doesn't move.

"You seem to have found your friend," the troll says.

Oak gives him a slow, considering smile. "And are therefore left without a reason not to partake in your hospitality."

The troll camp is set in a large clearing, where buildings of stone and clay have been constructed around a massive bonfire. Sparks fly up from it, then fall as black rain, smudging whatever they touch.

The houses are cleverly and artistically made. The stucco-like clay has been sculpted into shapes—spirals and trees and faces, all in the same pale mud color, decorate the dwellings. High up on the walls, circles of mostly green and amber glass have been inset, creating the effect of stained glass windows. I draw closer and see that they are parts of bottles, and spot a few in brilliant blues and crimsons.

The scale of everything is intimidating. As tall as Oak is, the trolls are at least a head taller. Most are well over eight feet, with bodies that are green or the gray of the stone they become.

We're greeted by a troll woman, large and heavy of limb, who introduces herself as Gorga, the speaker of the village. She has an axe strapped to her back and her hair in braids tipped with silver clasps. She wears a skirt of leather, with slits up the sides for easy movement.

"You're hurt," she says, taking in our bedraggled appearance. "And cold. Stay the day with us, and we will provision you and guide you to your destination safely next nightfall."

That sounds like an offer entirely too good to be true.

Oak meets her eyes with great sincerity. "Your generosity appears boundless. But perhaps I could prevail upon you to tell me more about this place. And yourself."

"Perhaps," she says, looking pleased. "Share a cup of strong tea with me. I will give you some good black bread and honey."

I glance over at Tiernan. He gives me a half smile and a shake of his head, inviting me into his amusement at Oak playing the courtier. "Let's get something hot to eat and sit by the fire," he says, clapping me on my shoulder. "He doesn't need us."

We walk together, me limping a bit. A few young trolls bring us cups made of stone, heavy in my hands. They are full of a warm liquid that looks like tea but tastes like boiled bark. I sit on a rock near the firepit. The heat is such that the stones are warm.

I am on my second cup when Oak joins us, holding a honey sandwich that he takes apart to offer us each a slice. "The troll king, Hurclaw, is off courting, according to Gorga. She was rather cagey about who, exactly, he was intending to marry. She was also rather cagey about what would happen if we tried to leave."

"So we're prisoners?" I whisper.

He sighs. "We are indulging the fiction that we are not."

I take a bite of the sweetened black bread. Then I take two more, practically stuffing the thing in my face.

"For how long?" Tiernan asks.

Oak's smile is tight. "As short a time as possible. Let's all keep our eyes open. Meanwhile, Wren, maybe I can look at your leg."

"No need," I say, but he ignores me, rolling up the bottoms of my pants. There's blood, but it's truly not so bad. That doesn't stop him from asking for bandages and hot water.

Since I left the mortal world, no one cared for my wounds but me. The gentleness of his touch makes me feel too much, and I have to turn my face, lest he see.

An old troll man arrives carrying a wooden bucket full of water, sloshing over the lip when he moves. He has a patch over one eye and white hair in two long braids on either side of his head. In his ears, a half dozen gold hoops glitter.

"Let me take that," Oak says, getting up.

The troll man snorts. "You? You're little enough to take a bath in it, like a babe."

"Nonetheless," says the prince.

The old troll shrugs and sets the bucket down, indicating Oak should give it a try. He lifts it, surprising the troll.

"Put it on the fire to heat," he directs the prince. "It's for your lady."

Oak places it on the hook of the metal tripod over the flames.

The old man sits to watch it boil and takes out a roll of bandages from his bag, handing it over.

Oak kneels by my feet. He has dipped one of the bandages in the water and uses it to wipe off the blood and clean the cut. His fingers are warm as he wraps, and I try to concentrate on anything but the feel of his hands on my skin. "I worried you might have been poisoned back in the woods."

A troll child comes to sit next to Oak, saving me from having to answer. He shyly asks one question and then another; a second child comes over with more questions. Oak laughs as the kids compare the points of their ears with his, touch the small horns growing from his brow and the smooth keratin of his hooves.

"Grandfather," one of them says in a high, childish voice that belies his size. "Will you tell the prince a story?"

I was almost certain they knew who Oak was, but the confirmation does nothing to quiet my nerves.

"You want a story to pass the time, princeling?" the old troll man asks.

"I do love a tale," Oak says.

"Perhaps the story of the kings trapped in stone," I put in. "And the curse."

The troll man looks toward me, narrowing his eyes, then back toward the prince. "Is that truly what you want?"

He nods. The children's giggling has ceased, and I worry I have broken some taboo by asking.

He begins with no hesitation, however. "There are two versions of this story. In the first, the kings are fools. That's the story featured in songs we sang and plays we put on when I was a young man and given to laughter. When leaving the forest for longer than a handful of days seemed unimportant.

"They were supposed to be brothers, these troll kings. They shared power and riches peaceably for many years. Decked out in gold mined from deep in the earth, they had everything they wanted. That is, until they met a mortal boy, a goatherd, lithe of limb and with a face that ought to have been carved in marble. So comely that both the troll kings desired him above all others.

"He wasn't the sharpest knife in the drawer, but the pretty goatherd had a wise mother, and she told him that if he chose one of the brothers, the other would surely prefer him dead rather than see his brother have what he wanted. If the goatherd wanted to live, he had to be sure never to choose.

"And so, the goatherd and his mother came up with a clever plan. He offered his love to the troll king who could hurl the largest boulder. First one and then the other threw larger and larger rocks until they were exhausted and no one could tell who had won.

"Then the goatherd told them that whosoever could defeat the other in a game of wrestling would have his heart. And so the brothers fought each other all through the night, and when the sun came up, both were turned to stone, and the goatherd was free to give his love where he pleased."

I can imagine the funny play that might make, and how much it must annoy the cursed kings if they know about it. "What's the serious version?"

The old troll clears his throat, and there is a pride in his face that makes it clear that however he laughed over the first story in his youth, this is the tale he prefers. "It is similar in many respects. It still concerns two troll kings, but in this case, they were never brothers. They had always been enemies, engaged in a war that spanned many decades. After so much slaughter on both sides, they decided they would wager the war on a contest between the two of them. And so, they met on the field of battle and threw themselves at each other. They crashed back and forth, so evenly matched that as soon as one got a good blow in, the other would get the next. As morning came closer, there were cries from both sides to abandon the contest. But each troll knew that if he cried off, defeat would be his reward. And so, they held on to the last and became stone, locked in the embrace of battle.

"There is still one more variation. It is said that before they declared war on each other, they had been lovers whose passion for each other had turned to hatred, until their desire to best and possess the other was all-consuming." He smiles at me with crooked teeth.

I look over at Tiernan. He's staring at the fire as though he cannot help thinking of his own lover, now his enemy.

"You're a good storyteller," Oak says.

"I am *the* storyteller," says the old troll, as though the prince's praise is immensely inadequate. At that, he gets up and wanders off, taking most of the children with him.

"This forest is cursed," I whisper to Oak.

He frowns at me, probably thinking I mean it in the same vague way that everyone else has when they refer to the Stone Forest.

Tiernan rises, walking off. The story seems to have bothered him.

I hurry on speaking, words tripping over one another in my haste to get them out. "That's what the troll meant when he said *leaving the forest for longer than a day or two seemed unimportant.* Because there's something keeping them here."

"Then where's Hurclaw?" he asks.

I shake my head. "All I know is that if he isn't in the woods, then he must have found a way to stave off the consequences, at least temporarily. But I think that's why he wants to wake the old kings. Not because he's mad. Because it's the only way to end the curse."

Tiernan returns with bread and a soup of barley and onions. I see a few trolls skinning fallen reindeer and smell the cooking of freshly butchered meat. Music starts up, a rowdy tune.

There's a raucousness in the air that wasn't there before, the wild edge of revelry. The smiles of the trolls who look in our direction have a sharpness in them.

"We've been offered pallets for the night inside the speaker's home," says Oak carefully.

"That seems kind," I say.

"A fine way to put it," he says.

Tiernan is eating some of the reindeer meat, chewing on the bone. "We sneak out of here at first light," he says, his voice low. "That's when they can't follow lest they turn to stone."

We are interrupted by a handsome troll woman who comes over to the prince, laughing at how small he is and offering to braid his hair. Though it is not particularly long, he lets her, with a grin at me.

I remember his hands in my hair, combing out the tangles and braiding it, and feel a shiver all down my neck.

Just before dawn, the speaker arrives.

"Speaker Gorga," Oak says, rising. He has three little braids in the back, one coming undone.

"Let me conduct you to my home, where you can rest," she says. "Next nightfall, we will bring you safely across the snow to your destination."

"Generous," Oak says.

Tiernan glances around as we move through the village, alert to opportunities.

When we arrive at her house, she opens the door, beckoning us inside. A clay stove vents into the ceiling above and gives the place a cozy warmth. There's a pile of logs by the fire, and she adds more, causing the stove's embers to blaze up.

Then she waves us to a bed covered in furs of many sorts stitched together. I will have to hop to get up on it. "You may sleep in my bed tonight."

"That's *too* generous," Oak tells her.

"It is a small thing." She takes down a stoppered bottle and pours the contents into four little cups. "Now let us have a drink together before you rest."

She lifts her cup and throws it back.

I pick up mine. The herbal, almost licorice scent hits my senses. Sediment shifts in the bottom. I think of my fears that first night when Oak offered me tea. And I think about how easy it would be to put the poison at the bottoms of certain cups, instead of in a bottle, to make it appear we were all drinking the same thing.

I glance at the prince, wanting to give him a warning but unable to come up with a way to do so without Speaker Gorga noticing. Oak drinks his in a gulp and then reaches for mine, plucking it out of my fingers and drinking it, too.

"No!" I cry, but I am too late.

"Delicious," he announces, grabbing for Tiernan's. "Like mother's milk."

Even Speaker Gorga looks alarmed. If she had measured out the doses carefully, then the prince just drank three times what she'd calculated.

"Forgive my greed," Oak says.

"*My lord*," Tiernan cautions, horror in his face.

"Perhaps you would like another round?" Speaker Gorga suggests uncertainly, holding up the half-full bottle.

"I might as well, and the others have yet to have a taste," the prince says.

She pours more into the cups. When I look into the depths, there is sediment, but significantly less. The poison, whatever it was, was already in the vessels. Prepared ahead of us even entering the room.

I take mine and tip it against my teeth, but do not drink. I make myself visibly swallow twice. Across the table, Oak has gotten Gorga's attention with some question about the fruits encased in ice, and so I am able to drop my hand beneath the table and surreptitiously pour out the contents onto my cloak.

I do not look down, and so I'm not sure if I've gotten away with it. Nor do I dare look at Tiernan to see if he has managed something similar.

"Why don't I leave the bottle?" Speaker Gorga asks, putting it down. "Let me know if there is anything else you require."

"What more could we ever want?" Oak muses.

With a small, tense smile, she rises and leaves.

For a moment, we sit just as we are. Then the prince stands, staggers, and falls to his knees. He begins to laugh.

"Throw it up," Tiernan says, clapping Oak's back.

The prince manages to make himself retch twice into a stone bowl before slumping down beside it. "Don't worry," he says, his amber eyes shining too brightly. Despite the cold, sweat has started on his forehead. "It's my poison."

"What have you done?" I ask him, my voice harsh. When he only smiles dreamily, I turn to Tiernan. "Why would he do that?"

The knight appears equally horrified. "Because he is madder than the troll king."

I open and close drawers, hoping to find an antidote. There's nothing that looks even vaguely promising. "What was it? What does he mean, *his poison*?"

Tiernan goes over to one of the cups, sniffs it, then shakes his head. "I don't know."

"I was born with blusher mushroom in my veins," the prince says, the words coming out slowly, as though his tongue is not quite his own. "It takes a great deal of it to affect me for long."

I recall what he said the night he'd been poisoned with deathsweet. *Alas, that it wasn't blusher mushroom.*

"How did you know what it was?" I demand, kneeling beside him, thinking of how recently he'd had another poison in his blood.

"I was desperate," he forces out. "I was just so afraid that one of you...that *you*..." His words trail off, and his eyes seem to be staring at nothing. His mouth moves a little, but not enough for sound to come out.

I watch the rise and fall of his chest. It is very slow, too slow. I press my fingers to his clammy forehead, despair making everything feel as though time is speeding and crawling all at once.

Just thinking requires pushing through a fog of dread. *He knows what he's doing,* I tell myself. *He's not a fool. He's not dying. He's not dead.*

Tiernan looks up at the shadows changing in the bottle glass high above us. A pinkish, soft light filters through, showing me the anguish on his face.

Dawn.

He tries the door. There's no visible lock, but it doesn't open. Barred. And there are, of course, no windows through which sunlight might strike Gorga and turn her to stone. He throws his whole weight against the door suddenly, but it doesn't budge.

"This is her house, not normally a prison, so whatever is keeping us inside has to have been moved for that purpose," I say, standing, numbly working through the possibilities as I speak. I recall the heaviness of the door, the thickness of the wood. "It swings outward. She's probably put something against it."

"Does it matter?" Tiernan snaps.

I frown. "I guess not, since we should just take off the hinges."

He stares at me for a moment and gives a panicked, despairing laugh. "I am not going to live it down, you being the one to come up with that."

There are many things I don't know, but I know a great deal about imprisonment.

Tiernan takes apart the hinges with a knife, making quick work of them, while I wrap Oak in a too-large woolen blanket. Giving in to temptation, I brush his bronze hair back from where it has fallen over one eye. At my touch, he gives a shiver.

*See*, I tell myself. *Not dead.*

"We won't be able to carry him far," I warn, although that must be obvious.

Tiernan has pried the door off to reveal a massive boulder blocking our way. It's more round than square, though, and there are gaps along the sides.

"You're small. Wriggle through and find something to put him on—a cart, a sleigh, anything. I'll try to move him," Tiernan tells me.

"I'll be quick," I say, and wedge myself into the gap between the boulder and the outer wall of the house. By climbing up a little and moving slowly, I manage to ease my way out.

It is strange to find the troll village so quiet as golden light spills over it. Since Gorga is the speaker, I assume that she has more than most of the others, so I figure I ought to start my search with her place. I creep around the back of her house. A small stone-and-clay outbuilding rests near the edge of the clearing. When I wedge open the door, I see a sled inside, and rope.

*A sled.* Exactly what we need for Oak.

*He'll be fine, he'll wake in time to find his father, to be yelled at by Tiernan, and for me to...*

The thoughts of what I will do after he wakes fade at the scent of rot in the air. The cold tamped it down, but it is definitely coming from something nearby. I move past the sled, deeper into the outbuilding. Whatever is decaying seems to be inside a chest in the back.

It's unlatched and opens easily when I push up the lid.

Inside are clothes, armor, and other supplies. Swords. Arrows. All of them stained with gore, blackened by time. Things worn by victims who have come through this forest before. My heart thunders, imagining my own clothes among them along with Oak's glittering golden mail. Then, gritting my teeth, I stick my hand inside and fish around until I come up with a tabard that looks like the sort worn by Madoc's soldiers. Possibly it belonged to Lihorn, whose head we found staked out on the snowy plain. I manage to find clothing that reminds me of what the huldufólk who used to serve Lady Nore wore, some of them blood-spattered.

My heart races at the evidence of what's happened to other travelers. I heap a few onto the sled and pull it back to the house. Tiernan is standing in the snow, Oak leaning against him as though he's passed out after a night of too much wine.

"We need to *go*," I whisper.

Using the clothes for padding, we strap him to the sled. Tiernan drags it behind us as we creep out of the troll encampment as quietly as we are able.

As we get closer to the tree line, I feel the curse try to steer me the wrong way, to make my steps turn back toward the forest's heart. But now that I am aware, the magic has a harder time putting my feet wrong. I cut in front of Tiernan so that he can follow me. Each step feels as though I am fighting through fog until we hit the very edge of the woods.

I look behind me to see Tiernan hesitate, confused. "Are we—"

Behind him, on the sled, Oak's body writhes against the ropes.

"It's this way." I reach for Tiernan's gloved hand and force myself to take it, to pull him along with me, though my legs feel leaden. I take another step. And another. As we hit the expanse of snow, my breaths come more easily. I release Tiernan's hand and squat, sucking in air.

On the sled, Oak has gone still again. "What was that?" he asks, shuddering. He looks back at the woods and then at me, as though he can't quite remember the last few minutes.

"The curse," I say. "The farther we are from the forest, the better. Come on."

We begin moving again. We walk through the morning, the sun shining off the snow.

An hour in, Oak begins to mutter to himself. We stop and check on him, but he seems disoriented.

"*My sister thinks that she's the only one who can take poison, but I am poison,*" he whispers, eyes half-closed, talking to himself. "*Poison in my blood. I poison everything I touch.*"

That's such a strange thing to hear him say. Everyone adores him.

And yet, I recall him running away at thirteen, sure so many things were his fault.

I frown over that as we trudge on, bits of ice catching in my hair and on my tongue.

"You're tough, you know that?" Tiernan tells me, his breath clouding in the air. "And quick-thinking."

Perhaps this is his way of thanking me for guiding him out of the woods.

"Not just some rabid animal, unworthy of being your companion on a quest?" I counter, still resentful over him tying my ankle to the motel bed.

He doesn't defend himself. "And not hideous, even. In case you wondered what I thought, which I am fairly sure you didn't."

"Why are you saying all this?" I ask, my voice low. I glance back at Oak, but he is staring at the sky, laughing a little to himself. "You can't possibly care what I look like."

"He talked about you," Tiernan says.

I feel like an animal after all, one that's been baited in its den. I both dread and desire him to keep talking. "What did he say?"

"That you didn't like him." He gives me an evaluating look. "I thought maybe you'd had a falling-out when you were younger. But I think you *do* like him. You just don't want him to know it."

The truth of that hurts. I grind my sharp teeth together.

"The prince is a flatterer. And a charmer. And a wormer around things," Tiernan informs me, entirely unnecessarily. "That makes it harder for him to be believed when he has something sincere to say. But no one would ever accuse me of being a flatterer, and he—"

He bites off the rest because, there, in the distance, rising out of the snow, is the Ice Needle Citadel.

One of the towers has fallen. The castle of cloudy ice, like some enormous piece of quartz, was once full of spires and points, but many of them have cracked and splintered. The jagged icicles that were once ornamentation have grown into elephantine structures that cover some of the windows and cascade down the sides. My breath stutters. I have seen this place so many times in my night terrors that, even half-demolished, I cannot help but feel like I am in another awful dream.

Rays of sunlight strike the snow, melting an ice layer that freezes and re-forms every day. As I take a step, I feel the sheet break, a craquelure spreading from my feet.

This time, I do not fall. In that reflective, glittering brightness, though, it is hard to hide.

During our trudge toward the Citadel, Oak untied himself and crawled from the sled, declaring he was well enough, and then proved that his definition of "well enough" wasn't the same as "well," since he has spent the time since staggering along as though drunk.

Titch found us again, swooping low and settling on Tiernan's shoulder. The knight sent the hob off to scout ahead.

"Let's stop here," Tiernan says, and Oak collapses gratefully into the snow. "Wren has suggested we change clothes."

"I do appreciate your commitment to us looking our best," says the prince.

By now, I am used to Oak and do not think for a moment he doesn't understand the plan. I haul out the uniforms I stole from Gorga. For myself, with my bluish skin, I take the dress of one of the castle servants. Huldufólk, like Lady Nore, have gray skin and tails. My skin isn't quite right, and I have no tail, but its absence is hidden by the long skirts.

I wrap the bridle in a strip of cloth around my waist, then tie it on underneath the dress like a girdle. My knife goes into my pocket.

I change quickly. So does Oak, who shivers as he pulls rough woolen pants over his smooth linen ones. They hang low enough that his hooves look passably like boots when half-covered with snow. Tiernan shivers almost continuously as he pulls on the new uniform.

"You're still likely to be identified if anyone sees you close-up," I warn Oak.

He is the prince, after all, with hooves not unlike the former Prince Dain's.

"Which is why I should go in, not you," says Tiernan for what feels like the millionth time.

"Nonsense; if they catch me, they won't immediately put my head on a spike," Oak returns.

He's probably right. Still. "Yes, but they're *more likely* to catch you," I say.

"You ought to be on my side," he says, looking hurt. "I was poisoned."

"That's another good reason for me to go in your place," Tiernan puts in.

"Pragmatist," says Oak, as though it's a dirty word.

We get as close as we dare and then hollow out snow into a cavern to wait in until nightfall. Oak and Tiernan pull their hands and feet tight to their bodies, but the prince's lips still take on a bluish color.

I unclasp the cloak that I've been wearing and pass it to him.

He shakes his head. "Keep it. You'll freeze."

I push it at him. "I'm never cold."

He gives me an odd look, perhaps thinking of me lying with him by the fire, but must be too chilled to debate.

As they go over our plan one more time, I start to believe that this is possible. We get in, steal back Mab's remains, and leave with the general. If something goes wrong, I suppose we have the deer heart in the reliquary, but since Oak's bluff seems like a long shot, I hope we don't have to rely on it. Instead, I concentrate on remembering that I still have the power of command over Lady Nore.

And yet, as we approach the Citadel, I cannot help but recall being lost in this snow, weeping while tears froze on my cheeks. Just being here makes me feel like that monster child again, unloved and unlovable.

As night falls, Tiernan crawls out of our makeshift dwelling. "If you're going in, then at least let me be the one to go down and make sure all is how we expect it."

"You need not—" Oak begins, but Tiernan cuts him off with a glare.

"Wren ought to stay behind with the heart," Tiernan says. "If you're not planning on confronting Lady Nore, then it doesn't matter if Wren can command her, and Wren's no use to you in a fight."

"I could be useful in avoiding one," I remind him.

Oak does not seem moved by Tiernan's argument. "If she's willing to come, then she's coming."

Tiernan throws up his hands and storms off through the snow, obviously angry with both of us.

"I do think I may need you inside the Citadel," Oak tells me. "Although I wish that wasn't the case."

I am glad he wants me there, though I am no knight or spy. "Perhaps all three of us could go in," I venture.

"He needs to stay here, lest we get caught," Oak says. "He'll keep the heart with him and bargain for our return with it."

A moment later, Tiernan ducks his head back inside, the owl-faced hob on his shoulder. "You two can climb the side to the birdie entrance. Titch has been watching the patrol shifts, and they're sloppy. Makes it hard to know when they are going to happen, but there's a window of opportunity when they do."

Oak nods and pushes himself to his feet. "Very well, then," he says. "No time like the present."

"One more thing," Tiernan says. "There are trolls on the battlements, along with those stick creatures and some falcon soldiers."

"But I thought the trolls were trapped...," I begin, but trail off because there are so many possibilities. They could be trolls that do not come from the Stone Forest and are therefore not subject to its curse. But when I think about the heaps of clothing, and the mounted heads, I wonder if what we witnessed were the remains of sacrifices meant to appease the ancient troll kings to open the way from the forest.

*My blood was spilled for the glory of the Kings of Stone who rule from beneath the world, but my body belongs to the Queen of Snow.*

At that unsettling thought, I follow Tiernan and Oak out of our snow tunnel and into the frigid air.

We stay as low to the ground as we are able. In the dark, it's easier to approach the Citadel without drawing much attention to ourselves. At least until we see a great and horrible spiderlike construction of ice and stone, flesh and twig, lumbering through the night.

We hear a piercing scream, and I see that the spider has a huldu woman in its pincers. They are too far away for us to help her. A moment later, her screams cease and the stick-spider begins to feed.

"If that thing can eat," Oak says, "then it's truly *alive*. Not like one of Grimsen's ornamental creations with fluttering wings that move like clockwork. Not like that head on a spike, repeating the same message over and over. It hungers and thirsts and wants."

*Like me.*

Oh, I do not want to be here. I hate this place. I hate everything about it and everything it might teach me about myself.

Enormous braziers burn on either side of the Citadel gate. We wait in the snow until there is movement on the battlements.

Tiernan flips a knife in his hand. "I'll create a distraction at the garrison while you and the prince go up that wall."

This is my last chance to avoid returning to the place of my nightmares. All I have to do is tell Oak I changed my mind. Tiernan would be thrilled.

I think of Bogdana's words to me in the woods. *The prince is your enemy.*

I think about the feeling of Oak's breath against my neck, the way his fox eyes looked with the pupils gone wide and black. I think about how desperate he must be, to come all this way for his father, to gulp down poison, to risk his life on an uncertain scheme.

I think about the bridle wrapped around my waist, the one I tried to steal. The one he gave me to keep.

I have to trust him. Without me, we cannot command Lady Nore.

"We should go straight to the prisons," Oak says. "Get Madoc. Go from there."

"Better not," I tell him. "We don't know how hurt he's going to be, and we can move faster without him. If we get the reliquary, then we can free him and move him to the sled directly."

Oak hesitates. I can see the conflict between getting what he came here for and getting everything. "All right," he says finally.

"If you're not back by dawn," Tiernan says, "then you know where I will be with the reliquary." With that, he heads off through the snow.

"How exactly is he going to create a distraction?" I ask, attempting to walk with my head down, as though I am a servant who belongs to the Citadel and am returning from a dull errand—perhaps gathering crowberries. Attempting to behave as though Oak is a soldier walking me inside.

"Better not to ask," the prince says with a slight smile.

Up close, the outside of the Citadel is not a single piece of cloudy ice, but one composed of blocks, which have been melted smooth. Oak sticks his hand into his pack, and I recognize the grappling hook and rope from Undry Market.

He's eyeballing the spires, looking for the correct one.

"There," I whisper, pointing up.

The entrance, three stories above us, isn't visible when standing beneath it, as we are. It looks like an arch, the mirror of those that surround it.

"You ready?" he asks.

I'm not. When I think of Lady Nore, it's as though my mind becomes full of scribbles, blotchy and looping, scratching through all my other thoughts. I nod in answer, because I don't trust myself to speak when I have no ability to tell anything but the truth.

Oak throws the grappling hook. Built for ice, the sharp edge sticks in hard. "If I fall, you must promise not to laugh. I may still be a little bit poisoned."

I think of Tiernan and how exasperated he would be if he heard those words. I wonder exactly how much *a little bit* means. "Maybe I should be the one to go first."

"Nonsense," he says. "If you weren't behind me, then who would break my fall?" Then he grabs the rope, presses his feet to the side of the Citadel, and proceeds to walk himself up the wall.

I roll my eyes, grab hold, and follow far more slowly.

We stop at the edge of the tower, and he winds the rope and removes the hook, while I peer down into the chamber through the opening. I hear distant strains of music. That must come from the great hall, where the thrones sit, and where instruments strung with the dried guts of mortals, or ones inlaid with bits of their bones, had been played to the delight of the Court of Teeth. This sounds more like a lone musician, though, rather than the usual troupe.

As I look down, a servant rushes through, holding a tray filled with empty goblets that clatter together. Thankfully, they do not glance up.

I press my hand to my heart, grateful we weren't descending at that moment.

"This time you go first," Oak says, sinking the hook into new ice. "I'll cover you."

I think he means that if someone spots me, no matter if they are a servant or guard, he's going to kill them.

"They taught you a lot of things, your family," I say. The sleight of hand, the wall climbing, the swordsmanship.

"Not to die," he says. "That's what they attempted to teach me, anyway. How not to die."

Considering how often he throws himself directly into the path of danger, I do not think they taught him well enough. "What's the number of times that someone tried to assassinate you?"

He gives a one-shouldered shrug, his attention on the tableau below. "Hard to know, but I'd guess there were a few dozen attempts since my sister came to power."

That would be more than twice a year for every year since I met him. And that scar on his neck suggests that someone got very, very close.

I think of him as he was in the woods at thirteen, wanting to run away. Angry and afraid. I think of him lying on the sled this morning.

*I poison everything I touch.*

Every time I feel as though I know him, it seems there is another Oak underneath.

I shimmy down the rope, dropping when I am close enough to the ground not to hurt myself. My feet make a soft, echoing noise when they hit the floor, and I am struck by the nausea-inducing familiarity of the place. I spent not even two years here, and yet the very smell of the air makes me sick.

A massive bone chandelier hangs in the center of the room, candle wax dripping hot enough to melt indentations in the floor.

While the exterior of the Citadel is formed of giant slabs of clear, bright ice, some of the interior walls are enhanced by having things frozen inside the ice, resulting in something like wallpaper. Stones suspended, as though forever in midfall. Bones, picked clean, occasionally used to form sculptures. Roses, their petals forever preserved in their full flowering. This room's walls have two faerie women frozen inside them, preserved so that they never decayed into moss and stone, like the rest of the Folk. Two faerie women, dressed in finery, crowns on their heads.

The Hall of Queens.

I had never known that Lady Nore might have joined their number, if not for me. A fresh horror, on top of all the others.

I can't help feeling like a child again, with time seeming to dilate around me. Every hour, each day had felt endless, telescopic. The spaces were distorted in my memory, the halls shorter, the ceilings less high.

My wrists still show knots of skin where Lord Jarel pierced them to drive through the thin silver chains that leashed me. If I touch my cheeks, I can still feel, right underneath the bone, the marks of scars.

I do not realize how long I have been staring until Oak lands beside me, the clatter of his hooves louder than my soft-shod feet. He takes in the room, and me.

"Do you know the way from here?" he asks.

I give a quick nod and begin to move again.

One of the dangers of the Citadel is that the ice throughout varies in translucence, so there are places where movement is visible between rooms, or even through floors and ceilings. We could be semi-exposed at all times. Therefore, we must not crouch or attempt to hide. We must move in such a way that our faint outlines do not betray us.

I lead us into a hall, and then another. We pass a thin window of ice that looks out on the interior courtyard, and I glance through it. Oak pulls me back into shadow, and after a moment, I realize why.

Lady Nore stands outside, in front of sculptures of stick and snow. A line of ten, some in the shapes of men, some beasts, some creatures that are neither. Each one's mouth is filled with sharp, jagged icicle teeth. Each one has stones in place of eyes; a few have them pressed into sockets of flesh. I spot other horrible things: a foot, fingers, bits of hair.

From a bag, Lady Nore takes a little knife in the shape of a half moon. She slices her palm. Then she takes a pinch of bone gravel from a bag at her waist and smears it onto her bloody, open hand. One by one, she walks to the snow sculptures and presses those bits of bone, shining with wetness, into their mouths.

And one by one, they awaken.

They are like me. Whatever they are, they are *like me*.

And yet, these stick creatures seem like living puppets and little else. They stay in their neat rows, and when she orders them inside, they go obediently, as though they'd never had any other thought. But I do not understand why, if the magic of Mab's bones is animating these creatures, they are not conscious in the way that I am.

Although I may have been made from snow and sticks and blood, there is some difference that allows me to behave like a disobedient faerie daughter, when these creatures seem to make no choices at all.

But then I recall the spider hunting the servant and don't know what to suppose.

The sound of footsteps is the only warning before two guards turn the corner.

Oak puts his hands on my shoulders, pushing my back to the wall.

"*Pretend with me*," he whispers. And then he presses his mouth to mine.

A soldier kissing one of the serving girls. A bored ex-falcon attempting to amuse himself. Oak hiding our faces, giving us a reason to be overlooked. I understand the game.

This is no declaration of desire. And yet, I am rooted in place by the shocking heat of his mouth, the softness of his lips, the way one of his hands goes to the ice wall to brace himself and the other to my waist, and then to the hilt of my knife as they draw closer.

*He doesn't want me. This doesn't mean he wants me.* I repeat that over and over as I let him part my lips with his tongue. I run my hands up his back under his shirt, letting my nails trail over his skin.

*I have been trained in all the arts of a courtier.* Dancing and dueling, kissing and deceiving.

Still, I am gratified when he shudders, when the hand he was bracing with lifts to thread through my hair, to cup my head. My mouth slides over his jaw to his throat, then against his shoulder, where I press the points of my teeth. His body stiffens, his fingers gripping me harder, pulling me closer to him. When I bite down, he gasps.

"You there," says one of the soldiers, a troll. "Get to your post. If the lady hears of this—"

When Oak draws back, his lips are flushed red. His eyes look black beneath golden lashes. I see the marks from my teeth on his shoulder. He turns and drives a knife into the troll's stomach. The troll falls soundlessly as Oak turns to slash the other's throat.

Hot blood spatters the ice. Where it lands, steam rises and a constellation of pockmarks appear.

"Is there a room nearby?" the prince asks in a voice that shakes only a little. "For the bodies."

For a moment, I stare at him stupidly. I am reeling from the kiss, from the swiftness of the violence. I am not yet used to Oak's ability to kill without hesitation and then look chagrined about it, as though he did something in slightly poor taste. Spilled a rare vintage of wine, perhaps. Mismatched his trousers to his shirt.

Although I cannot be anything other than glad he killed them swiftly and soundlessly.

I lead him across the hall, into a strange little chamber for keeping supplies to clean and polish and provide for the needs of the Gentry in this part of the castle.

Inside, the frozen carcass of an elk hangs in one corner, slivers of meat cut off. On the opposite wall are wooden shelves, packed with linens, cups, glasses, and trays, as well as dried herbs that hang in bundles. Two barrels of wine sit on the ground, one opened, a ladle resting on the lip.

Oak drags both guards in. I grab up one of their cloaks and a table-cloth from the shelves to go back and mop up the blood.

As I do, I check to see if there are any translucent parts of ice through which anyone could have witnessed what happened. If they did, it would have appeared like a violent shadow play, and therefore not entirely unusual in the Citadel. Still, if someone was searching for us, it might be a problem.

I notice nothing to give us away, so I stash the soiled fabric back in the room. Oak has pushed the bodies into a corner and covered them with a cloth.

"Is there any blood on me?" he asks, patting down the front of his woolen shirt.

It was a fine spatter, and though it struck his clothes, the pattern is nearly invisible in the dark fabric. I find a little in his hair and wipe it off. Rub his cheek and just above the corner of his mouth.

He gives me a guilty smile, as though expecting me to take him to task for the kiss or the murders. I cannot guess which.

"We're almost to the stairs," I tell him.

On the landing, we spot two more guards on the opposite end of a long hall. They are too far to make out our faces, and I hope too far off to see anything inauthentic in our costumes. I keep my gaze straight ahead. Oak nods to one, and the guard nods in return.

"Brazen," I mutter under my breath, and the prince grins.

My hands are shaking.

We pass the library and the war room, then walk up another set of stairs. These spiral steeply for two floors until we come to Lady Nore's bedroom, at the very top of the leftmost tower.

Her door is tall and pointed at its apex. It is made of some black metal, frosted over with cold. The handle is a deer hoof.

I reach out my fingers, turn it. The door opens.

Lady Nore's bedroom is entirely new, the room washed in red. It takes me a moment to realize where the color is coming from. Viscera. The flayed-open bodies of Lady Nore's victims on display all around her, frozen inside the walls so that light could filter through them and give the room its odd, ruddy tint.

Oak sees it, too, eyes wide as he takes in the awful space. "Well, a reliquary full of bones can't be out of place among all this grotesque art."

I give him a grateful glance. Yes. That's right. All we need to do is find Mab's remains. Then we can escape with his father. And perhaps I will no longer feel trapped by the Citadel, no longer be frozen in my past, as though I were one of the bodies in the wall.

A large bed sits in the middle of the floor, the headboard and footboard of carved onyx in sharp, spear-like shapes. Over the cushions rests a coverlet of ermine. A brazier burns in one corner of the room, warming the air.

Opposite hangs a mirror with a black frame in the shape of intertwining snakes. Beneath that is a dressing table, with jewels and hairpins strewn across its surface. I find an inkpot and a golden comb in its drawers.

I expect everything here to be perfectly arranged, as it was in the memory of my childhood, but when I turn to Lady Nore's enormous wardrobe, built of ebony wood and inlaid with teeth from many beasts and beings, I see that several of her dresses lie on the floor. They are great, grand things in scarlet and shimmering silver, with droplets that appear like frozen tears. There are whole gowns of black swan feathers. But the closer I look, the more I notice the stains, the rips. They are as old as the broken towers of the castle.

The mess makes me suppose that Lady Nore readied herself quickly and without the help of servants. There is a desperation in all this that seems at odds with her sitting at the cusp of vast power.

Oak puts a hand on my arm. I startle.

"You all right?" he asks.

"When they first took me from the mortal world to the Court of Teeth, Lord Jarel and Lady Nore tried to be nice to me. They gave me good things to eat and dressed me in fancy dresses and told me that I was their princess and would be a beautiful and beloved queen," I tell him, the words slipping from my lips before I can call them back. I occupy myself with searching deeper in the closet so I don't have to see his face as I speak. "I cried constantly, ceaselessly. For a week, I wept and wept until they could bear it no more."

Oak is silent. Though he knew me as a child, he never knew me as *that* child, the one who still believed the world could be kind.

But then, he had sisters who were stolen. Perhaps they had cried, too.

"Lord Jarel and Lady Nore told their servants to enchant me to sleep, and the servants did. But it never lasted. I kept weeping."

He nods, just a little, as though more movement might break the spell of my speaking.

"Lord Jarel came to me with a beautiful glass dish in which there was flavored ice," I tell him. "When I took a bite, the flavor was indescribably delicious. It was as though I were eating dreams.

"*You will have this every day if you cease your crying*, he said.

"But I couldn't stop.

"Then he came to me with a necklace of diamonds, as cold and beautiful as ice. When I put it on, my eyes shone, my hair sparkled, and my skin shimmered as though glitter had been poured over it. I looked wondrously beautiful. But when he told me to stop crying, I couldn't.

"Then he became angry, and he told me that if I didn't stop, he would turn my tears to glass that would cut my cheeks. And that's what he did.

"But I cried until it was hard to tell the difference between tears and blood. And after that, I began to teach myself how to break their curses. They didn't like that.

"And so they told me I would be able to see the humans again— that's what they called them, *the humans*—in a year, for a visit, but only if I was good.

"I *tried*. I choked back tears. And on the wall beside my bed, I scratched the number of days in the ice.

"One night I returned to my room to find that the scratches weren't the way I remembered. I was sure it had been five months, but the scratches made it seem as though it had been only a little more than three.

"And that was when I realized I was never going home, but by then the tears wouldn't come, no matter how much I willed them. And I never cried again."

His eyes shine with horror. "I should never have asked you to come back here."

"Just don't leave me behind," I say, feeling immensely vulnerable. "That's what I want, for the game I won all those years ago."

"I promise you," he says. "If it is within my power, we leave together."

I nod. "We will find the reliquary and ruin her," I tell him. "And then I will never come back."

But as we open drawers and comb through Lady Nore's belongings, we find no bones, no magic.

"I don't think it's here," Oak says, looking up from a box he's poking through.

"She might keep it in the throne room," I venture. Even though we must go down steps again and slip past guards, I will be glad to be out of this terrible room.

"My father might know where it's kept," he says. "I know you don't think—"

"We can try the prisons," I say reluctantly.

As I turn to give the chamber one last look, I notice something strange about her bed. The base of it is ice, and I am sure there's something frozen *in* it. Not red but ivory and brown.

"Oak?" I say.

He turns, looking in the direction that I am. "Did you find something?"

"I'm not sure." I walk across the floor. Pushing back the covers, I see three victims frozen there. Not taken apart, like those in the walls. I cannot even tell how they died.

As I stare, one, impossibly, opens his eyes.

I shrink away, and as I do, his mouth parts and out comes a sound that is half moan and half song. Beside him, the other two awaken and begin to make the same noise, until it rises in a ghostly chorus.

Sounding an alarm.

Oak grabs my shoulder and pushes me out the door. "A trap," he says. "Go!"

I run down the stairs as fast as I am able, half-slipping, my hand bracing on the wall. The clatter of Oak's hooves is right behind me.

We make it to the second landing before ten guards appear— ex-falcons, huldufólk, nisser, and trolls. They fan out in a formation around us, weapons drawn. Oak's back presses against mine, and I hear the rattle of his thin blade pulling free from its sheath.

# CHAPTER
# 15

O ak kills two trolls and a nisse before another of the trolls gets a knife to my throat.

"Halt," he calls, pressing the blade down hard enough to sting. "Or the girl dies."

For a moment, the prince's eyes are so blank that I don't know if he can hear the words. But then he falters, letting his blade sag. He looks as though it was a fight to come back to himself.

None of them get too close, even then. Blood still drips from that needle-thin blade of his. They'd have to step over the bodies of their comrades.

"Throw down your sword," one of the other soldiers calls to him.

"Vow she won't be harmed," Oak says, breathing hard. "Also me. I would like not to be harmed as well."

"If you don't drop that blade, I'll cut her throat and then yours," the troll threatens. "How's that for a promise?" He's so close to me that I can smell the leather of his armor, the oil on his knife, and the stink of dried blood. I can feel the heat of his breath. The arm across my neck is as solid as stone.

I try to think past my panic. My own knife is still in my hand, but the troll has gripped the wrist holding it.

I could bite his arm, though. My sharp teeth could rend even a troll's flesh. The shock of pain would either cause him to cut my throat or loosen his grip. But even if I was lucky, even if I could use that moment to slip out of his hands and run to Oak, what then? We'd never make it out of the Citadel. We would most likely never make it out of this hall.

The prince's sword dangles from his fingers, but he doesn't let it drop. "I was invited here and instructed to bring Mellith's living heart to your lady. I think she would be extremely disappointed to find you'd robbed her of her prize. Dead, I can hardly give it to her."

A shudder goes through me at the thought of Lady Nore getting what she wants, even though I know this is a game, a con, a hustle. Oak doesn't really have Mellith's heart. The danger lies in her seeing through his deception.

And it doesn't matter if it gets me into the room. All I need is to be able to talk.

Oak goes on. "You've almost caught us. You have to make only one small concession, and I will go with you, docile as a lamb."

"Throw down your blade, prince," says one of the ex-falcons. "And no harm will come to either of you by our hands while we escort you to the throne room. You can beg for Lady Nore's mercy and explain why, were you invited to the Citadel, we found you running from her bedchamber."

Oak lets the sword fall. It clatters to the floor.

One guard wrenches the knife out of my hand, while another takes a skein of rope and winds it between my lips, knotting it at the back of my head. As they push me along, I try to chew it apart, but though my teeth are sharp, I am bound well enough that we reach the throne room with the rope still in my mouth.

They have not bound the prince, but he walks surrounded by drawn blades. I cannot tell if that is meant as a sign of respect for his person or if they don't want to take their chances by getting too close.

All I know is that I must find a way to *speak*. Just a few words and I will have her.

The troll pushes me before Lady Nore so that I fall on my hands and knees.

She rises from her seat at a long, food-laden table. We have interrupted her banquet.

Lady Nore's white hair has been tied up on her head in a complicated arrangement of plaits, although a few have come down. Her gown is an opulent confection of black feathers and silver fabric that deepens to black at the floor. Ex-falcons crowd around her, formerly loyal soldiers to the Grand General of Elfhame, now hers to command.

When I look at her, I am filled with the same hate and fear that paralyzed me throughout my childhood.

And yet, there is fresh madness in her yellow eyes. She is not the same as she was when I saw her last. And disturbingly, I see myself in her. Resentful, and trapped, and full of thwarted desire. The worst parts of me, and all my worst potential.

New also are the two gray hands that she wears as a necklace. Horrifyingly, I see the fingers move as though alive, caressing the hollow of her throat. More horrifyingly, I suspect them to have once belonged to Lord Jarel.

Behind her, on a pillar of ice, is the cracked reliquary that must contain the bones and other remains of Mab. Strangely, tendrils, like roots, grow from the case, one with a bud on it, as though flowering.

On Lady Nore's left side sits a troll with a crown of beaten gold and a mantle of blue velvet stitched with silver scales. His clothing is leather, richly worked, with a pattern that reminds me of those we saw in the Stone Forest.

Hurclaw, who has somehow evaded the curse of the Stone Forest. Who has brought his people to help guard the Citadel. But why throw in his lot with Lady Nore? If what Oak got from Gorga was correct, Hurclaw is here to *court* her. If so, perhaps her power makes for a compelling dowry.

He and his trolls make up the majority of those seated, along with two huldufólk ladies, and Bogdana. She is in her usual ragged black robes, her hair as wild as ever. When she sees me, a strange gleam enters her eyes.

On the table before all of them are silver plates and goblets of ice filled with black wine from the night-blooming fruit of the duergar. Black radishes, soaked in vinegar and cut into thin slivers to show off their pale insides. Trays of snow drizzled with honey so that the honey freezes and can be lifted and eaten like a cracker. Jellied meat, with an uncomfortable resemblance to the walls of the Citadel with things frozen inside.

A single musician plucks at the strings of a harp.

Despite the feast, and the guards, and stick soldiers standing at attention along one wall, the room seems empty by comparison with what it was once like, when Lord Jarel was alive. There ought to have been tables filling the hall, with guests to make toasts. Cupbearers. Entertainers. A court shaped entirely to Lady Nore's whims. Have they all fled?

She looks past me, to Oak. "Heir to Elfhame, let's skip through the unpleasantness. Have you brought me Mellith's heart?"

Her guards are still tensed for the possibility of violence.

"I would hardly come here empty-handed with my father's life in the balance," Oak says. His gaze moves from the severed hands at her throat to the troll king.

I gnaw at the rope in my mouth, my desperation mounting. In a moment, she will ask him a question he cannot answer. I must speak. If I can speak, then I can still get us out of this.

But with Hurclaw's soldiers all around us, there is a new danger. If he guesses I can control her, he will order me shot.

"So you *do* have it?" says Lady Nore. "Unless you failed your quest, little prince."

My heart speeds. My sharp teeth are working through the rope, but I won't sever it in time to stop him from having to answer. This plan seemed risky, but now it seems doomed.

"Let me say it in full so you will not worry over being deceived," Oak says. *"I have brought Mellith's heart."*

I am stunned enough to stop chewing. The prince can't say that. His mouth shouldn't be able to form those words. He's one of the Folk. He cannot lie any more than the rest of us.

And yet, I saw the deer carcass cut open, watched him buy a reliquary from the smiths. I know it is no ancient heart he brought to the Citadel.

*Try to believe, whatever happens, whatever I say or do or have done, that my intention is for us to all survive this.* That's what he said to me on the boat. Was this what he meant? Was he willing to give away Mellith's heart if it meant we all lived?

If he *did*, and the deer heart was for the purpose of deceiving *me*, then he is about to hand over immense, terrible power to Lady Nore. The kind of power with which she could threaten Elfhame. With which she could carve up the mortal world that she despises.

And I have no way to stop him.

"Where is it, then?" Lady Nore asks, a snarl in her voice.

Oak does not flinch. "I may have it, but I am not so foolish as to have it on me."

Lady Nore scowls at him. "Hidden? To what purpose when you must hand it over to get your father?"

He shakes his head. "I would watch him leave, along with Wren, before I gave you anything."

She frowns, studying him. Her gaze flicks to me. Then she laughs. "I could quibble, but I can be magnanimous in my victory. How about I turn Madoc out of the prisons and into the snow right now? I hope he does well with cold, since I fear the clothing he is wearing is quite thin. And unfortunately, some of my creatures hunt the lands around the Citadel."

"That would be unfortunate, for all of us," Oak says. However firm he manages to keep his voice, he looks young, standing in front of her and Hurclaw. I worry that this is a game he cannot possibly win. "But I have an alternate proposal. Tomorrow night, my representative will meet us three leagues from here, near the rock formation. You will bring Madoc, me, and Wren. There, we can make the exchange."

"So long as you understand you won't be part of it, Greenbriar child. You are to remain here, in the Citadel, until I am done with you."

"And you're planning on doing what exactly? Making me a hostage to get some concession from my sister?"

"And not from the High King?" Lady Nore asks. She walks around the table, toward us.

Oak scowls, clearly confused. "If you like. Either one."

"They say that sister of yours has trapped him in some bargain." Lady Nore's words are light, but I can see that underneath it, nothing must have galled her as much as being outmaneuvered by a mortal. If anything other than the death of Lord Jarel has driven her mad, it's that. "Why else marry her? Why else do whatever she wants?"

"She's going to *want* to wear your skull for a hat," Oak warns. There is an uncomfortable shifting among the ex-falcons. Perhaps they are recalling their own choice to denounce her, their own punishment. "And Cardan is going to laugh and laugh when she does."

Lady Nore curls her lip. "Three things I need. Mab's bones, Mellith's heart, and Greenbriar blood. And here I am with two, and the third so close that I am able to taste it. Do not fail me, Prince of Elfhame, for if you do, your father will die and I will still get what I want."

Oak raises both eyebrows. However he actually feels, his ability to make himself seem unimpressed is immensely satisfying.

Lady Nore goes on, as though thrilled to have someone to whom she can deliver this speech. "Were it not for your father's weakness, we might have won the war against Elfhame. But I have a truer ally now and vast power. I am ready for revenge."

"King Hurclaw," Oak says, his gaze going toward the troll king. "I hope that Lady Nore hasn't promised you more than she can give."

A small smile quirks a corner of his mouth. "I do as well," he says in a deep voice.

Lady Nore scowls, then stands and walks to me. Oak's jaw tightens. His hand fists at his side.

"I suppose the prince thought that *you* could stop me." A terrible smile curls on her lips as she touches the frayed rope pressed between my teeth like a bit. "Little did he know what a sniveling creature you are."

I hiss, low in my throat.

To my surprise, she begins to loosen the cords I've been chewing. I part my lips the moment they fall away, desperate to speak. I am about to blurt out the stupidly unspecific *I command you to surrender.* But before I can get words out, she presses a petal into my mouth. I feel a twisting, worming sensation on my tongue. Whatever it is seems to move on its own, and I grit my jaw. The thing snakes around for another moment, then settles.

She lets go of the rope, smiling maliciously.

I shudder but finally can speak. I try to get the words out, but my tongue moves without my volition. "I renounce—" I begin to say before I slam my teeth down, trapping it painfully between them.

Lady Nore's awful smile grows. "Yes, my dear?"

Somehow she's woven a spell of control into the petal, no doubt plucked from the vine of the reliquary, where it grew impossibly from dry bones. If I try to speak, I will give up dominion over her.

I bite down harder on my tongue, to still it. It wriggles in my mouth like an animal.

"Bogdana told me how you lived," she says. "In your wretched little hut, at the edge of the mortal world, scavenging for scraps as though you were a rat."

I cannot reply, and so I do not.

There is a flicker of unease in Lady Nore's eyes. She glances toward Bogdana, but the storm hag is watching me from her place at the table, her expression unreadable.

"You dull little thing, open your mouth. I can give you what you most desire," Lady Nore snaps.

*And what is that?* I would ask were it safe for me to loosen my tongue. Instead, I keep it clamped between my teeth.

"I cannot make you human," she goes on. "But I can come very close."

I can't say part of me doesn't wish that were true. I think of the phone call, of how much easier it would be to slip into that old life if it didn't mean hiding or lying, if I didn't have to worry over them screaming at the sight of me.

She is still smiling as she walks to me and puts a finger against my chin. "I can put a glamour on you strong enough that not even the King of Elfhame is likely to see through it. I have the means to do that now, the power. I can make you forget the last nine years. You will return to the mortal world an empty vessel, free for them to project humanity on. They will decide that you were kidnapped, and whatever was done to you was so terrible that you blocked all memory of it. They won't press. And even if they do, what does it matter? You will believe every word you tell them."

I flinch away from her hand.

My greatest wish, the deepest desire of my heart. It infuriates me how well she knows me, and yet how she holds back every last mote of the comfort I so desperately crave.

Her yellow eyes study my face, trying to determine if I am hers yet.

"Are you thinking about the prince? Oh, do not suppose I don't know where you were when your own people died in the Battle of the Serpent. Hiding under that boy's bed."

My gaze is flat. I was a child, and I got away from her. I refuse to feel anything but glad about that. *He wanted me there*, I would say if I could speak. *We were friends. We are friends.*

But I can't help thinking about Mellith's heart, about what he told me in the boat.

*. . . whatever I say or do or have done . . .*

"Do you think he will protect you now? You're *useless*. The heir to Elfhame has no reason to spend any further time with an untutored savage of a girl. But think, you wouldn't have to remember him. You wouldn't even have to remember yourself."

"I'm not half as practical as you suppose," Oak says. "I like many useless things. I've been called useless myself from time to time."

Lady Nore doesn't turn her eyes from me, even when I give a little, unexpected laugh that almost makes me release my teeth's grip on my tongue. Lord Jarel's hands tighten on her shoulders as though in response to her mood. "His kindness will evaporate as soon as you need it. Now, child, will you take the bargain and trouble me no more? Or will you force me to deal with you more harshly?"

I imagine giving up. No more peering through windows, mourning the loss of a life that could never again be mine. No more hopeless desire. No more uncertain future. No more terror. Let her have Mellith's heart and Mab's bones. Let Elfhame rot and the Prince of Elfhame rot with it. Let her raze whatever parts of the mortal world she chooses. What would I care when I couldn't remember any of it?

I think of the Thistlewitch's words. *Nix Naught Nothing. That's*

*what you are.* That's what I would be. I would be consigning everything I've been, all I've learned and done to meaninglessness. I would be
accepting that I don't matter.

I spit in Lady Nore's face. The spatter is bright with my blood
against her gray skin.

She curls her lip and raises her hand, but does not strike me. She
stands there, shaking with fury. "You bite your tongue to spite me?
Well, I will lesson you. Guard, cut it out of her mouth."

One of the hulderfólk comes forward, taking hold of my arms. I kick
and claw, fighting as I never have before.

*"No!"* Oak struggles, but two ex-falcons grab him. "If you hurt her,
you can't expect me to just turn over—"

Lady Nore whirls toward him, pointing a finger. "Tell me where
Mellith's heart is *this moment*, and I won't cut out her tongue."

Three more guards help subdue me. I twist against their grip.

Oak lunges for the troll nearest to him and grabs her sword, drawing it from the sheath. The prince is still surrounded, but now he is
armed. A few hulderfólk and nisser draw bows.

Hurclaw waves his hand. "Show the boy it is no use," he says.

"Come forward, my creations," says Lady Nore, and the soldiers of
sticks and mud and flesh stride across the floor of the great hall. The
guards step back, letting the creatures take their places.

"Seize him," says Lady Nore.

The stick soldiers rush at Oak without hesitation. He slashes one,
cutting it in half, and then whirls to stab another. His sword sinks in
deep to the branches of the thing's body. It continues to come forward,
then twists aside, trying to wrench the sword out of Oak's hand with
the force of its own movement, even as doing so is tearing it apart.

Oak pulls the blade free, but three more throw themselves on it so a fourth can grab him around the throat.

This time the guards bind his hands behind his back with a silver cord.

When he meets my eyes, his expression is anguished. He cannot help me.

I fight as they press me down to the floor. Bite when they try to pry open my mouth.

But it's all for nothing. Two soldiers hold my wrists, and a third hooks a barbed instrument through the end of my tongue. He pulls it taut.

Then a fourth begins slicing through it with a curved dagger.

The sharp, searing pain makes me want to cry out, but I cannot with my tongue nailed in place. My mouth goes from dry from being held open to full of blood. Flooded with it. Gagging. Drowning. I choke as they release me, the scream dying in my throat.

Scarlet flows over my chin. When I move, flecks of red fly.

The pain swallows me whole so that I barely can concentrate, but I know I am losing too much blood. It spills from between my lips, slicks my neck, stains the collar of my dress. This is going to kill me. I am going to die, here on the ice floor of the Citadel.

Lady Nore takes a slow walk around my crumpled body. She takes another small piece of bone from her bag and presses it against my lips, then past my teeth. I can feel the wound closing. "You might not think so, but this is for the best. As your mother and your sworn vassal, I must trust my own wisdom in the absence of direct orders."

Blood loss and shock have made me dizzy. I feel light-headed. I stagger to my feet and think very seriously about sitting back down. Think very seriously about collapsing.

Since she cannot lie, in some twisted way, Lady Nore must truly believe that what she wants is what I *ought* to want.

Still, I do not need a tongue for her to read the rage in my eyes.

Her lips turn up at the edges, and I see that she isn't so different from before. She doesn't want me dead, because once dead I can no longer suffer.

"The prince doesn't even know what you are," she says with a glance toward Oak. "Barely one of the Folk. Nothing but a manikin, little more than the stock left behind when a changeling is taken, a thing meant to wither and die."

Despite myself, my gaze goes to Oak. To see if he understands. But I cannot read anything but pity on his face.

I might be only sticks and snow and hag magic, but at least I did not come from her.

I am no one's child.

That makes me smile, showing red teeth.

"My lady," says King Hurclaw. "The sooner Prince Oak sees his father released, the sooner we will have what we want."

Lady Nore gives him a narrow-eyed look. I wonder if the troll king realizes how awful she can be, and if he isn't careful, how awful she will be to him.

But for now, she obediently waves at the guards. "One of you, lock her in the dungeon, wicked child that she is, that she may think on her choices. Prince Oak and I have much to discuss. Perhaps he will join us at the table."

One of the ex-falcons comes to stand behind me. "Move."

I begin to walk unsteadily toward the doors. The throb of my tongue in my mouth is horrible, but the bleeding has ebbed. I am still drinking saliva that tastes like pennies but no longer feeling as though I am drowning in it.

"I would say that you lost yourself along the way, but you lost yourself far before that," the storm hag tells me as I pass her. "Wake up, little bird."

I open my mouth, to remind her that what I've lost is my *tongue* and perhaps my hope.

She grimaces, and for a moment, a fresh wave of fear and dizziness passes over me. It must be very bad to make Bogdana wince.

"*Move*," the guard repeats, shoving between my shoulder blades.

It's not until we make it to the hall that I glance behind me. Up into the purple eyes of Hyacinthe.

# CHAPTER

# 16

For a moment, we just stare at each other.

"I told you it would be wise to send me here, and since you gave me no commands to contradict it, I came," Hyacinthe says, low, so only I can hear.

I cannot speak. Staggering a little, I lean against the wall. The pain is hard to think past, and I am not sure if he is on my side or not.

"Be glad I did," he says, swinging his spear toward me, the point inches from my throat. "Folk are watching. Move."

I turn my back on him and walk. He makes a show of shoving me into going faster, and I do not have to pretend to stumble.

Several times, I try to turn, to catch his eye, so I can read the intention there, but each time he pushes me so that I must resume walking.

"Is Tiernan with you?" he asks when we reach the prison gate.

Loyal, that's what Hyacinthe called himself. Loyal to Oak's father. Hopefully loyal to me. Maybe loyal to Tiernan, too, in a way. Hyacinthe didn't trust Oak's honey-tongued charm. Maybe he wants to save Tiernan from it.

I nod.

Together we march down the icy passageways, to the prisons. Dug down into the frozen ground, they stink of iron and wet stone. "He's the one with Mellith's heart?"

A dangerous question. Given Hyacinthe's dislike of Oak, I am not sure whether he would like to see Lady Nore get what she wants or not. Nor am I sure *what* exactly Tiernan has. Also I am finding it hard to concentrate with the pain in my mouth.

Since I can't figure out a way to communicate any of that, I shrug and gesture toward my lips.

He frowns, frustrated.

The cells are largely empty. When I lived in the Citadel, they were teeming with those who had displeased Lord Jarel and Lady Nore—bards who chose ballads that offended, presumptuous courtiers, servants who made errors large and small. But now, as understaffed as the castle is, there is only one other prisoner.

Madoc sits on a wooden bench, leaning against the stone wall, far from the bars, which stink of iron. His leg is bandaged in two places, hastily and poorly, as though he was the one who did it. There is a cloth over one of his eyes, a little blood seeping through the fabric. His green skin looks too pale in the flickering lamplight, and he's shivering. He's probably been uncomfortably cold for weeks.

Hyacinthe unlocks a cell beside the general's and ushers me inside. I enter, careful not to let my skin touch the iron bars.

"I will get you out of here," he whispers to me as I slip by him.

"When things are prepared, you will be given a key. Meet me in the alcove across from the great hall. I have a horse."

I look a question at him.

He sighs. "Yes, that creature. Damsel Fly. Despite her pretty name, she's fast and sure-footed."

And then he closes the door. I am grateful he didn't bother to search me, didn't discover the bridle banded around my waist, beneath my servant's uniform. I am not certain what he would do with it.

I head for a bench, a sudden feeling of light-headedness making me worry that I will fall before I get there. Though I am not still bleeding, I lost a lot of blood.

Hyacinthe's gaze flickers toward Madoc, and he looks pained. "Are you well, sir?"

"Well enough," the redcap says. "What happened here? She looks like she took a big bite out of someone."

I am surprised to find that makes me laugh. The sound comes out all wrong.

"Her tongue," Hyacinthe says, and Madoc nods as though he's seen that sort of thing before.

Although I knew Hyacinthe had been part of Madoc's army, I forgot that meant they might know each other. It is strange to hear them speaking like comrades, especially with one of them the jailer and the other in a cage.

As he departs, the redcap glances in my direction.

"Little queen," Madoc says with a crooked smile. Despite not sharing blood with Oak, the mischief in his expression is familiar. "All grown up and come to devour your maker. I can't say as I blame you."

I am fairly sure he's missing an eye. I remember the old general from the endless meetings and parties where I sat in the dirt or was tugged on a leash. I remember the calm of his manner and the hot wine he gave me, as well as the gleam of his teeth whenever there was blood.

Like now, when I spit on the ground rather than swallow what's in my mouth.

Hyacinthe says something else to Madoc, and I put my head down on my arms, sprawling over the bench. Another bout of dizziness hits me, and I close my eyes, expecting it to pass. Expecting to be able to sit up. But instead, I am pulled down into darkness.

When I come back to consciousness, it is to the sound of Oak's voice. "She's breathing steadily."

By the time I am able to focus, though, it is Madoc who is speaking, his voice a deep rumble. "You might be better served if she didn't wake. What happens when she discovers how you've deceived her? When she realizes her role in your plan?"

I try not to move, try not to let a twitch of muscle or a tightening of my body give away that I am conscious and listening.

Oak's voice is full of resignation. "She will have to decide how much she hates me."

"Kill her while you can," says the old general, softly. He sounds regretful but also resigned.

"That's your answer to everything," Oak says.

"And yours is to throw yourself into the mouth of the lion and hope it doesn't like your savor."

Oak says nothing for a long moment. I think about the way he took an arrow while grinning reassuringly, how he gulped down poison. How, back in Elfhame, he apparently draws out assassins by being an excellent target. Madoc's not wrong that Oak throws himself at things. In fact, I am not sure if Madoc realizes the extent of his rightness.

"I despair of you," says the redcap finally. "You have no instinct to take power, even when it is offering you its very throat to tear out."

"Enough," says Oak, as if this isn't the first time they've gone through this argument. "This—*all of it*—is your fault. Why couldn't you just have the patience to stay in exile? To resign yourself to your fate?"

"That's not my nature," the redcap says softly, as though Oak should have known better. "And I didn't know it would be you who came."

The prince gives a shuddering sigh. I hear rustling. "Let me look at those bandages."

"Stop fussing," says Madoc. "If pain bothered me, I went into the wrong trade."

There is a long silence, and I wonder if I should pretend to yawn or something else to indicate that I am waking.

"I'm never killing her," Oak says softly, so softly I almost don't hear.

"Then you better hope she doesn't kill you," the general replies.

I lie very still for a while after that. Eventually, I hear the shuffling of a servant and the clank of platters, and use that as an excuse to give an awkward moan and turn over.

Oak's hooves clatter against the floor, and then he's on his knees in front of me, all golden hair and fox eyes and worry.

"Wren," he breathes, reaching through the iron bars, even though they singe his wrists. His fingers run through my hair.

*What happens when she discovers how you've deceived her? When she realizes her role in your plan?*

If I hadn't overheard what he'd said to his father, I would never have believed he had a secret so terrible he thought I would hate him for it.

The servant girl places bowls in front of the cells, on the ground. Cruel, since the bowls are too big to fit between the bars, which means that one must put one's wrist against iron with every bite. Our dinner appears to be a pungent, oily soup that has barley in it and probably the meat of seabirds.

I shift myself into a sitting position.

"We're going to get out of this," Oak tells me. "I'll try to pick the lock if you loan me your hairpin."

I nod to show I understand and unclasp it.

His expression grows grave. "Wren—"

"Stop fussing at *her* now. She can't even complain over it." The redcap smiles in my direction, as though inviting me into laughing at his son.

Who he told to kill me.

The prince withdraws his hand from between the bars and turns away. He doesn't seem to notice the burn on his arm as he pushes himself to his feet.

What could he have done that's so awful? All I can think of is that he really does have Mellith's heart and that he really is planning on turning it over to Lady Nore.

"Hurclaw is a problem," Madoc says as he watches Oak bend the sharp end of my pin and slide it into the lock. "If it wasn't for his people,

I believe I could have escaped this place, perhaps even taken the Citadel. But Lady Nore has promised that she will soon be able to break the curse on the Stone Forest."

"Take the Citadel? That's quite a boast," Oak says, twisting the pin and frowning.

Madoc makes a snorting sound, then turns to me. "I am sure that Wren here wouldn't mind taking Lady Nore's castle and lands for herself."

I shake my head at the absurdity of the statement.

He raises his brows. "No? Still sitting at the table and waiting for permission to start eating?"

That's an uncomfortably accurate way of describing how I've lived my life.

"I was like that once," he tells me, his sharp lower incisors visible when he speaks. I know this conversation is an effort to assess an opponent and keep me off-balance. Still, the thought of him waiting for anyone's permission is ridiculous. He's the former Grand General of Elfhame and a redcap, delighting in bloodshed. He's probably eaten people. No, he's definitely eaten people.

I shake my head again. Oak looks over at us and frowns, as though his father talking with me makes him nervous.

Madoc grins. "No? I can hardly believe it myself, in truth. But I spent most of my life on campaigns, making war in Eldred's name. Did I enjoy my work? Certainly, but I also obeyed. I took what rewards I was given, and I was grateful for them. And what did I get for my trouble? My wife fell in love with someone else, someone who was there when I was gone."

His former wife, whom he murdered. The mother of his three girls. Somehow, I'd always assumed that she left him because she was afraid, not because she was lonely.

Madoc glances at Oak again before returning his attention to me. "I vowed I would use the strategy I studied for my own benefit. I would find a way to take all that I wanted, for myself and for my family. What a freeing thought it was to no longer believe I had to deserve something in order to get it."

He's right; that would be a shockingly freeing thought.

"Stop waiting," Madoc says. "Sink those pretty teeth into something."

I give him a sharp look, trying to decide if he is making fun of me. I lean down and write in the dirt and the crust of my own dried blood: *Monsters have teeth like mine.*

He grins as though I am finally getting his point. "That they do."

Oak turns away from the lock in frustration. "Father, what exactly do you think you're doing?"

"We were just *talking*, she and I," Madoc says.

"Don't listen to him." He shakes his head with an exasperated look at his father. "He's *full* of bad old-guy advice."

"Just because I'm bad," Madoc says with a grunt, "doesn't mean the advice is."

Oak rolls his eyes. I note he has a new bruise at the corner of his mouth and a wound on his brow that has caused blood to crust in his hair. I think of him fighting in the throne room, think of the pain when my tongue was cut out. Think of him watching.

I go to the bowl of soup, although I cannot stand to put anything into my mouth. Still, if I can get the dish into the cell, even if I tip out half the food, I can pass what's left to Oak and Madoc.

As I begin to tilt it, though, I see something metal in the soup. Setting the bowl down again, I stick my fingers into the oily liquid and feel around. I touch the solid weight of a key and remember Hyacinthe's words about getting me out of the Citadel.

Forcing myself not to look at Oak or Madoc, I palm the object. Then I tuck it away into my dress and retreat to the bench in the back of my cell. Oak has no luck with the lock. Neither of them seems inclined to eat the food.

I listen to them talk a bit more about Hurclaw, and how he argued with Lady Nore over some sacrifices that Madoc didn't quite understand, and what would become of the bodies. Oak looks toward me several times, as though he would like to speak with me but doesn't.

Eventually, Madoc suggests we rest, since tomorrow will be "a test of our ability to adapt to evolving plans," which puzzles me. I know that Tiernan will arrive at the proscribed meeting place, with whatever it is in that reliquary.

The old general lies down on the bench while Oak stretches himself out on the cold floor.

I wait until they're sleeping. I recall how he caught me in the woods and wait a very long time. But the prince is exhausted, and when I fit the key into my lock, he doesn't wake.

I shove the heavy door, and it opens easily, the iron stinging my hand. I slip out, then tuck the key in a corner of their cell so that they will find it if I don't return.

In the hall, I slip off my big boots. And then I walk, my bare feet quiet on the cold stone. The guard at the prison gate is sleeping, slumped over a chair. He must be used to having Madoc as his only charge.

Up the steps, rays of early-morning sunlight turn the castle into a prism, and every time the shadows change, I worry over being given away.

But no one comes. No one stops me. And I realize that this was my fate from the start. It wasn't going to be Oak who stopped Lady Nore. It was always supposed to be me.

I do not meet Hyacinthe. I head for the throne room. As I tiptoe into a corridor that looks on the great hall's double doors, I see they are closed and barred, with two stick soldiers standing at attention. I can think of no way to get past them. They do not sleep, nor do they seem alive enough to be tricked.

But no one knows the Citadel like I do.

There is another way into the great hall, a small pass-through tunnel from the kitchens where refuse is tucked away by servants—empty cups, platters, messes of every sort. The cooks and kitchen staff fish them out later to clean them. It is large enough for a child to hide in, and I hid in it often.

I move toward the kitchens. When I see guards passing, I duck into shadows and make myself unobtrusive. Although it has been a long time, I am well-practiced at being unnoticed, especially here of all places.

As I move, I have a strange dissonance of memory. I am walking through these halls as a child. I am walking through my unparents' house at night, moving like a ghost. That's what I've been for years. An unsister. An undaughter. An unperson. A girl with a hole for a life.

How appropriate to have my tongue cut out, when silence has been my refuge and my cage.

I creep down to the kitchens, on the first level of the Citadel. Their heat is what makes the prisons warm enough to survive. I would have thought the fires there, perpetually burning, would have melted the whole castle, but they do not. The base of the castle is stone, and what they do melt refreezes into a harder layer of ice.

I see a nisse boy, sleeping in the ashes before the fire, tucked into a blanket of sewn-together skins. I slip past him, past casks of wine. Past baskets of crowberries and piles of dried fish. Past jars of salted and pickled things and bowls of dough that are covered with wet towels, their yeast still rising.

I squeeze myself into the pass-through tunnel and begin to crawl. And although I am larger than I was the last time I was in it, I still fit. I slip by tipped-over wine goblets, dregs dried inside, and a few bones that must have fallen from a plate. I emerge at the other end, inside the empty throne room.

But as I push myself to my feet, I realize that I have failed again because the reliquary is gone.

I walk over to the place where it was, my heart beating hard, panic stealing my breath. I was foolish to come to Lady Nore's throne room alone; I was foolish to come to the Citadel at all.

There is a withered leaf on the ground, and beside it something that might be a pebble. I lift it between my fingers, feeling the sharp edge of it. It's what I hoped—a piece of bone.

The Thistlewitch said that with Mab's bones, great spells could be cast. That she had the force of creation within her. And although I have never been adept at magic, if Lady Nore could use Mab's power to create living beings from sticks and rock, if she could use it to control my tongue to make it speak the words she wanted to hear, then surely there is enough magic in this to allow me to grow my tongue back.

I put the withered leaf in my mouth first. Then I place the bone on the cut root where my tongue used to be, close my eyes, and concentrate. Immediately, I feel as though my chest is being squeezed, as though my ribs are cracking.

Something is wrong. Something is wrong with me.

I fall to my knees, palms pressed against the ice of the floor. Something seems to twist inside my chest, then split, like a fissure opening in a glacier. The hard knot of my magic, the part of me that has felt in danger of unraveling when I push myself too hard, splits completely apart.

I gasp, because it *hurts*.

It hurts so much my mouth opens on a scream I cannot make. It hurts so much that I black out.

For the second time in less than a single day, I wake on a cold floor. I've been there long enough for frost to settle over my skin, sparkling along my arms and stiffening my dress.

I push myself to my hands and knees. The remains of stick soldiers are scattered around me, among berries and branches and chunks of snow that might have once been stuck in their chests.

What could have happened here? My memories are tangled things, like the stems growing from Mab's bones.

Kneeling and shaking with something that cannot be cold, I put my hand against the ice beneath me, noting spiderweb patterns, as though it were the shattered glass of a windshield, broken but not yet come apart. Staggering across the throne room, I crawl to the tunnel.

There, I close my eyes again. When I open them, I am not sure if it is moments later or hours. I feel leaden, sluggish.

With astonishment, I realize *my tongue is in my mouth*. It feels odd to have it there. Thick and heavy. I cannot decide if it is swollen or if I am just oddly conscious of it.

"I'm scared," I whisper to myself. Because it's true. Because I need to know if my tongue belongs to me and will say the things I mean it to. "I'm so tired. I'm so tired of being scared."

I recall Madoc and his advice. To sink my teeth into something. To take this castle and all of Lady Nore's lands for myself. To stop waiting for permission. To stop caring what others think or feel or want.

Idly, I imagine myself in control of the Ice Citadel. Lady Nore, not just beaten, but *gone*. Elfhame, glad of my service. So glad they are willing to name me the queen of these lands. And had I control of Mab's remains, if I could harness the power that Lady Nore has? Perhaps I would be someone his sisters might consider a fitting bride for Oak then, with a dowry like that.

The fantasy of buying my way into being acceptable to his sisters should make me resentful, but instead fills me with satisfaction. That even Vivienne, the eldest, who shuddered at the idea of my being bound to her precious brother, might desire me to sit at their table. Might see my sharp-toothed smile and smile in return.

And Oak...

He would think...

I catch myself before I build a sugary confection of a fantasy.

One in which, once again, I seek permission. Besides, I do not control the Citadel, no less Lady Nore.

Not yet.

I walk out the doors of the throne room and up winding ice steps toward the floors above. I hear voices just as I turn.

A patrol of two ex-falcons and a troll spots me. For a long moment, we stare at one another.

"How did you escape the dungeon?" one of them demands, forgetting I cannot speak.

I run, but they grab me. The chase is over fast. It's not as though I was really trying to get away.

Lady Nore is in her bedroom when I am brought before her. Three falcons—real birds, their curse as yet unbroken—sit on the serpent mirror above her dressing table and on the back of her chair.

My gaze goes to their hooked beaks and black eyes. All Lady Nore has been able to do for them is feed them and wait. But having broken Hyacinthe's binding, I wonder if I could break theirs. If I could, would they be loyal to me, as they are to her?

I wonder what it would be like, to never have to be alone.

"Sneaky little girl," says Lady Nore indulgently. She reaches out and twirls my hair around her finger. "This is how I remember you, stealing through my castle like a thief."

*Poor Wren*, I hope my expression conveys. *So sad. And her mouth hurts.*

Lady Nore sees only her simple daughter, sculpted from snow. A disappointment many times over.

Now that my tongue is regrown through the strange magic of Mab's bones, I could open my mouth and make her into my marionette, to dance when I pulled her strings.

And yet, instead I bow my head, knowing she will like that. Stalling for time. Once I begin, I will have to get everything exactly right.

"And quiet," she says, smiling at her own jest. "I remember that, too."

What I recall is the depth of my fear, the tide of it sweeping me away from myself. I hope I can mimic that expression and not show her what I actually feel—a rage that is as thick and sticky and sweet as honey.

*I'm tired of being scared.*

"Say nothing until I allow it," I tell her. My voice sounds strange, hoarse, the way it did when I first spoke with Oak.

Her eyes widen. Her lips part, but she cannot disobey me, not after the vow she made before the mortal High Queen.

"Unless I say otherwise, you will give no one an order without my express permission," I say. "When I ask you a question, you will answer it fully, holding back nothing that I might find interesting or useful— and leaving out any filler with which you might disguise those interesting or useful parts."

Her eyes shine with anger, but she can say nothing. I feel a cruel leap of delight at her impotence.

"You will not strike me, nor seek to cause me harm. You will not hurt anyone else, either, including yourself."

I wonder if she has ever been forced to swallow her words before. She looks as though she might choke on them.

"Now you may speak," I say.

"I suppose all children grow up. Even those made of snow and ice," she says, as though my control of her is nothing to be overly concerned with. But I see the panic she is trying to hide.

My heart beats hard, and my chest still hurts. My tongue still feels wrong, but so does the rest of me. She is not the only one panicking.

"Summon the two guards outside the door. Convey to them that they should bring Oak here." My voice shakes a little. I sound uncertain, which could prove fatal. "Tell them nothing else, and give no sign of distress."

Her expression grows strange, remote. "Very well. Guard!"

The two outside the door turn out to be former falcons. I recognize neither of them.

"Go to the prisons, and bring me the prince."

They bow and depart.

I have stood apart from the world for so long. That has made it hard for me to navigate being in it, but it has also made me an excellent observer.

I stare at Lady Nore for a moment, considering my next move.

"You may speak, if you wish," I tell her. "But do not raise your voice and, should anyone come into the room, cease talking."

I can see her considering not to say anything out of spite, but she breaks. "So, what do you mean to do with me now?" Around her neck, Lord Jarel's fingers scuttle.

"I haven't decided," I say.

She laughs, though it sounds forced. "I imagine not. You're not really a planner, are you? More of a creature of instinct. Mindless. Heedless. A little low cunning, perhaps, the way animals sometimes surprise you with their cleverness."

"How can you hate me so much?" I ask her, the question slipping out of my mouth before I can snatch it back.

"You should have been like us," says Lady Nore, her posture rigid. The words come easily, as though she has been thinking on them for a long time. "And instead, you are like *them*. To look at you is to see something so flawed it ought to be put out of its misery. Better to be dead, child, than to live as you do. Better to drown you like some runt of a litter."

I taste tears in the back of my throat. Not because I want her to love me, but because her words echo the worst thoughts of my heart.

I want to smash the mirrors and make her stick the pieces in her skin. I want to do something so awful that she regrets wishing I was anything like her.

"If I am so low," I say, my voice a growl, "then what are you, to be my vassal, and lower still?"

When the door opens, I turn toward it. I probably look furious.

I can see the confusion on Oak's face. He looks rumpled and must have been sleeping when they took him. He is brought into the room, wrists bound, by one of the ex-falcons.

"Wren?" he says.

In that moment, I realize I have already made a bad mistake. The guard stands there, waiting for orders, but Lady Nore can give him none. If I tell her what to say now, my power over her will be obvious—not to mention the restoration of my tongue—and the soldier will alert the others. But if I do nothing, and Lady Nore gives him no commands, it won't take him long to discern something is wrong.

The moment stretches as I try to come up with an answer. "You can go," Oak tells him. "I'll be fine here."

The former falcon makes a small bow and leaves the room, closing the door behind him. Lady Nore gasps, furious and shocked in equal measure.

My own surprise is just as great.

The prince looks at me guiltily. "I can imagine what you're thinking," he says, moving his wrist to cast off the silver binding. "But I had no idea what my father's plan was. I didn't even know he had a plan. And it turns out that it wasn't enough of one to win."

I recall Oak's words in the prisons. *This—all of it—is your fault. Why couldn't you just have the patience to stay in exile? To resign yourself to your fate?*

So Madoc had known he was going to be kidnapped—perhaps from Tiernan, who would have gotten it from Hyacinthe, or maybe even from Hyacinthe directly—and he'd let it happen. All so that he could recruit his own soldiers back to his side, take Lady Nore's Citadel, and impress Elfhame enough to let him back in.

The falcons had been loyal to him once, and so it made some sense—arrogant sense, but still sense—for Madoc to wager that weeks spent in the heart of the Citadel would allow him the time to win them over.

*Hurclaw is a problem. If it wasn't for his people, I believe I could have escaped this place, perhaps even taken the Citadel.*

Madoc hadn't planned on Hurclaw's trolls, which left the former falcons outnumbered. Not to mention the huldufólk and nisser.

And the monsters of stick and stone.

"And now?" I ask.

Oak's eyes widen satisfyingly at the sound of my voice. "How are you *speaking*?"

"I used a shard of Mab's bones," I tell him, and if I shiver a little at the memory, he cannot guess the reason.

"So you're saying that while my father and I were asleep, you found the reliquary—all by yourself—and then single-handedly subdued

Lady Nore?" He laughs. "You might have woken me. I could have done something, surely. Applauded at the right moments? Held your bag?"

I am flattered into a small smile.

"So," he asks, "what order ought I give the guards, now that you're in charge?"

Lady Nore sits rigidly, listening. Realizing, perhaps, that I do not need to have more than low animal cunning. All I need is an ally with a little ambition, one who will be a little kind.

Or, perhaps, realizing for the first time that she does not know me half so well as she thinks.

"Tiernan plans on meeting us still, correct?" I ask.

Oak nods. "It could be a way to get Hurclaw's people in one place and surround them. We'd have the element of surprise, and the stick creatures on our side."

I nod. "There's Bogdana to think of, too."

I push my feelings about what I overheard he and Madoc discuss aside and talk through possible plans. We go through them again and again. I command Lady Nore to have the guards fetch Oak's things for him. Send a message to Hyacinthe. Have servants bring me the sweet ice Lord Jarel used to give me, and send wine and meat pies to Madoc.

Then I send for Lady Nore's maidservants to help me get ready.

The door opens soon after to two huldufólk women, Doe and Fernwaif. Their tails swish. I remember them from my time here, sisters who had come to work for Lady Nore in recompense for some deed done by their parents.

They were kind, in their way. They did not prick me with pins just to see me bleed, as some of the others did. I am surprised by how sunken-eyed they look. Their clothing is worn at the hems and sleeves. I think of the briar-and-stick spiders hunting across the swells of snow and wonder how much worse it is to be in the Citadel now than it was then.

I choose a dress from Lady Nore's closet and sit on a fur-covered stool while Doe pulls it over my head. Fernwaif arranges my hair with combs of bone and onyx. Then Doe brushes my lips with the juice of berries to stain them red, and does the same to my cheeks. It happens in a blur.

*Kill her while you can.*

Oak and I have been playing games for a long time. This game, I have to win.

Outside, we meet more guards and Madoc, brought up from the prisons. I look for Hyacinthe, but he isn't there. I can only hope he received my note. A former falcon hands over a brace, hastily made from a branch. Madoc props it under his arm gratefully.

I see Lady Nore, mounting a reindeer, reliquary in her arms. Her hair, the color of dirty snow, blows in the wind. I see the gleam of greed in her yellow eyes, and the way Lord Jarel's grim gray hands tighten on her throat.

When I was here as a child, I was afraid all the time. I will not give in to that fear now.

We set off through the drifts. Oak maneuvers himself close to me. "Once this is over," he says, "there are some things I want to tell you. Some explanations I have to give."

"Like what?" I ask, keeping my voice low.

He looks away, toward the edge of the pine forest. "I let you believe—well, something that's untrue."

I think about the feeling of Oak's breath against my neck, the way his fox eyes looked with the pupils gone wide and black, the way it felt to bite his shoulder almost hard enough to break skin. "Tell me, then."

He shakes his head, looking pained, but so many of his expressions are masks that I can no longer tell what is real. "If I did, it would serve nothing but to clear my conscience and would put you in danger."

"Tell me anyway," I say.

But Oak only shakes his head again.

"Then let me tell *you* something," I say. "I know why you smile and jest and flatter, even when you don't need to. At first I thought it was to make people like you, then I thought it was to keep them off-balance. But it's more than that. You're worried they're scared of you."

Wariness comes into his face. "Why ever would they be?"

"Because you *terrify* yourself," I say. "Once you start killing, you don't want to stop. You like it. Your sister may have inherited your father's gift for strategy, but you're the one who got his bloodlust."

A muscle moves in his jaw. "And are you afraid of me?"

"Not because of that."

The intensity of his gaze is blistering.

It doesn't matter. It feels good to pierce his armor, but it doesn't change anything.

My greatest weakness has always been my desire for love. It is a yawning chasm within me, and the more that I reach for it, the more easily I am tricked. I am a walking bruise, an open sore. If Oak is masked, I am a face with all the skin ripped off. Over and over, I have told myself that I need to guard against my own yearnings, but that hasn't worked.

I must try something new.

As we trek across the snow, I am careful to walk lightly so that I can stay on top of the icy crust. But it still spider-webs with every step. My dress billows around me, caught by the cold wind. I realize that I am still barefoot.

Another girl might have frozen, but I am cold all the way through.

# CHAPTER
## 17

Ahead of us, Lady Nore rides a shaggy reindeer. She is in a dress of scarlet with a cloak of deeper red over it, long enough to cover the back of the deer. The reliquary sits in her lap.

The troll king is mounted on an elk, its horns rising in an enormous branching crown of spikes over its head. Its bridle is all green and gold. He himself has coppery armor, beaten into that same strange pattern again, as though each piece contains a maze.

I think of how Tiernan must have passed these last two days. At first, hoping we would return, and then panicking as the night wore on. By the time day dawned, he would have known he had to come with the heart and play out Oak's scheme. He might have embroidered the plans as he sat in the cold, angry with the prince and terrified for him. He had no way to tell us.

And we had no way to tell him that Madoc had recruited so many of the former falcons to his side.

Lady Nore swings down from her reindeer, her long scarlet cloak dragging through the snow like a shifting tide of blood.

"Take the storm hag," she orders, just as we planned. Just as she was commanded.

Stick soldiers grab for Bogdana. The ancient faerie sinks her nails into one of them. Lightning strikes in the distance, but she has no time to summon it closer. Her hands are caught by more stick creatures. The storm hag rips apart a stick man, but there are too many and all are armed with iron. Soon she is pressed down in the snow, iron manacles burning on her wrists.

"What is the reason for this betrayal?" Bogdana shouts at Lady Nore.

Lady Nore glances at me but does not answer.

The storm hag croaks. "Have I not done what you asked of me? Have I not conjured you a daughter from nothing? Have I not helped you make yourself great?"

"And what a daughter you have conjured," Lady Nore says, scorn in her voice.

Bogdana's eyes go to me, a new gleam in them. She sees something, I think, but is not yet sure what exactly she's seeing.

"And now, prince," Lady Nore says, returning to the plan. "Where is Mellith's heart?"

Oak is not armed, although the former falcon at his side carries the prince's sword where he can easily get it. And though his wrists appear to be tied, the cords are so loose that he can free himself whenever he wishes. The prince looks up at the moon. "My companion is supposed to be here presently."

I glance around at the assembled Folk. Part of me wants to give the signal now, to take command of Lady Nore's stick creatures and force the trolls into a surrender. But better for Tiernan to be in sight, to be sure he won't arrive at the wrong moment and jump into the fray, not knowing friend from foe.

I shift nervously, watching Lady Nore. Noting the hands of Lord Jarel around her neck, a reminder that if she could find comfort in something like that, her other actions may be impossible for me to anticipate. My gaze goes to King Hurclaw, tall and fierce-looking. For all the rumors of his madness, I understand his motives far better than hers. Still, the thirty trolls behind him are formidable.

"Perhaps you are used to your subjects biding at your pleasure, heir to Elfhame," Hurclaw says, "but we grow impatient."

"I am waiting just as you are," Oak reminds him.

Twenty minutes pass before Tiernan appears, walking over the snow, Titch on his shoulder. It feels far longer than that with Lady Nore glaring at me and Hurclaw grumbling. Madoc leans heavily on his stick and does not complain, although I worry he might collapse. At perhaps half a league off, Titch springs into the air, flapping wide wings.

The owl-faced hob circles once, then lands on Oak's arm and whispers in his ear.

"Well?" demands Hurclaw.

Oak turns to Lady Nore, as though she really is the one in charge. "Tiernan says that Madoc should begin walking toward him with a soldier, as a show of good faith. Tiernan will meet them."

"And the heart?" she inquires, and I bristle. My commands had to be more open-ended for her to perform in front of Hurclaw, but she's clever and will be looking for a loophole. I told her to behave like herself, but not to say or do anything that would give away that I had control over her. In this game of riddles and countermoves, I fear I have not been careful enough.

"He carries it in a case," Oak says. "He'll pass it to your soldier. Then Suren and I are to go to him."

Lady Nore nods. "Then make haste. Let the exchange begin."

Before, she said she wanted to keep Oak. Now she seems as if she's planning to release him. Will that seem strange to Hurclaw? Will he even notice? I slant a look at him, but there's no way to know his thoughts.

The hob takes to wing again, speeding over the snow toward Tiernan. "I have informed him you agreed to this plan," Oak says.

I doubt very much that's what he told Titch.

"With this heart, you can make the troll kings live again?" Hurclaw asks, narrowing his eyes at Tiernan and the case in his hands. "You can end the curse on my people?"

"So Bogdana told me, once, long ago," Lady Nore says with a glance toward the storm hag, whom the stick soldiers have hauled to her feet. "Though I sometimes wonder if she wanted it for her own reasons. But I remembered her story of the bones and the heart, remembered that they would be entombed beneath the Castle of Elfhame. And when the heart wasn't there, I knew that only a member of the royal family would be allowed to search through the tunnels extensively enough to find it—or to know if it had been deliberately moved. So I took Madoc and gave them a reason to look."

She nods at a former falcon, and he begins to help Madoc across the snow. I see the general lean toward him and say something. Their pace slows. We wait with the wind whistling around us and the hour growing later. Tiernan halts when he reaches Madoc and hands the case with the deer's heart inside to the soldier.

The soldier starts to walk back to us. Madoc and Tiernan remain, as though expecting that Oak and I will really be coming to join them in a moment.

Bogdana watches, amusement lifting a corner of her mouth despite the shackles she wears.

"What a delight it would have been," Lady Nore says in a tone of barely concealed malice. "To have had all that power and to have known it was Madoc's son who gave it to me."

The troll king looks at her, and I realize my mistake. I have instructed her to say nothing that will *give away* the power I have over her, but I failed to take into account that she could make airy, passive-aggressive statements implying a great deal.

"What does that mean?" Hurclaw asks.

"You ought to ask my daughter," she says with the sort of sweetness that is meant to cover the taste of rot.

His gaze goes to me. "I thought she had no tongue."

Lady Nore only smiles, and he nods to one of his Folk.

The troll soldier lifts a bow. He shoots before I can do more than raise my hand in warding.

The arrow slices through the pad of my thumb and strikes me in the side, slicing through flesh. The impact unbalances me. I hit the snow, falling to my hands and knees. I gasp for air, feeling the agony of trying to get a breath. I think one of my lungs was struck.

Scarlet stains my side. The snow is blooming red with it.

Oak starts to run toward me when the troll archers train their bows on the prince and Hurclaw calls for him to halt. The prince stops. I can see he has his sword, the restraints tying his hands are gone.

The former falcons are fanning out, and I see Hyacinthe weaving between them, moving in my direction.

This is all wrong.

"Prince," Hurclaw's voice booms. "Bring that heart to me, or I will fill you both full of arrows."

I want to call out, to order Lady Nore to command her troops to defend me, but I cannot seem to make the words come. This *hurts*.

It hurts like when—

The bone shard in my mouth—

My chest—

The ice spider-webbing under my fingers as I moved—

Oak glances at me with those trickster's eyes, panic in them. Then he inclines his head to the troll king. Walking to the former falcon, the prince takes the box with the heart from him.

And whispers something.

Hurclaw swings down from his mount.

Oak approaches him. They are close now, too close for arrows aimed at the prince not to strike their king.

Hurclaw lifts the latch with a flick of one clawed nail. A moment later the troll stumbles back, grabbing for his throat, where a needle-thin pin sticks out from his skin. The heart, dark and shriveled, falls into the snow. A deer heart, nothing more.

It was the case that mattered, the case that Oak commissioned from the blacksmith in Undry Market.

*Once, the Bomb told me a story about poisonous spiders kept inside a chest. When the thief opened it, he was bitten all over.*

The case was the trap.

I remember the care with which Oak set the lock, back in the cave. He must have been fitting a poisoned dart, ready to kill Lady Nore if all our other plans failed.

"Now!" shouts the soldier who'd been given the prince's whispered orders.

The falcons have made a careful circle behind the trolls. At the signal, they draw their weapons and rush in.

There is fighting all around me. Arrows and blades. Screams.

I push myself to my knees. "*Mother*," I say, forcing it out.

That was the word meant to end the masquerade of control.

"All who follow me, you shall follow Suren's commands from this moment forward and forevermore," Lady Nore calls out, following my instructions exactly as she was supposed to, at least until she pitches her voice low. "If she can make any."

"Stop the trolls," I shout, pushing myself to my feet. When I cough, blood spatters my fingers.

"You are the one to order me captured, child?" Bogdana calls to me. "You?"

I snap off the end of the arrow, gritting my teeth against the pain. Freeing my other hand.

Hurclaw is trembling all over. Whatever the poison, it is acting fast.

"You played us false," the troll king says. "You never had Mellith's heart at all, did you?"

"He cannot lie," says Lady Nore, standing amid the carnage, watching it as though it is distant from her. "He told us he brought it north with him. He has it."

*What happens when she discovers how you've deceived her? When she realizes her role in your plan?*

"Call off your people," Oak tells Hurclaw. "Call them off, and I will give you the antidote."

"No!" The troll king lunges for Oak. They topple together onto the snow. Oak is skilled, but nowhere as strong as Hurclaw.

*She will have to decide how much she hates me.*

Oak, who abandoned looking for the heart after he went to the Thistlewitch. Who tried to send me away, who hadn't wanted to need me.

*He'll steal your heart.* Wasn't that what Bogdana said in the woods?

My mind drifts dizzily back to the feeling of something inside me unraveling.

To lying on the cold ice floor of the throne room. Memories flood me until it seems as though I am in two places at once.

I am another little girl, unwanted and afraid.

*Hag child,* a woman's voice says. *You will take Clovis's place in her bed tonight.*

The feel of heavy blankets, embroidered with stags and forests. Warm and soft. And then waking to agony, to breathlessness. To my mother looming over me, bloody knife in her hand. To the joy, the relief I felt before the feeling of betrayal so vast it consumes me.

My real mother. My beautiful mother. Bogdana.

I hear her voice. But she is not speaking to me now; she is talking to someone else, a long time ago. *I will make sure your heart beats in a new chest.*

I am terrified. I feel the agony of her nails reaching into my chest.

I blink, and it is as though I am seeing double, still half in that memory, half in the snow at the edge of night.

Mellith's heart is mine.

I ought to have known it since waking on the cold floor of the throne room. Since those dreams, which felt too real. Since the power sang through my veins, just waiting for me to reach for it.

I was afraid of magic from the first moment that Lady Nore and Lord Jarel stepped into my bedroom in the mortal world. And I couldn't stop being afraid of myself. Afraid of the monster I saw when I glimpsed my reflection in still pools, in windows.

But all I am is magic. Unmagic.

I am not nothing. I am what is beyond nothing. Annihilation.

I am the unraveler. I can pull apart magic with a thought.

An object flies from nearby. I have a moment to tell that it is made of bronze with a cork in one end before it explodes.

Flames scorch the ground. The wicker soldiers are on fire. Lady Nore screams.

I fall again. The heat on my face is scorching. My skirts are ablaze.

Tiernan is running through the snow toward Oak.

I struggle to my feet. And as I do, I see that though some of the stick creatures burn, it doesn't slow them. They fight on. A monstrous multilegged thing is ripping a troll apart, limb by limb, like a child taking apart a toy.

Hurclaw's body lies in the snow. It has gone very still.

Oak wipes dirt off his mouth with one arm and looks toward me as he gets up. I feel as though I am staring at him from very far away. There's a roaring in my ears. Now that the magic is loosed inside me, I do not think I can call it back.

And he knew. *He knew.* He'd known the whole time.

He used me like a coin in a trick. Used me so that he could say he brought Mellith's heart north, because it wasn't a lie.

I take a deep breath, pulling power toward me. The fire at the bottom of my dress goes out.

I close my eyes and focus my thoughts. When I open them, I let my power slice through enchantments. The stick things fall apart into a scattered field of blackened branches and twigs, forming a circle around me. The scent of smoke is still thick in the air.

"What have you done?" Lady Nore says, her voice coming out high.

The falcons and the trolls pause. Two run to their king and attempt to rouse him from where he lies.

Bogdana begins to cackle.

"Oak," Tiernan says, having made it to his friend's side. "What's happening to Wren?"

They're all watching me now.

*Nix. Naught. Nothing. That's what you are. Nix Naught Nothing.*

"Do you want to tell them, or should I?" I ask the prince.

"When did you—" he begins, but I cut him off before he can get the question out.

"When Lady Nore and Lord Jarel wanted a child to help their schemes, Bogdana tricked them." It is my turn to tell the fairy tale. "She made them a child of snow and sticks and droplets of blood, just as she told them she would. But she animated it with an ancient heart."

I recall enough of the Thistlewitch's story. I glance at Bogdana. "Mab cursed you. Is that right?"

The storm hag nods. "On my daughter's blood, that I should never harm any of Mab's line. Only Mellith could end my curse, but I could not give her new life without being asked to do so, nor could I speak of doing so without being questioned."

"You couldn't—this can't—" Lady Nore cannot bring herself to admit how deceived she was.

"Yes," I tell her. "I am what is left of Mellith. Me, whom you tortured and despised. Me, with more power than you've ever had. All of it at your fingertips. But you never bothered to look."

"Mellith. Mother's curse." Lady Nore spits the words at me. "That ought to have been your name from your making."

"Yes," I say. "I rather think you're right."

Tiernan tugs at Oak's shoulder, urging him to move. Madoc calls from across the snow. But the prince stands still, watching me.

Now I know the game he was playing, and who was the pawn. And flowing through me, I feel the endless power of nothingness, of negation.

"Will you trade Greenbriar blood for your own?" Lady Nore says. "You could have brought Elfhame to its knees. But I suppose it's me you want on my knees."

"I want you *dead*," I roar, and with no more than the force of that desire, she is spread apart on the snow. Taken apart. Unmade as surely and easily as a stick man.

I look at the red stain. At the storm hag, whose black eyes are glittering with satisfaction.

Horror chokes me. I hadn't meant to . . . I didn't think that would . . . I didn't know she would *die* just because I wished it. I didn't know I could do *that*.

The urge to shrink into myself, to hide from what I have done, is overwhelming. My shoulders hunch, my body curling in on itself. If

I was afraid of my anger before, now it has become something terrible beyond measure. Now that I can take all the pain I have ever felt and make everyone else feel it, too, I am not sure how to stop.

Hurclaw stirs. Either the poison wasn't meant to be lethal, or the dosage was for Lady Nore and is not enough to kill someone so much larger.

"Free Bogdana," I tell Hyacinthe. He does, removing the iron shackles from her wrists. His expression is wary, though. I wonder if he regrets his vow. I told him he would.

"Now take the antidote from Oak and give it to the troll king."

Hyacinthe stomps through the snow. The prince hands over a vial from his pocket without protest, his gaze still on me.

It takes a few moments for Hyacinthe to administer the liquid and a few more for Hurclaw to sit up.

I turn to the troll king as he staggers to his feet with the support of one of his subjects. "I can give you what she could not. I can break the curse."

He gives a grunt of assent.

"And in return, you will follow me."

Hurclaw, seeing the destruction around him, nods. "I await your orders, my lady."

"As for you three," I say, and look in the direction of Tiernan, Madoc, and Oak.

It is too late for them to run, and we all know it. No one can escape me now.

*Go,* I could tell him, and send him back to the safety of the isles of Elfhame, where he can return to being charming and beloved. A hero, even, bringing with him his father and the news of Lady Nore's demise. He could say he had an adventure.

Or I can keep him here, a hostage to force Elfhame to keep away. And mine.

Mine the only way I can ever trust, the only way I can be sure of.

"Heir to Elfhame," I say. "Get on your knees."

Prince Oak goes down smoothly, his long legs in the snow. Even bows his horned head, although I think he believes I am playing. He's not afraid. He thinks this is my revenge, to humiliate him a little. He thinks that, in a moment, all will be as it was.

"The others may go," I say. "The general, Tiernan, and any falcon who wishes to depart with them. Tell the High King and Queen that I have taken the Citadel in their name. Oak stays here."

"You can't keep him," warns Madoc.

*Sink those pretty teeth into something.*

I reach for the bridle, moved from around my waist when I dressed so that I might have it at hand. The leather is smooth in my fingers.

"Wren," Oak says, with the kindling of fear in his voice.

"There will be no more betrayals, prince," I tell him. He struggles at first, but when I whisper the word of command, he stops. The straps settle against his skin.

Madoc looks at me as though he would like to cut me to pieces. But he cannot.

"You don't need to do this," Oak tells me, softly. A lover's voice.

Bogdana grins from where she stands near the red stain of Lady Nore's remains. "And why not? Are you not the Greenbriar heir, the thief of her inheritance?"

"Don't be a fool," Tiernan says, ignoring the storm hag. He glances at the gathered soldiers, at the trolls, at everything he would have to fight if he tried to stop me, and narrows his eyes. "Jude might not have come for her father, but she will bring all the armies she can muster here to war with you for her brother. This can't be what you want."

I stare at him for a long moment. "Go," I say. "Before I change my mind."

"Best to do as she says." I can see Oak weigh his options and make the only real choice left to him. "Get my father back to Elfhame, or if Jude won't lift his exile, to somewhere else where he can recover. I told Wren I wouldn't leave without her."

Tiernan's gaze rests on the prince, then on me, then goes to Hyacinthe. He nods once, his expression grim, and turns away.

A few of the other knights and soldiers follow. Hyacinthe strides across the snow to my side.

"You may go with them, if you wish," I tell him. "With Madoc, and with Tiernan."

He watches as his former lover helps his former general across the snow. "Until my debt to you is paid, my place is here."

"Wren," Oak says, causing me to turn toward his voice. "I'm not your enemy."

A small smile turns up a corner of my mouth. I feel the sharpness of my teeth and roll my tongue over them. For the first time, I like the feeling.

CHAPTER

18

Bogdana leads the way to the Citadel. Hyacinthe walks by my side. When the servants bow, it is not out of mere courtesy. It comes from the same fear that caused them to make obeisances before Lady Nore and Lord Jarel.

Fear is not love, but it can appear much the same.

So too, power.

"Write to the High Court," urges Bogdana. "As its faithful servant, you've retrieved Mab's remains, ended the threat that Lady Nore presented, and set the former Grand General free. And then ask a boon—that you might remain here in her old castle and begin a Court of your own. That will be our first step. If your message gets there before Tiernan, the High Court could grant it all before they know better."

Bogdana goes on. "Tell them that the prince is with you, but sustained an injury. You will send him back to Elfhame once he is rested and ready."

Hyacinthe gives me a quick look, as though checking to see that I am the same person who so despised captivity as to help him escape from it.

I am not sure I am the same.

"Do not presume to give me orders," I tell the storm hag. "I may owe you my life, but I also owe you my death."

She steps back, chastened.

I will not make the same mistakes as Mellith.

"As soon as Tiernan and Madoc reach Elfhame, they will inform the High Court that we're keeping Oak prisoner," Hyacinthe says. "No matter what boon the High King and Queen have granted you, they'll demand his release."

"Perhaps a storm will delay their progress," I suggest, with a nod toward Bogdana. "Perhaps Madoc's injuries will require treatment. Many things can happen."

All around the hall, birds still perch. Soldiers doomed to feed on kindness. To kill nothing or be forever winged. I close my eyes. I can see the magic binding them. It is tightly coiled and weaves through their little feathered forms, tugging at their tiny hearts. It takes me a moment to find the knots, but when I do, the curses dissipate like cobwebs.

With ecstatic sighs and gasps, these falcons discover they are in their own faerie bodies once more.

"My queen," one says, over and over. "My queen."

Surely, I am easier to follow than Lady Nore.

I nod but cannot smile. Somehow as satisfied as I find myself with what I have done, it does not touch me. It is as though my heart is still locked away in a box, still buried underground.

I find myself inextricably drawn to the prisons. There, in his iron cage, I see Oak lying atop the furs I had sent down. He looks up at the ceiling, cloak pillowed beneath his head, and whistles a tune.

I recognize it as one of those we danced to back at Queen Annet's Court.

I do not shift from the shadows, but perhaps some small movement exposes me, because the prince turns toward where I am.

He squints, as though trying to make out my shape. "Wren?" he says. "Talk to me."

I don't reply. What would be the point? I know he will twist me around his finger with words. I know that if I give him half the chance, love-starved creature that I am, I will be under his spell again. With him, I am forever a night-blooming flower, attracted and repelled by the heat of the sun.

"Let me explain," he calls to me. "Let me *atone*."

I bite the tip of my tongue to keep myself from snapping at him. He meant to keep me ignorant. He tricked me. He lied with every smile. With every kiss. With the warmth in his eyes that should have been impossible to fake.

I'd known what he was capable of. Over and over, he'd shown me. And over and over, I believed there would be no more tricks. No more secrets.

Not anymore.

"You have good cause to be furious. But you couldn't have lied, had you known the truth. I was afraid you'd have to lie." He waits, and when I say nothing, rolls into a sitting position. "Wren?"

I can see the leather straps running across his cheeks. If he wears the bridle long enough, he'll have scars.

"Talk to me!" he shouts, standing and coming to the bars. I see the gold of his hair, the sharp line of his cheekbones, the glint of his fox eyes. "Wren! *Wren!*"

Coward that I am, I flee. My heart thundering, my hands shaking. But I can't pretend that I don't like the sound of him screaming my name.

# ACKNOWLEDGMENTS

I am lucky to have had a bevy of encouragement and advice on this book.

I am grateful to all those who helped me along on the journey to the novel you have in your hands, particularly Dhonielle Clayton, Zoraida Córdova, Marie Rutkoski, and Kiersten White, who helped me kick around the outline of this book as we swam in a pool in the autumn. Even more so, I am grateful to Kelly Link, Cassandra Clare, Joshua Lewis, and Steve Berman, who helped me rip the manuscript apart and stitch it back together in winter (and several other times). And to Leigh Bardugo, Sarah Rees Brennan, Robin Wasserman, and Roshani Chokshi, who helped me rip it apart again in the summer.

Thank you also to the many people who gave me a kind word or a bit of necessary advice, and who I am going to kick myself for not including right here.

A massive thank-you to everyone at Little, Brown Books for Young Readers for returning to Elfhame with me. Thanks especially to my amazing editor, Alvina Ling, and to Ruqayyah Daud, who provided invaluable insight. Thank you to Nina Montoya, who gave me a different perspective. Thank you as well to Marisa Finkelstein, Virginia Lawther,

Emilie Polster, Savannah Kennelly, Bill Grace, Karina Granda, Cassie Malmo, Megan Tingley, Jackie Engel, Shawn Foster, Danielle Cantarella, and Victoria Stapleton, among others. And in the UK, thank you to Hot Key Books, particularly Jane Harris and Emma Matthewson.

Thank you to Joanna Volpe, Jordan Hill, Emily Berge-Thielmann, Pouya Shahbazian, Hilary Pecheone, and everyone at New Leaf Literary for making hard things easier. And to Joanna, Jordan, and Emily for going way above and beyond, reading through this book and giving me a bevy of critical (in both senses of the word) notes.

Thank you to Kathleen Jennings, for the wonderful and evocative illustrations.

And thank you, always and forever, to Theo and Sebastian Black, for keeping my heart safe.